The Rich Woods

A Novel
WITH ILLUSTRATIONS

By

Charles F. Gill

Other Books by Charles Gill

THE AUTOBIOGRAPHY OF CHARLES F. GILL

LONGEARS, THE MOON & ARTICHOKES

 CHARLES F. GILL was born and raised in Richwood, Ohio and presently lives with his wife, Karen, in Saratoga, California. This is his third book and all are available at lulu.com.

Charles.gill@comcast.net

Foreword

Dear reader,

Is it possible that this book was written only for you? Many books are written with the author's intention that there be a wide distribution of his work, that it will be read by many, and that it might even provide a financial reward. That is not the case with this book. It would be my great desire if this small work would survive long enough to find its way to you – preferably one of my descendants – who have lived beyond my lifetime never having known me, and that through this note in the bottle adrift in the sea of time, you would come to know me together with a handful of my ancestors. Your reading of this collection of short stories might then give our spirits a rebirth, a renaissance, a gift of life. In return, I hope that you would come to know and love the earthly vessels that carried the few quarts of life force and DNA that flow through your arteries, veins and capillaries.

I make no apologies for the inaccuracies of fact in this novel, either of the omission or commission type. After all, my pilgrimage on this earth is of short duration compared to the combined lifetimes of those about whom I write. The Kingdom of Navarre and the city of La Rochelle are real places, but whether the LeMaître family ever lived at either of them, I do not know. It certainly was possible. You can be sure, however, that they were Huguenots and fled France to the Isle of Jersey, and from there across the Atlantic to Zachia Swamp in Maryland, making their way through West Virginia to Crossroads, and then on to Richwood.

When I ponder the changes that have taken place in the last

century, knowing that my grandparents never heard of a television, a computer, or a cell phone, I cannot help but wonder what marvels you, my reader, know of and experience that are beyond my grasp and imagination. More importantly, were you able to save the planet from its own self-destruction?

Charles F. Gill
Monterey, California
July 23, 2007

In the mid-sixteenth century, except for Philip II of Spain, women ruled the western seaboard of Europe – HM Mary Stuart, Queen of Scots; Regent Dowager Queen Catherine de Medici of France; Elizabeth I, Queen of England, France and Ireland; and Queen Regnant Juana III d'Albert of Navarra.

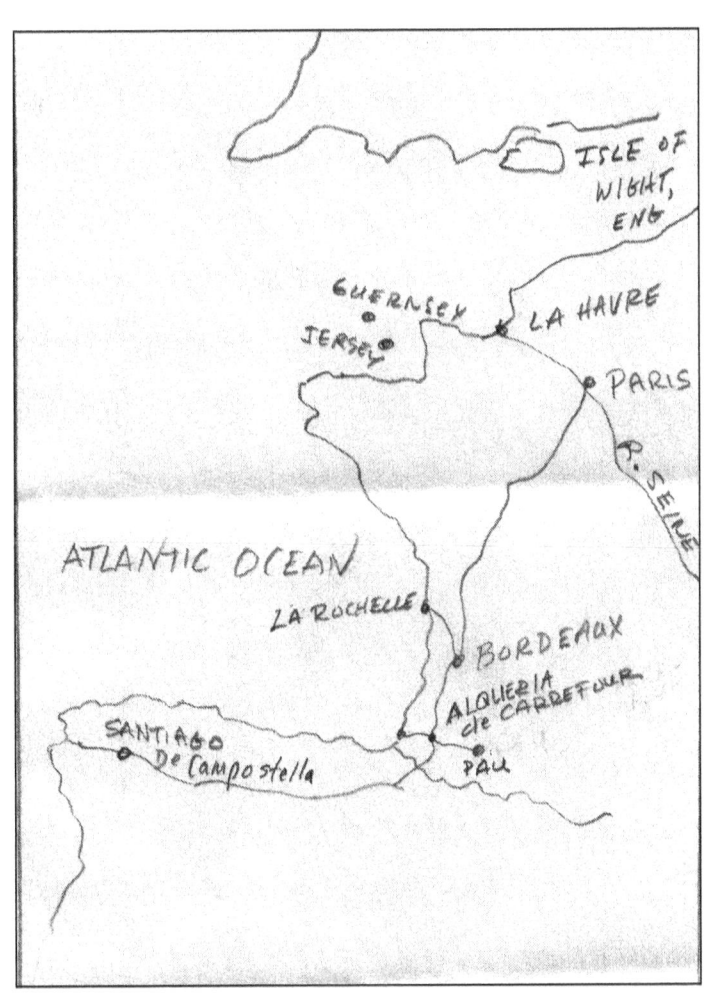

Part I

Navarre

I t wasn't that she minded chasing after this missing goat; rather she hated leaving the remaining flock alone. And it wasn't as though this particular one was lost, just because it had wandered off; it had done it many times before only to be found at the top. It was as if she and Emu, her longhaired chamois, had this prearranged agreement: if we become separated, we'll meet at the top. Nevertheless, that didn't prevent her from being anxious; wild boar and wolves were always out there looking for something to devour, and she would not rest until Emu had been reunited with her small herd.

She was used to these hills; she climbed them almost daily, chasing after her cud-chewing bovines. Whenever she reached the top, she could see the ocean far off in the west and wished that someday she might arrange to leave her goats with Señora Gonsalves and take a boat down the Gave de Pau to the port city of Ville-de-St-Pier.

Mornings were usually shrouded in mist and rain, but not today. It was a warm, spring crack of dawn, and the eastern sun reflected against the flecks of metal in the rocks like thousands of tiny mirrors mixed in with the salt and pepper granite.

She had spent the night at the pasture below and had risen only a short time earlier, eaten a piece of bread and some cheese from her knapsack and bathed at the small creek, a tributary off the Gave. Her name was Alecka, she was an orphan, and most of the time she lived alone in the wilderness, gathering watercress, fruits, roots and honey, setting and checking her traps and tending her small flock of goats. Sometimes she would spend a few days visiting with Señora Gonsalves, who also lived alone in the wilderness. Señora Gonsalves was a spiritualist and could communicate with the dead.

Alecka had just turned fourteen two months earlier. She was not particularly tall, but she appeared so, with a lean, muscular body. Her small breasts had barely developed, and her dark brown skin was dry and rough, too rough for a girl her age. She had several cuts, nicks and bruises on her arms and legs resulting from her constant scrambling on her hands and feet over the rocky hillside. One scrape in particular, where she had banged her knee against a sharp rock, was throbbing. Her thick, dark brown hair, frequently a trap for leaves and twigs, was long and wavy and hung nearly to her hips. She made her own clothing and sandals, as she had very little money, only a few coins tucked away in her knapsack that she got for selling an occasional wether. She rarely needed money, however, only when she wanted to buy beans or rice in nearby Ordulla. She would often trade milk for cheese and flatbread with Señora Gonsalves.

Off in the distance to the north, she could see where two roads intersected. The first ran east to west along the Gave, continuing a short distance to Ordulla and on to Ville-de-St-Pier, toward the ocean. At the crossroads, there was a flat-bottomed ferry crossing the Gave, connecting north to south. This road was a route through the mountain pass leading to Santiago de Compostela in Galicia, where the head of James, the brother of Christ, was brought following his martyrdom. The cathedral there had become the third most important site in Christendom after Jerusalem and Rome.

It was now the month of May, the pilgrimage had already

begun, and she could see the brown-robed pilgrims, loaded with backpacks, bedrolls and walking sticks, making their way along the route.

Alecka was born Catholic, but she never attended mass. Señora Gonsalves had become her only resource as to spiritual matters.

Emu was the newest and youngest of her small goat flock. Alecka had found her in the wild while she was very young. Emu was a chamois, a bovid, similar to the other goats, but with shorter horns, which curved slightly backwards, a coat of brown fur, and a white face with pronounced black stripes below her eyes. She would not mate Emu with any of her bucks since the resulting hybrid would most likely be sterile. Most people considered young chamois chevon to be quite tasty, and Emu would bring a good price should she ever decide to sell her. However, if she could find a buck chamois she would probably mate her. Emu was the most difficult of her goats to manage. Her climbing skills far exceeded those of the rest of the herd, and she had a genetic tendency to flee and climb to higher ground at the slightest provocation.

Alecka continued calling out Emu's name, climbing higher, starting to perspire even though hard, crusty patches of the winter snow tucked in crevices protected from the morning sun still lingered, giving a false impression of the warm air.

For a moment, as she paused, she thought she could hear the clanging of Emu's bell, barely audible, yet distinct. Often, but not now, the animal would bleat. Alecka's ear was tuned to the unique sound of each bell of each of her goats. It would remain silent when the goat stood still, followed by quick reverberations as the spirited animal darted either up or down the hillside, dodging rocks and brush.

"Darn you, Emu!" Alecka cursed, not really meaning it. "Wait until I catch up with you. Do you want me to sell you?"

3

Arriving at a small plateau, Alecka wanted to stop, but she pressed on as the tinny clanging grew louder.

Her scraped knee continued to throb, and she knew from experience that if she didn't soon get to a creek or lake where she could clean it, she would develop an infection, but she was used to that too.

As she walked across the plateau, she couldn't help worrying about the herd she had left below with Blue, her sheepdog. They were practically the same age, and like Alecka, Blue had also escaped the massacre. That was when her entire family had met their deaths – only she and Blue had escaped. Señora Gonsalves had taken them both in to her home.

Blue knew his job – to protect the herd – and he did it well, and usually he couldn't be distracted. Still, Alecka found it difficult each time she had to leave the herd to fetch a lost lamb or goat, set or check her traps, or track down a new member for the herd. Blue and Señora Gonsalves remained her only supporting companions.

The clanging grew louder and soon Emu appeared, unaware that she was missing, busy pulling the leaves off the branch of a small shrub. Alecka rushed toward her and quickly threw her arms around the animal's soft brown neck while at the same time thanking Quetzalcoatl, the god of nature and one of the creators.

She quickly placed a rope about her chamois' neck and began their decent to the pasture below. Nevertheless, as they made their way down the rocky steps, Alecka's feeling of exhilaration was short lived; she saw a large black buzzard overhead – an ominous sign. This set her heart pounding as she tugged at Emu, impatiently struggling to get the two of them down to the bottom. Hastily, she rushed down, running on the straight-a-ways, jumping down to each successive boulder, often sliding on her fanny while hanging on to the braided leash tied around Emu's neck, at the same time keeping her eye on the buzzard overhead. She didn't see the rabbit scrambling from her path or hear the owl that hooted as they passed beneath its perch, and she didn't feel the swishing of the bushes and brambles against her body, or the throbbing from the unattended abrasion on her knee. She was totally concentrated on getting to her herd and to Blue.

As the pasture below came into view, only minutes away, she couldn't see either her flock or her red-haired sheepdog. She hoped that they hadn't strayed far.

She began shouting, calling the dog's name. Placing two fingers in her mouth, she forced a loud, shrill whistle that could be heard over the sound of the rushing waters of the creek where she had bathed earlier. Without any response she regarded the ground closely, the mashed grass where she had slept during the night and where her herd had grazed. The buzzard continued to circle overhead, waiting patiently to score. She was scarcely surprised when she discovered a trail of blood; but she was abruptly shaken when the trace led to tufts of golden red hair.

Blue lay motionless only a few meters away, and there, at the edge of the thicket, stood a gray wolf pulling and tugging at the carcass of one of her goats. It was Atol, a nanny, her udders full of milk.

Alecka screamed at the wolf and began throwing rocks, hoping to scare it away. It stopped only long enough to pull its head back against its shoulders, show its teeth and growl at her for a moment. Then without fear or concern for Alecka's threats, it continued to rip and tear at its kill.

Alecka kneeled before Blue and took hold of his lifeless body, his eyes bulging, his blue tongue hanging out of his mouth, and his matted coat caked with a paste of dirt and his own blood.

The wolf, appearing relaxed, lay on his stomach, protected from the overhead sun beneath a spreading oak, his back legs stretched outward and his front paws clutching a chunk of red chevon. He pulled and tore at the flesh voraciously, swallowing without chewing, and always keeping an eye on Alecka.

The young girl lifted up her longtime companion, carried him out of the sun to the edge of the pasture, and began piling rocks over him, keeping a careful eye on her foe. Blue had one blue and one gray eye – that's how he got his name. They had been off together, she and Blue, visiting with Señora Gonsalves when her family was slaughtered – their home, barns, creamery and winery torched, and their livestock slain. And now, years later, Blue was dead too.

She continued to gently pile rocks, stone and loose dirt on her best friend, allowing her tears to drip over his resting place. Blue's body lay quietly, but his spirit was very much alive. She could still feel his presence, his panting, his soft red tongue dangling at one side of his mouth, his blue and gray eyes looking up, seeming to whisper, 'I love you Alecka.' She saw him sitting, alert, watching, always on duty. She watched as he darted to the front of the herd, circling it, keeping each of her animals in check. She felt his wet slobber on the ball that he loved to fetch, she smelled his wet fur following the rain, and she heard his barks, his whines, his scratching, even his snoring. She knew that he was very much alive and that they would continue to be companions forever.

Even though he ate ravenously, the wolf was in no hurry to finish; he was going to enjoy this feast for as long as it took.

When Alecka had finished, she sat down to rest and scanned the area for any sign of her other goats, still keeping an eye on the wolf. Sheep, she thought, when disturbed, would normally remain together and follow a leader away from danger. Goats were much more independent, each going in separate directions at the first sign of trouble. She knew it would take her a while to round them up. She still had the entire afternoon to look; the sun remained high overhead.

She sat, staring at her adversary. At first, she considered charging after him with her knife, but she wondered if she had the strength or the skill to survive his counterattack. Her blade once imbedded in his heart or through his neck would certainly be a victory for her. However, she might not get a chance if his jaws caught her by the neck first.

The wolf could see her anger, and he returned her stare; the two remained fixed on each other. The time passed slowly and the wolf continued to tear at the bloody carcass, glancing at Alecka intermittently.

When he had finished, she thought he would get bored and wander away, but instead he lowered his head on his outstretched font limbs and continued to gaze at her. Gradually, the tension between the two began to lessen, and they each seemed less threatening to the other. As the sun slid into mid-afternoon, shady clouds appeared and the sky began to drain. The air began to reek of damp mushrooms, and a cool breeze floated across the tall grasses and into the thicket. Alecka slowly came to an understanding: the wolf attacked her goat, and her dog went to its defense, this was how it was supposed to be. She felt the sadness of having lost her friend, perhaps somewhat guilty for having left him alone for so long and certainly disappointed that this turn of events had occurred, but she no longer felt anger or resentment toward the wolf.

Emu, Lemoa, Pesaru, Unanu, Arce, Arriola, Bera, and Garai – these were the names of her remaining goats. Emu, of course, was the chamois; Atol and Pesaru were a pair, a doe and buck that she had purchased from Señora Gonsalves, but Atol was now gone – the rest were their kids. Alecka eventually was able to round them up and lead them down toward the valley. Since she no longer had her sheepdog to manage the herd, she thought she might need to cut a long green sapling to snap over their heads – she would never use it against them. She couldn't remember how long it had been since she had cut a switch. However, it wasn't necessary; her goats climbed down the mountain path, each finding its own way over and around the rocks, apart, yet still together.

An unsettled sun struggled to make up its mind, going in and out from behind the clouds while the light mist that filled the air could care less. A bevy of mountain finches chirped together in an adjacent shrub, and Alecka kicked an occasional rock as she passed by just to see how far it would go. Each of the goats, one at a time, raised their tails and released small turds onto the ground and effluvium into the air while Señora Gonsalves, off in her small alqueria several kilometers away, skimmed chèvre from the milk and poured it into molds. Once the older members of her herd saw the direction they were headed, they knew where they were going – home to Alecka's baserrias familia along the Gave de Pau.

They reached the top of the last small hill, and the place where Alecka had once lived came into view. She already knew that much of it had been destroyed – she had returned there several times before but had never stayed.

As she approached, she could see that most of the stonewalls of the house remained intact, however, the red tile roof had collapsed and much of its wooden structure had been burned – unburned members and ashes remained spread, disheveled everywhere. She stopped at the side of what was left of one of the barns and gazed at the remains of the winery and several other wooden outbuildings, but it appeared to her as if the spring-fed well hadn't been damaged. Near the end of summer, the well usually went dry so water was saved into wooden storage tanks – these too had been destroyed. The vineyard on the hillside at the rear of the house had survived even though the two years of neglect and lack of pruning had produced a large amount of leggy overgrowth.

As the afternoon started to fade, Alecka began gathering pieces of burned poles and lumber, and she managed to reassemble a small corral for her goats – there was enough vegetation growing, for a while at least, to keep them busy without wandering off. She lowered a cracked wooden bucket down into the well using a piece of rope that she found lying on the ground. Raising it back up, she was careful not to bump the sides or knock dirt into it. When her goats had finished drinking, she refilled the pail, raised it to her own mouth and drank. When she was done, she emptied what remained over her head.

The vineyard was only a few meters from the well, and she walked to the edge to examine the vines and the young grapes that were just beginning to form. They were a Bordeaux clone of Cabernet, on good rootstock, and planted in gravely alluvium soil. The crop was modest and the vines were healthy. It seemed like she ought to try.

She could remember the times when her father and brothers had tended them, tying the new growth to the stakes in the spring, checking the sugar content in the fall, and pruning following the harvest. If they were picked too early, the juice might be too acidic, and if too late, then the juice might lack the acidity needed for a balanced wine. It was all a mystery to her – she would need help.

She knelt down, picked up a fist full of dirt, and held it in both hands, letting it gradually fall between her palms back to where it came from. It was dry, rocky and solid, but it had served their family for several generations. The Romans had come and gone, and so had the Iberians. Her family had outlasted them all, she reasoned, and now was not the time to walk away.

That night she began to clear the house of all the burned wood, ashes and rubbish, and whatever was not serviceable she piled outside and built a large bonfire out of. She discovered a small cask of wine, which went along just fine with the last of her bread and cheese, further adding to her gusto the notion of returning the farm to what it had been before that roving band of brigands had laid plunder to it. Her enthusiasm carried her late into the night until she became quite drunk, finally falling asleep outside in the corral with her goats, but not until she had experienced for the first time a burning desire to find a husband for herself.

The next morning, at the break of dawn, there was no rooster to crow, no sleeping in late. She awoke to the nudging of Arriola, the youngest of Atol's kids, whose nose was in Alecka's back, pushing, shoving and cajoling her mistress. Her stomach was growling and there was no more bread and cheese for breakfast.

She raised a bucket of water from the well for her herd, and when they had had their fill of the cool stuff, they all set off down the road to visit Señora Gonsalves and tell her about Alecka's decision to revisit the homestead. Perhaps she was also going for some advice, and some beans and rice, just to help until she could get things going. With only two milk-producing goats, she wouldn't have much to sell or for cheese. It might be possible for her to make enough soft cheese – soft cheese was the fastest to cure – to sell in a short period of time, but there could be no wine until late in the year at the very earliest.

Over the next few months Alecka disassembled the remains of the several buildings, restoring the parts, the tiles, the timbers, poles, nails, hinges, locks and windows, scrubbing and scraping, and then reassembling them all into a much more modest building.

Emu sold for a better price than she had expected, and word began to circulate around Ordulla that the goat girl of the mountains had returned, and she was rebuilding the farm out on the road to Pau. The two nannies that Señora Gonsalves had lent Alecka were now pregnant and soon to deliver, as well as two of her own does, Arriola and Bera.

Suitors began showing up at her doorstep, and she was quick to receive them, even if it were only to get what work she could out of them, while to her chagrin – due only to her high expectations and not any lack of sexual hunger – she remained virgin.

By the following spring, she had seventeen new kids and she was selling her new wine, bread and cheeses to the pilgrims that passed. Then one day a pilgrim stopped by for some wine and cheese and never left. His name was Guillemot LeMaître.

She had been outside, near the barn, tending to one of the new kids when he arrived. He was tall, handsome, and well-dressed, conservatively in a simple dark suit, wearing a wide-brimmed hat and leather boots. He was mounted on a small spotted horse, and his long legs almost reached the ground – certainly not the typical pilgrim, on foot or mounted on a donkey, which passed by now on a daily basis. She watched him dismount as she stopped what she was doing and wiped her hands on a towel that she wore around her neck.

He secured his horse to the post at the front of the barn and walked toward her. "Pardon, mademoiselle!" His voice was as bold as his appearance was conservative. *He sounds as if he's from east of here*, she thought to herself. She began to notice a rumble in her stomach and spoke.

"I am the proprietress, monsieur. May I help you?"

"The coxswain at the ferry suggested that I stop at your door. He says that here is the best chèvre and wine in this valley, and that the mademoiselle is a feast for the eyes. He surely must have been referring to you if I may be so bold to say so."

"You are so kind to say. If you're looking for good wine and cheese, you've come to the right place," she responded, feeling her bowels beginning to swell.

"My name is Guillemot LeMaître, mademoiselle. I have come from Tarbes, and I'm on my way to Santiago."

Suddenly, unplanned and certainly ill timed, she felt her insides exploding, so much so that she reasoned that if she didn't make a run for the outhouse, she would soon regret not having done so. It had to have been the beans she had for breakfast; sometimes they reacted that way with her. The pressure from her bowels continued to build, and her warm smile slid into a forward gaze, her eyes open wide as she flexed the muscles of her ass, trying very much not to fart lest she might soil her pants.

"If the chèvre is half as good as..." Then he stopped, realizing that she was gone; he could see her running for the privy.

Actually, he didn't immediately catch on as to why she had vanished so abruptly. It wasn't until he saw her enter the small square-shaped building with moon-fashioned slits on the door and sides that he realized she was making a mad dash for the outhouse. He was quickly amused by her situation and chuckled to himself, wondering if he should remain and pretend to be unaware, or if he might venture over to the shaded porch at the house and wait for her to return. He chose the latter.

She seemed to be taking an unusually long time so for that reason Guillemot walked from the porch to the well, then to the edge of the vineyard, then back to the barn, and leaned up against the shaded wall facing the privy. He continued to wait, patiently staring out toward the grapevines and the corralled sheep and goats when he remembered the small metal flute that he carried in his vest pocket. He withdrew the instrument and began to play.

As she listened to the sweet sound drifting in through the moon-shaped slits, Alecka knew that he was nearby, and she felt embarrassed. She had finished and wished that he would go away so she could return to her chores. The music stopped abruptly. She waited a few more minutes, pulled up her leggings beneath her skirt, cracked the door and took a peep. She saw that he was still leaning against the side of the barn, and she quickly pulled the door shut, creating a soft thud. He resumed his playing and she began to wonder if this might be Pan, the horned shepherd god who wandered the hills and mountains playing his panpipes. No, it couldn't be Pan, wooly and goatlike from its waist down to its hooves; human and masculine above. This visitor was neither longhaired nor unkempt, she thought.

She wished now that she hadn't waited so long. She was ready to open the door and march past Guillemot when she heard him call out, "Mademoiselle, I'm sorry that you are not feeling so well. Is there anything I can do to help? I could bring you some water from the well."

She slowly opened the door and shouted back, "No thank you, monsieur. I'm fine now. I'm coming out," and she stepped into the bright sunlight, squinting for having been in the dark for so long.

As she approached him, he stepped forward from the wall and began to walk toward her. She again noticed how handsome he appeared.

The long line of suitors that had arrived over the previous months had all been disappointing and remained in total contrast to the young man that now stood in her presence. He offered her his arm as they turned and walked to her porch together.

He was several inches taller than she was, and she felt his strong arm while walking next to him. When he spoke to her, he seemed to quell her nervousness, and she began to feel comfortable being near him, able to talk to him without becoming tongue-tied.

When they arrived at her porch, they remained standing, talking to each other for nearly an hour before she realized that she hadn't offered him to sit down. She made tea and served him cornbread that she had baked early that morning. As evening set in, she prepared corn soup for him and served some of her best wine.

Later they sat together on the porch in the warm summer night, listened to the crickets and the frogs from the nearby Gave and watched the full moon that was delivered personally to them by Luna herself. The aroma of musty mushrooms seeped into the air, evidencing the presence of Pan, that invisible god of rustic music. Eros, that mischievous, winged child armed with bow and arrow, was also present, spreading desires and irresistible emotions. When all her children had completed their work, Aphrodite emerged, robed the two in beautiful vestments, gently lifted them into her arms and dropped them tenderly into Alecka's bed, where they remained for seven days, emerging only for brief moments for other bodily functions.

On the eighth day, they arose and left the bed much like bears leaving a cave following hibernation, having not consumed either food or water for the duration. They both walked to the well and brought up a bucket of water, and when they could drink no more, Alecka went to the henhouse and retrieved a basketful of eggs while Guillemot built a fire in the stove in the kitchen. Together they cooked a giant omelet made of eggs, milk, cheese, and spices from her garden. When they finished breakfast, Alecka noticed that the smell of musty mushrooms was gone.

One month later, they were married in a small church in Ordulla, and before moving into the Alqueria du Carrefour, Guillemot returned to his home in Tarbes, which has long been known for its horses, in order that he might tender his resignation as schoolmaster there. Additionally, he needed to sell his house. He returned with a wagonload of his personal belongings such as his small library of books and a lute that had been fabricated especially for him by a luthier from Bologna.

Theirs had been love at first sight. He possessed manly charm, was bright, and was in love with her. He saw her as beautiful, energetic, certainly uninhibited, and in love with him. They both had resources; she had the farm, and he had an education and a home in Tarbes that was easily converted into cash. They were both excited about the opportunity that appeared to be theirs, believing that together they could accomplish something that neither of them could do separately. Exactly nine months later, their first son, Jean-Luc, was born. Señora Gonsalves consented to being the boy's godmother.

"Hurry, Alecka!" Guillemot called from the horse-drawn wagon parked in front of the house. "We'll never make it in time; mass will be over before we get there." Jean-Luc had just turned a year old and Alecka was rushing to get him dressed.

"We'll be there in just a minute," she yelled back, wishing that she hadn't agreed to attend mass this particular morning.

They were both born Catholic and neither was very religious. Guillemot's pilgrimage to Santiago had only been an excuse to leave Tarbes – he had been looking for an adventure. Before she met her husband, Alecka only went to mass while her parents were living. Guillemot stopped attending when he began as a student at the university. However, Frère Richard, from the local parish, had been calling on the young couple regularly, encouraging them, with only limited success, to return to the church.

Alecka finally appeared at the door and stepped down from the porch, while Guillemot quickly jumped down from the wagon to help her and the baby up to the driver's bench. With the three of them aboard, he grabbed the reins, released the footbrake, and shouted to the horse, "Allons-y!" and they headed down the lane to the road that would take them into Ordulla.

The lane was bumpy, full of potholes and protruding rocks and the wagon, which had been designed for hauling hay not people, had no shock absorbers.

"I don't like leaving the farm unattended," Alecka shouted over the sound of the road noise. "We've worked too hard just to come home someday and see the entire herd gone or the house burned to the ground." This was a common theme for her and was her biggest objection for going off to mass on Sundays.

"I've been thinking." Guillemot's voice was quivering from the vibration of the wagon, but he knew that she was right. "If we were to hire some help, we could increase our productivity, and we wouldn't have to spread ourselves so thinly. We have several hectares on the other side of the road that we aren't using except grazing."

"Guillemot, maybe time will take care of all this. More than a month has passed since my last display; I think we're going to have another baby. The day will come when we'll have plenty of help."

With that, Guillemot pulled the wagon to a halt and set the footbrake. "Alecka, you should have told me sooner! You should not be out here being thrown around on top of this wagon. He put his arms around her as she continued to hold their son, who had fallen asleep in her arms, and spoke softly to her. "Darling, I love you – very much." He waited for a response that took too long to come and then asked, "Are you happy?"

"Yes, darling, and I love you. But I don't think our lives are about happiness. The gods have been good to us, but I can tell they want us to be strong; they have something bigger waiting for us."

"You've been talking to Señora Gonsalves, haven't you?"

"She is all we need; she hears what the gods are saying and all we need to do is live our lives accordingly. *C'est vrai simple.*"

After they sat there quietly for several minutes, Guillemot released the brake, turned the wagon around, and returned to the farm. They never returned to the Catholic Church. There was a new religion spreading all over Europe, not on the old way, the way of the Basque, the Celts, or the Moors, rather it was modeled on John Calvin's reform at another crossroads, Geneva. The adherence of a large number of the nobility to the movement gave it political meaning and would soon add fuel to religious persecution.

Guillemot pulled up to the front door of the alqueria, this time in the new carriage he had just purchased. The extravagant acquisition would have been cause enough for excitement but for the passenger that it was carrying. Having not been warned ahead of time, Alecka stepped out of the front door and was taken aback seeing her husband dismounting from the bright shiny four-wheeled coach with the strange-looking gentleman who remained seated. Guillemot walked around to the side, where his passenger remained, and invited him to step down and be introduced to his wife.

Alecka could see his strange manner of attire: silk pantaloons, a short-waisted long-sleeved jacket, and a round brimless cap. He wore his coal black hair in a long ponytail that hung almost to the small of his back, and he had a long stringy goatee with so few hairs that her first impression was, *Why bother?*

"Alecka, I would like you to meet M. Sun-Wen-Wong. M. Wong, this is my wife Alecka."

As they shook hands, Sun-Wen-Wong lowered his head in a gesture of formal salutation. "M. Wong has consented to remain with us for a while to help us with the household chores, and to watch over Jean-Luc. He has agreed to remain for a short trial period, and then if we are happy with each other, we will move to a more permanent arrangement."

Reluctantly at first, Alecka soon came around to accepting the man from the east into their household. Of course, it was necessary to add a room onto the house for his, as well as their, privacy.

Sun-Wen-Wong prepared their meals, introducing an Asian style of cooking that both Guillemot and Alecka quickly accepted. He took care of Jean-Luc during the day, and Alecka was able to tend more freely to the goats and the preparation of their cheeses. When they began setting out new rootstock in the pasture across the road, he joined in and helped. He was well educated, had brought with him his own small library of books, written in Cantonese, and was able to share with Guillemot his ideas on religion, philosophy and politics. When the trial period had ended, they mutual agreed to continue the relationship, however, Sun-Wen-Wong's only stipulation was that he be given one day off each week, to which Guillemot and Alecka agreed.

Beginning with the time that Alecka's parents had been killed, Señora Gonsalves had become an important person in Alecka's life. Following the marriage, Alecka thought of Señora Gonsalves often, but there always seemed to be too much that needed to be done at the farm – the goats, the baby, and now tending to the sales of wine and cheeses to the passing pilgrims all required her continuous presence.

Now that Sun-Wen-Wong had joined their household and had proven to be responsible and helpful, she decided that she would spend a few days visiting her dear friend, the godmother of her firstborn.

She headed off by horse (the same horse Guillemot had ridden the day they met), bareback, down the lane, turning toward Pau, taking with her only a change of clothes and several bottles of wine in her knapsack. She loved to ride fast, and she brought her mount to a quick pace, knowing that she wouldn't be able to do that much longer. Her small barefooted body was more suited to this small equine than her lanky husband.

She felt the cool breeze on her face, her bare arms and legs. It slipped in each morning along the valley floor, coming from the ocean. It was that breath of air that cooled the grapes and kept them from burning in the hot Navarre sun. Her long thick hair, no longer a haven for twigs and leaves and glistening in the warm orange landscape, flowed behind.

Several kilometers along, she slowed the pace, looking for the unmarked trail that would lead her up the gentle slopes of the pine-covered mountain to her friend's small cottage. Then it appeared, and she knew it right away because she had taken the path many times before. No particular terrain features stood out, such as a large boulder or a hollow tree, she was guided only by a simple feeling of familiarity.

She charged into the dark opening, working her way upward, keeping her head down so as not to hit any low branches until she was forced to dismount and lead her horse the rest of the way. It was no longer a path, and gradually the trees thinned out, leaving the low scrubby brush and rocks in the clear daylight, the higher Pyrenees on the horizon – Alecka knew the way well.

As she came near to the small cabin, she could see the smoke overhead from the fireplace and an occasional goat along the way, each a part of Señora Gonsalves' small herd – they ran freely during the day and then came in on their own at night. A sheepdog, which looked a lot like Blue, came dashing out to greet Alecka and jumped up with excitement.

"Hello, Sirius, you good boy, you, how have you been?" She dropped her reins to the ground, leaned down and began petting the dog, digging her fingers deep into his thick coat.

Señora Gonsalves emerged from her door and called Sirius back to the house. "Come on, boy, let Alecka be." The two friends greeted and embraced. "It's about time you made it up here. Since you got married, I rarely get to see you. Hey, what do you have there?"

"I brought some of our wine. Let's open a bottle and you can tell me what you think."

"That sounds like a good idea. I'll get us a couple of glasses."

Alecka handed her the four bottles from her knapsack, took a seat at a small wooden table and looked around the room. Hanging from rafters there were several bundles of dried flowers, and bundles of different herbs and spices. She could recognize only one or two: rosemary and thyme. Not far to the side there were goatskins, a spinning wheel, a butter churn and her cheese making equipment. Señora Gonsalves took a seat across from Alecka and began to pour.

She seemed somewhat older than when Alecka had last seen her. Her hair, which had gradually been graying, was now completely white. Nevertheless, It was beautiful, long, thick and wiry, extending down her back and over the sides of her shoulders. Her once smooth, olive complexion was a little puffier than Alecka remembered. Always somewhat buxom, her rounded breasts and bottom always attracted the attention of the warm-blooded Navarre men. Alecka could tell that she hadn't gained any weight, had managed to keep that attractive look and could still capture the eyeballs and lust of most of the men at any pub, bistro or church – Catholic or reformed.

Señora Gonsalves raised her glass, twirled the wine about, peered deeply therein, and then looked at Alecka in the eyes, "*¡A tu salud!*"

"*¡Salud!*" Alecka responded. She waited a few seconds as Señora Gonsalves sloshed the wine in her mouth, seemingly in deep concentration, and then asked, "Well; what do you think?"

"*¡Magnífico, espléndido!* What more can I say? Your father would be proud to know all that you have done. But, my dear, there is more to come, much more. As I have told you many times before, your family bears its curse, but do not fear, the gods are looking at you with much favor, my pretty one. Nevertheless, much is expected of you. Do not worry about any of this, you will not be given any more than you can handle."

Alecka reached for the bottle and poured a second glass for each of them. "After this glass, I shall not have any more, as I am with child, but you can have more if you wish."

"No, Alecka, two is my limit. Say…how about a game of tarot? Wait here and I'll get the cards."

They played together until late and then went to bed. They snuggled together the way Alecka had slept with her mother in earlier times beneath a woolen blanket. "I have missed you so much, Señora Gonsalves."

"I have missed you, also, Alecka. *Buenos noches*." They kissed and then went to sleep.

Prince of Navarre

One child at a time, their family grew until there were three boys and two girls: Jean-Luc, Louise, Philippe, Guillaume and Eugénie. They were schooled at home by their father, and by the age of eight each of them was conversant in Basque, French, Spanish, Portuguese and Latin. By the age of ten they knew rudimentary German and English. The curriculum also included mathematics, geography, history and literature. Their religious education took place each Sunday at The Reformed Church in Ordulla. However, their father schooled them at home with Catholicism and Islam, while Sun-Wen-Wong lectured on the teachings of Lao-Tsu and Confucius. They each rotated jobs in the family business: goat husbandry, the winery, the cheese making, and the store where the wine and cheese were sold, thus they were each familiar with all parts of the business.

Jean-Luc, the oldest, was usually in charge of the goats, making sure they were fed, milked and exercised, in addition to keeping the barns clean. Of the brothers and sisters, he was the least interested in his studies, and the one that complained the most about his chores.

Louise was born one year after Jean-Luc and was the brightest of the children. Her greatest passion was painting. Guillaume, like his oldest brother, preferred working with the goats to cheese making, but at grape-picking time, all the family joined in, Sun-Wen-Wong included. Eugénie was the baby of the family.

Jean-Luc remained at home and eventually took over the farm, Louise became a famous Parisian painter; Philippe became a professor at a university, and Guillaume became a partisan in King Henri's court.

He could hear riders tearing through the thicket, at least four or five of them it seemed, and they were headed in Guillaume's direction. Equestrians on this mountain usually meant that members of the royal family were hunting boar, and that he should stay clear. There were plenty of places to hide and the young fourteen-year-old boy slipped in behind a large boulder in the midst of a grove of malato trees and low-growing underbrush.

As their shouts and the tramping of the horses grew increasingly louder, Guillaume watched a fat, tusked, squealing pig come scurrying through the brush from their direction and heading towards him. He pulled himself in tighter, keeping his hand on his knife, crouching lower, hoping not to be seen either by the swine or by its pursuers.

The pig, seeing the boulder and the thicket surrounding it, without knowing that the spot was already taken, dove in, colliding with the innocent onlooker.

The porkish invader leered at Guillaume as if he had just walked into the women's privy. It turned, without saying excuse me, and bolted for the door. Making its hasty retreat, the pig suddenly met its challenger head-on.

The man's horse was immediately spooked and reared back, slipping on loose rock and tumbling to the ground with the rider's leg firmly squashed between the horse and the ground.

The pig, seeing that the sides had changed, instinctively charged the downed horse, ramming him first with his snout while squealing and kicking his feet, and then tearing at it with his teeth.

The trapped rider, feeling the spray of the horse's spurting blood, tugged unsuccessfully to free his leg while shouting for help from his friends, who had not yet caught up with him.

Guillaume looked on. For a moment he remained silent, then reaching for his knife he darted towards the pig and began screaming loudly. With two giant steps, he leaped on the back of the swine and pushed his long hunting knife deep into the soft spot at the rear of the boar's head, piercing its brain. The pig fell limp onto its side, its tongue dangling from its mouth, a fountain of blood spurting from its head upward onto the rider and running off onto the ground, mixing with the existing pool of horse's blood.

The remaining riders finally arrived; each one stunned at seeing their companion trapped beneath the dying horse and wondering who the boy was that was pulling his knife from the pig's head.

Guillaume quickly climbed off the dead boar as the others dismounted, and he began tugging at the flailing horse, its head waving back and forth while it struggled to get up. Together, they were able to lift the stressed stallion enough to pull free the young man, who had now passed out from perfervid pain. Once liberated, they leaned him against the large boulder that Guillaume had hidden behind earlier, and a tall, older gentleman, the last to arrive, loosened the young man's collar and attempted to straighten his leg, which was broken in several places. Another of the company removed his knife from his belt and proceeded to finish off the suffering horse by slitting its throat.

"*Je m'appele* Admiral Gaspard de Coligny," the older man spoke, looking first at Guillaume and then at the injured man while giving him wine from his goatskin bag. "And this is Henri de Bourbon, first-blood prince of Navarre, that you have so nobly rescued. You will certainly be rewarded by the queen when she hears of this. What is your name, young man?"

"*Je m'appele* Guillaume LeMaître. I live with my parents at the bottom of this mountain, near the crossroads by the river. We have a farm and vineyard there and sell wine and cheese to the passing pilgrims."

Coligny scratched his head and thought for a moment. "Yes, I know of your place, I have stopped there before to rest. Your father and mother, they are well known for having the best wine and cheese in this region, and I too have enjoyed their produce."

"If it would please you, the place is near and would be convenient for his royal highness....."

"Of course, that would be wonderful. You are a perfect

gentleman."

Coligny managed to immobilize the prince's injured leg by applying a makeshift splint made from several saplings wrapped with material torn from one of their shirts. He then gave the prince more wine, placed him on a sled, and prepared him for the trip down the mountainside to Alqueria du Carrefour.

Eduardo and the Duke of Alençon, the younger brother of King Charles IX, lifted the dead pig up onto the rear of one of extra horses, brought for this purpose, tying it down securely with ropes that stretched beneath the horse's belly. The pig's blood continued to splash onto the rock-strewn ground.

They each took turns leading the homemade gurney down the hillside, Eduardo going first. Alençon led his horse as well as the horse carrying the boar. The admiral walked alongside Guillaume, leading his stallion. He was quite tall, perhaps 185 centimeters, and thin. His dark eyes seemed to bulge forward from his long suntanned face, which terminated at his chin with a pointed beard. He wore a small-brimmed, red hunting cap and a brown brocade jacket that hung to his knees with side vents for his jeweled sword, which had never left its scabbard during the turmoil.

"I want to thank you for the tremendous service that you have provided to the prince, and to the kingdom itself, first for your bravery and then for having accommodated us so graciously."

"You are so kind. Please think nothing of it, Admiral. I did what had to be done."

Guillaume's youthfulness reflected in the warm morning sunlight along with his light shoulder-length hair, bleached from the sun. His soft olive skin clung to his lean athletic body, made muscular from having spent most of his years climbing the hills and chasing after goats, wild boar and rabbits. He wore a woolen shirt, pantaloons, and sandals of goatskin strapped to his ankles.

His bone-handled knife, which he had wiped clean and returned to his belt, had been given to him by his father on his last birthday, and Guillaume was anxious to return home to tell his father how he had used it to kill the boar. He was used to bringing home birds and rabbits he had trapped, a skill passed on to him by his mother, but this day he was bringing home a boar on the ass of a prince's stallion.

As they worked their way slowly down the slope, the admiral paid close attention to both Henri and to Guillaume, stopping from time to time to rest. At one such stop alongside a stream, Guillaume spotted some watercress growing on the opposite side. He waded across to pull several handfuls and washed the roots clean in the water before returning to Coligny and offering him some of it. "Here, try this, fresh produce from the highlands of Navarre."

"You are quite resourceful, young man. And I enjoy watching you move about, not at all intimidated by our presence."

"Oh, I am, Admiral Coligny, it's just that I prefer that you do not see it. Here, would you like some more watercress?"

"Yes, thank you, Guillaume. It's quite refreshing. We must continue; it is getting late."

Eugénie stepped out of the barn and could see the four figures walking slowly down the road leading the horses and the gurney. Thinking that she could see Guillaume among them, she ran into the house exclaiming, "Guillaume is coming, and he isn't alone, it looks like there are four horses!"

Alecka stopped churning the butter, wiped her hands on her apron and rushed to the door to see what her daughter was talking about. Having seen their royal attire, she turned back into the house, out the back door to the vineyard and yelled out to Guillemot to come quickly. Then she rushed back to the front door and waited. As the group came closer, she could see her son, the man walking alongside with his brocade jacket and his jeweled saber, the Arabian horses, the dead boar, and of course the young blood-soaked boy carried on the gurney, his leg wrapped in the hastily made splint.

"Bring him inside; he can have your bed, Guillaume!" Alecka led the way, rushing to pull back the blanket that covered the bed as Coligny and Eduardo carried the gurney into the small dark farmhouse. "What happened, anyway? Did the pig get him?" Then suddenly she stopped and realized that the boy on the gurney was someone special. "Who is this young man?"

"Mother, this is Prince Henri of Bourbon, and standing next to you is his adviser, Admiral Coligny."

Alecka quickly fell to her knees in obeisance in front of the young prince as Guillemot walked in behind, unobserved.

Guillaume continued the introductions. "Your highness, this is my mother, Alecka, and coming in the door here is my father, Guillemot LeMaître. In the room behind you are my brothers and sisters, and then there is our housekeeper, Sun-Wen-Wong."

The prince had awakened, and with a grimace on his face he acknowledged the introductions. "Madame... please... rise, it is I who should be kneeling to you, mother of the one who saved my life. And you... M. LeMaître... I am truly honored to meet you and to be in your household. You have a very lovely family, I can see."

Sun-Wen-Wong entered the room, bowed, and seeing the contortion on the prince's face turned to Coligny. "I have had some experience with broken bones. If you like, I would be glad to examine the prince's leg."

"Yes," the admiral responded. "Please, go right ahead."

"It would be good if everyone would leave the room, except of course Admiral Coligny, you certainly can stay. I would feel much better if there were not so many looking on."

Alecka instructed Eduardo and Alençon to bring the pig around to the back of the house so she might begin to dress it. Eugénie looked on at Eduardo with dreamy interest, much like a young schoolgirl having her first crush. Guillemot and Jean-Luc took the horses to the stable to unsaddle and feed them.

Sun-Wen-Wong then approached Prince Henri, smiling and bowing before speaking. "Your highness, I am Sun-Wen-Wong, and I would like to examine your leg." He was dressed in traditional blue-colored silk Chinese garb with a round cap. His long black ponytail hung to the small in his back. He had the look of a professional, assured and confident, and spoke as if he were certain of what he was about to do.

"I will be very gentle. However, I will need to remove first the splint, then your bloodstained clothing. I will then feel your leg and attempt to see if and where it is broken. I will probably need to set the broken bone and then put a cast on your leg to hold it while it heals. Do you understand all that must be done? I can give you some wine to help you though this."

The prince shook his head in agreement, and the Asian housekeeper proceeded to remove the splint and examine the leg. When he had finished his examination he reported to the admiral that the bone was broken in two places, and that the admiral would need to hold the patient as the broken leg was reset.

It was now nearing late evening and the sun had dropped beneath the horizon, leaving the room almost dark. Sun-Wen-Wong lit several candles along with three joss sticks and began waving the burning incense over the prince while reciting a prayer in his native Cantonese. The smell of sandalwood would soon overcome the damp odor of the room. He then offered the boy a beverage he had prepared containing an herbal solution. No one could hear the bleating of the goats outdoors or the scurrying of the rabbits to their holes in the ground as young Prince Henri let out a bloodcurdling scream. Coligny held him securely while Sun-Wen-Wong carefully manipulated the broken parts into position, and after a few minutes it was done. Sun-Wen-Wong then instructed the admiral to remain with the patient and keep him from moving while he prepared a mixture of plaster for a cast.

When he returned, he brought with him some herbs, some wooden braces, some cloth and a bucket of wet plaster of Paris he had mixed. He then proceeded to light new incense sticks and to sprinkle the herbs on the bare leg, allowing much of it to fall onto the bed. He wrapped the braced leg tightly with the cloth pieces and applied the plaster to the cloth, pressing it into the material, smoothing it with his hands. When he had finished, he bowed and thanked the prince for being his patient before returning to his room.

Alecka and Louise were both at work in the kitchen when Sun-Wen-Wong had finished. It was late and no one had eaten. The kitchen table was too small to seat everyone, so Alecka announced that dinner was ready, but that the kitchen table was reserved for Guillemot and their guests, Coligny, Alençon, and Eduardo. Eugénie and Louise would do the serving. Everyone else would have to pick up a plate, take some pork, some bread and a glass of wine, and find a place wherever.

When they had finished eating, Eduardo made his way to the stable taking his bedroll with him and laying it out on a bed of straw in the loft. Gaspard du Coligny and Guillemot LeMaître took a seat on the porch. The night air was damp and Llargi, the quarter moon, shone through the fog and mist that was making its way up the valley from the coast. She seemed to stick to each morsel of mist that hung in the sky, making the night air appear to sparkle. The herd of goats in the nearby corral was quiet, settled down for the night, allowing the crickets and bullfrogs from the nearby Gave to be heard. The spirits were quite active. Mari and her consort Sugaar could almost be heard sleepwalking through the hills above the vineyard. They would periodically generate thunderstorms and lightning, but not this night; tonight Ortz, the moonlit mist would prevail. Pan, the invisible, two-legged goat, entered the bedroom where the two sisters were sleeping and carried Eugénie off to the loft in the stable, leaving behind a musty mushroom smell.

The admiral was enjoying the good feeling he was experiencing with the LeMaître family. *How simple life could be here in the country,* he thought to himself. The two men discussed arrangements for Henri to remain there at Alqueria du Carrefour until he was ready to be moved, and for the coverage of his expenses.

Their conversation turned to politics and the war of religion. Admiral Coligny began to explain the current crises. "Since Charles IX was the intended target at Meaux, and her sole aim has been to protect him, Catherine de Medici, as regent, has dropped her policy of toleration and issued an edict withdrawing all freedom of worship for Huguenots; she has ordered all Huguenot ministers to leave the country. She has now ordered the arrest of Condé and me. I suppose from her perspective this was a sensible move as we are the two main military leaders in the Huguenot ranks. Catherine has tried to negotiate a settlement, but each time she makes conciliatory moves towards us, she angers the Guise family, the leading Catholic family. She seems to have herself into a position that whatever she does, she is greeted with suspicion and a compromise towards one side provokes the other.

"A peaceful settlement would greatly benefit France, however. Catherine is now considering a masterful move to weaken the power of the Guise family. She plans to marry her daughter, Marguerite de Valoir, to Philip II of Spain. This would give her influence in the court of Madrid at a time when Spain is considered a major military power, and the Guise family cannot voice a complaint as Philip is known to be a staunch Catholic."

The next morning was the day of the spring equinox; the sun began its journey across the sky from below the Earth's horizon but remained hidden behind a thick, gray curtain of fog that had poured in from the coast and up the Gave de Pau. The distant hillside grasses appeared more blue than green. The LeMaître family watched as Coligny, Alençon and Eduardo slowly rode their horses down the lane to the road. They turned left and rode on to the province of Béarn, and to the court of Queen Jeanne d'Albret.

Henri de Bourbon was suddenly awakened by the activity on the porch. Feeling mildly hung over from the wine that had been administered to him hours earlier, he sat up and lifted his injured leg, now weighed down with plaster, with both hands and eased it onto the wooden floor. Then with both hands pressed against the edge of the bed, he pushed himself up onto his other leg into an erect standing position, balancing himself with hands and arms extended in opposite directions. Someone had left a makeshift crutch at the foot of the bed, and Henri nearly lost his balance in reaching for it. Once the padded prop felt comfortably tucked into his armpit, he tried it, experimentally shifting the weight of his body onto it instead of his injured leg. Satisfied that it would hold him, he scanned the room, seeing for the first time since his arrival the primitive farmhouse where he had spent the night and where he would spend the next few weeks while he recovered. The cool morning air breezed past his face as he made his way toward the bedroom door, toward the laughter that he could hear coming from the front of the house.

"Oh, look, he's up and walking!" Guillemot was the first to see him, and the others all turned to watch the young prince hobbling delicately toward the front door.

Having never knowingly entertained royalty before,

Guillemot remained formal and dropped to one knee, *"Bonjour, mon prince."* Then, without thinking, he rushed toward the prince ready to offer any support he could as the others voiced their expressions of good morning.

"Hello!"

" Bonjour!"

" Good morning, how are you?"

The prince looked up, smiled, and as if he were saying 'thank you' he spoke as he often did in Catalan, *"Bon dia!"* and then regarded the riders off in the distance.

"Coligny asked us to tell you that he said 'goodbye.' He did not want to wake you. He left a note on the table for you. Here, it is," Guillemot said while handing the note to the prince.

> *Duty calls, my prince; there is much to do. I'm on my way to see King Charles, in Paris; he may be our only ally, our only way to Catherine. See you soon.*
> *–Coligny*

The young Henri of Navarre read the note slowly and watched his three companions disappear into the distance. The fifteen-year-old Navarre, first prince of the blood, knew that he should be with them, not standing there on a wooden crutch. The hunt had been a mistake – poor judgment on his part. The Huguenot cause was at its height; the gray-haired admiral Coligny was leading the Reform. It had been Navarre's idea for the hunt, and the queen had been firmly against it. She had consented only if Coligny would accompany him and then return promptly to court.

By the time he had finished reflecting, his three companions were completely out of sight, and he turned to Guillaume and spoke. "It looks like you and I are going to be friends for the next few weeks. Why don't we sit down and you can tell me about yourself."

Louise, the older of the two sisters, was quite tall like her brother and father, was flat-chested and she wore her hair wrapped in a bun on the back of her head. She had a pretty, oval-shaped face, thin lips and a small pointed nose. Her soft, pale white skin rarely saw the sun – she avoided it at all costs.

It was Marsday, and one week had passed since the prince had arrived. Each night at the dinner table, Henri was aware that Louise was staring at him. He was used to people looking his way, and most of the time he thought nothing of it. Nevertheless, her gaze seemed different, almost as if she were reading his thoughts. At court, he had become known as a *vert-galant* for his prowess as a lover. She was pretty and the right age; nevertheless, he knew that it would be very inappropriate to get involved with a member of the household. She seemed quiet most of the time and rarely joined in the dinnertime conversation. On the few occasions that she did have something to say, her remarks seemed to be brief and forceful, often with an element of wit.

On this occasion, the conversation centered on the queen's famous edict that abolished popish services throughout Béarn and introduced Protestant worship. Louise daringly offered an open criticism before the prince.

Following the meal, Henri approached her and thanked her for her honesty. He then asked, "Each evening I am aware of your gaze; I'm not sure what you are looking for."

"I am a painter, Your Highness, and I have been studying your face. I would like very much to paint it. Are you aware that your features are quite striking?"

"Yes, I am," he said, looking directly into her eyes and smiling.

"Your eyes in particular; they seem to burn through

whatever you are looking at."

"I've been told that before, but I'm more than flattered to hear you say it."

"I would like to capture that young would-be king look of yours, full of genius and character like your mother. I pray though that you would have her consistent piety."

"I pray that I would have her courage! Yes, I desire that you paint my portrait, but I've not seen your work, and what if I don't like it?"

"If you don't like it, it is probably because it is reflecting some truth that you don't want exposed. I once heard the story that King Henry VIII sent his court painter, Hans Holbein, to paint the portrait of Anne of Cleves. He returned with her image, falsely enhancing her beauty. Relying on the image, he sent for her to become his queen, but on her arrival she looked quite different, so much so that Henry had the marriage annulled. When questioned, Holbein replied that if she were to become queen, she must appear to be beautiful."

"Then beauty is not always truthful?" Henri asked.

"Why do you ask? Truth is always beautiful, even when painful. You of all people should know that. Tonight I will grind my pigments, and perhaps tomorrow we can meet on the porch. Unless, of course, you and Guillaume are going fishing. Good night, Your Highness."

Henri lay in bed that night thinking about Louise, her temerity keeping him awake. Only his mother could speak to him in that tone and manner.

Early the following morning, Henri began to investigate his new surroundings, and he made his way slowly out past the well to the nearby vineyard. Even though he was in fine physical shape, he needed to stop and rest after hobbling only a short distance. He stood motionless putting all his weight on the crutch. The ground seemed dry and dusty. The warm springtime sun forced drops of perspiration out of the pores on his forehead. He looked up and was impressed to see how the rows of grapevines remained perfectly even and parallel as they extended up the hillside. Most of the old growth had been pruned back following last year's harvest, and the new growth was fresh and green; the grapes were barely showing. Many times he had ridden past the vineyards in Béarn, but he had never seen the vines up close. He wished he could make his way farther up the hill.

Jean-Luc finished milking the goats and stepped out from the barn into the warm morning air. He saw Henri leaning on his crutch several meters up on the sunny hillside and called out to him. "Prince Henri, is everything OK?"

Henri turned and looked downhill toward Jean-Luc and waved. "Yes, all is fine."

Jean-Luc took long strides, making his way up the slope to Henri. As he came close, he removed his hat and unconsciously slapped it against his leg as if he were shaking the dust off it. "It's still too early, the grapes are just starting to form. Can I help you make it back to the house?" He was slightly out of breath, but he tried not to show it.

Henri said, "This walk turned out to be more difficult than I expected. Yes, I suppose."

Jean-Luc was about two centimeters taller than Henri. He placed his hat back on his head, reached around and took Henri's right arm, placing it around his neck and over his shoulder before putting his own arm around Henri's waist. "All right, you hand me that crutch and hang on to me. We'll make it back in no time."

Slowly they worked their way down the hill, stirring the dust as they went, with Henri using Jean-Luc's body as a substitute leg.

Small chipmunks and lizards stuck their heads out of their holes as the prince passed their homes, this being the first time they had ever had a royal visit. Grape berry moths flew in formation overhead while spider mites and stink bugs crawled out on the edge of their leaves hoping to get a better look.

As the two neared the front porch, Henri could see Louise and Eugénie sitting together. Eugénie was plucking her psaltery, while Louise gazed out at the two young men making their way toward her. Whereas Eugénie slouched in her chair holding her instrument, Louise sat erect and poised with her hands in her lap. If one were to look very carefully, one might see a slight glimpse of amusement in the layer immediately beneath her expressionless visage at seeing this goat farmer lugging the future king of Navarre, perhaps even one day king of all France, down the vineyard hillside.

As the prince approached that invisible line of differentiation separating ruler and ruled, both sisters rose. Eugénie placed her instrument on her chair, and they both curtsied. "Good morning, Your Highness," their soprano and alto voices rang out in spoken harmony.

He limped forward two or three more steps, stopped and removed his arm from around Jean-Luc's neck. Leaning on his crutch and looking directly at Louise, then at Eugénie, and back at Louise, he returned the greeting. "Good morning, ladies." Then, without moving his body, he turned his face first up into the sun, then awkwardly scanned the mountain vista. He smiled and remarked, "How good it is just to be alive! How good it is to have friends." Then he leaned forward and with the aid of his crutch, he maneuvered himself onto the porch. "Ladies, please be seated; I do not want to make to a spectacle of myself, neither do I want to disturb you any further. I will just go inside and sit for a while."

He then started for the doorway but stopped. He turned

toward Louise and said, "Louise, did you, by chance, grind those pigments? I'm looking forward to the portrait – do you remember?"

Louise looked startled. She straightened her bodice (which didn't need straightening) and said, "Of course I remember. But I did not think you were serious, perhaps just teasing me. Oh my! Now I do feel embarrassed. Can you forgive me?"

"It's nothing grave, and please don't be embarrassed. Perhaps you could make it up to me by allowing me to watch you prepare the material. I would like that." Without waiting for a response, Henri went inside. Louise returned to her chair, and Eugénie took her psaltery from the floor, sat down and began to play.

If Louise took after her father, Eugénie was the image of her mother – medium height, athletic build with small but well-defined breasts and hips, long wavy hair and dark olive skin with large eyes beneath thick bushy eyebrows. In a foot race, she could outrun all her brothers and sisters except for Guillaume, who was the tallest and fastest member of the family. She could throw a knife and turn a sheep on its side for sheering as well as any man. Eugénie was energetic, full of life and rather gregarious, and she had a natural talent for music. She could play an assemblage of instruments – the bagpipes, a psaltery, a shawm, a lizard, and the lute. Nothing could ever be hidden from her antennae, and she was quick to notice the tête-à-tête taking place between Henri and Louise.

She continued to pluck softly on the psaltery on her lap and after a few minutes she spoke to her sister. "I heard that he has a mistress."

Louise continued looking straight ahead as if she were admiring the distant mountains. "That is of no concern to me, even if it were true." Then turning her gaze toward her sister she continued, "And it should not be of any interest to you either.

Where did you hear such a thing?"

"Oh, rumors; you know how they go around. But the pear does not fall far from the tree, especially when it's a handsome prince."

"You think he's handsome, do you?"

"Indeed, he's adorable, but in a strange way. His pointed nose and chin could be scary when he gets older, but, for now, his wavy hair and rosy cheeks, and his tight ass, I would bed with him even if he weren't a prince."

"Eugénie! Where did you learn to talk like that?"

"Don't tell me that you aren't just as interested! Your slip is showing. The difference is that I might actually act on my feelings."

The conversation came to a sudden halt as Alecka stepped out onto the porch. "There are several pilgrims heading down the lane, and one of you needs to go wait on them. Eugénie, you take care of the travelers, and, Louise, you need to start on the cheese. The milk has been sitting long enough. And I couldn't help but hear you two talking; I do not want either of you bothering our guest. Do you hear me?"

Guillaume enjoyed fishing. He viewed it as time alone when he could get away from all that was going on at the farm, or when he had something he wanted to work out in his mind. He knew fishing was something Henri could do while waiting for his leg to heal. The two would often start out early in the morning, cross the road, sit on the banks of the Gave, spend the morning talking, joking, and occasionally bringing in one or two of the salmon or trout that were plentiful. Henri was always excited when he brought home a salmon or a trout for Sun-Wen-Wong to prepare.

He enjoyed Sun-Wen-Wong's cooking – rabbit soup, beans and pintxos, and chow mein. He frequently served a sauce that

Navarre had never tasted before, which was much like a hollandaise sauce except that he replaced the lemon juice with a reduction of wine, vinegar, shallots and tarragon. When he asked what it was called, Sun-Wen-Wong thought for a moment, smiled, and answered, "Béarnaise sauce." He also gave France one of its more famous recipes, poule au pot – stuffed chicken boiled with vegetables. The prince was reputed to have said that he didn't want anyone in this realm to be so poor as to not be able to afford a poule in the pot once a week.

Prince Henri's leg slowly began to heal.

The first picking of the grapes had begun, and each year there was always a grand *fête de la moisson* at the alqueria. Friends and neighbors were invited, and an ox was butchered and buried with hot coals in a pit where it cooked slowly all day. Even Señora Gonsalves came, bringing her dog, Sirius, and her small herd of goats. She would remain for a fortnight before returning to her mountaintop.

Frère Richard arrived from Ordulla bringing his violin, and Sun-Wen-Wong arranged for his sister, Shuang Xiao, to arrive from Ville-de-St-Pier. Several families came prepared to perform skits.

Henri demonstrated how Guillaume, on that well-known day, had killed the boar, and Eugénie and Louise, to everyone's laughter and amusement, did their rendition of Jean-Luc helping Prince Henri down the vineyard hillside.

There was music, singing and dancing, and of course the most important event was the stomping of the grapes. This year was more special than any before because by now the entire region knew that there was a prince living with Guillemot and Alecka LeMaître.

In the midst of the celebrations and festivities, the revelers danced gaily into the night around a bright bonfire. No one noticed the two riders from Béarn that had just arrived and had turned their royal horses onto the lane leading up to the alqueria, riding slowly towards the place of merriment. Once they were close enough and had become illuminated by the bonfire, the eyes of the throng turned toward them, and because they could tell straightaway that the strangers were from the queen's court, the music and dancing stopped.

Henri had been with Louise on the far side. When he walked around the blaze to get a better look, he recognized them at once and called out their names. "Eduardo, Alençon, *bonsoir! Que fait vous ici?*"

They dismounted and the three embraced. Jean-Luc took their horses to the barn, and Eugénie rushed to bring wine for the guests.

Alençon, the king's youngest brother, was in high spirits now they had finally arrived. "We weren't sure if we were going to be able to find this place in the dark. It was lucky for us that you had the bright fires burning or we would probably have ridden on past. Henri, you look good. I see *les beaux campagnes* have done you well – no crutches, no limp, a beautiful woman at your side, you look fully recovered."

Louise was no longer at his side; rather she was standing off to the edge. She knew that Alençon had just referred to her, so she straightened her posture and blushed lightly, which no one noticed.

Henri was aware that his hiatus there at the alqueria had lasted longer than was necessary and felt compelled to justify not returning directly to court once his leg had healed. *"Ah, la Campagne!* The food, the wine, the good people of this valley, I have never been so happy. And you, my friend, how have you been?"

Alençon answered, "Well. The wars have been quiet – too quiet perhaps."

Free-spirited and barefooted, Eugénie, her legs and feet stained purple from stomping grapes earlier in the day, returned with two mugs of wine, handing one to Alençon and the other to Eduardo. She looked straight at Eduardo, remembering the night that she had spent with him in the stable, now wondering if he had ever thought of her after he left.

Eduardo could tell that she was a bit giddy from too much to drink. She reached out and took his free hand, "Have you had anything to eat? There is plenty at the table, please help yourselves."

Eduardo smiled. "I'm starved. Why don't you take me to the table and show me what's good?"

Henri replied to Alençon, "I'm sorry to say, I had almost forgotten about the wars. And the queen, how is she doing, and Coligny?"

"Coligny is in Paris, with my brother Charles. They are working on a plan to take the war to the Netherlands, trying to distract the Spanish. Catherine doesn't like the idea at all. Your mother, she's still at Pau and doing fine. Why don't we move over here, out of earshot of the others?" He took his first taste of the wine Eugénie had given him. "This is new wine? – *Pas mal!*"

Once they were alone, Alençon took on a serious look. "Henri, the reason we've come is to bring you back to court. Your mother, the queen, has finalized an agreement with Regent Catherine for you to marry my sister, Marguerite de Valois."

"What! Marry a Catholic? Has she lost her mind? This is the most ridiculous thing I have ever heard of. She must think that this will bring peace to us Huguenots. How do you feel about this?"

"You would become my brother, there's nothing wrong with that."

"Do they expect me to convert?"

"I don't think so. They are working on getting a dispensation from the Pope, but it doesn't look promising. They want you to marry anyway, but outside the Notre Dame – not inside. I really can't answer any more about it; they just asked me to come get you. How soon do you think you can be ready?"

"I'll let you know."

Henri walked away from Alençon, poured himself a mug of wine and returned to where Louise was standing.

Alençon could see Henri's disappointment and took a seat by himself around the bonfire, only to be quickly joined by others that were anxious to meet him. Eduardo and Eugénie had already headed to the barn.

Henri and Louise had become good friends throughout the summer months, and of all the LeMaîstres Louise was who he enjoyed being with the most. He had been careful not to become too attached to her and until this night, out of respect to Guillemot and Alecka, had never attempted anything sexual with her. Their relationship had developed during the times that they had spent together while she painted his portrait. She would paint, and he would talk. She had wanted to know about his being a prince, a future king, about life at court, his reputation as a *vert-gallant*, his mother and father, and other matters inside his mind.

The yellow-orange flames were beginning to die, and Henri and Louise felt the evening dampness as they walked away toward the vineyard. The moon, a waxing crescent, was positioned slightly above the horizon, somewhere between the earth and the sun. There were no clouds to hold in the day's warmth, leaving a clear black sky full of bright shining stars.

"I can tell something is troubling you, Henri," she said. They both began climbing up the knoll, the same hill he had climbed that first morning. "Won't you tell me what it is?" she urged.

"I need to figure it out myself first," he replied.

Up the hill they climbed, higher than he had climbed before. She caught herself as she slipped on a loose stone and listened to it tumble downhill in the cool, dense air. "If by yourself, do you mean that I should leave?"

Henri paused and then spoke. "No, do not leave."

When they reached the top, they both sat in a small clearing in the dirt where there were no vines. They looked down at the remaining fire, now a pile of embers. "What is it that you need to figure out, dear Henri?"

He waited for a few minutes before responding, and then while looking off into the northern distance, he told her what he had just learned, that his mother had arranged for him to marry the king's sister, Margaret. "You, your family and friends have all been so kind, not just to me but also to each other. I am suddenly finding it painful to leave this place. Nevertheless, I must face the fact that I was born to be king."

She took his hands into hers and looked directly into his face, where she could see his struggle, and wished that she could comfort him. They remained quiet for the next few minutes, and then he stood up, walked to the edge of the knoll and stared off at the distant southern Pyrenees. His concentration was disrupted by the sound of a bat zigzagging near his head. Selene appeared as a thin sliver, her lunar crescent as a crown set upon her head. Her great love was the shepherd prince Endymion.

"Come, lie with me, Henri," Louise called to him.

"In a moment, my love." He continued to gaze out to the south and then after more time had passed, Louise called out to him again.

"Henri, if you want to be alone, please tell me and I will leave."

She could barely hear him respond. "No, do not leave me. I need just a little more time."

Still seated, and as more time passed, Louise looked down

the hillside. She could almost make out Jean-Luc adding some kindling to the dying embers below, and some larger sticks and then some larger logs. As the logs were beginning to catch and the flames were getting brighter, she could hear the musicians begin to play once again, and the people below began to dance around the fire.

Then Henri returned to her, sitting down next to her so close that their hips and shoulders were both touching. "Thank you for staying with me," he whispered softly to her.

Nearby, a woodpigeon cooed a very pleasant, soothing sound. The surrounding air seemed warmer than before as he put his arms around her and kissed her. She responded, turning her body toward him and returning his kisses. This was her first time with a man, and she was burning with desire. She accepted his tongue into her mouth. He placed his hands beneath her chemise onto her tiny breasts, and then she allowed him to undress her. Her loins were wet, and she felt for the first time in her life the excitement of being naked before a man, and of seeing his nakedness, his aggressiveness, of being gazed upon by him, of experiencing that man's mouth on her breasts and the wetness on her hands as she searched out and nervously took hold of his member. At last, he mounted her from behind, the side of her face pressed against the earth, and she felt the pain of being opened for the first time, a throbbing soon followed by an uninterrupted stream of pleasure.

When they had both finished, they fell into a deep sleep and when they awoke, they both felt cold, shivering from being naked in the damp air. They quickly dressed and returned down the hill, each to their own room in the house, each to their own bed.

Henri needed time to prepare himself for the return to court life and to express his appreciation for all that everyone had done for him while he had been there. He had established friendships not only with the LeMaître family but also many of the families surrounding the alqueria. The following days, he spent time with all those with whom he had become close. He went fishing with Guillaume, and he helped Sun-Wen-Wong prepare the final diner the night before he departed. After diner, they took out their musical instruments, Guillemot, his lute; Sun-Wen-Wong, his xiao, an end-blown flute; and Eugénie, her psaltery, and when they ran out of songs that they knew, they made up new ones.

On the last day, Henri and Louise rode horses into the hills, taking a picnic lunch with them. They both accepted that their romance was soon to be over when he returned with his friends back to Castle Pau. They also knew that they would each continue to carry the memory of their romance long after. While they rested their horses and lay together on a blanket at the edge of a stream, Louise told the story of Tristan and Iseult two star-crossed lovers. Tristan had to forego his love for Iseult, who was obligated to his uncle, King Mark of Cornwall.

The following morning, Henri, Alençon and Eduardo left for Pau before the sun had a chance to get out of bed. Alecka packed a few provisions for them, some of her good chevre, flat bread, fish jerky and of course some of her fine red Béarn wine, and the three had passed the turnoff to Señora Gonsalves hilltop home before the sun had raised its head.

The tree-lined road followed the Gave the entire distance to the castle. Pau had been developed at a strategic location where there was a ford for flocks being driven up to summer pastures on a Roman road between Bordeaux and Saragossa.

Down the long, palm-tree-lined Boulevard des Pyrénées they rode with the streets running east and west. They passed through the Place Royale, a thirty-acre park planted with beech trees stretching along the high bank of the Gave. They passed over the stone bridge and into the castle. On the left of the entrance was the donjon or Tour de Gaston Phenbus, and on the right was the Tour de la Monnaie.

Life returned to normal at the alqueria. Word came that Queen Jeanne had died; Henri was now king. (A popular rumor of the time alleged that Jeanne had been poisoned by Catherine de Medici, his future mother-in-law.) Henri was to wed Marguerite of Valois in Paris, and Henri requested that Guillaume accompany him to Paris along with 800 other Huguenot supporters for the wedding. The messenger sent an Arabian horse to Guillaume as a gift. Guillaume felt obliged to attend because of their friendship and headed off to Castle Pau.

When Guillaume arrived, he learned that the king had departed several days earlier, and he quickly left in an attempt to catch up. He arrived in Paris on the day following the wedding and witnessed the streets filled with celebrants, both Catholic and Huguenot. There were no spare beds in the city so he was forced to find a place to sleep in the street, along with thousands of others. Throughout the night there were minor skirmishes between the revelers, but nothing serious erupted until word came that Catherine had sanctioned the brutal assassination of Coligny and six Huguenot leaders.

It was dark; the sun had slipped below the horizon hours earlier as Guillaume rode his tired horse into Paris. Everywhere he looked there were people, men and women alike, their orange faces reflecting the light of the numerous fires that were burning in the streets. Some were dancing to the music of a guitar or a musette, celebrating, and others were trying to get some sleep, lying in the street because there were insufficient beds in the city for the large number that had come for the wedding. He rode beyond the Île de la Cité to the Louvre and stopped along the Seine, where he decided to look for an unoccupied spot to water and feed his horse and to bed down for the night. There was no feed for his horse, only water from the river.

"Did you hear?" The young man nearby directed the news to Guillaume. "They killed Coligny. They shot him and then they threw the body out the window."

"Do you mean Admiral de Coligny?" Guillaume questioned.

"Yes, Admiral Gaspard de Coligny as well as six other Huguenots. They say that members of the Guise family did it; Catherine put them up to it."

"Coligny was my friend; he spent time at my home near Ordulla. He was a good man. Tell me, did the wedding take place?"

"Yes, several days ago. But they say that Queen Margot won't have anything to do with Henri because he's not Catholic. He's being held prisoner, Catherine wants him to convert to Catholicism and renounce his Protestant faith."

"Do you think he will renounce?"

"If he wants to keep his head he will."

"I do not have a good feeling about all this. We probably should leave."

"Why, what do you think might happen?"

"I do not trust Queen Catherine. She is constantly changing sides."

Guillaume thought he could hear shouts and cries coming from near the front of the Royal Palace – screaming, cursing, and what sounded like metal clashing, swords clashing. It started out slowly and then became louder. There were also the sounds of horses, their hoofs pounding against the cobblestone street, a mixture of snorts and blows out of the nostrils; a neigh, whinnies and squeals, as if from a closed mouth, and screams – loud and long – a loud roar of rage. *How rare*, he thought, *to hear a domesticated horse scream.*

"What is it?" he asked the young man.

"Oh, these skirmishes have been taking place all night. I don't think it's anything – I wouldn't worry. You know the festivities and all, people drink too much, so it's bound to happen."

Guillaume said, "I don't believe this is a scuffle, monsieur; it sounds to me that people are being killed, and I think it's moving in this direction. I'm going to move to a safer spot on the other side of the river. I think you would be well advised to move on too."

The young man said, "The bridge is at the front of the palace, and that's where all the commotion is coming from. If you go that way, you're heading right into the disorder. You'll need to follow the river in the other direction to find the next crossing."

Guillaume said, *"Merci;* that is the way I'll go," and began saddling his horse, the Arabian given to him by Navarre. He was beginning to wish that he had left this particular horse and its expensive saddle back at the alqueria along with his expectation of joining his friend Navarre in celebration.

The upheaval grew nearer and louder, and Guillaume quickly mounted and began to make his way downriver. Many more along the waterway began to realize that the fracas was developing into something much larger and the street was filling with others who were withdrawing. The street soon became full to capacity, people of all ages, men and women with children running in different directions; so much so that his horse was becoming frenzied and Guillaume had to dismount. Soldiers then began appearing from the side streets bearing drawn swords, some with poleaxes and spiked maces.

As Guillaume forcefully made his way through the crowd, he kept one hand on the reins of his horse and the other on the handle of his sheathed rapier, the one given to him by the prince, the prince that had taught him how to use it.

It soon became apparent that all were to be slaughtered; no one was to be saved, and Guillaume watched heads tumbling to the ground as the soldiers slashed and hewed. He could hear their dead skulls bounce and see their faces forever locked in a look of surprise with half-spoken cries of *si'l vous plait* frozen on their lips; their severed corpses limply snaking toward the cobblestone pavement. No one could escape the spray of uncapped jugglers across the face or body or the stench of uncontrolled bowels and bladders, all merging and combining to form a slippery slime on the hard street.

Guillaume moved through the crowd holding his horse's bridle tightly close to its mouth both to keep it from rearing back and to keep someone from pulling it away from him. Suddenly someone grabbed him, wrapping arms around him from behind while a second attempted to pull the horse's reins from his hands. Guillaume reacted quickly by throwing his arms and hands outward while keeping hold of the reins, breaking the grip from behind. Then another grabbed him; Guillaume drew his dagger and quickly plunged it into his attacker's stomach. As his assailant fell to the ground Guillaume remounted his horse and charged aggressively though the crowd with his sword drawn beating off both the royal soldiers as well as crazed civilian members of the mob fighting to escape.

For a short period, the crowd thinned and there were fewer soldiers. It appeared as though he would make it out of the city, but as he neared the gate there were more soldiers. The gate had been locked and there was no way over the wall. He reversed his direction and began to ride aimlessly, looking for any way out of the city or a place to hide.

It was almost daylight, that brief period in the morning before the sun rises when there is just enough light to know that it will not be far behind. The air was moist and cool, a wet heavy cloud hung over the city. Royal soldiers rode in twos and threes up and down the Paris streets looking for survivors, and those that had escaped the melee. Their tired horses, dripping wet and covered with white froth, stepped over the many bodies strewn throughout. Except for the soldiers, the streets seemed deserted, and Guillaume still hadn't found a place to hide. He rode slowly past several small shops – *une tailleur; un boulanger; and un boucher.* They all seemed closed and vacant. He stopped in front of a bookstore, dismounted and looked inside through the window. Seeing no one, he forced open the door, led his horse inside, and then remained out of sight behind a row of bookshelves.

He wondered how long it would be before the soldiers began going door to door. There were living quarters in the rear of the store, and Guillaume wandered back to make sure there was no one there that might give him away. He found the remnants of a loaf of bread and a small amount of wine, which he quickly consumed. He came across a pitcher of water and several apples, which he gave to his horse. There he waited, hoping that with time he would be able to make an escape, where or how he didn't know.

After several hours, he could hear the soldiers knocking on the door to the adjacent shop, yelling and demanding entry. When no one responded, they pushed through the door and entered. Estimating that now was as good a time as any, he mounted his horse, charged out onto the street and ran away, looking for a new place to hide.

Hearing him, the soldiers quickly gave chase, but their horses were no match for the Arabian stallion.

At last, Guillaume came to a wooded area adjacent to the river. It was still within the city walls, but a place where it would be easier to hide than in the city streets. When nighttime arrived, leaving his horse behind, Guillaume slipped into the river, and floated away, hiding among the numerous corpses.

Tired and exhausted, Guillaume managed to stay afloat while the river carried him downstream. The river was full of decaying bodies and other floating debris. Within his reach was a barrel and several pieces of a broken chair. The chair pieces were too small to hold his weight and the barrel was too difficult to hang on to, at least for any extended time.

Nearby, a man was hanging on to a wooden ox cart that was partly submerged and upside down. The man had managed to pull the top half of his body onto it, leaving his legs submerged. He appeared to be dead so Guillaume swam closer to get a better look, and as soon as he placed his hand on the corpse, it slid into the water and sank to the bottom.

Guillaume climbed on to the floating structure much the same as the man before him and began to kick with his legs, thereby accelerating his forward movement along with the downstream current. His loud splashing muffled out most other sounds, and when he stopped kicking for a moment, he could hear cries coming from the shore; clearly, the massacre wasn't yet over.

As he looked toward each bank, it all appeared dark except for an occasional fire. The stench of the floating debris in the river created a nauseous feeling in his stomach, so much so that he began to throw up what little food he had eaten earlier in the day, leaving him with dry heaves.

Too tired to kick, he began to paddle with his arms and hands, but that too gave way to fatigue, and he resumed kicking. Too tired to pay much attention, Guillaume soon fell asleep.

When he awoke, it was daylight, and he had floated beyond the city walls and gates into the Normandy countryside. He had drifted onto the side of the river among the cattails and bulrushes, and his ox cart was hung up on a fallen tree that had been rotting there for some time. The shoreline was thick with trees and low-growing underbrush.

Guillaume climbed ashore and sat on the bank with his feet hanging down, reaching two or three centimeters below the surface of the water. He had no idea how far he had come, only that the river ultimately led to the seaport city of La Havre and Honfleur. Far from being out of harm's way, it seemed best for him to continue.

His stomach was making those grinding groans that stomachs make when they don't receive any food, especially after being used to receiving regular input, as was the case with Guillaume. He wasn't a bit overweight, he was quite trim and he was young; he ate well and received plenty of strenuous exercise on the farm. It would have been easy for him to consume a plateful of pork chops and vegetables and two tall glasses of goat's milk, come back an hour later and do it again. At this moment, his only hope was to find some berries, so he began to make his way into the thicket. He found several raspberry bushes; however, the fruit was sparse, barely edible so he continued to press on, pushing aside the low-growing tree branches and wiping away the many spiders' webs that welcomed him into the Norman forest.

Eventually he arrived at a small clearing where he discovered an area with wild strawberries growing, so he spent most of the remaining daylight hours there. He knew that if he stayed too long, beyond nightfall, he would have a difficult time finding his way back and locating ox cart, so in the late afternoon he retraced his steps to his makeshift raft.

The news of the massacre had traveled quickly to Navarre, just as it had spread throughout all of France. Guillemot, Alecka, and Guillaume's brothers and sisters were obviously quite concerned, and Guillemot struggled trying to decide if he should travel to Paris and try to find Guillaume. Jean-Luc wanted to go with him, but that would have left only Alecka and Philippe to defend the alqueria. So, after two days had passed, it was decided among the family members that Jean-Luc would go to Paris alone.

On the following day, Venus' day, he saddled a horse from the barn and packed very lightly, taking only a bedroll and a few provisions such as a bag of water, cooked rice and some strips of dried fish. It would be more than a week before he arrived in Paris, so Guillemot gave him a few coins to obtain more provisions along the way.

The afternoon had been warm, and Guillaume wished that he didn't have to return to the cold river. As primitive as it seemed, the floating oxcart had proven to be his best means of travel, even though it was taking him in the opposite direction to home. He reasoned that he was now probably far enough away from danger, but he wanted to take no chances. He stepped back into the black night, the cold river, climbed onto the raft and pushed himself away from the riverbank, kicking with his legs and paddling with his arms through the bulrushes until he reached the downstream current. Once there he relaxed and allowed the river to carry him.

As he watched the evening sky, he could scarcely see the banana-shaped moon as it appeared and disappeared behind the clouds. It began to rain lightly, but it was of little concern as Guillaume had accepted his total wetness. He was as lonely as lonely could be, and he wished he could see his brothers and sisters, and his mother and father – were they in danger? And Henri – was he still alive?

Hours later houses began to appear along the edge of the river. Occasionally one would have lights, but it was early in the morning and most were asleep. Slowly Guillaume coasted along as the houses became closer together and the foggy dawn began to emerge, revealing the small village of Rouen, where years earlier Joan of Arc had been tried and executed. There were probably no soldiers here, so he should have no trouble; besides, there was no way of determining who was Catholic and who was Huguenot. In Paris that was different – anyone one on the street that night was presumed to be Huguenot. Now, he was miles away and free – he only had to find a way home.

He paddled his raft to the shore and climbed on to the grassy bank. The sun had just broken through the clouds and morning fog and glistened brightly in his blond hair and on his several-day-old growth of red facial hair. He stretched his arms and legs and held his face toward the morning light, feeling its warmth against his cold, wet clothing.

He walked along the riverbank toward the harbor until he came to an area where there was a large amount of activity. Freighters were being loaded and unloaded; luggage carts filled with suitcases, trunks and personal effects sat ready to be taken aboard a passenger ship parked alongside the quay.

Guillaume entered the first café that he came to; it was already filled with people having *petit déjeuner*. It was a long narrow room with picnic tables lined along the wall to the right, and a bar and counter along the wall on the left. He took a seat at the counter and placed a small silver coin in front of him.

The woman behind the counter was middle-aged and big-boned with dark brown hair. Her Celtic-Breton accent made it difficult for Guillaume to understand her, and he had to ask her to repeat herself when she asked him what he wanted to order. He ordered a breakfast of fish and chips, and when he had eaten it, he asked for a second helping. She told him that she would only charge him half price for the second helping.

An older-looking man sitting next to Guillaume had the appearance of a seafarer, wearing a heavy wool coat with broad lapels, a double-breasted front, large wooden buttons and slash pockets. He said that he was the captain of the *L'Eau de Vie de Cidre* – a small freighter headed for Bordeaux in the Bay of Biscay carrying a load of calvados.

Guillaume reluctantly explained his difficulties, having fled the massacre in Paris and his need to return home to Navarre. The captain indicated that he could use an extra hand to help unloading cases of calvados at each of the ports of Cherbourg,

Brest, La Rochelle and Bordeaux, and after seeing Guillaume to be strong and fit, he asked him to come aboard and work for his passage to Bordeaux.

The older-looking man stood up from the counter and introduced himself. "My name is Captain Mason Yerington, and my ship is docked outside this café, near the end of the second wharf, you can't miss her. We'll be leaving this morning in say, two more hours, so if you have anything to take care of, do it now, but don't be late. Say, I didn't hear your name."

"Guillaume LeMaître." Guillaume stood up and responded with his hand outstretched.

Shaking hands with the young man, the captain said, "Well, I'm glad to meet you, LeMaître. When you get aboard, we'll get the paperwork started. There won't be much though, since you're working only for passage. The company always wants to know who's on board, though. I don't know what difference it makes." He then released his grip, tossed a silver tenth-gros onto the counter, turned and headed for the café door.

Captain Yerington looked as if he were about sixty years old. His face was puffy, with hair growing from his ears and nostrils and deep wrinkles across his forehead and cheeks resulting from a lifetime career that had exposed him to the maritime elements – the sea, the wind, the salt and the sun. His thick, white eyebrows matched his wavy hair, extending out from under the edges of his wool stocking cap. He had a small benign lump growing on the right side of his face not far from his nose and a deep dimple in his chin. He appeared to be two or three centimeters shorter than Guillaume, but it was difficult to tell for sure because he seemed to be stooping forward slightly as he walked out the door.

Guillaume had nothing to do for the remaining time before the ship was to sail, so he walked along the waterfront, gazing in the windows, poking his head in open doors and then he found a comfortable spot on the second wharf where he could get a good look at the *L'Eau de Vie de Cidre*. It appeared to be an ancient two-masted ship with square sails and castles rising above the stem and stern, quite similar to the ships sailed by Columbus to the New World. There were several men aboard loading cargo into the hold, and Guillaume could see Captain Yerington standing outside the door of the sterncastle talking with one of the crew.

Guillaume paced back and forth along the dock, anxious to get going, and when he could wait no longer he stepped onto the gangplank and made his way up to the deck.

"Welcome aboard, LeMaître! I was hoping that you would show. The crew has just about finished stowing the cargo below, and they'll be getting ready to shove off shortly. Why don't I show you where you can find a berth and then you can get look around and get familiar with the ship?"

The two walked across the deck to the sterncastle, opened the door and entered. It was a large room with several bunk beds and two hammocks hanging nearby.

"Say, LeMaître, why don't you stop by later this evening? I would like to talk to you about what happened in Paris. We can have a drink or two of calvados." Then he turned and walked back to his cabin, leaving Guillaume to take one of the unoccupied bunks.

That night, Guillaume explained to Captain Yerington all that had happened in Paris, beginning with the day that Prince Henri had been thrown from his horse, continuing with the time that Henri had remained at Alqueria du Carrefour, his invitation to the wedding, and then the massacre in Paris. They discussed the war. Yerington disclosed that his family too was of the Reformed faith and he feared for their safety, particularly since he is frequently away. Yerington had several sons, all of which were fully-grown and had left home. Only his youngest daughter, Florence, remained.

La Rochelle

G uillaume stood on the port side of the ship, along with several other crewmembers, looking east through the fog, where he was nearly able make out the two towers marking the entrance to the harbor. The sun appeared above the fortress, looking like a dull pearl through the thick haze. It was early Sunday morning and the gulls and terns were wildly circling the ship, making their loud shrieking sounds, welcoming the sailors to La Rochelle. A brisk tail wind was carrying the *L'Eau de Vie de Cidre* into the port several knots faster than normal, and they would soon need to trim the sails.

Yerington steered the ship while Guillaume stood on the

quayside holding the bowline, waiting to toss it down to the dockworker that stood ready to secure it to one of the wooden bollards. All the sails were now stowed except for one small triangular one near the stern, where Yerington used both it and the long-handled rudder to steer alongside the pier. He had done it hundreds of times before and could nearly do it with his eyes closed. He could get it very close in, usually on the first try and without any damage either to the ship or to the dock.

Once the ship was secured, the gangplank came down and two men from the port authority came aboard to meet the captain. They walked off to Yerington's cabin to take care of the paperwork and pay the port fees.

In the meantime, Guillaume joined the crew and began getting the hold opened and the cargo ready to be inspected and unloaded. As the cover to the hold was removed, the strong, concentrated smell of oak and distilled spirits leaped out and upward, filling the deck with the brandied aroma of calvados. Smiles immediately appeared on the faces of Guillaume and all the crewmembers, each one taking in a deep inhalation of the air with hopes of getting an instant buzz. It was a ritual done at each port, and like the brandy below it would never grow old, only better with age. The strong fragrance was even more pronounced below, like climbing into a brandy snifter.

Once all the port requirements had been completed and the captain had met with the warehousemen, the crew could begin unloading. The oak barrels were all resting in rows, secured by wooden cradles more than half the length of the ship (the remainder was for the galley), three tiers high along the keel and with only one tier along the edges. Each barrel had to be removed one by one and placed onto a railed, wooden pallet and lifted out by a hand-operated cargo crane and boom. The crane was secured to the pier and operated by two men who would crank a large wheel, one on each side, lifting the pallet from the hold, swinging it around to the pier, and then lowering it to the ground, where it would be reloaded onto a cart and taken inside the warehouse. The unloading went quickly, and after several hours, the men were free to go, having been given instructions to return the next evening by 1700 hours. Yerington then wiping his hands on a small towel and standing next to Guillaume on the wharf turned toward him and spoke. "Let's hurry, we still have time to make it to church."

Guillaume, not knowing what else to do, followed along. He walked at a quick pace, sometimes next to and other times behind Yerington, through the narrow stone streets, past the warehousemen, past the sailors, some sitting and some standing around, past the pimps and whores walking the wharf, past the boulangeries, the patisseries and cafés; the bookstores, the shoe shops, and the confectioners; the coal man, the carpenter and the newspaper boy. They turned to the left, and then to the right, and then straight ahead up the hill through a narrow stonewalled passageway to the gray and white granite steps of the Reformed Church of La Rochelle.

It was a large church with a cross at the top of a tall steeple. As they approached, they could hear the congregation singing inside, and they entered quickly, walking down the center aisle past the rows of benches until they came to the row where a woman and a girl were standing, singing with the aid of a hymnal between them.

The man and wife standing next to the aisle immediately recognized Yerington and made room for the two of them to squeeze by and take their places next to what appeared to Guillaume to be the captain's wife, who seemed surprised to see the captain. The young girl appeared equally astonished. She glanced at Guillaume, smiled and then quickly returned her gaze to the hymnal.

La Rochelle was populated predominately by Huguenots; it

was here that Queen Jeanne d'Albert and Prince Henri had found refuge when threatened by the Pope's army a few years earlier. Guillaume felt safe here as he looked around the sanctuary. It was a very plain-looking church with none of the regalia present in most Catholic churches. The parishioners were also very plain-looking, wearing mostly dark suits and dresses. The most extravagant piece of attire seemed to be the lace bonnets worn by several of the ladies. He tried to get a better look at the young girl standing between Yerington and his wife, but even looking out of the corner of his eye it was impossible to see her, especially with Yerington blocking the view. When he leaned back, he could see that she was not wearing a bonnet; her auburn-colored hair flowed down her back.

The singing ended and the minister began to pray. He prayed for the ships at sea, the soldiers that guarded the city; he prayed for the king and his regent; he prayed for the sick and the poor, the rich and greedy, the accusers and the accused, the old and the new; he prayed that it would rain, but not too much, and that all wrongs would be made right.

Guillaume became fidgety standing there waiting for all the praying to end, and when it did the two ushers were called forward to the small table positioned below the lectern where the minister was standing, to take the offering. Each usher picked up a basket with a long handle and began extending it in front of each parishioner, permitting an offering to be deposited. When it was presented to Guillaume, he dropped a tenth-gros into the basket and hoped that it was the right amount to avoid any attention being directed toward him. It was then moved to Yerington. Guillaume again looked out the corner of his eye, trying to get a glance of what the captain had offered, but the older man inserted his entire hand in the basket, making it impossible to see. It was then moved past the young girl and Yerington's wife to the next gentleman. When the offering was completed, the ushers returned the baskets to the table and then another prayer was given by the minister. The message was followed by another prayer, and then the service ended with the benediction.

Just as Guillaume rose from his seat, the man who had been sitting next to him introduced himself. "Bonjour, monsieur, I don't believe I know you, my name is…"

None of this was unusual for Guillaume, after all, he too was a Huguenot, and he had attended services in Ordulla with his family, and the liturgy was quite similar. His family was not noticeably religious, however, and they did not attend every Sunday – perhaps once or twice a month was the norm. After all, the freeing aspect of the Reformed Church was not only the permission of guilt-free sexual intercourse between husband and wife, but also the avowed personal relationship between man and God. When Henri had arrived at Alqueria, they all seemed to attend more frequently, not because they were feeling more religious, rather it just seemed like the right thing to do. He was never introduced to anyone as a prince – he was just presented as Henri, a friend who was spending the summer with them.

Guillaume would sometimes feel closeness with God. He certainly believed in God, and no one had to convince him that God created the Heavens and Earth. He believed that Christ was the Son of God even though he didn't quite understand it. The Holy Spirit was another issue; no matter how hard he tried, Guillaume was never able to comprehend whom or what it was, what it did, or why it was even necessary. Nevertheless, his lack of understanding did not prevent him from being what he considered a good Christian. Now, here he was, with Yerington, dragged into church without any warning, where he knew no one, wishing that he had declined the offer when it was presented to him back at the wharf.

Even though the service had ended, no one was leaving. It

appeared as if everyone was compelled to stay and socialize. Guillaume preferred to be apart from it and gently worked his way up the aisle, through the standing, chatting flock to the front door, where he remained waiting for the Yeringtons to come out.

Standing on the top step, he was able to look out over the rooftops of the houses and buildings below him to the wharf where the ship was docked. The fog had burnt off and the noon sun was warming the cool Atlantic coastline. He slowly stepped down to the bottom of the steps, stood off to the side and watched the congregation slowly emerge until at last he saw the young girl appear. She was no longer with her parents and started down the steps, carrying her prayer book in her arm, unaware that she was headed in Guillaume's direction. The sun shone through her hair, causing it to glow.

When she reached the bottom, she saw Guillaume and walked up to him. "You are the man that came with my father, aren't you?" Her rosy cheeks stood out against her pale complexion.

"Yes, I met your father in Rouen. My name is Guillaume LeMaître, and I come from Navarre. And you, what is your name?"

She had freckles on her cheeks just beneath her eyes. Offering her hand she replied, "I am Florence. I am pleased to meet you, Guillaume of Navarre."

He couldn't help but notice her freshness. He was still wearing the same clothes he had worn both before and after Paris. He reached out and shook her hand, feeling her warm, tiny, white-gloved hand inside his palm. He hoped that she did not notice his fingernails. "Your father has spoken highly of you. It would seem, though, that he understated your pleasant appearance."

"I am flattered, Monsieur LeMaître," she said, smiling, slowly withdrawing her hand and aware of how warm and confident his grip felt. "My father never brings anyone home for church. Will you be sharing our Sunday meal?"

"It would be my pleasure, but he has not yet invited me."

"Then I will invite you. Oh, look, here he and mother come now."

Yerington approached Guillaume and began to make introductions. "Guillaume, I would like for you to meet my wife, Madam Mercedes Yerington, and my daughter, Mademoiselle Florence Yerington." Referring to Florence he continued, "I call her 'Mabelle'. And this young man is Monsieur Guillaume LeMaître from Navarre. We met in Rouen."

Guillaume turned to Madam Yerington and smiled. "I am very happy to make your acquaintance, Madam Yerington. You have a lovely family, a beautiful church and a very nice town. I am so happy to have been invited by your husband." He turned toward Florence, smiled and spoke. "And the mademoiselle and I spoke briefly before you arrived. Yes, Captain Yerington, you have a very lovely family."

Madam Yerington spoke to Guillaume. "Now that the captain has arrived and brought this handsome young man to our home, and…oh…I forgot, Reverend Gainsbourg is also going to be calling on us this afternoon; what a wonderful day this has turned out to be! I can hardly wait to tell Conception to begin preparing our Sunday meal. She's a pearl, an excellent cuisiniere! She makes a wonderful gazpacho, you know, very simple: trout, leg of lamb, cheese and dessert. It's delicious, it's her specialty."

Once they all arrived at Yerington's townhouse, the most pressing thing was for the captain and Guillaume to take baths and put on a clean change of clothes. As Conception began preparing the afternoon meal, Madam Yerington began heating water for the bathtub. It was a warm sunny day and the tub was moved from the kitchen to the back porch, where hopefully the two men could enjoy (one at a time) some semblance of privacy.

Guillaume climbed in first wearing only his underwear. Florence curiously peered down from her upstairs bedroom window. Once he was safely submerged from the waist down, he removed his underwear and tossed them on the ground. There was nothing for her to see except his bare back, and that was nothing new to her, she had seen men often with their shirts removed. But this was different and she found it quite difficult to turn away or step back from the window. She began to feel an excitement that she had never experienced before. She wanted to touch herself and resisted, but when he stepped from the tub and she saw his total nakedness, she could no longer deny the temptation.

When Guillaume returned to the living room, he was dressed in one of the captain's white shirts and a dark suit. He had shaved and his long sandy hair, still wet, hung to his shoulders.

Madam Yerington walked into the room, saw him, and remarked about how nice he looked after cleaning himself up. Then Mademoiselle Florence entered the room and took a seat without saying anything. Her mother saw her and exclaimed, "Mabelle, your face, it's all flushed! Are you all right?"

Before either of them could say anything, there was a knock at the door and Mercedes went to answer it. It was Reverend and Madam Gainsbourg.

The reverend removed his hat and held it in his hand; he and Madam Gainsbourg simultaneously gave an enthusiastic greeting. *"Comment allez vous,* Madam Yerington?"

Mercedes, throwing her hands into the air very excitedly, said, *"Merci, Merci! Je vais bien!* Come in, come in. We are so happy to have you pay us a visit. Conception is almost ready with the meal." Then stepping back one or two steps and turning her head toward the front room she called to her husband. "Mason, Mason! It's the Reverend and Madam Gainsbourg;

come quick, come quick! Mabelle, you too, come and greet our guests."

As the Reverend and Madam Gainsbourg entered the front room, Guillaume rose from his seat and was introduced. They all took seats, Guillaume on the rocking chair where he had been sitting, and the Reverend and Madam Gainsbourg on the divan. Minutes later, Florence served them lemonade, and when she had finished, she took the reverend's hat and hung it on the hat hook behind the front door. She was aware that Guillaume was watching her closely, and she tried to ignore it until he called her over. "This is wonderful lemonade, a little tart, a little sweet. Are you, by chance, the one that made it?"

"Why yes, I did. I'm glad that you like it. Would you like some more?" she asked.

"If it wouldn't be too much trouble. I certainly am thirsty, and this is so refreshing."

"Well then, it seems that we are out of lemons. Perhaps you could help me by picking some fresh ones from the tree out in the back of the house. Come with me and I'll show you where."

The two walked to the garden in the rear of the house, passing by the bathtub that had now been turned on its side to dry. It was a narrow parcel, the width of the townhouse; however, it was deep. The sides were lined with various fruit trees – an apple tree, a peach tree, both sweet and sour cherry, and at the far end a lemon tree loaded with bright yellowish-green lemons. As they began to pluck the ripe fruit, they sensed a certain amount of nervousness and spoke very little. Florence pulled up the bottom of her laced apron and placed the lemons into it. A small asp had wrapped itself around one of the branches, and it startled Mabelle. She squealed, letting loose her apron and allowing the fruit to fall to the ground. Guillaume quickly put his arms around her, hoping to comfort her, and said, "Do not be afraid, lovely princess, it won't harm you."

"It scared me," she whispered. She liked having his arms around her and she didn't want him to take them away.

"Let me pick these up for you," he spoke softly into her ear while continuing to hold her.

"Just hold me like you are doing."

The following afternoon, Captain Yerington and Guillaume returned to the ship, hoping that the crew would all show up on time. That morning it had been very foggy, but it had burnt off by noonday and now it was a pleasant afternoon with a light breeze out of the north. Once the crew, fresh water and food were aboard, the captain gave the signal to untie the ship, and he set a course out between the two towers and then south toward Bordeaux.

However, by late evening the sky had filled with heavy dark clouds. The storm that followed did not last long, but it was enough that Guillaume had to hang his head over the fantail several times.

They arrived at the port city of Ville-de-St-Pier the following day, and Yerington asked Guillaume if he would stay on and make the return trip to Rouen. There, they were to reload with more calvados and sail on to the Baltic Sea, making stops at Oslo, Stockholm, and Copenhagen. Guillaume, however, was eager to return home and said farewell to the captain.

Ville-de-St-Pier

Guillaume walked hollow-hungry with his duffle bag over his shoulder along the deserted wharf all but tripping over one of the bollards. He could see and feel the morning fog, and the briny sea breeze coming in from the Atlantic, and he could hear the sound of the barking sea lions, the creaking dock, and the rhythmic slap of the riggings against the masts of the *L'Eau de Vie de Cidre*, but something was missing. Where was everyone? The port was usually full of people, the stevedores and fishmongers, street characters, gypsy musicians, Portuguese anglers and Italian bocce-ball players. He saw and smelled nothing to eat, no smell of boiling crab. Most of the shops close to the quay were still shuttered, and there were just a few of the usual street vendors hawking their merchandise. He had hoped to buy a horse, but when he arrived to where the horse vendors usually gathered, this place too was deserted. The morning fog was heavier than usual and this added to the cold feeling of the normally active port.

He turned and headed up the hill toward the central part of the town and only came across a pipe-blowing goatherd, his dog, and three heavy-bagged goats.

Guillaume continued up the hill and entered a small café, the 'Café Gaulois', which also seemed vacant except for the young girl behind the counter and two customers sitting alongside the wall drinking coffee, smoking pipes and talking together. The small room had the sour smell of drunkenness and seemed rather sad and gloomy, and after eyeing the place, Guillaume took a seat at a table along the opposite wall, near the small front window.

After several minutes, he realized that the girl hadn't yet come to wait on him, so he turned toward the counter hoping to catch her attention, but she was gone. He had not seen anyone arrive or leave through the front door, which appeared to be the only visible place of entry. The back wall behind the counter seemed continuous without any doorway. Guillaume was in no hurry, but he couldn't help but wonder what had happened to her.

The two men at the other table began talking loudly, distracting Guillaume's attention, and he turned his head in their direction. The older man was shouting and pounding his fist on the table when they both stood up and continued arguing loudly. The girl then appeared mysteriously from behind the counter and yelled with a deep gravely voice at the men to be quiet or leave. The room hushed; the younger man reached into his pocket, removed a coin and tossed it on the table before walking to the door and departing.

The girl then appeared at Guillaume's table ready to take his order. *"Vous desirez, monsieur?"* Her voice was deep and hoarse.

The small amount of light that made its way through the small salt-crusted window landed directly on her, revealing a woman much older than she had appeared in the darkness at the back of the room behind the counter. Guillaume wondered if she was the same person. Up close, she appeared coarse with a deep scar across her heavily freckled face starting at her right temple and running down to her upper lip. Her light brown hair was shoulder length and heavily speckled with gray, and she wore a tattoo of an anchor across her right bicep, drawing attention to her masculine looking arms. *Now I see why those men got quiet so fast*, Guillaume thought to himself and then asked, "Was that you behind the counter when I walked in?"

"Oui; Vous desirez, monsieur?"

"I saw you and then you were gone."

"I must have been behind the counter cleaning the cupboard. No menu today, I'm serving only eggs and country ham. Would you like that?"

"Yes, sounds perfect. Say, by the way, I'm looking for a horse, and I was unable to find any for sale along the wharf. Oh, and a cup of coffee, black, please."

"I can't help you with the horse, but I will bring you the coffee *tout de suite.*"

Just as she returned to the counter, the older man along the other wall rose from his chair and positioned himself in front of Guillaume's table. He was tall, thin, and lanky, with a pointed gray beard growing from his chin, and was wearing a stocking cap. He leaned forward on his arms, placing his hands against the table, his face level with Guillaume's. His cheeks and nose were red and puffy with deep pores filed with blackheads. His breath reeked of wine. "I couldn't help but hear you across the way. You are looking for a horse?" His face was animated as he spoke; eyes opened wide as his lower jaw shifted one way and then back, his lips puckered. Then before Guillaume could answer, the old man removed his hands from the table, cupped his mouth and whispered, "You aren't a Protestant, are you?"

Guillaume politely responded with a question of his own. "Tell me, sir, I know that Ville-de-St-Pier is as much Catholic as it is Protestant, so you tell me, what should I say?"

The old man winked as if he understood; he too was more concerned with form over substance and remarked, "If you want to keep your head you better be for a Mass. This city is crawling with soldiers belonging to the Duke de Guise. And with Coligny dead and King Henri and Condé both held prisoner in Paris, the city has no defense."

"I see," said Guillaume. "Yes, I would be for a Mass. And you, sir, would that be the same for you?"

"Of course I would," replied the older man as he pulled a pewter crucifix hanging around his neck out from his shirt. "Now about that horse, how much would you be willing to pay?"

The woman appeared at the table. *"Voila, monsieur,* your coffee. Your ham and eggs will be ready in a moment." She reached in between Guillaume and the old man, setting the hot cup on the table.

Guillaume's eyes turned from the man to the steaming cup to the waitress, *"Merci beaucoup!"*

The old man turned with a grin to watch her walk back to the counter. He winked at Guillaume and placed both his hands on his crotch while making a humping gesture with his torso. When she was about to turn around and catch him, he returned to his leaning position at the table, recomposed a serious business look on his face and spoke. "How much did you say you would be willing to pay?"

"I didn't say. I haven't seen the horse. Is it nearby?"

"Yes. I would be glad to take you there. It is just a short walk, a few blocks from here near the Opera House." He then stuck out his hand and introduced himself. "I am Antoine Duprat, at your service! And you?"

Guillaume spoke while rising from his chair and extending his hand. "I am M. Guillaume LeMaître, and the pleasure is mine." After a slight pause he continued, "M. Duprat, are you in the horse business or are you only being a good citizen and helping me out?"

"Well, it's kinda both. I don't have any horses of my own, but I know where you can buy one, and you need me to help you get the right price. You see, I know Sr. El Gascón, who runs the livery, and he will listen to me because I bring many people to him. In addition, I know the difference between a carthorse and a draft horse, a racehorse and a hobbyhorse, a saddle horse and a sea horse. Do you know horses, M. LeMaître?"

"I know a little. I come from Tarbes, and I know the difference between a gelding and a mare, a sawhorse and a pommel horse, a thoroughbred and a Trojan horse, a Chincoteague and a Shetland, Exmoor and Eriskay, Estonian and East Bulgarian. And I know that one ought not to regard a gift horse in the mouth; neither should one get on one's high horse."

"Oh well, then, of course you do know – fine horses they are that come from Tarbes. I know fine horses."

"Voila, your eggs and country ham, monsieur!" She placed the plate on the table in front of Guillaume. He thanked her and she then looked at Duprat, "Is there anything I can bring you, Monsieur Duprat?"

Duprat smiled through the side of his mouth, revealing a narrow slit through which Guillaume could see was nearly devoid of teeth and, the few that remained were mostly green, black and heavily stained. Duprat turned and slid onto a chair opposite Guillaume and with a more serious look, answered, "No, I'll just sit here with M. LeMaître. You just go about whatever you were doing; I'll be just fine. Unless of course…"

"Sorry, M. Duprat; what you are lookin' for is farther up the street, not that you could do any better there than you could here."

Duprat wanted to take it no further and ignored her insult tearing a small piece from one of the baguettes and stuffing it into his mouth. "Now, tell me M. LeMaître, is there a particular kind of horse that you are looking for?"

"I'm simply looking for a ride home, to Ordulla, a horse that can get me there," and when he finished his breakfast, he reached into his purse, removed a silver tenth-gros and tossed it on the table, turning to see if the woman was looking. She returned a silent smile and he spoke. "Au revoir, madame."

"Merci, monsieur, au revoir."

Guillaume turned to the old man and spoke, *"Allons-y,* M. Duprat, let's find me a horse," and the two walked together out the door into the persistent fog.

Guillaume looked down the street toward the wharf, and he thought could almost see the *L'Eau de Vie de Cidre.* The two then headed up the hill to the Opera House and over several blocks to the left to the livery. It was easy to tell that they were near as the fog kept a tight grip on the stinging tangy smell of the corrals, and there were increasing amounts of horse droppings imbedded between the cobbles of the street. Suddenly, they were almost on top of the dull blue-gray barn and could see the sign over the large double doors in bold red letters, *'Pension Pour Chevaux, Sr. El Gascón, propriétaire'.*

Duprat went inside to talk to Sr. Gascón. Guillaume remained outside, leaning against the corral fence and looking at the four or five horses standing motionless around a tree close to the barn, hooves and legs covered with mud.

The two men soon walked out together to the corral and met with Guillaume to discuss which ones were for rent and which were available for sale. Guillaume could see in through the doorway, and in a separate stall stood a beautiful Arabian that looked very much like the one given to him by Prince Henri, the one he had left behind in Paris.

Gascón spoke first. "You can have either one of the two on the right for fifty real each. That's a real fair price, and you won't do better anywhere else."

"And what about Mr. Duprat's fee?" Guillaume questioned.

"That's included in the price, M. LeMaître. So what do you think? Do you like either one of them?"

"Tell me, Sr. Gascón, may I see that Arabian?" Guillaume pointed inside.

"Oh, M. LeMaîstre, I see that you know horses, even from a distance. One of the Duke de Guise's men, a lieutenant I believe, left behind that stallion. He traded it for a fresh horse and indicated that he would return for it later."

The three walked to the stall where the smooth shiny horse was boarded. The horse instantly recognized Guillaume and came close to the stall gate, where Guillaume began to stroke his neck and mane while the horse made quick nervous steps in place, pulling at the tethers attached to each side of the stall. Guillaume noted its size and markings and he knew that this was in fact his horse. After a few minutes, Guillaume looked at Duprat and asked, "How much will you take for this animal?"

"I'm sorry, the lieutenant said he would be back for him so he isn't for sale. If he were, though, this horse would probably bring close to 700 real. Guillaume was aware that he had only 230 real in his purse."

"When did he say he was returning? Perhaps he's not coming back," Guillaume suggested.

"Well, he said in a couple days, and that was over a week ago. Still, I don't want any trouble. If he returns and I don't have the horse for him, I hate to think about what he might do. I'm sorry, señor, I can't let you have him. He's worth a lot of money, and I could make out real well, but I don't want to take the chance."

"Sr. Gascón, I will give you 1000 real, and you can certainly tell him that you relied on what he told you, that he would return in two days, and after you waited over a week and he still didn't return, it was impossible to turn down such a good offer as what I'm offering you. Think about it."

Gascón struggled with the offer; it certainly was a lot more than he ever expected to get. Guillaume, on other hand, struggled wondering where and how he was going to come up with the real should Gascón accept his offer. For close to an hour the two discussed and bargained – Gascón would almost accept, but then he would change his mind. Duprat would join in from time to time and attempt to soften Gascón.

"You've got every right to sell it; he's abandoned that beautiful horse. Why would anyone be so reckless?" argued Duprat. "He doesn't deserve it."

At last, it looked as if he had decided and said, "I'm sorry, I just can't do it. All the money in the world isn't worth it. You have to understand, I have a wife, kids and they need me. I'm sorry."

"Yes, I understand. You have to do what you have to do. The truth is that horse once belonged to me. I was forced to abandon it two months ago. That horse was a gift to me from King Henri – he was a prince at the time. I saved his life, and he gave the horse to me in repayment. I'll not bother you any more, though. Come on Duprat, let's allow Sr. Gascón to get back to work."

Guillaume walked to the door, stepped outside, and began to walk in the direction of the Opera House when Gascón came running after him. "Wait!" he called out. "Wait, I've changed my mind. You can have the horse, but for 1200 real."

Except for the increase in the stakes, Guillaume's bluff had succeeded. His hard won victory was yet to be realized since the coins in his purse came nowhere close to meeting the agreed price. What little was there he had received from Captain Yerington earlier that morning. He knew his only hope of coming up with the money was to return to the ship and convince Yerington to loan him the rest. It was a long shot – that he knew. He wasn't even sure if the ship had pulled out of the harbor yet, but it was certainly worth the try.

Guillaume stopped, turned toward Gascón and waited for him to catch up. Gascón appeared nervous; there were heavy drops of perspiration across his forehead. He looked as if he were facing the lieutenant instead of Guillaume. There was a smile on Duprat's face. It appeared to be his day; little did he know that there was more work to be done. Gascón believed that it was over and offered his hand to Guillaume. "Monsieur, I accept your offer; upon payment, the horse is yours."

"Thank you very much. I am pleased that we have been able to come together as to the terms. Now if you will excuse me, I will contact my banker and return with the money. This should not take long. Duprat will remain here as my representative until I return. You will be here how long?"

Gascón responded, "I'll be here the rest of the day."

Guillaume headed off, lugging his heavy duffle bag in the direction of the Opera House, where he turned right and then started down the hill in the direction of the wharf. The fog had partially lifted, but there was no clear vision of the dock below and he remained optimistic that the *L'Eau de Vie de Cidre* had not yet pulled away. Nevertheless, he picked up his pace as if every second counted.

As he passed by the Café Gaulois he could see that the door was open wide, but he rushed by too quickly to see if there was anyone else inside or if the same woman was working. *There was something I liked about that dreary place,* he thought to himself as he hurried past. That thought quickly disappeared as he began to perspire, and he wished he had left his duffle bag back at the stable, but then again, he reasoned that if he should not be able to get the money from Yerington, he would have no reason to return to the *Pension Pour Chevaux*. Yes, it was better this way, he thought.

Dashing down the steep cobblestone street, his mind returned to the horse. It wasn't only that it was such a splendid animal, but also it had been a gift from his friend, King Henri. Beginning at the moment that he had left it on the bank of the Seine, he had been troubled over how he would explain it. He had been plagued with the nagging notion that he had proven himself unworthy of such a princely stallion, and now he was somehow presented with an opportunity for redemption. If only he could get there in time and convince Yerington to help. Only a few more meters and he would be there.

Suddenly, almost at the bottom, the ball of his right foot landed on a loose cobble. As the small rounded stone shifted, his toe sank into the opening and the weight of his downward forward motion sent him sailing through the air, landing him on his hands and knees. The duffle bag that hung from his shoulder flew in a different direction and continued to roll for one or two meters. With no time to waste or to think about it, he scrambled to his feet, grabbed his bag and continued on his way.

He arrived at the end of the street, out of breath, and turned onto the dock where he was able to see that not too far off the ship was about to depart. Through the misty haze of drizzle and fog, he could see Yerington on the deck giving directions to a crewmember as the sails were being unfurled and the gangplank was being stowed. Guillaume called out as he ran, trying desperately to catch Yerington's attention. When he was unable to approach the ship any closer else lose sign of the captain, he stopped, dropped his bag on the ground and formed a funnel with his hand around his mouth and repeatedly called out to the man. A raspy hoarseness began to shroud his voice as Yerington walked from the port side to starboard, deaf to Guillaume's call and out of view. It seemed that all was about to be lost. Guillaume ceased calling and all fell silent except for the shrieking gulls and the whoosh of exploding sails. The rippling water of the bay quietly splashed, slurped and echoed against the pilings and stringers beneath the dock; wood-eating termites silently gnawed away at a nearby bollard, and an organ grinder could barely be heard in the distance.

Guillaume remained standing with his arms at his side

waiting for the vessel to pull away when Yerington appeared port side and shouted down to Guillaume, "Ahoy there! Is that you, LeMaître?"

"Yes, Captain Yerington. I'm sorry to bother you, but I need to talk to you. I need your help. Can I come aboard?"

Yerington gave a sigh of impatience, lowered his head then turned it to one side. He cast his gaze back toward the young man on the dock, *"Bon Dieu d'bon Dieu!* Guillaume, the ship is ready to leave. What do you want?"

Guillaume paused without turning away, wondering if he should try to get aboard first or simply yell out that he needed the loan. Before he could answer, Yerington roared, "Good God, son, what is it?"

Guillaume looked back toward Yerington and put his hands around his mouth again. He took a deep breath and shouted with all the strength his lungs could muster, "I need a loan – 1000 real will do it – can you help me?"

From the very first day that Yerington met Guillaume, he had felt a fatherly fondness for the young man. He enjoyed Guillaume as the son he never had. He was pleased to take him to his home at La Rochelle, and he was happy that Guillaume had been attracted to his daughter. Guillaume was bright, a hardworking Protestant boy, and he did not appear to swear or exhibit any other bad habits. Yerington had wanted Guillaume to remain on board and finish the tour, but he understood that he needed to return home, if only to make sure that everything was fine with his family. When Yerington took him on back at Rouen, the agreement was that Guillaume would work for his passage to Ville-de-Ste-Pier, but then he ended up giving him a 235 real bonus. Yerington wanted to do anything that he could to help Guillaume, but to hold up the ship like this at the last moment was more than he wanted to deal with. He walked away from the edge of the ship, paced for a minute or two, and then resumed his position at the railing, "Guillaume! Meet me at the gangplank; I'll be right down." Then he turned and walked away, out of Guillaume's view.

In a matter of minutes, two crewmembers began pulling the ship in tighter with ropes strung through the eye of each of the bollards at the fore and aft of the ship against those on the dock. Once completed, they lowered the gangplank and Yerington appeared and climbed down onto the quay, where he stood face to face with Guillaume. "I have no idea what you are up to, and I have no idea if I will ever see you again except that my instincts tell me that you can be trusted. Here is the money, son; *Dieu te garde.*"

Little was spoken between the two. Guillaume accepted the purse and thanked the man. Yerington did an about-face and returned to the ship. Guillaume returned immediately to the *'Pension Pour Chevaux'*.

Antoine Duprat was the first to see the young man heading toward the stable, dragging his duffle bag along. Duprat's standing commission arrangement with Gascón was for 6%, which for this transaction amounted to a weighty 72 real, substantially more than the three coins he usually received for the typical sale. Therefore, it was understandable that Duprat was excited when he saw Guillaume walking slowly toward him, and it explained why he was quick to rush out and greet him. "M. LeMaître, how did you do? Did you get the money?"

The trip down the hill, the fall, his nervousness associated with Yerington being there and lending the money and the climb back up the hill all wore on Guillaume. He walked past Duprat, ignoring his questions, and headed straight for the barn, where El Gascón was standing next to the stallion.

Gascón was proud to have such a steed in his stable, and he was grooming it in preparation for Guillaume's return with the money. The horse gave a short quick whiney and began pawing at the ground when Guillaume entered the barn. Guillaume placed his bag on the ground next to the open stall where the horse had been tethered, and then he approached the horse with a fresh regeneration of energy. "Yes, I'm back," he said while looking directly into its large dark brown eyes and stroking its neck and mane. "We'll be out of here in no time and on our way to the alqueria. "You'll be home and we'll see Alecka and Guillemot, Jean-Luc, Eugenie and Louise."

After Gascón finished fitting the horse with a bridle and saddle, Guillaume handed him his purse. It was quite heavy with a mixture of different coins, including several *écu au soleil,* Spanish colonial Mexican dollars and double excelentes. Gascón looked into the purse, beamed and withdrew a double excelente, biting down on it with an upper and lower canine. He smiled and then returned it with the others.

Guillaume secured his duffle bag behind the saddle, shook hands and exchanged farewells with Gascón, then mounted the horse. As he rode out between the barn doors, he ducked, careful not to bump his head, and Gascón shouted out to him, "Follow this street north until you come to the Gave and then turn right. *Vaya con Dios, amigo.*" He slapped the horse on the rear and waved goodbye.

Guillaume turned and waved, *"Adios, Gascón."*

Return to Alqueria Du Carrefour

T he southwest was a Huguenot stronghold and there wasn't much threat from the Catholics, especially in the countryside. Nevertheless, Frère Richard continued to visit Alecka and Guillemot in an attempt to sway them back to the Catholic Church. His extreme tactic was to remind them of the time when brigands had killed her parents and destroyed their home. He seemed to allude to them that it could happen again. Alecka couldn't help but wonder if this was what Señora Gonsalves meant when in earlier times she had said, "But, my dear, there is more to come, much more."

Alecka's life at the alqueria had been good – she had married a wonderful husband and raised five children. Unless something was to happen to her family, she had nothing to complain about.

She couldn't help but worry about Guillaume; she hadn't heard from him for almost a year, and she feared that he might be held prisoner at court in Paris, or worse yet he might not be alive. Jean-Luc had gone to Paris shortly after the massacre to look for him but was unable to locate anyone who had seen him. He returned home without news to report – good or bad.

By the time Guillaume finally returned home, he had learned that La Rochelle was under siege. The city had refused to pay taxes to the king because of the massacre and refused admittance to the royal governor. The king declared war and sent in an army led by Henri d'Anjou, and included Henri de Navarre as a hostage.

Guillaume longed to see Florence and eventually returned to La Rochelle only to learn that Captain Yerington was out at sea in the Mediterranean. He rented a small flat in town and waited for Yerington to return, reluctant to call on her without the captain's presence or permission.

Since it was a port city easily supplied by sea with a near-impregnable harbor, it was difficult for d'Anjou to reduce the city, and by early spring the siege was called off. Yerington finally returned and gave permission to Guillaume to marry Florence provided he would go to work for Yerington on a permanent basis. Guillaume agreed, and within a year they had their first child, Thomas. Over the next few years, they had two more boys, Robert and William, and two girls, Alecka and Louise, and once the family was complete, Yerington died. Guillaume became the captain of the *L'Eau de Vie de Cidre* and continued to distribute calvados and wines of the various French and Italian domains throughout the Atlantic, the Baltic and the Mediterranean.

None of Catherine de Medici's children produced any legitimate heirs to the throne, and following the death of her last son, King Henri III, King Henri de Navarre, a distant cousin, became the most beloved of all French kings. In order for Henri to secure his position as king, he necessarily converted, allegedly saying, "Paris is worth a Mass."

Guillaume attended the coronation and the two saw each other for the first time since their time together in Navarre. In 1598, King Henri issued the Edict of Nantes, which offered amnesty to Huguenots and protection against persecution.

Part II

The New World

Abraham LeMaître
Isle of Wight, Great Britain

May 12, 1657
M. et Mme. John LeMaître
15 Rue Sainte-Croix-de-la-Bretonnerie
St. Mary's Parish
Isle of Jersey, Great Britain

Dear Papa and Mama,

I know that this is quite sudden and unexpected, but when you receive this, I will have left for America. I will explain all to you later, but for now, you must know that I do not mean to be disrespectful to you and that I love you both.

Abraham

Abraham LeMaster
Zekiah Swamp
St. Mary's Province
Maryland

July 18, 1658
M. et Mme. John LeMaîstre
15 Rue Sainte-Croix-de-la-Bretonnerie
St. Mary's Parish
Isle of Jersey, Great Britain

Dear Papa and Mama,

I have not received any response to my last letter, wherein I explained all that had occurred before my departure for America. Did you receive it?

Things are happening very rapidly since I last wrote. I am now working for Richard Edelen on his plantation, and I am fast discovering opportunities wherein I might obtain a piece of land for myself, not to buy, but to rent, at least for a short period. I feel certain that it will not to be difficult for me to do well here. I must admit that learning to speak English is sometimes very frustrating. Papa, I should have listened to you when you tried to teach it to me early on. If you notice, on the return address, I am using the Anglican spelling for my last name. I hope this doesn't upset you too much.

I guess the most exciting thing to happen to me is that I am now married. Her name is Elizabeth Alice Cooksey. I think that you will both like her very much. We were married in the First Anglican Church of Baltimore.

Abraham

Abraham LeMaster
Zekiah Swamp
St. Mary's Province
Maryland

July 18, 1659
M. et Mme. John LeMaître
15 Rue Sainte-Croix-de-la-Bretonnerie
St. Mary's Parish
Isle of Jersey, Great Britain

Dear Papa and Mama,

Elizabeth and I are both very excited, as we are about to have our first baby. I hope that it will be the first of many to come. We have already decided, Mama, that if it is a girl, we are going to name her Sarah, after you. We have managed to acquire, for rent, fifty acres near the edge of Zekiah Swamp. It is on the western edge of the frontier, and we are among the Indians, you do not need to worry for I believe them to be peaceful. I know that the name does not lend well, but to us it is paradise. We hope to have our house built before the end of summer.

I have already begun clearing the land, getting it ready for planting. Tobacco is the only solid staple commodity of this province, except maybe furs and skins of beavers, otters, muskrats, raccoons, wild cats, and elk or buffalo. The tobacco seeds are planted early spring, January and February in beds and then later, around April or May, the young plants are transplanted into the ground. Tobacco is used in this province like money.

Abraham

The Chesapeake Bay

The three-mast ship, twice the size of the *Mayflower*, carrying ninety-eight surviving passengers, twelve crewmembers and five African slaves taken on board in Barbados, pulled into the harbor at St. Mary's City at the most southerly tip of the finger of land where the Potomac River enters the Chesapeake Bay. The passengers and crew crowded the north side of the deck, anxious to get their first glimpse of Maryland and its forest, birds and Indians. This colony, a proprietorship granted by King Charles I to Lord Baltimore, extended north from the Potomac to the 40th parallel, having been a portion cut from the Virginia province to the south that continued from the eastern coast of America to the sea in the west, wherever that might be.

The speedy passage from the Isle of Wight, England had taken less than two months, sailing down the western edge of France and Spain to the Canary Islands off the coast of Africa, then west across the Atlantic to the island of Barbados, and then north along the coast of America to the Chesapeake. The actual time at sea was seven weeks and two days, the remainder having been spent at Barbados. Except for several stormy days at the beginning of the voyage when many of the passengers became sick, the seas had remained reasonably calm. The ship's galley was well stocked for the journey with sufficient supplies of flour, meat, dried fruit and vegetables, water, and beer. Nevertheless, the conditions were crowded and several of the passengers died from fever and dysentery. Two babies were born aboard, the first while only five days out, and the second the day before arrival at Barbados. Of the surviving passengers, only fifteen were women, whose ages ranged from four years to thirty-two, not counting the baby girl born while off the coast of Spain. Of the five Africans put on board at Barbados, four were male and one was female, the lot of them stored in the hold with the rest of the cargo.

Several ships were making regular trips, ever since the first voyage of the *Ark and the Dove* some twenty years earlier. They ventured back and forth between England and Maryland bringing people with experience in the kinds of work that could help build the new colony – carpenters, bricklayers, shipbuilders, blacksmiths, unskilled workers, and occasionally a priest or minister, all eager to find a start in the New World. At first, carpenters were in most demand; however, any person willing to work hard was welcomed. In the end, most that came to Maryland had no special skills or money for their passage and arrived as indentured servants.

Abraham had just turned seventeen two months earlier. He was not particularly tall, but he appeared so, with a lean, muscular body. His frame was still forming and would add an additional two inches in the oncoming year. His chin had the peach-fuzz beginnings of blond facial hair that would eventually change to red later on in his life. His face and arms bore several marks and scratches from his continuous itching throughout the long voyage. One scrape in particular, on his left forearm, was infected and needed to be drained and cleaned. His thick, dark blond hair was long and wavy and hung to his shoulders. He usually wore a faded blue beret pulled down over his ears, but today the air was warmer, and he wore it perched lightly on top of his head with a slight tilt to one side. He also wore a heavy wool coat brought from home that was now showing its age with torn pockets that he had attempted to repair with his needle and thread kit, also brought from home. His few other possessions remained tucked away in the knapsack he had slung over his shoulder.

Nearly a century earlier, Abraham's great-great-grandfather, Guillaume LeMaître, Captain of the *L'Eau de Vie de Cidre*, had retired, sold his shipping business and purchased a farm on the Isle of Jersey off the northeastern coast of Mont-St-Michael, a place that he had stopped at many times on his voyages throughout the English Channel. The farm had been passed down through three generations, and Abraham's father, John LeMaître, having spent his whole life working the farm, was anxious to retire and leave the farm to his sons Isaac and Abraham.

However, Abraham wasn't interested. Leaflets advertising the Chesapeake Bay Colony were commonplace and had been pasted all over England and Ireland for nearly twenty years, and Abraham, living on the remote Isle of Jersey, had come across one of the brochures. It seemed exciting to him and he didn't want to remain on the farm or the island for the rest of his life. So after waiting several weeks near the time the next ship was leaving the Isle of Wight, he announced to his parents that he had decided to leave for America. His father would not hear of it and demanded that Abraham put it out of his mind. Abraham agonized over the thought of disobeying him, but as the days for departure drew near, unbeknownst to his father, he approached his mother one last time and said goodbye. She gave him her blessing and handed him a small purse of silver coins.

Elizabeth Cooksey

lizabeth Alice Cooksey stood to the left of her parents, the Reverend and Mrs. Cooksey, about one hand apart, her right hand on the rail, the other clutching her small travel bag. She stood smiling cheerfully as the ship steered near the quay, gazing at the small wooden buildings of St. Mary's City in the not too far distance. Even though it was an early autumn day, there was an air of coolness about, and if one were to pay any attention to it, one could almost see one's breathe.

The gulls circled the ship, making shrieking sounds, and small waves of water made plunging thuds against the dock as the crew completed furling the sails – all but the small lateen sail to maneuver the ship into place. Moments later, the eastern sun rose above and behind the skyline and Elizabeth let go of the railing to shield her eyes from its brightness. Often she peered off to her left, where she could see Abraham, who also stood along the rail looking towards land. With her parents standing beside her, she was unable to make any sort of gesture to attract his attention, and she wished that he would look in her direction.

She had spent most of the night reading, unable to sleep, knowing that the ship would be arriving soon, then falling asleep for two or three hours. She had awakened to the sound of the lookout in the crow's nest shouting, "Land ho!"

She had climbed into the dress she had removed before falling asleep and rushed to the railing along with several other early risers. It was still dark and only the distant lights of St. Mary's City were visible, yet there was enough excitement for the onlookers to remain with their eyes fixed on the shoreline. Eventually, one at a time the crowd thinned as they returned in the early morning dawn to their spots below to prepare for landing and disembarkation.

Elizabeth shoved each of her personal effects into her travel bag and waited for her parents to finish dressing and packing. She impatiently removed a piece of bread and cheese that she had saved from her meal the previous night and pinched small morsels away from the dry loaf, nervously placing them into her mouth.

"Please hurry, Daddy, Mama!" she prompted while pacing in the few inches of space that had been their home for the past two months.

"We're going as fast as we can. It will still be there, I promise," her father answered, looking at Mrs. Cooksey and smiling. "Why don't you go on up to the deck, and we'll be right behind?"

As she started up the steps, Elizabeth looked back at the large room, still filled with passengers, their beds, and their few possessions, a few lit candles throughout, knowing that this would be her last glance at what would be an experience she would never forget. She could see Charles and Maude Freedman, who had become friends with her mother and father, and she wondered if they would see each other again in the New World. Charles was a lawyer and had hopes of establishing himself in Maryland. A man whom she knew only as Mr. Martin was still gathering his stuff; she had played chess with him several times during the voyage, and she wondered if she would ever see him again. She had known almost everyone aboard and had spent time with each, more or less. Some had been interesting to talk to, and others not so much, but as much as she tried not to, she found herself drawn to Abraham, who, unfortunately, had failed to make a favorable impression on her parents.

Just as she started back up, she stopped again and ran back down to where her bed had been. She reached behind a narrow opening in the wall from which she pulled a small doll. "Thank goodness! I would have really missed you," she exclaimed, speaking directly to the wooden toy that had been carved for her on board by another of the passengers. She couldn't remember his name, but he was always whittling on pieces of wood and then giving them away. The doll was very simple – a head, body, two arms and two legs. The arms and legs hung loosely, each connected by a pin from the shoulders and hips that allowed them to swing back and forth. Under normal circumstances, she would have been too old to play with such a simple toy, but this had been a different time and place and any article of amusement was welcomed gladly.

As she started back toward the stairs, she met Filbert Smith, a man she would have preferred to avoid. He stopped and stepped to the side, allowing her to proceed ahead of him. He removed his hat and spoke. "Good morning, dear Elizabeth. And how are you this fine morning?"

"Just fine, Mr. Smith," she replied, and without looking at him she dashed up to the deck, taking hold of her long floor-length dress and finding a spot along the railing.

Reverend Cooksey

T he Reverend Douglas Cooksey, with his wife, Anna Alice, and his daughter, Elizabeth Alice, was arriving to replace the ailing Rev. Thomas Gervais, head of the First Anglican Church of St. Mary's. Rev. Gervais had been sick for the past two years and had solicited a replacement some time back without any response until six months before when he had received word that Rev. Cooksey would be forthcoming. However, Rev. Gervais did not live long enough to see his replacement, at long last fatally succumbing to a pneumococcal infection. The long delay was partially explained by the difficulty of long distance communication between the two dioceses, but more important was the difficulty in finding a willing replacement with sufficient credentials to govern the frontier church. Rev. Cooksey had been selected along with three other ministers for the assignment, and all three had rejected the church's offer of the archbishopric. Numerous meetings between the reluctant candidates and the church governors failed to make any progress, and ultimately the church was forced to make a strained choice between the nominees, and even that process was painfully slow, finally being decided by prayer accompanied by the drawing of straws. The Rev. William Whitehead's name was drawn and he, at last, accepted the appointment gracefully, believing that it was truly the will of God that he drop everything and move to the colony. However, the day that his ship was to depart, Rev. Whitehead dropped dead of heart failure.

Rev. Cooksey had the next longest straw. Considering the problems at hand, he now seemed to be the perfect selection – at thirty-eight he was considered to be middle-aged, athletic, fit and in good health. Seeing the position that the church was in and without any reasonable excuse to offer, he accepted the appointment and made the announcement to his disappointed family that they would be selling the family home and moving to Maryland.

Unless Rev. Cooksey was wearing the official church attire, the long black robe over white shirt and collar and the flat brimmed hat worn by ministers of that time, it would be difficult to recognize him as a man of the cloth. A bon vivant, he was tall and handsome with shiny, slicked-back red hair and striking features, eyes that could penetrate brick walls, with dimpled cheeks and a strong jaw and a deep indented chin dimple. He could out-fence or ride a horse as well as most any soldier of either the Royalist or the Parliamentary cavalry and he was always armed with a tale to tell that could only be told after the ladies were no longer present.

Anna Alice Cooksey was an admiring compliment to her husband – always well dressed but never overstated, quick to respond but never overshadowing, carefully flirtatious but always faithful. She saw it as God's calling that she rise to the highest level of any situation while remaining subject and subordinate to both God and her husband. When she discovered that Abraham's mother had given her blessing contrary to that of his father, she was silently outraged – in the beginning anyhow.

She was known for the role that she frequently played in several of the church social functions such as at Christmas and Easter, as well as her role as hostess for secular events held from time to time at their home in London. She supported the arts as well as charity programs for the needy. London's loss would be the colony's gain.

Both Rev. and Mrs. Cooksey were aware that throughout this lengthy cruise, their only daughter was seen spending more and more time with M. LeMaître, whom they quickly dismissed as unworthy of her position yet one who seemed nice enough and safe. They hoped that this would be simply a temporary relationship, tolerable only considering there were no other women or men her age aboard except for Lieutenant Jones, of the ships crew, and several bonded passengers that would certainly have nothing in common with her. Neither of her parents forbad her to meet with M. LeMaître; however, they did discuss with her that this friendship would necessarily terminate once they arrived at St. Mary's City.

Abraham and Elizabeth considered their relationship platonic, and for the majority of the voyage they regarded her parents' admonitions as unprovoked. But that was all to change when they arrived in Barbados.

Abraham and Elizabeth seemed to be in between adolescence and adulthood, unaware of either, one day running and laughing, playing tag on the deck, scampering up the rigging frequently pulling on each other, and being called down by the captain and told to "act your ages!" Sometimes they would footrace against each other, with Abraham giving Elizabeth a few feet of handicap. Other times they sat together quietly as she would read to him chapters from *The Canterbury Tales* or the poetry of Margaret Cavendish, or they would talk about their former lives, their friends, and their likes and dislikes. Once he admitted to her that he thought she was the most beautiful woman he had ever met. Even though she was embarrassed, she liked very much hearing him say it, and the only response she could muster at that moment was to say that she liked him more than anyone she had met before. Those remarks produced a warm feeling in both of them that would last a few more weeks.

They became friends with Lieutenant Jones and with several of the younger bonded passengers, including Edward Beckwith and Thomas Cranfield, and by the time they reached Barbados, the friendship among their small group had grown and developed more in those few weeks than any other had developed over the previous years of all their lives.

Barbados

The trade winds are regular, dependable winds that blow east to west at the twenty-degree latitude. Rather than sailing a direct route from England to Maryland, it was advantageous to travel the longer route first to Africa then rely on the 'westerlies', not too light and not too strong, across the Atlantic to the Caribbean. With the words "land ho," the passengers rushed to the rail, fighting for position to get a glimpse of the small pimple of land barely visible across the distant grayish-blue meniscus.

The weather conditions could not have been better as their ship slowly carved its way into the warm, glassy Caribbean waters. The small wooden vessel – its masts creaking, its exhausted travelers gazing silently with anticipation, its captain reassured not only that it was a safe passage, but that they were able to locate this small island with only the aid of the stars, its crew pleased that there was sufficient beer to make the journey, and that there would be rum waiting only hours away – barely left a wake as it seemingly skated across the shimmering surface.

Pushed closer and closer, those spectators along the rail and those tall enough to look over the heads of those in front began to make out the small, coral land mass. They watched it grow and unfurl its white sandy beach; its long, slender palms stretched and leaning outward toward them as if beckoning them to come closer, welcoming them, culling them into the exotic, a land only spoken of by crusty sailors and tasteless journals. This island respite was long awaited by most of the eager passengers, yet denounced by the Reverend Douglas Cooksey, especially as he accompanied his wife and daughter. Had they not been along, he too would have been celebrating their arrival.

The ship maneuvered its way from the east to the west side of the island in the very small channel at Holetown, formerly known as Jamestown, where the captain dropped anchor offshore. (Later ships would be served at nearby Carlisle Bay.)

Prior to their disembarkation the captain gave a briefing to everyone aboard. "The purpose of our stay, ladies and gentlemen, is to acquire fresh water and supplies and for everyone to enjoy a short stay on this warm island. The ship will be departing for Maryland in two days at 1800 hours; anyone not aboard will be left behind. The tenders will come and go back and forth from the ship to shore at 800 hours and 1800 today, and 800 hours and 1600 hours tomorrow. I must remind you that even though this is British territory, you must be careful, as there are those who will gladly relieve you of your purses. Enjoy the ocean water, swim in it; it is not only warm and refreshing, but it can heal those sores that many of you are complaining of. This island has quickly become the largest producer of sugarcane in the world, and its accompanying byproduct, rum. I must warn you, especially you who are indentured, do not get so messed-up that you do not make it back to the ship."

In the first tender, the captain rode with several crewmembers and the first-class paying passengers, leaving Lieutenant Jones behind and in charge. Rev. and Mrs. Cooksey and Elizabeth disembarked together in the second group while Abraham, Edward Beckwith and Thomas Cranfield followed later.

Edward Beckwith and Thomas Cranfield

E dward Beckwith was in his mid-twenties, came from London, and worked with his father in his print shop on Beeker Street.

The printing press had been around for almost two hundred years and after its initial introduction by Gutenberg, printers were kept busy printing mainly Bibles and religious tracts. Many people went into the printing business and went right back out again, there was still a low literacy rate in Europe – most people didn't know how to read at all. The situation was improved by the introduction of the book fairs. London was an early center for printing and so it sponsored a book fair, which drew publishers, booksellers, collectors, and scholars, who could find what they needed for their livelihoods.

Edward was a journeyman printer, having worked with his father beginning at an early age and could expect some day to take over his father's business. He was of average build, average height, had brown hair, a round face and no real distinguishing physical characteristics. He did enjoy reading and was quite inquisitive, quite informed on world news, at least when it became available, and he was usually able to hold his own in an argument.

Thomas Cranfield, age seventeen, also came from London but had no skills. He rarely saw his father, who was a sailor serving under Admiral Robert Blake in the Anglo-Spanish War at Cádiz; his mother barely eked out a living selling fish along the waterfront of the Themes River.

Thomas, much more aggressive than his brothers and sisters, was determined to escape out of his life of poverty and take his chances in the new world. Several years earlier, he had been trampled by a runaway horse, resulting in a badly broken right leg. He was lucky not to have lost his leg, but he now walked with a limp, a handicap that would continue to make life difficult for him. He wore a navy blue pea coat given to him by his father.

Both Edward and Thomas met for the first time when they boarded the ship at the Isle of Wight. They were together this late morning along with Abraham as the tender they were riding in pulled up to the wooden dock at Holetown.

Lavinia

"What do we do first?" questioned Edward, climbing on to the quay and looking back at the other two.

"I don't know, except that I'm hungry for some real food, I'm sick of that slop they've been giving us," Thomas answered as he followed Edward out of the tender.

Abraham joined in, "Why don't we look around and see what's here?"

"I've got to get my land legs back first," laughed Edward as he suddenly realized that he almost had to relearn how to walk on firma terra.

Along the dock, there were several wood-framed buildings with gray wood siding and shingle roofs which looked as if they might be warehouses of some sort. As they walked by the large sliding doors, they could see bales of sugarcane stacked high to the ceiling. There were dark-skinned workers unloading bales from a horse-drawn cart through the opened door at the rear of building. As they came to the end of the boardwalk and buildings, they could see the long stretch of beach lined with palm trees swaying lightly in the breeze.

"Now that's what I want, just to lie in that warm sand, and when I get hot, jump into that frothy surf. Just look at it!" exclaimed Abraham.

Edward was a couple steps ahead of the rest. "Do you see what I see?" There were people of all ages on the beach, some were white – the Dutch were the first Europeans to settle the island – and some were various shades of bronze, some were swimming in the surf, others were sitting beneath the palms, others were lying in the sun. Nevertheless, what had caught Edward's eyes were women seemingly of all ages exercising their right to the same 'topfreedom' as men.

Thomas had heard stories from his father's sailor friends about the bare-breasted beaches along the Mediterranean, and he wanted to move in closer for a better look.

Nearby, a beach vendor was selling rum-filled coconuts. They each bought one, and then the three walked across the white sand to the water's edge near a group of young Bajan women sitting on a large, woven reed mat. They were laughing and having a good time playing Wari, a popular board game played with 'nickernuts', the marble-like seeds of a spiny native shrub (Caesalpinia bonduc and C. major.)

The boys removed their shirts, shoes and socks, and one at a time entered the surf. Like three puppies they romped and played together, glad to be off the ship, splashing and diving in the briny waves, laughing boisterously while all the time glancing back and forth toward the beach.

Edward tired first and returned to the place where they had left their clothing, and soon Thomas and Abraham followed, except that Abraham approached the three girls. He had no towel and was dripping water in the sand. He pushed his long blond hair back, beginning at his forehead, and smiled. All three were attractive, each with long black hair and bronze skin. The one nearest him wore a white gardenia in her hair, a silver toe ring and a colorful loincloth tied to her waist. She sat with her legs stretched out. Off to her side was a pile that looked like towels and sarongs that each had removed.

He was the first to speak but only meaningless dribble that no one understood. As he spoke, the one that wore the gardenia with her legs stretched out lifted herself slightly from the ground, repositioned her legs beneath her, and sat up straight. They were aware of each other's awkwardness and she began to giggle.

As he gazed down at her, Abraham could not help but stare at her nakedness, even if it was from the periphery of his vision as he concentrated on aiming his stare toward her eyes. She could tell that he was just off the ship and would be gone in a few days or hours; guys like him came and left all the time.

"We no speak English," she uttered, barely understandable.

"I no speak *anglais;* speak *français*," suddenly discovering within himself some extra needed buoyancy as he lowered himself to his knees without sitting on his legs.

She looked at the others and sniggered again. "We...no...know...you." She spoke each word slowly and separately.

Abraham placed the palms of both of his hands onto his chest and spoke. "Abraham," repeating it distinctly three times.

"A-bu-am," she imitated, and the other two repeated his name to each other several times.

At first glance, Abraham was neither exceptionally handsome nor bad looking. His attractiveness was in his natural smile and in his confidence, once he was able to locate it. Like starting a fire with a piece of flint, once he could get a spark to land on the tinder, he could sprinkle on the kindling – soon, he thought, she was beginning to feel his warmth. He pointed his hands in her direction, palms up as if to say 'What is your name?'

She turned, looking toward her two friends, and shrugged her shoulders. She then looked back at Abraham and said "Lavinia. I Lavinia, you A-bu-am." She then pointed to the girl sitting next to her and said, "Cereus," and then to the one opposite, "Chandin."

The sun was soon overhead and the girls moved back toward the tree line beneath some lower growing palms. The ground was hillier there with small dunes and patches of grass. Edward and Thomas eventually joined them and they all worked on learning each other's names and how to play Wari. The boys made several trips to get refills of rum in their coconuts, and when all the meat had been eaten, they returned for more. Eventually, the girls began to share the rum, and by late afternoon they were all becoming pleasantly intoxicated. It was then that the captain, Rev. and Mrs. Cooksey, and Elizabeth came walking along, returning from spending the afternoon in Holetown. They had had lunch at a small restaurant in town, had walked to a nearby sugarcane field, and were returning to catch the end-of-day tenders back to the ship.

"Elizabeth, isn't that young Abraham over there rolling around with those naked savages? Doesn't he have any sense of decency? I had a feeling that he wasn't any good. Just look at him! I dare say that this is the last you will be seeing of him. Come now; let's get back to the ship. I believe that I've seen enough for one day."

"Your father is right, Elizabeth, you are not to share his company any more. Do you understand me?" Her mother echoed the reverend's sentiments while looking directly at her, holding her arm.

"Yes mother, I understand." To all that could see her, Elizabeth maintained a stiff upper lip, but inside her heart was hurting, she wanted to run away and never see the captain, the reverend, her mother, and especially Abraham again.

Abraham watched from afar as they climbed into the tender, the captain assisting Elizabeth and the reverend helping Mrs. Cooksey, she holding on to her flowered parasol. When they were all seated, the coxswain stood and gave the command to the oarsmen, and Abraham watched them return to the ship, bobbing up and down in the surf, all eight oars in synchronized motion.

Abraham awoke and sat up on the hard, single bed. It was the next morning and the sun was shinning in between the louvered slats in the window, casting alternating lines of light onto the bed. Rays of light also squeezed into the room between the gaps in the thin wallboards – a simple form of construction used for housing on the island. The walls were quite plain with no pictures or decorations, a few clothes hanging on several hooks added the only color to the otherwise bare room. From the waist down he was covered with a light blanket, and Lavinia sat next to him, facing him with one foot on the floor. Her breasts seemed larger than they had on the beach, especially as she leaned over him, lightly pressing her fingers against his lips while she whispered 'shhhhh' as if to keep him from saying anything. After a few minutes, she stepped off the bed, quietly opened the bedroom door and peeked out. When it appeared safe, she left the room to make certain that everyone in her family had left. A small gray chameleon scampered up the wall by the doorway and stopped just below the thatched roof. It turned around and brandished his tongue at Abraham, then disappeared into the roof.

When Lavinia returned, she was wearing a simple sarong and carrying a tray with a bowl of mixed fruit – melons, guava, and small finger-sized bananas that she had prepared. She also had a small dish containing raw oysters and shrimp. Pressed between her upper right arm and body, almost at her armpit, she had a small, round loaf of bread. Still keeping the loaf tucked under her arm, and while holding the tray and balancing it carefully, she climbed onto the bed and set the tray between the two of them. She then reached into the bowl, withdrew a slice of melon and raised it to Abraham's mouth, waiting for him to take a bite. As he bit, the juice ran down the side of his face and down the bottom edge of her forearm. They both laughed and he reached for a slice of pineapple, wiping it against her lips until she decided to take a taste. The juice flowed down the side of her mouth, her neck and in between her breasts. Abraham gently wiped the liquid with his fingertips and then placed his fingers into his mouth. He felt fluttering and nervousness in his chest, and he placed Lavinia's palms against his heart so that she could feel his excitement.

They continued to sit facing each other, touching and caressing, running their fingers through each other's hair. Then they began to smear each other with the rest of the fruit, crushing it between their bodies, tasting the fruit and their perspiration. The fragrance of the sweet fruit merged with the musty, mushroom odor that poured out from their excitement.

When they had finished the fruit, they began sharing the shrimp and passing the oysters from her mouth to his and back again, mixing their tongues together with the soft-bodied mollusks. After they had consumed all the food, they began to taste one another's parts, and when every cavity had been fully explored, and he had inserted himself into her every conceivable opening, and all their body fluids had been exchanged, they folded into each other's arms and slept.

Two hours passed and Lavinia stood beside the bed nudging Abraham to wake up. When he opened his eyes, she pointed to his shirt and trousers, which she had picked up off the floor. The bed was still wet from the fruit and semen. Abraham slowly dressed, and when he had finished they embraced again and gazed into each other's eyes. Hers were large and black, and she could see that he had one blue eye and one gray one; they sat deep in his head.

He reached out one of his arms, comparing her bronze skin next to his. *She is even more beautiful than Elizabeth*, he thought to himself. He knew that he would never forget this past night and morning. *If there is any such thing as paradise, this had to be it,* he decided.

Together they walked outside of the small house. It was in the middle of a row of cottages on the edge of a sugarcane field, each the same size with roofs made of palm fronds lashed onto bamboo slats. At the shady side of the house, there was a bush full of tiny finches fluttering, making their squeaky chirps, a mix of colors like a vase of mixed wildflowers, yellow, white, red and chocolate. The tall green leaves of the cane, like elephant grass, were blowing in the warm wind, the trade winds that had blown him to paradise, to Barbados.

They walked together along one of the alleyways that cut through the middle of the field and led back to town. Lavinia reached over and broke off a small section of cane, stripped it and then handed it to Abraham. He had never seen cane before and he didn't know what to do with it, so she took it back, pulled a strip away with her teeth and then began chewing on it, swallowing the sugar water it produced before handing it back to him. He quickly caught on and tore off a long stock to take back to the ship with him. He wished that he could take her with him as well.

When they came to the end of the field they arrived at the residential area of Holetown, the streets were neatly paved with cobbles, just like in England. In the center of town there was a large square surrounded by the usual stores that you would expect in any town – a bakery, a candle maker, a cobbler, a produce and fish market, and several alehouses. Running parallel to each of the four sides of the square there were two streets running in each direction, creating a matrix of twelve streets, mostly residential with a few commercial buildings containing upstairs residences. The square was filled with people, some standing and visiting with one another, and others seated on the several benches placed throughout. Some were locals doing their shopping, and others from the ship were rummaging through the shops looking for bargains.

At the far end of the square, a platform rose about three feet above the ground, and Abraham could see that there was an African standing on it, naked and chained to a pole. There was a man standing next to him who wore a long coat and a tall hat. Abraham wanted to move closer, but Lavinia tried to steer him away. It was obvious that she didn't want him to watch, but he insisted and she followed.

As he got closer he saw several other Africans standing on

the ground, each naked and chained to a post. Several of the posts contained more than one slave, and one contained what appeared to be a family – a male, female and a young boy that could have been a son. Each post had a number from one to ten. There was an auctioneer standing on the platform who was receiving bids from the crowd below, and as Abraham got as close as he could, he heard the auctioneer shout, "Sold! To the man in the front row for one hundred and fifty pounds." Abraham could see the buyer as he stepped forward; it was Filbert Smith, from the ship.

She wanted to explain the slave trade to him, but was unable, how they were first captured by the Dutch, and then later the English, from Sierra Leone, Guinea, Ghana, the Ivory Coast, Nigeria and Cameroon and brought to this island – a major Caribbean distribution point – and then sold out to the local plantations and to the colonies along the Eastern Seaboard. The production of sugar, tobacco and cotton was heavily reliant on the indenture of servants. White civilians who wanted to emigrate overseas could do so by signing an agreement to serve as a planter in Barbados for a period of five or seven years. To meet the labor demands, servants were also derived from kidnapping, and convicted criminals were shipped to Barbados.

Descendants of the white slaves and indentured labor (referred to as Red Legs) still live in Barbados to this day. They live amongst the black population in St. Martin's River and other east coast regions. At one time they lived in caves in this region.

As they crossed the square toward the dock, Abraham could see that the tenders had not yet arrived, so he and Lavinia sat together near the beach on a grassy dune wanting to hold off until the last possible moment. They both knew that he would never be back, and that they would never see each other again. Then when there was no more time, he reluctantly returned to the ship.

It was the perfect time to set sail – the tide was going out and the wind, coming from the southeast, had suddenly shifted. However, it would be the warm ocean currents that would propel them north, the third leg, zigging and then zagging their way across the Caribbean and along the Eastern Seaboard, arm wrestling the whole way with the norteasterlies, the currents emerging as ultimate victor.

The captain waited anxiously for the final tender to return to the ship before giving instructions to the crew to unfurl the sails and lift the anchor. Most of the passengers were on deck, a few of the men were waving to newfound sweethearts on the not so distant beach, others stood near the rail simply watching whatever might be there to see.

Two young islanders in an outrider canoe bobbed about below on the small waves at the portside of the bow diving for coins, however, not so many coins were forthcoming. What little money each passenger carried would certainly be needed in the coming days, and those who were more fortunate had little inclination to be so extravagant.

It had been a friendly place with plenty of attractions for wayfarers such as were aboard, a warm, exotic island setting, yet quite English. There were taverns, brothels and even decent cafés, and then there were also restaurants where even the Reverend and Mrs. Cooksey were comfortable. There was certainly a shortage of men needed to work the cane fields, so anyone not returning to the ship, such as occurred with Edward Beckwith and Thomas Cranfield, could easily stay behind, but there remained their unpaid indentures.

Abraham stood at the rail scanning the beach, then the dock, and then he shifted his gaze back to the beach again, searching for the bonze-skinned islander with whom he had shared the past two days. Had she been anywhere in sight, he would surely have seen her. He thought for a moment that he had seen her still sitting on the dune where he had left her, but then she was gone. Then he thought perhaps that she might have moved closer to get a better look while he boarded the ship. There were several Bajans standing along the surf's edge, some in water even up as high as their waists, so he carefully studied each, hoping to locate the orange and white flowered sarong that he knew she was wearing. Search as he might, he would not see her because she had left.

Lavinia had remained on the sandy dune and watched Abraham make his way slowly toward the quay. It had been an exciting two days with him. To begin with he was pleasurable to be around, and he made her laugh; he was courteous and treated her with respect. Even though they didn't share a common language, he was able to charm her from the start, and as their time together progressed, they were able to communicate with each other without words. However, she accepted the reality that she would never see him again.

As she walked back along the long lane through the cane field, she began thinking about what she would say to her parents. There were few secrets in her house; it was too small. They would want to know with whom she spent the night, who had kept her from her work that day. They would not want to hear that he was an Englishman off the ship on his way to America. They would not understand how she could have been so foolish; at least that was what she anticipated they would say. Unable to rework an acceptable version of her story, she decided that she would simply tell them the truth; they would have to accept it, and she would accept the outcome.

As she approached the house, she could smell bacon frying. Some smells spoke of the love of her parents, and bacon was one of those smells. It was familiar and comfortable and reassuring and meant that all was well at home. They might be disappointed in her, and she might have to listen to their harangue, but all was well – the bacon told her that.

Abraham was no longer on deck when the last tender pulled alongside. Having failed to locate Lavinia on the beach, he gave up and went below. Had he remained on deck he would have been shocked, just as were the majority of those standing about that evening. Most that had gone ashore during the day and witnessed the Africans being auctioned in the town square had been greatly disturbed by it. By now, most had put it out of their minds until they saw that it was Filbert Smith standing in the last tender watching the five slaves he had purchased being brought aboard and stowed in the hold with the rest of the cargo.

Like animals, each was wearing an iron collar around their necks, which was chained to their wrists, and shackles on their ankles, the five were herded onto the deck and down into the hold to be chained to the floor.

The Disappearance of Beckwith and Cranfield

Earlier that afternoon, Robert Wentworth stopped for a pint at one of the alehouses on the square. He was a small sugar plantation owner and had arrived in town for the specific purpose of acquiring a slave at the auction that afternoon. Having successfully concluded his business and chained his newly acquired property to his wagon, he walked across the square and entered through the swinging doors of the One Eyed Owl. Barbados was a free port and the One Eyed Owl was a public house often filled with newcomers, floaters and immigrants, refugees and squatters, soldiers and sailors, locals and natives, of European, African and Caribbean persuasion, mostly male.

Opposite the front door and straight on was a long, carved oak bar which had originated from a public brothel in Barcelona opened in Cañet Street in 1452 by Simon Sala, not far from Las Ramblas.

The air was permeated with an alcoholic vapor mixed with the brume and haze of Cuban cigars and the stench of body odor. The crack of clashing billiard balls across one of the two cloth-covered carom tables could be heard above the mélange of voices, some laughing, some cursing, while others were engaged in normal conversation. Other than the bar, the most notable of the fixtures was the piece of green felt hanging on the wall above the billiard table, supposedly the 16th century billiard cloth that had once wrapped the body of Mary, Queen of Scots.

Of all the saloons in Holetown, this was Robert Wentworth's favorite place, just as it was for many of the other single townies, mainly because of Polly Fisher, the proprietress. Polly had inherited the tavern from her father, who had started it some ten years back but had passed away the year before. He had bumped his shinbone while at work, tearing the skin. Infection had set in and the doctor, who was also the town vet as well as the barber, was unable to cure it, ultimately leading to gangrene and the removal of his leg.

Polly had helped her father from the start, so she had a good feel for running the business and, with the help of the heavy club she kept behind the bar, handling any out-of-line customers. She was several years younger than Robert Wentworth, and by Holetown standards, attractive, and she had not yet made up her mind as to which one of her several suitors, if any, she would ultimately decide on. Robert Wentworth was hopeful.

Edward Beckwith and Thomas Cranfield, Abraham's friends from the ship, had nothing better to do that afternoon than to sit there at the tavern and pass the time while waiting for the ship to depart. When Robert Wentworth arrived, he walked straight into the pub and directly to the bar across from where Polly was standing. There were no vacant seats, so he made a place and squeezed in, placing his right boot on the brass rail and one elbow onto the bar. But Polly was bouncing about the bar like a Bajan butterfly, too busy for any small talk with Robert Wentworth, so he introduced himself to Edward and Thomas and a conversation developed among the three.

He seemed most interested in their story about their enlisting for passage to Maryland, their indenture with Johnson Miller and their hopes for obtaining a parcel of land, a new suit and an axe at the termination of their contract. After listening carefully and then giving the matter due consideration, he offered to match their indenture. If they were to stay and work for him, he would in return agree to pay off their bond, or at least give them an indemnity against any future litigation that might come their way for failing to show up in St. Mary's City. This would enable them to work and live in the warm Caribbean rather than in Maryland, where the winters were extremely cold. He further emphasized that, even though he was still single, there were twenty men for every one woman in Maryland whereas they could easily find themselves a Bajan woman that would make an acceptable wife.

The captain had given a fair warning to all the passengers about drinking too much rum and missing the ship, and it could probably be said that the rum had some influence on their decision to miss the ship and remain on the island.

After a handshake and several more pints, Edward and Thomas climbed into the back of Robert Wentworth's mule-drawn wagon and rode out to his plantation to begin work the next day. Moses, just purchased that afternoon, sat chained to the side rail.

Robert Wentworth sat on the driver's seat holding the reins loosely as the two mules pulled the four passengers along the bumpy alleyway. The wagon was quite large, capable of hauling two tons of cut cane. The four wooden spoke wheels were mounted on two iron axels connected to the iron leaf springs, and there was a grease bucket hanging on the outside, near the front, for lubrication. Overhead in the night sky the illumination of a nearly full moon enabled him to steer the wagon around the many potholes in the uneven road. Still, not all the potholes were escapable and both driver and passengers had to hold on tightly, as the wagon had no tolerance for comfort. Nevertheless, Robert Wentworth was used to the alleyways and could navigate them as well as anyone.

He was in good spirits. He had negotiated a good price for Moses, one hundred and seventy-five pounds, and he had convinced the two white boys to come to work for him, although he wasn't quite sure about the gimp with the deformed leg. He might have to pay for their indentures, then again, he might not – he would have to wait and see. He had done this before and gotten away with it, but now he realized he might be pushing his luck too far. Most of the planters that had come to the island were, after all, adventurers, mercenaries, opportunists and risk takers, and he had taken his share of risks – sickness, too much or not enough rain, not enough help and falling sugar prices. In the beginning, he employed mostly indentured servants coming from Ireland, but those were more and more difficult to come by and were being replaced by slaves from Africa.

Moses was young and strong and would be good for many years. The turnout at the auction had been small and there wasn't a lot of competition, only Filbert Smith, from the ship. On a busier day, Moses would have gone for at least two hundred pounds, maybe even more. He had belonged to a plantation owner in an adjacent county that had died and the widow was selling off everything, taking her four children and moving back to England. Moses had been married for a short time and had no children. His wife had worked in the house and he in the fields. His wife had been purchased two weeks earlier without Moses, and he had become quite angry and depressed, but that wasn't going to be a problem for Robert Wentworth, as he had taken separated husbands before.

The ship hadn't been long at sea when Johnson Miller realized that part of his investment, Edward Beckwith and Thomas Cranfield, was not aboard. There was no turning the ship around; Johnson Miller would have to deal with the matter on his own once he arrived at St. Mary's City. He spoke first with Anem Bendin and Henry Bishop, who said that they had seen them on the beach with Abraham, that he had returned to the ship the first day, but they didn't remember anything about the two on the second day. Abraham reported that yes, they were together on the beach, that he thought they went off with two of the Bajan women, but he couldn't be sure. Filbert Smith said he had seen them at the tavern later on the last day talking with Robert Wentworth, a plantation owner who had been bidding against him at the auction.

Johnson Miller was furious because his own land grant was based on bringing five able men, now he only had three. He would in the coming days claim that his damages amounted to not only the price of their passages but also the future value of the portion of land that he wouldn't receive. Filbert Smith silently chuckled to himself, patting himself on his own back for having had the insight to purchase five slaves that could be chained to the floor.

Johnson Miller went about the ship questioning just about anyone that would talk to him about his missing indentured servants, and ultimately he came across Charles Freedman, the lawyer. Charles suggested that they wait until they arrive at their destination and see what services could be made available for the extradition of Beckwith and Cranfield. He was sure that the matter could be handled, but he wasn't sure at what cost – whether it would be worth it or not – and advised that Johnson lighten up, at least until they arrived at their destination.

Abraham was aware that Elizabeth was no longer as available as before. He also knew the reason why. Each time she appeared on deck she was with either one or both of her parents, and he continued to look for an opportunity to get her alone so he could at least talk to her and see what he might do to redeem himself. After all, he wasn't looking to marry her; he just wanted to continue with their friendship. He penned a short note to her.

Elizabeth,

I know that I was very foolish, and I want to apologize to you and your parents. It there any hope that I might be forgiven? I miss you very much and the fun that we had together.

Abraham

He still had her copy of *The Canterbury Tales,* so he placed the note inside the front cover and then asked Mr. Martin, her chess partner, to deliver it to her, to which he agreed. The same day he returned with her note that simply said, "I'm sorry."

Zekiah Swamp

Charlestown was the most important tobacco port on the Potomac River. Below Charleston, the Wicomico River marked the border between the southern Ste. Mary's County and the northern Charles County, running south some thirty-seven miles and draining into the Potomac River. Its source was the Zekiah Swamp, rich in wildlife, including great blue herons and summering bald eagles. It is also known for having many insects, including mosquitoes, and for being inhabited by the Zekiah or Pangaio Indians.

Between Zekiah Swamp and Charlestown, Lord Baltimore reserved two Manors of 6,000 acres each, one about the town of Pangaia, the other including the town of Zackaio. These towns were Indian settlements. Most of its white inhabitants lived along the Potomac and its estuaries, and the tide of settlement moved inland year by year. The lowest reaches of Zekiah Swamp lay well inside the frontier plantations.

Abraham's back and legs ached as he stooped over and removed a small tobacco plant from the wooden flat, transplanting it into the black loamy earth. The worst of the pain was in his lower spine, and once the plant was firmly in place he stood and tried arching his back and stretching his arms upward. He looked behind at the half-completed row, and then off to his flank at the hundreds of rows that had been planted over the past several days as if taking a moment to admire his work would serve as a balm to his tired body. It is good to feel good about one's labors – it helps get one through the hard times. He also knew better than to allow the luxury of being too much in awe of his work; this moment of weakness could only hinder the timely completion of getting all the young tobacco plants that remained into the ground. Such distractions could easily justify the taking of longer breaks and quitting early. Not having an overlord standing at the side of the field, his work was as much psychological as physical. Having taken control of his thoughts he squatted down and removed the next plantlet from the wooden box, inserted it into the ground, then the next and the next before duck-walking a step or two, dragging the flat behind and then withdrawing the next sprout. He could usually manage to complete the process three or four times before having to move. Each plant had to be removed carefully, so as not to damage the tender roots, and inserted into the ground that he had tilled earlier. With each empty flat, he would retrieve another from off to the side.

He had never planted anything before, not even on his father's dairy farm on the Isle of Jersey. It was well into spring and the danger of frost burning the tender leaves had passed – at least he hoped. The seedlings had remained all winter in flats stored in both his cabin and in a small lean-to shack. The soil was moist and black, moist because his fifty-acres was surrounded by multiple tributaries of the Potomac; black because the land had never been cleared, was rich in nutrients having been formed through the combination of the physical and chemical decay of glacial material, vegetation and animal life, earthworms and burrowing animals.

Sweetscented was considered the best tobacco in the world and brought a better price than Oronoco, the other type of tobacco grown in the Chesapeake region. It would be months before he would see any profit. Was it worth it? Of course it would be; those who had come before him were doing well and they were acquiring more and more land from the profits. Land was easy to come by – he had already proven that. The hard part was finding the labor to do the work. He had the land but no one to help, no one to talk to, no one to share his pride but for the animals of the forest, the fox, the rabbits, the deer, and the turkeys. He couldn't help but admire his work, and he wished that he had a wife.

Abraham had received his fifty acres, just as the flyer in Brittany had promised, soon after arriving at St. Mary's City. Had he paid the way for five others, besides himself, he would have received one hundred acres. Receiving this plot was not without conditions – he had to agree to five years of indentured servitude and an annual rent of 600 bushels of corn each year. The land had originally been granted to Edward Evans of Ste. Mary's County, two hundred acres of land by assignment from Richard Edelin, the assignee of William Boarman, the assignee of Thomas Nobley due Nobley for transporting Samuel Haley, Mathew Hinch, James Weatherly and Thomas Whinley into the province.

Abraham had begun work early each morning clearing the land. He also needed to spend time gathering food, primarily fish from the nearby creek and small game such as squirrel, rabbit and raccoon. As the tobacco plants would soon grow, he would have to groom his field, topping each plant by cutting off the flowers to speed the maturation of the lower leaves. By late August, the plants would be ready for harvest, and the tobacco would have to be cut by hand. When first cut, they are brittle and must lie in the sun and wilt slightly. After the plant is pliable, the base of each stalk must be split with a steel spear. Six or eight plants would then be threaded through the split in the plant's base on a wooden tobacco stick. The sticks would be loaded, again by hand, onto a flatbed wagon and taken to the barn to hang and cure. It would be a hot and risky job. When the fall harvest was complete, he would then need to devote all his time to clearing the land in preparation for the spring planting.

Abraham watched the remaining sliver of the sun slide slowly below the horizon, turned and walked unhurriedly back to the cabin. Even with the sun gone for the night, the sky had yet to give up the light as the full moon arrived just in time for the second shift (the night creatures and fowl) soon to arrive. It had rained the night before and the ground had been wet all day; his shoes and trousers were caked with mud, so before entering his small house he removed all his clothes and draped them over an outside chair near the door. He had shared this small dwelling with the flats of seedlings that he had spread throughout the single room during the past few months, so tonight would be his first night alone. There were sufficient embers remaining in the hearth for him to revive a small flame with the help of a few dry leaves and soon he had a warm fire ready to keep him company through the darkness. After finishing his dinner of cornbread and cheese, he crawled in between the covers ready to fall asleep. When he lay down, he was aware of how much he needed a wife.

It could be easily said that Abraham's near marriage to Martha York would have been a marriage of convenience. Her father, John York, had several daughters and only one son. His entire plantation was devoted to tobacco and none to corn. John had a yearly obligation of 500 bushels, but he didn't want to give up any portion of his land for raising it. When Abraham offered to provide him with the 500 bushels for the next four years in trade for one of his daughters, John accepted the offer. John was quite pleased with the agreement and threw in a horse just to 'sweeten the deal', but he also made it quite clear to Abraham that if he were to default on payment when due, he would quickly foreclose on the both the horse and Martha.

Martha was several years younger than Abraham, but even so, she seemed much older than her actual age. She certainly seemed of adequate age to bear children, and she was pretty enough to look at – brown hair, brown medium-sized eyes, not set too far apart, an oval face with a pale complexion and thin lips, ten fingers, ten toes and good body conformation. When her father introduced her, Abraham was immediately taken by her charming smile and her poise. She wore several ankle-length waist-fastened petticoats beneath a bodice and a skirt, the bodice buttoned all the way down the front with lace collar and cuffs. Her hair was worn up and pulled tightly back beneath a coif.

"I am very glad to meet you, mademoiselle," Abraham said, gently kissing her hand. "Your father told me how beautiful you were, now I can see." The words rolled out in English with a creamy 'Jersey Norman French' accent.

Martha was also mildly pleased. Even though his attire was somewhat frayed, and his soft face wore a thin unshaven crop of peach fuzz, he stood tall, with handsome features and dark, wavy blond hair that he wore stylishly slicked back. His demeanor reflected confidence, ambition and a *joie de vivre*. She couldn't help but notice how strange it was that one of his eyes was blue and the other gray; she was unable to dismiss it as an anomaly both bizarre and beguiling.

As soon as he had left, she spoke to her father. "Oh Daddy, he's handsome all right, and what a charmer, but to live out there in the swamp in a small cabin. I had no idea that he would be this poor. And he can barely speak English."

"You'll see, my dear sweet Martha. This young man will do well and you will have the luxury of building a life together with him that will bring you much satisfaction. I can see it in him. He reminds me of me!"

Each Sunday, Abraham mounted his newly acquired horse and rode to the York plantation and then together with the family to the First Anglican Church. They all sat together, filling up the pew box that John York had purchased at the time the church was being constructed. Then they returned home for the single meal of the day. Afterward, they would go to the parlor to visit. John's wife, Betty, would play the piano and one of the daughters, usually it would be Martha, or Olivia, would recite a poem or a bible verse that she had learned that day. On the first afternoon, Martha sang the *Agincourt Carol*:

> *Owre kynge went forth to Normandy*
> *With grace and myght of chyualry;*
> *Ther God for hym wrought mervelusly;*
> *Wherfore Englonde may calle and cry,*
> *Deo gracias.*

During that period of courtship, Abraham and Martha sat together near the front window of the parlor, which was a respectable distance from the others, and this enabled them to get to know each other better. There, he could look at her more closely, and she at him, not only at each other's physical being but also they were to discover the deeper qualities that each possessed. She could see that he hadn't always been poor, that he had come from a good family in Europe, that he had been schooled at home by his mother and understood, perhaps, a little Greek and Latin. He wasn't fluent in either, that was for sure. Beneath his recently acquired frontier unevenness, she saw his charm and pleasant disposition. He was able to see that she was quite intelligent, that she was well read, especially for being so young; she particularly enjoyed reading Chaucer, Shakespeare, Sir Thomas Malory, and John Milton. She had strong opinions about several subjects that were traditionally only discussed by men – issues such as Maryland's proprietary system of government, slavery and the wars of religion.

Abraham eventually managed to acquire a newer suit and he began to look more and more as though he was a part of the family. The last week before the wedding, they sat together before the parlor window, her hands in his, and he professed his love for her, telling her how much she meant to him. Martha was moved to tears and realized that she too was falling in love with him.

It could have been a grand wedding; many of the earliest settlers, now successful plantation owners, would have attended. Many of them had started out much the same as Abraham, with only fifty acres and five years of indebted servitude, and they looked on upon him with sodalist favor and considered him as one of their own, eager to support and protect the couple, knowing that it would not be easy for them.

However, on the last Sunday before the wedding was to take place, following church services, Martha wanted to see the cabin where they would be living and take a few items of clothing. Abraham loaded her trunk onto the back of a small cart hitched to the horse that had been part of the bargain between Abraham and John, and they headed out the long plantation lane and then toward Zekiah Swamp.

Even though it was mid-afternoon when they arrived at the cabin, it seemed dark, the air sprinkled with mosquitoes and the sparkle of an occasional firefly. Abraham helped his bride-to-be down from the horse cart. She had ridden in that cart throughout the countryside many times before, always returning to her father's stable where a waiting groom would be there to receive her, where dinner would be waiting, where she had her own bedroom with clean sheets and towels.

Inside the cabin, the stale-smelling room was dark and cold and damp, so dark that what little sunlight there was outside seeped in miserly through the gaps in the timbers, and Abraham promptly built a fire in the hearth hoping to make the homecoming seem a bit warmer.

They sat quietly in front of the orange flames, Martha more uncertain than ever about her new environment, and Abraham sensing her anxiety. A nearby hoot owl could be heard outside above the muffled clicks of the crickets, most likely announcing the arrival of the bride, or perhaps some other message of sylvan importance.

As the flaming logs and the cabin mice began to settle, they sat near each other on Abraham's lumpy bed with both their feet flat on the floor. He had never noticed before its musty smell and he was sure that she was politely not mentioning it to him. They both sat together for a few short moments and then Abraham moved closer and turned to her. He took her hand and told her that he loved her and that this would pass, that she would not always be living in a cold damp cabin. He drew nearer to her and spoke softly. "This is the beginning of a great journey for the two of us, my darling, a chance for us to create our own dreams in this new world. I see rainbows everywhere, in the water, in the land, in the air we breathe and in the people around us."

Deep within her heart and soul, Martha wished that his words would take hold of her, that God would breathe down upon her but to no avail. She then realized that the smells and sounds, the mosquitoes and dampness, were too much for her to suffer. With an overwhelming sense of apprehension, she was unwilling to continue – the romance was over.

Stuck in the Mud

S everal years had passed since that time in Barbados when it seemed that Abraham and Elizabeth were never to see each other again, certainly never to marry, and least of all become the father and mother of several hundred thousand LeMaster progenies. When Abraham stepped off the ship, he went directly to work for Jon Smith. Elizabeth remained with her father, who became the bishop of the Anglican Church in St. Mary's City.

As a bonded servant, Abraham couldn't marry until the expiration of his term of servitude. Elizabeth, on the other hand, was free to marry, and she did, to Lieutenant Jones from the ship. However, being married to a sailor at that time was like not being married at all, and she remained living with her mother and father, the Rev. and Mrs. Douglas Cooksey, in the parish rectory. Her husband was constantly at sea and the couple never had any children; then one day when the ship arrived, she discovered that he wasn't on board. He had been in a fight at Polly's Tavern in Barbados and had received a fatal stab in the heart – he died on the spot.

Several months later, Elizabeth had been riding alone in her carriage, something she rarely did, from an afternoon visit at the home of Mrs. Bowling, whose husband was Captain James Bowling, now a large plantation owner in St. Mary's County.

She was returning to the rectory along the edge of Zekiah Swamp when the large wheels of her carriage became stuck in the mud in a low spot on the road. Her horse set its rear down in the mud and refused to go any farther. She attempted to rouse the horse from its seat with her buggy whip, cracking it frantically over its head without any success. She then climbed down into the mud, sinking in the slimy slurp up to her ankles, and began yelling loudly at the stubborn animal, which was behaving quite mulishly, to get up.

Her voice carried so loudly through the thicket that she attracted the attention of Abraham, who was about to wind up his chores for the day on the Jon Smith Plantation. He walked through the thicket, following the commotion, carefully avoiding the sticky thorns from the blackberry bushes, and stuck his head out into the roadway clearing quickly recognizing Elizabeth, whom he hadn't seen since they had been friends on the ship.

She was exasperated by the situation, and not knowing that she was being watched, she went to the front of the horse and grabbed hold of the leather bridal strap on both sides of its head and began to tug, but the horse remained uncooperative.

Abraham was amused and watched to see what she might do next. As she tugged, she began to place more of her body into each pull until her hands slipped from the bridal and she fell butt first into the mud, her hands sinking into the murk as she attempted to break her fall.

Out from the brush Abraham emerged, and slowly he approached the mud-covered woman with whom he had once had a friendship, nearly romantic, abruptly terminated. He reached out for her hand, expecting her to take hold of him as he pulled her from the sticky muck.

She looked up, her eyes met his, and she immediately recognized him. She took his hand. He seemed more filled-out from when she had last seen him. His white skin was now tanned. His arm seemed strong and was covered with bright yellow curly hairs as he pulled her upward. Her long hair flowed down her back and the mud made a sucking sound as she was lifted up. She seemed somewhat older.

"Do you remember me?" The words seemed to come from him without his speaking.

"Yes, I've thought of you often. How have you been?" He seemed even more handsome.

He escorted her out of the mud to a dry spot a few feet away. "Wait here until I can get your horse up on all fours. Can you tell me, what's his name?"

She had to stop and think. "I don't think he has a name; no one ever told me. He belongs to my father, and he never gave it a name."

Abraham returned to the horse and appeared to be speaking to it; at least he had his mouth close to one of its ears. Just then, suddenly, the horse snorted, rolled its rear legs to the side and then back under and up it rose.

Elizabeth smiled and called out to Abraham. "What did you tell him?"

He looked back at her and smiled. "I told him that he had to take you home or else."

"Or else, what?" Elizabeth asked.

Abraham climbed up onto the carriage seat and set the brake. "Or else I was going to remove his testicles, I told him," he shouted back as he climbed back down.

"I don't believe you, Abraham LeMaître! You just made that up." She tried to wipe some of the mud from her shoes with a small branch she picked up from the ground as she spoke. "What are you doing out here, anyway? You seemed to come out of nowhere."

"This is where I work and live." He walked toward her, off to the side, leaving the horse standing still in the middle of the road. "I work for Jon Smith; this road passes through his plantation, and I would guess that you just came from the Bowling Plantation?"

"You're just full of surprises. Would you please help me up onto the carriage?" She offered her elbow so he took it, and they started toward the horse and carriage.

"My cabin is on the other side of this thicket; there is a small lane leading in to it up ahead. Why don't you let me take you there and allow you to clean up before heading on home? I would be willing to drive you if you like."

She certainly was covered with mud, and she thought that it would be nice to clean up, but she was reluctant to go with him alone. That sort of thing just wasn't done; she told him that it would not be proper and he reminded her of how they had played together on the ship, and she reminded him of his behavior on the island. He then told her that he didn't want her to run off, that he had thought of her often, and now that he had found her, she could not just leave.

Elizabeth felt much the same and agreed to stop at his cabin, only long enough to clean up. It would be dark in a few hours, and she would have to be on her way. One month later, they were married.

Naiche: *The Indian Boy*

A t the edge of the field in the underbrush, Abraham could see an Indian boy half-hidden behind a tree watching him intently. Abraham continued working and pretended not to see the young boy, just as he had done several times before. It seemed as though the two were equally curious about each other. The first time the boy appeared he didn't try to hide but stood beside the tall sycamore in full view. Abraham thought that he must be around ten or eleven years old. He could see well enough to note that the boy wore a breechcloth, leggings and moccasins all made of animal skins; his hair was in long braids, with a porcupine roach and feather. He carried a bow, wore a quiver of arrows on his back and a long knife on his belt. After a few minutes, the boy disappeared.

That evening Abraham told Elizabeth about the young boy, describing his several appearances over the past month. He explained that at first he didn't know what to make of him – whether to be concerned or whether it was just curiosity. After all, there had been no reports of trouble with any of the local Indians. Still, Abraham carried his musket with him each day that he went to the clearing. He wasn't sure exactly why, but he had been cautioned repeatedly by his father-in-law to always be prepared for any eventuality, either human or otherwise. Having it nearby was also handy when a rabbit, squirrel or turkey happened to pass within range.

Elizabeth suggested that he make friends with the boy. There were many wild apple trees growing nearby and she had a few preserves remaining from the last season. Perhaps she could bake a pie, and Abraham could offer it to him. They could invite him in for dinner. Abraham might even inquire if the boy were interested in helping him clear the farm.

But then, Abraham considered, the boy may be friendly enough, but what about his family? He feared that he might be getting more involved than he ought to be. "I think we should just continue doing what I have been, simply allowing him to be and not make any big deal out of it."

Elizabeth argued in favor of making friends with the boy, and it was her wisdom that frequently prevailed. Just as they had discussed, she baked an apple pie, and Abraham set it out on a stump at the edge of the clearing exactly where the boy appeared each day. To their surprise, a raccoon managed to beat the boy to the stump and knocked the pie to the ground, gulping most of it down before Abraham became aware and scared it away. He rushed over and picked up the tin pie pan, dumped what little remained onto the ground and walked back to the cabin.

Elizabeth could only laugh and gave her husband a hug and a kiss on the lips. She then prepared a second pie, but this time she kept it in the house until the young Indian arrived, with the idea that either she or Abraham would take it out and present it in person. Except that he didn't come any more, at least for close to a month there was no sign of him.

Then, one evening following dinner, they were both sitting on the floor by the fire when there was a knock at the door. Abraham rose from his position and walked to the door, opening it slowly. He was surprised to see the young Indian boy standing there with who he thought might be his father and mother.

Nervously, Abraham welcomed the guests, inviting them to come in and offering them each one of the four chairs situated around the table.

However, the three remained standing, looking curiously

about the room, left then right, up then down. Kashiaka, the woman, who appeared to be a few years older than Elizabeth, maybe twenty-five, was particularly interested in the bed, which was secured in a small loft with a ladder leading up to it. She had a small oval face, with dark eyes and coal black hair hanging down her back in a single braid.

Maintaining a blank look, each of their six eyes scanned the room, slowly studying the walls, the green planks on the floor, the fireplace, the table, also made of green planks, and the few possessions placed throughout. Then, Woosah, who was as tall as Abraham, muscular, well proportioned and about thirty, began staring at the musket leaning in the corner of the stone fireplace.

Elizabeth broke the silence, "I just made fresh tea, it's chamomile. Would you like to try some?"

There was no response and she pulled the teapot away from the hearth and placed the four cups that were on the mantle onto the table. She began to pour, offering first a cup to each of her three guests and then one to her husband. As she handed each a cup she repeated, "Tea...tea; this is tea. Be careful...hot!"

Kashiaka realized there were only four cups and five people in the room. She looked at Elizabeth questioningly.

Elizabeth read her mind, smiled and responded, "Abraham and I will share one," and she hastily retrieved the cup from her husband, taking a small sip.

After each had taken a quick taste, Kashiaka and Woosah looked at each other and nodded with expressions of delight. They continued to blow across the top of their cups until the steam was gone, placing their cups on the table when they had finished.

Kashiaka looked at Elizabeth and spoke, "Tea." She was pleased she could utter the sound that she had distinctly heard, allowing her face to reflect her sincere appreciation for the kindness that she, her husband and son were enjoying.

Kashiaka and Woosah had known for some time that Elizabeth was pregnant, about to deliver, and they brought a gift for her – a cradleboard. Piscataway mothers, like many Algonquin mothers and Native Americans, carried their babies in cradleboards on their backs. It was made with a soft leather pouch mounted on a wooden board, colorfully decorated in reds, greens and ocher, and stitched with various size beads with leather shoulder straps. Woosah had been holding it the entire time he was drinking his tea.

When all the cups had been returned to the table, Kashiaka reached over to Elizabeth and placed her hands on her abdomen, signifying that she was aware Elizabeth was pregnant. Woosah handed the gift to Naiche, the boy, who then offered it to Elizabeth.

"For me?" she exclaimed, holding it up in the light of the fireplace, examining it closely. "It's adorable; did you make it? Obviously you did. Abraham, would you look at this, it's beautiful."

Then, feeling the need to reciprocate, Elizabeth searched about the room, looking for something that she could give Kashiaka, but nothing seemed to be good enough for what she had just received. Then she remembered the apple pies that she had baked a month earlier, the one eaten by the raccoon and the second one that they ended up eating themselves. She rushed to the cupboard and from behind the flour, sugar and jars of molasses, she pulled out two jars of apple preserves and returned to Kashiaka. "Here," she said, handing the jars to her new friend. "This could never compare to what you have given to us. Thank you so much."

Kashiaka, Woosah and Naiche all headed to the door while Abraham and Elizabeth followed close behind. The two groups waved to each other, and in a matter of moments, the Indians were gone.

The following day Naiche stood at the edge of the clearing as before. Abraham saw him and motioned for him to come closer. Abraham continued setting the young tobacco plants in the furloughs that he had prepared days earlier, and Naiche watched much as any boy might watch his own father at work, but squirmy and fidgety and unstill, and then he left as quickly as he arrived.

Each day Naiche would appear at the margin, and Abraham would motion him closer. Naiche would watch him plaster mud in the gaps between the timbers of the cabin walls, or cut firewood from the surplus of logs lying about, or pull weeds from the vegetable garden, or carry water from the nearby creek – a tributary of the Potomac.

Abraham would always greet him with a 'hello' or 'good morning' or 'bonjour', and Naiche would respond simply by smiling, move around restlessly and then leave without the simplest utterance.

One day Naiche appeared with a friend, Kusox, who appeared younger, shorter and less fidgety. Abraham just happened to have some rock sugar candy and broke off a piece for each of the boys. When Kusox returned to where the two boys lived, he told several of his friends and so they too wanted to go with Naiche to visit Abraham.

Then one day Abraham decided to teach Naiche to speak English. What made teaching difficult was that Abraham knew very little English himself, and he spoke with a French accent and was unable to form certain sounds, so Naiche learned to speak English with a French accent.

Richard Leimaster

All told, Abraham and Elizabeth had six children. Sarah and Mary, the two older sisters, came ahead of Richard, followed by one other younger sister and two younger brothers.

Richard grew up helping his father build their present manor house, which was built ten years after their first home, which Abraham built by himself, the drying barns, barns for the livestock and twenty-two cabins which housed their many slaves, as well as much of the indoor carpentry and furniture. He preferred carpentry to farming so Abraham employed their first-born son exclusively as a woodwright.

By the time Richard had reached his seventeenth year he had earned a reputation as the finest cabinetmaker in both St. Mary's and Charles Counties. For his service to the family business, Abraham gave him fifty acres of farmland adjacent to Betty's Delight, along the edge of Zekiah's Swamp, which Richard named LeMaster's Delight. He soon turned his marshy parcel into a productive tobacco plantation with its own manor house, drying barns and slave cabins. He would never take a direct interest in the actual production of tobacco – that was left to his wife, Martha, who quickly took charge.

Abraham and Richard, each with their separate manors, continued to share services with each other. Richard, the carpentry, and Elizabeth his mother, who had a head start developing a self-sufficient working plantation, provided their clothing with three household slaves whose exclusive responsibility was that of the millinery. They also produced butter and cheese. Eventually, Martha's garden and orchard developed and became the major source of most of the fruits and vegetables for both plantations. Abraham continued to provide the corn.

The Visitor

By the time Richard had arrived at his eighteenth birthday, all his brothers and sisters had been born. John, the youngest, was only a month old, and Ann was thirteen months; both were in the nursery. The rest of the family, including his mother Elizabeth, his brother Isaac, who was now five years old, and his two older sisters, Sarah and her husband, John Tennyson, Mary and her husband, Robert Barron, had gathered at the dinner table and Abraham, his father, was saying grace when there was a knock at the door. No one heard the knock except for Tessie, one of the kitchen slaves, who had been serving the meal. When she went to the door, there was a young light-skinned mulatto standing there with a small duffle bag resting on the porch floor next to his feet. He stood about five feet eight-inches, peering down at her with a slender build, holding a straw hat in his left hand, and his hair was closely cropped.

She wasn't accustomed to any person of color, even as light as this one, free or slave, ever appearing at the front door. She wondered who he might be standing there as confident as if he were part of the family, and before he had a chance to say anything, she spoke first, "I'm 'fraid you have to go around to the back; Masr don't allow a colored to come to the front door."

She started to close the heavy oak door when he reached out, placed his hand against it, stopping it, and said, "Tell your master that his son, Abram, has come from Barbados to see him."

Her eyes were bulging wide, the size of turkey eggs, so was her mouth as she looked up at him, staring briefly, not knowing whether to believe him or not. After gathering her wits, she instructed him to remain standing there, and said that she would call Master Leimaster.

She closed the door and started slowly for the dining room where Abraham had finished saying grace and was now ready to begin carving a large fowl, the main entrée of this afternoon birthday dinner.

The light shining in through the front door glass glistened against the polished hallway floor. Her mind raced; there was no easy way to announce the visitor. She was thinking whether to whisper it to him, call him away and tell him in private, or blurt it out in the usual manor. She wasn't used to making decisions like this.

As she walked though the hallway to the dining room, the floor planks creaked and her legs felt heavy, so heavy that she could barely lift each foot, as if she were walking in mud, and she could feel wet drops of perspiration on her brow. She paused in the doorway and could hear the cacophony of voices of all the family members gaily speaking to each other at the table. Slowly she approached Abraham and then, as if the words in her heart had a mind of their own, they jumped out.

"Masr, there is a gentleman at the front door, he say he know you and would like a word with you." She thought to herself that the words were good. Those seated at the table that heard paused and looked at her wondering whom the visitor might be, while the rest continued their conversations.

"Tessie, he'll have to wait until we finish our dinner, would you please show him to the parlor? By the way, Tessie, did he tell you his name?"

"No, Masr, I jus ask him his name but he not say," she lied; she hoped he would forgive her. Now she wore a serious look on her face and was unable to hide her nervousness. She stood wringing her hands, playing with her fingers and Abraham suspected that something was bothering her.

"Come now child, out with it. What's bothering you? I've never seen you quite like this."

She looked down, no longer able to regard his face. "Masr, he say he be your son!"

Abraham set the carving knife on the board, wiped his hands on the white cotton napkin lying next to the fowl and looked up at Tessie while replacing the napkin back on the table. "Thank you, Tessie. You may show him to the parlor and tell him that I will be in to talk with him when we finish celebrating Richard's birthday. That should probably be in another hour." Abraham pulled his engraved pocket watch from his vest pocket and checked the time. "Yes, Tessie, tell him that I will be there at about 3:30. And, Tessie, why don't you offer him some tea or an infusion? That would be nice."

"Yes, Masr, I will do that, right away."

She turned and left the dining room as Abraham took back the carving knife and carried cutting where he had left off. Tessie mumbled to herself as she walked back down the hall toward the front door, "Oh Lawd, have mercy, Masr in big trouble! He got another son, and he be handsome, not too dark, not too light. Masr sure be full of surprises."

When Tessie opened the door, Abram stood with his back to the door perusing the green tobacco fields on both sides of the lane leading up to the house that spread in both directions to the distant wood lines. He had walked all the way that day from Port Tobacco and had seen the many miles of the green stuff. In a way, the fields looked somewhat like the sugar fields in Barbados.

"Masr say you can cum in now." Tessie opened the door wide and Abram turned back around and then followed her in through the doorway.

"Thank you Miss..., I don't believe I caught your name." They walked a few feet until they came to the room that Abraham had directed.

"Tessie, everybody call me that. Masr give it me. I think it was Teresa, at first, but don't no one call me that." She slid open the sliding double doors, one to the right and the other to the left, and Abram followed her. The parlor wasn't a very large room, but it was quite comfortable with furniture spread about mostly along the edges except for the large sofa under the front window, which had two large, padded chairs positioned across from it with a coffee table in between. Abram headed for the first chair and waited for Tessie to offer him to be seated.

"Can I bring you some tea? We'se got good razzberry tea. But if you don't want that, I can bring some water."

"I would prefer the tea. Thank you, Tessie."

She turned and departed, closing the doors behind her. Before Abram sat down he couldn't help but notice the painting of the young boy on the opposite wall from the front window, and he walked up to examine it more closely. The painting was quite old and the oils had dried and cracked. The inscription at the base of the frame read, *Henri IV, Le Roi de la paix, France et Navarre, Louise LeMaître, 1568.* The boy appeared to be a few years younger than Abram and showed him as bushy-haired and broad browed, with alert eyes and a prominent nose

Back in the dining room, Elizabeth set directly to Abraham's left and pretended to not have heard, keeping her eyes on the large fourteen-inch blade, which was now slicing thin white sheets from the bird's breast.

Abraham commented to her about how it was perfectly well done, yet tender and juicy, and then he looked down at the other end of the table where Richard was sitting and said, "Richard, since you are the guest of honor, why don't you pass me your plate?"

Elizabeth couldn't stop thinking about what she had just heard. She looked upon Abraham, seeing that he seemed so calm and unaffected by the presence of the young man waiting in the parlor.

Richard's plate was made of pewter and had his initials etched in the center. He forwarded it to his father and said, "If you don't mind, along with my regular portion, I would like the gizzard."

Elizabeth sat quietly, withdrawn from the conversation that was taking place among Sarah, who sat next to her, Mary and her husband Robert, who sat directly across the table.

"You are too easy to please, my son." Abraham picked up the gizzard with his fingers and placed it alongside the slices of turkey. Then one at a time, each passed their plate forward to Abraham, who then carved and served each their special request – drumstick, breast, thigh or wing – while the mashed potatoes, sweet potatoes, squash and gravy made their rounds about the table.

Before Tessie could serve the hot apple pie, Elizabeth had become overly anxious, and then unable to restrain herself any longer she looked at her husband and asked, "Who is the caller that is waiting in the parlor? Is this something that I should be concerned about?"

Abraham reached over and took her hand. "I don't think so. This is most likely either someone playing a joke or it's some mistake. I'll take care of this shortly; there's nothing for you to worry about."

Abraham did not make a practice of telling lies, not even to cover up something, accordingly, Elizabeth felt comforted by his reassurance. "If this is a joke," she remarked abruptly, "I don't think that it's funny."

Abraham agreed, "Neither do I."

Following the dessert, Tessie began serving tea, and Abraham excused himself and walked down the hallway toward the parlor wondering who this person was that was waiting to talk to him. For a moment, his mind flashed on the two days that he had spent in Barbados and he stopped, remembering Lavinia, the bronze Bajan girl. *No, it's not possible*, he thought to himself, quickly dismissing the notion that he could have left a son behind on that island. When he arrived at the parlor door, he stopped again and recomposed his countenance before entering.

As he walked into the salon, the young mulatto rose from the sofa, stepped forward and introduced himself. "Abram LeMaître," he said, extending his hand.

Abraham reached out and shook it. "And I am Abraham Leimaster."

As they stood face to face, Abraham could see that the boy stood about an inch taller and appeared neatly dressed, wearing a white shirt with a ruffled collar, however, his most conspicuous feature was his one blue and one gray eye, the family feature that could scarcely be denied. Abraham continued to stare directly at Abram, looking for any other distinguishing trait or familial feature. For a moment he thought that he could see a slight resemblance to his father – in the mouth – but he couldn't be sure of it.

"Please," Abraham offered, "would you take a seat there at the sofa, and I'll take this chair here across from you."

After they both sat down, Abraham crossed his legs and drew up his trousers from the knee, revealing a pair of black polished leather boots, ankle length. "Well, tell me who you are and why have you come?"

"Permit me to begin by first saying thank you for seeing me. I know that my visit has come as a complete surprise to you, without any warning, and I would not have found it surprising had you turned me away. My mother's name was Lavinia

Beckwith. I was born in a small plantation cabin near Holetown, Barbados and raised by my mother and her husband, Edward Beckwith, until the age of five when he was arrested by the Barbados police and surrendered to a bounty hunter by the name of Filbert Smith. I understand they were both on the ship with you when you arrived in Barbados?"

"Yes, I remember them both."

"My mother explained to me at that time that Edward Beckwith was not my real father, and that they had married a year after I was born, that she had become pregnant by a Frenchman who had passed through the island on his way to Lord Baltimore's colony in Maryland. She said that his name was Abraham LeMaître, but she could never pronounce Abraham, so I became Abram. From that time on, I always wondered who my real father was, and I hoped that I would some time be able to search him out and discover him. Perhaps I might learn something more about myself.

"Edward Beckwith, while on the island, was quite ambitious and was able to start a small print business. He purchased printing equipment from London and was able to eke out a living first by printing Bibles and religious tracts, and later he started a local newspaper. He spent much of his spare time reproducing and selling other common publications, literature, prose and poetry. When he was arrested, the print shop was taken over by his property owner, who continued to print the weekly journal. I was able to acquire large numbers of my stepfather's books and publications, and for the next years, continuing until the present, I became an avid reader. My mother never remarried, and together the two of us worked on the plantation until last year when she died of an infection. Through my stepfather's books, the world has become a larger place than my small island, and with my mother's passing, I was no longer compelled to remain. The first piece of business in the reordering of my life was to search you out. I had no idea what would be the outcome, whether I would ever be able to locate you, if you were still alive, and would you talk to me, would you acknowledge me? I have not come to embarrass you, nor to ask you for money, nor for you to adopt me into your family. Forgive me if I seem overly bold; I have simply come as a boy seeking to find his father and to know something of him."

Abraham spoke, "Then if you find him and he acknowledges you, then what will you do?"

"As providence will have it," Abram quickly responded. "I plan to take this quest one pace at a time. If my father were to refuse me, then I would take notice and be on my way."

Abraham was reasonably moved by his son's presentment. He appeared to him educated and eloquent; he had demonstrated good judgment and foresight in the management of his affairs. Abraham continued, "Your coming here will not be easy for you or for me, or for the members of my family. This is not Barbados. This is Maryland, and even though you are not black, you are still of color and born out of wedlock. You may express that you did not come to embarrass me, but I can assure you that Elizabeth, my wife, whom I love dearly and would want to protect from such discomfiture, will suffer. And dammit to hell, I suppose, if I tell the truth, it is not you, but I who has brought this on. If I send you on your way, where will you go?"

"I will return to Barbados. Do not fret, all will be well."

"Then be gone. But I promise you this: if and when I have satisfied myself that you are whom you say you are, and I am confident that you are my son, I will confess all this to my dear Elizabeth. She already has wind of you. At that time, I will then notify you of my feelings in the matter, and we can discuss any further arrangements. In the meantime, do you have the financial means to return home?"

"Yes," Abram replied. "What I have is sufficient. It is late in the day; perhaps I might spend the night in your barn?"

"No," Abraham replied. "The time is not right. You must leave now, but take this. Here is enough for a good night's rest and meal at Port Tobacco. Now be gone." And with that Abraham showed his son to the door.

Only Sarah, Mary and their husbands remained seated at the dining room table, which Tessie had completely cleared. Elizabeth had gone to the nursery to look in on the infants, and Richard had left for the barn to check on a sick lamb. John and Robert, the two husbands, were having a separate conversation from that of their wives and were busy puffing on cigars such that the room was entirely smoke-filled when Abraham made his reappearance.

Abraham walked to the nearby credenza to get his favorite pipe and a pouch of tobacco and approached the two men. "If you prefer, we can move into the parlor. I wouldn't mind at all having a small bit of Madera." Both men nodded. "Sarah, would you let Tessie know that we would like three Maderas in the next room?"

Nothing more was said by anyone about the strange visitor, at least in the presence of either Abraham or Elizabeth, and neither Abraham nor Elizabeth talked about it to each other.

The next day Abraham rode to St. Mary's City and visited with Charles Freedman, his personal lawyer, and then with Filbert Smith, the slave broker/bounty hunter that was responsible for locating and retrieving Edward Beckwith. Beckwith had spent some time in jail, and following his release, he began working for the city's major newspaper, the *St. Mary's City Tribune*, where Abraham was able to meet with him and confirm many of the details of Abram's narrative.

The *Tribune* was housed in a two-story building with a narrow front that extended the entire length of the block from the main street. The printing presses were located on the upper level with the news, editorial and want-ad departments on the ground floor, and the newspaper's archives being stored in the small half-basement. The only light in the room came from the ceiling length windows that ran the length of each side of the building, where the morning sun came in on the left side and the afternoon sun on the other. The windows on the right would continue to be a light source only as long as the empty lot on that side of the building remained unimproved. A few feet in from the front door, there was a waist-high, polished red mahogany fence that kept the public separate from the office personnel and work areas.

A young man, about twenty-five, sat at a desk on the public's side of the fence, busy shuffling papers when Abraham entered the front door. He wore a visor that he had pulled down over his eyes, protecting them from the glare of the morning sun pouring in on him from the left, and he didn't look up as Abraham approached his desk in spite of the dull sound his boots made on the oak plank floor. The young man had earlier removed his suit jacket and hung it on a hook near where the fence was secured to the wall, revealing an elastic band on each of his upper arms, no doubt to shorten the shirt sleeve lengths. Because he had to both shuffle papers and meet with the public, he wore cuff protectors while he shuffled papers to keep the printers' ink from getting on his shirt, removing them only when he met with the public, which he was now about to do as a result of the gentleman standing before him. Furthermore, the fumes being emitted from the printers' ink seemed to create a frog in Abraham's throat, causing him, a man of the outdoors, to wonder how anyone could remain trapped inside under these conditions.

Abraham cleared his throat several more times, and when that failed to get the attention of the young man he said, "Good morning," and then waited for the young man to stop what he was doing.

When at last he looked up, he replied, "Yes, may I help you?" simultaneously removing his cuff protectors.

"Yes, you may. My name is Abraham Leimaster, and I would like to speak, if I might, with one of your employees, a Mr. Edward Beckwith."

"Is this about placing a want-ad? If so, I can help you with that."

"No, I'm afraid that this is a personal matter."

"Then you will have to wait until he breaks for lunch. He is now running the press upstairs and can't be disturbed." The young man reached for his pocket watch and continued, "That would be at noon, in another hour and a half."

"Just so I won't miss him, would you please let him know that Abraham Leimaster was here and would like to buy him lunch? Please tell him that he can find me at the restaurant across the street, what is it named?"

"Marie's."

"Yes, that's it, Marie's. Thank you, I'll be waiting for him."

At exactly the time indicated by the young man at the front desk, Edward Beckwith walked in the front door of Marie's and scanned the place looking for Abraham. He also wore a white shirt with cuff protectors, but without armbands, and a brown leather apron that looked as if it had had several years of useful life.

Abraham was sitting at a corner table off to the right, and he rose to great Edward, who quickly spotted him and turned toward him. They shook hands and both complemented each other on how youthful they had both remained even though Beckwith was now bald and donned a medium-sized potbelly that pushed his leather apron forward. When he smiled, it was also clear that he had neglected the care of his teeth.

They both took their seats and discussed pleasantries about what they were doing now, Abraham about his plantation and family, and Beckwith his work as a printer in Holetown, his subsequent time in jail and now his work at the newspaper. Abraham then recounted the recent visit by the young mulatto boy that had claimed to be his son, and that he was now looking to either confirm or refute the boy's story.

"It's all true, the story is anyhow. I can't vouch for the boy that showed at your door without seeing him though. You will need to bring him by and let me take a look at him, just to be sure."

Abraham appeared frustrated, "He's no longer here; I sent him away. I had no way of knowing."

"Hmm, that's too bad. I'm sorry that I can't be of more help. I can tell you this much, though. If it's him, he's a fine boy, serious, conscientious and hardworking. I would have been proud if he had been my own. And once he realized that I wasn't his real daddy, he always wanted to find you. He knew that one day he would find you, and he wanted to be ready for that day, so that you might accept him."

Abraham paused, wondering whether to ask or not, and then he questioned Edward about Lavinia. "I've thought of her often; did she ever talk about me."

"No, not to me, and not often, only to Abram. I think that was out of respect to me, yet she wanted Abram to know about his father. She was a beautiful woman, both on the inside and the outside."

"Once you had served your time, why did you remain here? You had a business, a beautiful wife, and a stepson that you yourself described as one that you would have been proud to call your own. What was stopping you from returning to Barbados?"

"The business was gone; I had lost it. And, in order for Lavinia to survive while I was in jail, she was forced to turn to prostitution. Once I was released, I had hoped to get enough money together to start a printing business in Port Tobacco and then bring the two of them here, where we could be together and start over, but then she wrote and told me that she was slowly dying of syphilis."

Abraham quickly injected, "But Abram said that the two of them worked on the plantation and that she died of an infection."

"He lied. Of course, you can understand."

Abraham paid the check and Edward returned to the presses at the *Tribune*. He walked out the door of Marie's about to return to Betty's Delight and spotted two horsemen riding into town leading a slave, on foot, with a rope around his neck. The three were approaching at a very slow pace. Abraham climbed into his carriage and started out on the road toward Zekiah Swamp when he realized that the man being led was Abram. He pulled alongside, came to a stop and saw that one of the riders wore a deputy sheriff's badge. Realizing that it might not be wise to identify the boy as his son, Abraham asked what they were doing with his property.

The deputy said that he had arrested him on the road to Port Tobacco as a runaway; that he had no documentation or pass. Abraham explained that the boy belonged to him, that he had been out looking for him, and the deputy, seeing that he was a genteel man of means, after discussing the matter with the other rider, released Abram to him, but only after collecting his fee of twenty-five pounds, which Abraham promptly paid on the spot.

Abram climbed into the carriage and took a seat next to Abraham. The rest of the afternoon was spent returning to the plantation, arriving quite late that night.

Abraham drove the carriage into the stable, where he was met by Hercules, the young black groom who had been asleep on a small cot that he maintained in the corner by the back door. Hercules was one of forty-five slaves on the plantation, and he usually waited in the stable whenever Abraham was out just to be ready to receive his horse on return. As Abraham pulled the carriage to a halt in the center of the stable, Hercules took hold of the horse by its bridal, holding it steady as Abraham and Abram climbed down.

"Hercules, I want you to meet my son, Abram." He spoke in a serious tone. "He's come to live with us, so I want you to show him the same respect that you would any other member of my family."

"Yessur masr, I will; you can be sure," he said, and he then went about disconnecting the horse and carriage. He was putting it into its stall for the night as Abraham and Abram walked to the house.

When Hercules had finished he closed the stable doors and dashed off to his cabin among the row of cabins where all the colored people lived on the plantation. He was a very fast runner and he arrived there in a short amount of time, passing by each small hut one at a time. Each cabin reflected a dim light through a single, opened, candle-lit window together with the sound of either a baby crying, a dog barking, or perhaps sounds of laughter, or arguing, or children playing.

Upon arrival at the wooden steps of his own small house, he pushed open the door into the tiny room, illuminated only by the fire in the fireplace, and stood in the middle of the room, pausing for a moment to catch his breath. His father was on the floor sharpening his axe with a whetstone; his mother was sitting in a rocking chair nursing his youngest brother, and his other brother and sister were both sitting up in their bed in the loft stretching their necks to see what was going on.

After taking a final deep breath, Hercules excitedly blurted it out. "Masr jus arrived home, and he brought with him a colored boy, and he say he be his son, Abram, most like the masr's." Still wheezing slightly he continued, "I not want to stare, but he seem half-and-half, not so dark. They both go to the house together. I wonder if Missus Elizabeth know about this?"

Unofficially, Tessie was the primary source of news and gossip. She had known about Abram the previous day, but for some strange reason she hadn't relayed this scandalous tittle-tattle about the young man who had appeared earlier at Richard's birthday party to anyone. Occasionally Hercules, too, would pick up interesting trivia and pass it on, and this evening, had Hercules been a reporter for the *St. Mary's Tribune*, what he had to tell would have made bold headlines.

Announcements of any type usually took place in some undefined area in front of their cabins, most of the time in a central location, frequently in front of Tessie's cabin. Within minutes of Hercules' arrival at home, the word was out and almost everyone rushed outside and formed into two groups, one surrounding Tessie, and the other around Hercules. If Master was the father, then they wanted to know who was the mother; was she one of them? No, it couldn't be, they reasoned, since each pregnancy as far back as anyone there was concerned was accounted for. After all, he was born before any of them had arrived at Betty's Delight. She must have been from another plantation. Tessie explained that Abram had come by ship from Barbados, which was the port that several of them had passed through years earlier. She said that he was handsome and that he talked like and had the manners of a white boy.

Tessie was born on the plantation fourteen years earlier and she lived with her mother, Eliza, and her father, Harlan, and two younger sisters, Clara and Berta. Because she had frequent breathing difficulties, Elizabeth brought her into the house rather than sending her out to the dusty fields that provoked her condition. This had turned out to be a wise choice as Tessie was a hard worker, a fast learner and required minimal supervision, and the Leimaster household all agreed that she could be trusted more than any of the other domestics. Elizabeth had been spending about an hour, three days a week helping Tessie learn to read and write with the proviso that once she became an adult, she would teach others. Tessie had a high forehead and wore her hair in multiple braids. She was at the age where she was experiencing erratic growth spurts, her spindly legs seemingly growing faster than the rest of her body, causing her to appear perhaps a little awkward. Her small breasts were beginning to push outwardly – a source of further embarrassment. Still, she always appeared neat and clean, as if she had just been scrubbed.

A particular circumstance in her adolescent years was a bit disconcerting to her. When she was about ten, Eliza, her mother, began walking off from the cabin into the woods late at night, repeatedly not returning until nearly dawn. Upon her return, Harlan would query her as to where she had been, and she would always respond that she didn't know. Her hair and clothes would often be covered with leaves and foxtails, which she would be unable to explain.

Harlan followed her one night along the path to the swamp and was surprised to see her completely undress and begin dancing naked in a small open meadow in the moonlight. She would swirl about wildly waving her arms, often chanting what seemed like an African mantra, a sound that she expressed repeatedly. Incapable of understanding her strange behavior, Harlan attempted to restrain her during the hours of darkness, tying her arms and legs to the bed. This only resulted in her thrashing and trouncing about, screaming loudly so much that everyone in the proximate cabins could hear, some wondering if Harlan were beating her.

Their three daughters were terrified upon hearing their mother's earsplitting screams. Before long, almost everyone, the coloreds living in the cabins as well as the Leimasters living in the plantation house, knew that Eliza was exhibiting very strange behavior. Harlan was certain that he had to bring to an end this nightly captivity since it was causing more troubles than it prevented, still, each night he would follow her to the woods and watch her carry out her ritual. However, he gradually became so tired of doing this and not getting enough sleep that he could scarcely stay awake while working in the fields, and Gabriel, the overseer, soon began to notice that his work performance was deteriorating.

Harlan concluded that there was nothing he could do to stop her. During the daylight hours, she went to the fields with all the others and performed to the overseer's satisfaction, and at home, she was good to Harlan and their three daughters, fixing the meals and repairing their clothes. She always responded to Harlan's sexual advances, she herself frequently initiating foreplay with him. Her enthusiasm in lovemaking was as fervent as her passion in the moonlight, so much so that Tessie often lay awake listening to the two of them, their sighs and moans eventually reaching a reverberating crescendo. Nevertheless, as soon as they had both finished their business, she was out the door and off to her spot in the moonlight. The cabin would become silent with only the sounds of the crickets and frogs in the nearby swamp filling the vacuum.

Tessie enjoyed her work at the plantation house, preferring to be there than at her cabin. She especially enjoyed the time that Elizabeth spent with her teaching her to read and helping her with other subjects that she was missing by not attending school. Before long, she became aware of how differently Elizabeth and the rest of the Leimaster family sounded when they spoke. When she would read aloud from one of Elizabeth's books, she would catch herself trying to pronounce certain words the same way as Elizabeth, certain words such as 'master' instead of 'masr'. When Abram arrived, she was quick to notice that he spoke white English freely without effort, and she wished that she could converse the same way.

Elizabeth enjoyed sharing her time with Tessie, receiving satisfaction that her efforts were genuinely appreciated while watching Tessie mature into a bright young woman. Elizabeth had taught each of her children to read and write, but they did not share the same enthusiasm for learning that Tessie had. She had hopes that Tessie would be a seed that would multiply and produce more Tessies, and the world would be better for it. Her husband and children were proud of her and supported her, just as they supported her many other activities that included the Ladies' Aid Society, Outreach to Native Americans, and The Christian Women's Temperance Union. Besides Tessie, she had several other students to whom she gave clavichord lessons on Saturday afternoons, and she held teas at their home on Sundays following church services which had become for several years a very popular social event frequented by some of the colony's most notable citizens such as the Bowlings, the Boarmans and the Edelens. None was more proud than her father, Rev. Cooksey, now retired from his position in the First Anglican Church. His daughter's popularity and his son-in-law's success as a plantation owner had provided him with a venue that enabled him to continue his sense of self-importance. He was now willing to overlook the Frenchman's previous indiscretions and push aside his own misjudgment.

The startling arrival of this Filius Nullius produced a sudden quandary, and from the onset no one in the Leimaster family was eager to discuss it, at least openly that is.

From that first moment when Elizabeth had overheard Tessie telling Abraham that there was a young boy at the front door claiming to be his son, she began sinking into pensive sadness, a melancholy, and when she had asked Abraham if what she had heard were true, he quietly reassured her that she need not be concerned about it. When she realized that the boy was

156

gone, she felt measurably relieved, yet there remained within her center a sentiment of uncertainty, as if a cancer had been removed yet there remained an unrelenting fear that it might return. She had hoped for an explanation. She had hoped that Abraham was waiting for a certain moment when they could be alone when he would speak openly to her about what had taken place. Nevertheless, neither that special moment nor an explanation had come soon enough for her.

The following morning he quickly left for St. Mary's City without saying where he was going or when he would be home. She bided her time all morning and noontime sitting near the front window watching and waiting for him to return. At about four o'clock that afternoon, she asked Tessie to bring her a small glass of port, and when she had finished it, she asked for a second. She felt warmed by it and walked out to the garden, insentient to her shoes sinking slightly into the freshly tilled glebe.

The daffodils and tulips were in full springtime bloom and she decided to cut a bouquet for the table and returned to the kitchen to fetch a knife and a basket. However, before returning to the outdoors, she stopped for one more glass, this time quietly pouring her own, hoping that Tessie wouldn't hear. As she sauntered toward the back door she felt lightheaded, less stressed, pleased that she had found the backyard plot as a refuge where she could relieve her mind of her husband's spurious issue.

When he returned with Abram, the two entered the back door of the house through the kitchen. It had been dark for some time and someone had placed a lantern on the counter that was emitting a warm orange light. The rest of the house seemed cold and silent; Tessie and the other household slaves had returned to their families for the night.

Father and son entered the dark hallway to the front room,

the same room where Abram had waited before, where Elizabeth had taken a seat after returning from the garden and had fallen asleep, sitting up on the divan by the front window. An almost empty bottle of tawny port rested on its side next to her feet having been kicked over earlier when she nodded off.

The hallway floor creaked under the weight of the two men, startling and awakening Elizabeth. Abraham opened the double parlor doors and made his way to the center of the room, which was illuminated only by a small band of moonlight shining in the window over the divan.

Motioning for Abram to wait by the parlor doors, Abraham then removed his gloves, placing them on a table close by, leaned his buggy whip against the wall and lit the oil lamp next to the divan. The white sulfuric smoke from his lighted stick-match permeated the air with the redolence of burning gunpowder. He drew near to Elizabeth, stopping in front of her and pausing for a moment.

She remained seated as he kneeled down on one knee, pushed the empty bottle aside, and reached for one of her limp hands, bringing it to his lips and kissing it several times before releasing it to her. Looking up at her, his face reflected a polyglot of feelings and emotions – sad, ashamed and contrite for having caused her such pain, unapologetic for having seeded this fruit of adultery, aware that any act of contrition would seem to dehumanize the young man that he was steadily coming to love. The warm, glowing light from the lamp failed to dissolve her icy expression.

"I would ask for your patience, your forbearance, dear Elizabeth. I had no idea that I had this son; and now he is here, I cannot, I will not turn my back on him."

Remaining seated, Elizabeth looked down at her husband and then turned toward Abram, who stood by the doorway. For the first time she caught a glimpse of his light brown skin. "I don't understand how this young man can be your son, unless have you been with one of our slaves. How long has this been going on?" she questioned, her voice getting louder.

"I swear I have always been faithful to you, my wife. Abram's mother was Lavinia, from Barbados, from before we were married."

Elizabeth rose from her seat and motioned to Abram. "Come here, young man, let me get a closer look at you. Abraham returned to standing as Abram stepped forward, appearing confident, keeping both eyes directed at her, holding his wide brimmed straw hat in his left hand. She noticed that he was dressed neatly in a clean white cotton blouse and knee length trousers. His hair was cropped close to his head; however, he had not shaved since the day of his arrival and it appeared to darken his unusually light Bajan skin.

"Abram, I would like for you to meet my wife, Elizabeth. Elizabeth, this is my son Abram."

She continued to look intently at him, not quite knowing what to make of the state of affairs, and then without thinking she put forward her hand to him. Faded images of Barbados fought for her attention – the beach, that trollop, her father, the minister. Abruptly becoming aware of her outstretched hand she made an effort to withdraw it, but not in time as Abram reached out mechanically, took it, and began to shake it slowly.

"I'm happy to make your acquaintance, Mrs. Leimaster," he said, slightly stuttering, his face radiating a warm smile, her tiny hand not quite disappearing in his solid grip.

Gazing straight at him she thought to herself musingly, *His smile, his visage, so much like that of Abraham when we first met, when we climbed the rigging together on the ship – Richard never received his father's look, how dare he give it away so cheaply!*

"Abram, you say. And what is your family name?"

"My birth certificate reads 'LeMaître'. I was never quite sure how to pronounce it."

"And your mother, what family name did she use?"

"Her father's name was Azcarta, and she took her husband's name, Beckwith, when they married."

"I see." Elizabeth did not want to continue and decided to excuse herself. "I'm sure you are very tired, and I must attend to my children in the nursery. If you will excuse me, Abraham will show you to your room. Good night." As she stepped away, her foot bumped the bottle, sending it spinning toward the center of the room.

Gabriel

G abriel was the plantation overseer. His wife had died years earlier of consumption, and he had never officially remarried. He shared one of the cabins with Elsa, who was several years younger and had also lost her spouse, but from a different form of consumption – corn liquor. After she buried him, she never took another drink.

Although Gabriel and Elsa did not give each other marriage vows before God, they had two sons together. Most everyone considered theirs to be a common law marriage, and there was never any shame pronounced upon them by anyone, white or black. Their cabin was on the right side of Harlan's, and the two of them were able to hear the commotion whenever Harlan would tie Eliza down to the bed to keep her from leaving. Gabriel was always concerned that Harlan might be killing her, and he took it on his own to look in Harlan's window from time to time when the screaming was happening just to make sure everything was all right.

Gabriel and Elsa were both vegetarians and both in top physical shape. His body was lean and his muscles were well defined, so much so that he appeared much younger in years. Elsa was never as fit as he; however, in the end, she outlived him by over twenty years.

He had been rewarded the position as overseer several years earlier for having saved Abraham's life. Gabriel was in his twenties at the time. He had always been a good worker and Abraham believed him to be trustworthy. When Abraham had special jobs or projects that needed to be done, and he couldn't get Richard to do them, he could usually rely on Gabriel. He had also earned the respect of the other slaves. When any special need would arrive among them, they would usually turn first to Gabriel either for a solution or for him to speak on someone's behalf to the Master.

Normally, the position of overseer on most small plantations belonged to a member of the family; however, Abraham's first two children were girls and Richard was so occupied with his carpentry work that Abraham had to either take on an indentured servant or promote one of his slaves. Since Gabriel had pulled him out from under a fallen tree one day while the two of them were clearing a tract of land he had recently acquired near the river, Abraham felt as though he owed him more than a pat on the back. Thereafter, every evening, Gabriel would go to the plantation house to get his instructions for the following day. If Abraham were not there, then usually Richard, whom Gabriel considered the second in command, would meet with him. Elizabeth would usually fill in when both Abraham and Richard were gone, but beyond that, Gabriel was on his own. With the arrival of Abram, that was to change.

"Gabriel...you know that I have always felt indebted to you...I owe you my life. I had hoped that making you the plantation overseer would...well; I guess you've heard...a son of mine that I did not know about has shown up at the house. His name is Abram." Abraham had invited Gabriel into the parlor to let him know that he was no longer the overseer, that Abram was replacing him.

Gabriel remained standing, holding his hat in his hand, taking in all that his master was explaining to him. "Yessir, Masr Leimaster, I understand. You've got to do what you've got to do. After all, he's your son. But what will I be doing now?"

"Well that's what I want to explain to you. You know that

162

small parcel, a couple acres more or less, on the other side of the swale? I want you to have it, you and Elsa. The two of you are both strong...you can do something with it...build a small house, plant a garden, maybe even plant some tobacco. It's all up to you – I'm giving you your freedom."

Captain Chaplin's Muster Call

That time in the early morning when the sky is filled with soft light, before the sun has a chance to climb above the horizon, when the cock crows and the tobacco leaves sparkle and drip with dew, mosquitoes, crickets and roly-poly bugs go into hiding beneath the rocks, ferns and grasses while the magpies and herons begin their search for early breakfast, he kissed Ann, his wife, and then tied his bedroll, powder horn and duffle bag containing a few personal items around the neck of his horse. He didn't have a saddle – the horse had been used mainly for tilling the soil, uprooting stumps or being hitched to their wagon. He and Ann had not been long in Frederick County – only two years – and it had taken most of that time to clear the land. It was now August, they had completed their small harvest, and the tobacco crop was hanging in the barn, drying, not that that made it any easier for him to answer Captain Chaplin's Muster Call. The settlement at nearby Conococheague was in dire need of relief having very recently been attacked by a large party of Indians near the mouth of Opeekon River, where seventeen persons were killed. The Garrison at Fort Frederick was too weak and sickly to send out so many as was deemed necessary for their security.

His gear secured, he placed his roundhat – with one side cocked up – on his head and took his wife of eight years again in his arms. While stroking her long strawberry hair that hung over her shoulders, he looked down through his wire-rimmed spectacles into her azure eyes as she returned his gaze, looking up into his mismatched pair, one gray, the other blue, seeing his prematurely wrinkled forehead, his dimpled cheeks peering out between his faint reddish facial hair. He spoke softly, repeating what he had previously told her. "I shouldn't be long...this muster is only for thirty days. If you need to reach me, try getting word to me over at Fort Baker."

"We'll be fine, Isaac. You know Red Hawk has promised he would watch over us, and I trust him," she spoke softly between kisses while maintaining her composure. "And we can always go to Flint's place." Then she began to weaken a little. "Oh, how much I will miss you! You will be careful, won't you?"

"Sure I will... I think you know me well enough." Smiling he said, "Perhaps, when I return, you will have some good news, and if not, we'll just try again." They wanted another child, especially if something were to happen to him. Thomas their oldest, was now five years and Benjamin, three. Leaning over a bit, he pulled her in tightly, placing his chin on her shoulder, the sides of their faces touching, and he squeezed her one last time before pulling away.

Isaac Leimaster stood five feet eight inches, a little taller than his wife, was medium build, athletic, and wore a brown wool coat, with pewter buttons, over his waistcoat, which hung to his mid-thigh, and brown wool drop-front breeches. He wore a white linen shirt with a gray neck stock, black leather shoes with large square-shaped pewter buckles and white knee-length stockings. He took hold of the homemade deerskin bridle that he had made two nights before and placed the bit, which he had hammered out of a piece of scrap metal, into the horse's mouth and then pulled the reins around its neck, allowing them to cross over its withers. With both hands, he grabbed some mane at the crest of its neck. Then in one smooth movement, he sprang off his left leg and pulling himself up, throwing his right leg over his mount. His horse, Molly, not having been ridden for some time, demonstrated an immediate objection by shaking her head, pawing at the ground with her front right foot and making a few snorts and whinnies while Isaac held his reins tightly, waiting for her to calm. He patted her on the neck and said, "There, there, Molly, it's all right."

Ann watched proudly from the porch. As the sun slipped above the horizon, she could see Isaac clearly until his mounted profile entered the tree line, and then she could only catch glimpses of him as he rode between the white oaks, the hemlocks and cedars, sometimes being illuminated by the few rays of sunlight that penetrated the forest canopy. Slowly he disappeared and she wanted to run to the edge of the timberline to see if she could get one last glance. However, she became distracted when she heard Benjamin from inside. He had awakened and she could hear his tiny feet running across the oak planks of the cabin floor. Standing at the threshold, he peered out at her in his knee-length cotton nightshirt, his forearm held over his forehead enough to shade the new morning sun, and then he ran down the porch steps and off to the side of the house where he lifted his jam jams and begun to pee.

When he had finished, he lowered his nightie and rushed toward his mother, who knew what was on his mind. She had been nursing since the birth of Thomas, and even though she knew it was time to begin weaning Ben, she was hesitant to do so. She enjoyed it – the closeness – the relief from the other toils of the moment, and he was gentle, not like Thomas, who bit and clawed leaving her sore and raw.

"Come here Ben," she spoke while taking a seat on the porch steps and loosening the strings on her bodice. "Climb up on my lap."

He was quick to find his familiar position, taking hold of her, taking in her warmth, drawing off her lacteal honey, clover and comfort. His eyes remained closed, occasionally opening them and gazing up at his mother for a quick moment then allowing them to return and flutter loosely. When he was younger, he would usually fall asleep, and she would break the suction with her thumb and place him in his crib, but now once he realized he was full – or bored – he released her and climbed down on his own.

As she was readjusting her top, she noticed that she was feeling hungry. Earlier that morning, she had fried eggs, potatoes and fatback for Isaac's breakfast, and after he had eaten, she made sandwiches with the leftovers to take with him. She had not taken anything for herself, and knowing that Thomas would soon be up, she decided to go to the barn and gather a few more eggs.

The barn was purposely built away from the house, and since it had rained the night before, the ground was quite muddy, so she walked carefully on the planks that Isaac had laid between the two structures. The boards were wobbly and she tried to be careful, but she slipped and tumbled, her feet flying our from under. As she fell, she cried out, her hands landed in the muddy ground, and the rest of her body plunged down onto her right leg. She started to get up, but she felt a large amount of pain. She was certain that the snap she heard had been her leg, and she feared that she had fractured it. Struggling unsuccessfully to pick herself up, she crawled towards a stump, hoping to be able to lift herself onto it, discovering that each time she moved a muscle, it brought torment to her injured limb.

She remained on the ground next to the stump. Even if she could get up, she knew she would not be able to walk on it. *Not even gone for an hour,* she thought to herself. *Now what am I going to do?*

"Benjamin! Where are you?" she shouted in the direction of the cabin and waited for a response. Hearing no reply she called again. "Benjamin, please baby, come here, I need you to help me. Thomas! Can you hear me?" Still, no answer came.

Slowly Benjamin walked out onto the porch carrying a small wooden doll. The doll was very simple – a head, body, two arms and two legs. The arms and legs hung loosely, each connected by a pin from the shoulders and hips that allowed them to swing back and forth. He paused at the step and glanced around looking for his mother.

"Benjamin! I'm over here."

Hearing her troubled voice, he turned in her direction and saw her sitting on the ground.

"Ben, I need you to wake Thomas and bring him to me. Could you do that?"

Hearing but not having understood, he stepped down to the ground and darted across the same shaky planks that his mother had taken on her way to the barn moments earlier. "Be careful, Ben! Those planks are wobbly; look what happened to me," she called out. "Please be careful!"

Ben may have toddled as any awkwardly three-year-old tot in a nightshirt; however, he did not need her cautioning. Slowly and calculatingly, his arms and fingers extended laterally and upward to ease his balance, he maneuvered himself off the planks, sinking into the soft muddy ground and felt the wet assortment of fallen forest mix and mud on his bare feet, the mire oozing between his toes. He was used to walking shoeless, and he took no offense to it. As he approached her he wanted to reach out and take hold of her.

However, fearing that he would cause further pain, she held out her hands to stop him and again asked if he would go get his brother. She explained that she had fallen and was hurt and that she needed his brother to help her. He responded by squirming in place, and when it appeared as if he either did not understand or was unwilling, he fidgeted some more, turned around and darted for the cabin, tightly clutching his wooden doll.

It seemed to Ann an eternity of time had passed before Thomas emerged at the door of the cabin, his nightshirt hanging to a level short of reaching his knees, squinting from the bright morning sun and being pulled along by young Ben. He stood a head and shoulder taller than Ben.

Trying not to express her anxiety she calmly called out, "Over here, Thomas, I've fallen."

Looking in her direction, he saw her leaning against the stump. He dropped his brother's hand and rushed down the steps in her direction. "Wh…what happened?"

Without any pause and before he reached the planks she answered, "I slipped on one of those wobbly boards; please be careful or you'll be down here with me!"

With the confidence of youth, he dashed across each board. "Don't worry. Mother, I'm used to them," and then he stepped off and stopped inches away from her.

"Does it hurt?" he questioned.

"Yes, it does, and I don't think that you're strong enough to lift me up. But let's try. I'll put one hand on this stump and put my other arm around your shoulders. You put your arm around my waist. Together, with me pushing on this stump I think that I can at least get seated on it. Do you think you can do that?"

Tom was a skinny boy, weighing less than fifty pounds, but he had the confidence of a boy twice his age. "Yes," he answered, "I can try." He moved next to her and crouched down so that she could place her arm over his shoulders. "I love you, Mommy; we can do it."

"I love you too, Thomas, and if I make a lot of noise, you won't be afraid, will you?"

"No, I'll be all right."

Ann reached up placing her hand on the stump behind her and then spoke to Tom. "I'm ready."

"I am too. One, two three, lift!" Ben remained watching off to the side.

Together they pushed and lifted and the sting of a hundred scorpions shot through her body beginning at the break in her lower leg. As she closed her eyes and winced, she cried out so loudly that no one could hear the squawks or swooshing of the fleeing birds.

Tom could taste the salty perspiration running from her armpit as his mouth became pressed against her. She could feel his spindly, yet muscular arm. Just at that moment when their struggling seemed hopeless, she found herself on the stump as if God himself had put his hands around her waist and lifted her. She remained still, leaning forward slightly with both hands next to her legs, both palms griping securely onto the stump, eyes remaining closed, silent, waiting for the throbbing to lose its edge. When she opened them she saw both boys standing in front of her, each with serious looks on their faces. She wondered how Thomas had ever lifted her. She couldn't remember becoming untangled from him.

"My heroes," she remarked, smiling at each. "Come here and let me give each of you a hug." As she lifted her palms from the stump, the slight movement stirred the pain again and a grimace appeared on her face. "Wait, I'll give you a hug later, all right?"

She wondered how she would get to the cabin, up the steps and to her bed. She needed a doctor or someone that could set her leg. Who would milk the goat, fix the meals?

Isaac followed along the Indian trail that would eventually take him to Baker's Fort. But first he wanted to stop at Flint's settlement, less than an hour away from his cabin. The path was narrow but wide enough for a very small wagon, well worn from years of use and was surrounded by low-growing ferns, scrub oak and madrone beneath a think canopy of tall sycamore trees. This trace followed Opeekon River, crossing back and forth several times as the stream meandered along, eventually dumping into the Potomac.

Isaac's land was adjacent to Flint's property, and both were bounded by the creek to the east. Flint had arrived in Maryland several years earlier as an indentured servant, and after he had completed his obligation was able to acquire other lands on the frontier at a very low price, speculating that it would eventually be worth a great deal more. He was correct. He had sold Isaac's seventy acres to him at about ten times what he had paid.

Isaac tied a bandana around his face to protect him from the ubiquitous mosquitoes that plagued him, lowering it below his chin whenever he came to a clearing. As his horse ambled along slowly, he kept his Brown Betty musket handy with the butt under his arm and the long barrel resting across his horse's neck, loaded and cocked, ready for any moment when he might need to defend himself. He also had a small pistol stuck in his trousers at the waist, together with a long hunting knife. He didn't think that he would need to use any of these weapons, at least for a while. Several tribes were becoming more and more warlike in the area, except for the Cherokees – they were much friendlier than the Mingos.[1]

---

[1] I cannot help but wonder why Isaac was able to leave his wife and two young boys home alone. Indian raiding parties were making the western frontier of Maryland a very dangerous place. The muster required all men between the ages of 16 to 60 to serve in the militia. The penalty for refusal to report for duty was ten pounds of tobacco. I wonder if Isaac left for Fort Baker out of patriotic duty, or because he didn't have the funds to forfeit. It seems, at least, that he could have sent his family to Flint's settlement or even to Fort Baker. After all, many settlers throughout the region were going to the nearest fortress for safety. Even so, how safe were the four of them, even when he was present? I doubt that he could have defended his family against a raiding party determined to set their cabin on fire and scalp them as they attempted to escape. His two single-shot Brown Betty and French Charleville muskets really did not constitute very much of a defense. I have a feeling that

Isaac arrived at a place where the path widened into an unpaved road full of potholes, with standing water where a large clearing opened on the left to Flint's settlement in the distance. He could see several buildings and smoke pouring from the chimneys on each side of the main plantation house. From the creek, he turned onto the long lane leading to the frontier mansion. The lane was surrounded by tobacco fields on both sides, where he could see several African slaves loading freshly cut tobacco bales onto a horse-drawn wagon.

The plantation overseer stood at the edge of the lane smoking a corncob pipe, wearing a tricorn, a wool coat over his waistcoat, his fowling piece propped against a willow tree as he watched Isaac slowly pass by. The two men nodded to each other, and Isaac raised his hand and motioned a perfunctory wave.

The three-story plantation house was a rectangular, eaves-front symmetrical building with a central entrance, 'five-over-four and a door' with roof dormers. The cladding was a combination of wood clapboard and brick covered with whitewash. There were several other buildings behind the main house, including the drying barns, the animal and feed barn, two henhouses and the slave quarters, which were a row of small cabins at the edge of the field that also had smoke pouring from their chimneys. There was a windmill twirling its blades in the light breeze, pumping water into a large wooden tank from which two cows stood nearby both licking a large block of salt. There was a large garden with several rows of corn and low-

---

they had become used to the difficulties and dangers of the frontier and possibly realized that there was not a whole lot more danger in his absence than what existed all along. They had chosen to live in the frontier because they believed that it offered them a great opportunity, just as it had provided for Isaac's grandfather a century earlier and they were willing to face the risks and challenges.

growing vegetables like beans and squash being attended by a slave, and near one of the barns was a corralled area containing several forms of livestock, including cows, sheep and a pig.

As Isaac and his horse approached the house, Belle Flint recognized him through the dining room window and rushed out to greet him. One of the servants followed her closely and quickly took his horse, tying it at one of the hitching posts.

"Good mornin', Isaac...not seen ya for some time now. Come down from that sorry beast of yours and let's get a look at ya."

Joseph Flint and his wife Belle were early settlers in the area. They came from Scotland and had acquired large tracts of land. They had quickly developed the flattest portions first, leaving the hillier and more difficult locations for last.

When Isaac came along several years later, he offered to purchase the south seventy acres that remained undeveloped, and Flint was quick to accept his offer. Although the parcel was not the best, Isaac acquired it at a fair price. Isaac and Ann remained somewhat isolated from the Flints; however, on a few occasions, when Isaac needed extra help, Joseph would provide a slave or two and occasionally the Leimasters would be invited for dinner, spending the night and returning home the next day.

Isaac returned the salutation. "Good morning, Belle, it's so good to see you. How have you and Joe been?"

Belle stood about an inch shorter than Isaac and was rather portly. She was usually dressed in work clothes, cotton shirt and wool pants, leather boots and a wide-brimmed hat. "Oh, I've been fine, always plenty to do, but Joe, he's been so miserable with the gout. Why don't you come on in to the house...had your breakfast, yet?"

"Yes, about an hour ago...eggs and fatback...Ann fixed it."

"Ah, yes, your pretty little wife...and how has she been? Any new younguns?

"No, just Ben and Tom, but we're working on it. We'd both like a big family."

The colored servant walked behind the two as all three entered the front door. Belle turned to him and gave a quick command. "Abraham, would you see that we have tea served in the parlor, and also would you let Mr. Flint know that he has company, that he needs to come to the parlor?"

"Yessum, Missus Flint, right away," he said and scampered off to the kitchen.

As the two entered the parlor, Belle removed her crushable wool-felt hat and tossed it onto the first chair by the door, shook her head and allowed her long red hair to fall behind her, nearly reaching the small of her back. Her face was beginning to sag a little, but Isaac could see that before she had put on all the weight, she had been a very attractive woman. "There, that feels better...have a seat, Isaac, over there. Abraham will be right along with the tea."

As soon as Isaac sat down, Joseph arrived. Tall and lean with gray hair and several day's stubble of facial hair, obviously several years older than Belle, he walked in, trying not to show his gout-induced limp, and headed straight for his southern neighbor, who had quickly stood again. Offering his hand, Isaac took it and Joseph spoke first. "Good morning, Isaac. So good of you to stop by. What brings you to our humble home?"

"Captain Chaplin's Muster Call. I'm on my way to Baker's Fort, and I thought I would stop by just to say hello." Isaac spoke while shaking Joseph's marathon handshake, pretending not to notice his stale breath.

"Oh, yes, that Indian problem...two of our boys, Joe and Henry, they are both preparing to leave also – Fort Frederick, I believe. They are excited about the bounty for scalps, four pounds apiece, six pounds for each one brought in alive I hear. Captain Chaplin, you said...isn't he that member of the Lower

House that's been trying to get funding for the frontier defense? This is all on account of the French; you know they're busy stirring up those savages. Well, Baker's Fort, that's not too far from here; I'm surprised you're not bringing your family with you, for safe keeping that is."

Abraham entered the room with a steaming pot of chamomile tea, and the air in the parlor was immediately infused with its aroma. He quietly sat the tray on the small table and poured a cup for each of them, and then waited to be excused. His only words were, "Sugar? Cream? Lemon? Yessum. Nossur. Right away, sir." Both Joseph and Belle remarked to Isaac about how pleased they were with Abraham, how he was so efficient and dependable.

Sundays were always a day of rest on the plantation and when the Flints went to church, Abraham would conduct services for the slaves out by their cabins. On inclement weather days, they would meet in one of the barns. He was the only literate colored on the plantation, and he would read from the Bible to them and then follow up with a sermon, usually preaching hellfire and damnation. There would always be lots of singing at their services, and they would become quite emotional and often get so carried away that Joseph would worry about the chickens not laying eggs or the cows not producing milk. But that never happened, so Joseph eased up and was thankful that they too were to be saved.

Belle looked in the direction of her punctilious possession, smiled and politely thanked him, "Thank you, Abraham, that will be all for now."

Isaac continued, "This muster is only for thirty days, otherwise I would be more concerned."

Flint was skeptical. "Washington should have been more concerned at Fort Necessity, and Braddock too…Ben Franklin warned him, but he thought he knew all the answers. Now the

French control Fort Duquesne at the three rivers."

Thomas returned from the cabin with the broom and small blanket that Ann had asked him to fetch for her. It had been nearly an hour since the two of them had struggled to get her onto the stump, and she decided that she was going to have to make it to the house irrespective of the discomfort. For padding, she wrapped the blanket around the end of the handle then planted the makeshift crutch on the ground between her injured leg and the stump. Then with one hand on the tree stub and the other holding tightly onto the crutch, she lifted herself up, shaking clumsily while keeping her weight off her injured leg. Once again, she felt shockwaves ripple through her body and then ease once she was able to establish her balance. Tom stood nearby, vicariously experiencing her distress as Ben played with his doll on the porch.

Getting up the steps and into the house took nearly an hour all told. Ann hadn't eaten since the previous evening and had consumed a lot of energy making her way from where she had fallen all the way to her bed. Ben was hungry and wanted to nurse, and she lay on her side and obliged.

She didn't think that Thomas would be able to catch a chicken, let alone wring its neck. Nevertheless, he could still gather eggs. Isaac had made sure there was plenty of game and dried fish in the house before he left, and the garden was replete with vegetables. The river was nearby, but Thomas would have to lug small buckets at a time. It would not be easy, but they would manage.

After asking Thomas to watch and not let the fire go out, exhausted, Ann closed her eyes and fell asleep.

Isaac was soon on his way. He hadn't intended to stay and visit, just to stop and pay his regards. However, the Flints were quite affable, and he had a difficult time pulling away.

It was still before midday and his shadow hadn't quite moved beneath him. The Flints had given him a fresh loaf of warm rye bread and a small skin of corn whiskey that he had looped around Molly's neck. There was still time for him to reach Baker's Fort before sundown. There were several other smaller plantations beyond the Flints that were along the river but none as impressive. Eventually the terrain became steeper, less developed, the trail narrowed again, and he found himself in the dark forest. He kept both his musket and pistol fully charged.

As he worked his way toward his destination, he wondered what Flint was referring to when he spoke of Braddock's defeat. He had known some of the prior events that had taken place. The British and French had both been at odds, each attempting to control the territory west of the Alleghenies. Virginia Lieutenant Governor Dinwiddie had dispatched Major George Washington to Fort Le Boeuf, along the Allegheny River, to deliver a letter to the French commander asking them to leave and to assess French strength and intentions. When he reached the fort, he was turned away by the French.

A year later, the British built Fort Prince George at the intersection of the Allegheny, Monongahela and Ohio Rivers, which was soon captured and destroyed by a larger French force that replaced the tiny British stronghold with a much larger and stronger Fort Duquesne. Washington had taken command of the Virginia Regiment and had been constructing a road toward Fort Prince George when he learned of its capture. Several days later, he encountered and attacked a French scouting party near Jumonville Glen and began construction of Fort Necessity at a large clearing known as the Great Meadows. The French soon forced Washington to surrender Fort Necessity but allowed him and his men to return without their armaments.

As the terrain became more rugged, the forest more dense,

and the trail less obvious, Isaac had to pay close attention not to lose his way. Molly wasn't used to carrying a rider, especially in rugged terrain, and she wasn't especially surefooted. He could hear many creature sounds coming from all around him and his imagination began to convince him that he was being followed by Indian scouts. He began to pick up the pace, hoping that Molly would not tire before reaching the fort, and he hummed church hymns to himself, hoping to distract his mind.

He eventually arrived at a clearing where there was a small settlement, amounting to a few houses and a store, and he stopped for a short rest. He tied Molly to a hitching post and looked in each direction, not seeing anyone except for a young girl of perhaps ten or eleven years playing on the floor of the porch at one of the cabins about thirty feet away.

She looked up and began to stare at him as he slung his musket over his shoulder. She was barefoot, skinny, dressed in rags and her sandy hair was wild as if it had never been combed. He spoke to her and she gave him no response. He waited a few moments and then asked her if the store was open, and she said that she thought it was, that he would just have to go in and see. She then got up from the floor and climbed onto a rocking chair. Her legs didn't reach the ground so she began to put it in motion by moving the upper part of her body back and forth. She continued to gaze at Isaac until a woman opened the door from inside the cabin and called to the young girl to come in. The woman didn't show herself so Isaac wasn't able to tell anything about her.

The young girl ignored the command and continued to gaze outward, rocking the chair by pumping her upper body back and forth, the rocker generating a squeaking sound against the porch planks. Once again, the woman opened the screen door and called out to the girl. This time, however, she obeyed, climbing down from the chair and taking two steps to the door still being

held open. She stopped and turned back again to see if Isaac was
still there.

Isaac stepped onto the landing of the storehouse and
attempted to open the latch, but it was locked. Then the squeaky
door of the house where the young girl was playing opened and
Isaac turned toward it and saw the barrel of a musket pointing
directly at him. Just as he hadn't been able to see the woman that

had called out to the young girl, he was unable to determine who was holding the weapon pointed in his direction until she called out to him.

"The storehouse is closed. What is it that you want?"

She leaned forward slightly, and Isaac could now get a glimpse of her. The late morning sun highlighted her golden hair and her shapeless brown cotton dress. "My name is Isaac Leimaster. I live several miles up the road, past Flint's settlement. I'm on my way to Fort Baker, Captain Chaplin's call. I just stopped for a rest. I mean no harm."

"You best be on your way. I've a good eye, and I'm not afraid to shoot," she declared and stepped out the door a few more inches. She appeared quite thin, her cheekbones and chin protruded from her freckled face. Her bony arms extended beyond her sleeves and seemed as long as her musket. He thought she must be quite poor, in her late-twenties, and he wondered why she was so afraid.

"Really, I mean no harm. I'll be on my way."

He stepped from the landing onto the soft grass that surrounded the hitching post when he was able to hear the faint voice of an older man. He thought he could hear him say that he knew of Isaac, that he had passed by here before. She stepped inside, the two voices argued for a moment, he could hear her swearing, and then she reappeared on the porch, still holding her musket.

With the look of having lost the squabble, she regarded Isaac and said, "You can come in…my father says he knows you."

"I'm sorry, madam, I don't mean to intrude, I wasn't looking for an invite, just to rest, and now I've done that. I'll just be gone."

"No, please…after the way I behaved, I won't feel good unless you have a cup of tea with us…and some oats for your horse."

It was a typical small cabin, plank floors with a stone fireplace on the right, surrounded by some iron cookware, a table and four chairs, much like Isaac's own home. There were three windows, one near the front door and one on each sidewall. On the left wall was a bunk bed and close by a twin bed. An older man lay awake on the single bed, his head propped up with several pillows. His face was pinkish white from having not been outside in a long time, dotted with brown age spots and yellow blotches, framed with long snow white, collar-length hair and a beard. The whites of his eyes, too, were jaundiced – perhaps from some liver disorder.

When Isaac stepped inside, the man struggled to sit up, causing him to pass gas. Roseanne, his daughter, rushed over to help him. Isaac noticed the dank musty redolence of the room, a mélange contributed to by the sod roof overhead, the smoky fireplace and the old man's poor health.

He could see that before his arrival the woman had been cutting vegetables on the table and placing them in an iron pot half-filled with water. The carcass of a partially roasted rabbit remained on a spit, near, but not directly over the few embers in the fireplace. He reasoned that it would soon be joining the stew. Roseanne reached for two small logs and placed them in the back of the hearth, where they would burn more slowly, and she then removed a teapot from the coals and poured hot water into two cups where she had deposited a few dried spearmint leaves to make a minty, refreshing drink that is highly satisfying.

"My name is Malachi Sidle, at your service." The old man's outstretched spindly hand reached upward in Isaac's direction.

Isaac promptly took it, shook it up and down two times, and repeated his name to the dying man.

"And this is my daughter, Roseanne, and my granddaughter, Sarah. Their husband and father were killed by Indians at Fort Necessity, the Great Meadow. Now alone, they have to contend with me. Did I hear you say you were responding to Captain Chaplin's Muster Call?"

"Yes, that's correct."

"And your family?"

"My wife, Ann, and my sons, Tom and Ben, are at home. I saw no reason to bring them with me."

"And you are probably right. I can tell you with certainty that the local Indians are forming alliances, and Fort Baker is going to be a tough place to defend. Your family is probably better off just staying put. I know Baker's Fort quite well, and it's small, so small that it won't hold everyone. Some folks will have to remain outside its walls. Those Indians were never a problem until the French began stirring them up. Gov. Dinwiddie didn't help matters either by sending Washington...the Indians had to pick a side, and it looked like to them that the French would prevail."

Malachi realized that he was becoming overexcited and lay back on his bed. From a small flask at the side of his bed he poured a modest amount of its contents into his empty cup. Isaac took a chair at the table, picked up his cup and began to sip the hot liquid.

Roseanne went about her business preparing the stew, occasionally taking a sip of tea. Sarah went back outdoors to the porch to play, and Molly noisily munched at her bucket of oats.

Ann awoke to a throb in her swollen leg that was keeping time with the tingle and twitter in her thumbs and fingertips. Her chest was vibrating also. Ben was sound asleep, having finished nursing some time earlier. She reconnected her bodice, reached down and placed her fingertips on the protruding bone that had all but punctured her tender skin. She was aware that her leg needed to be reset soon or it would begin healing in this disjointed manner. Locating either a doctor or a veterinarian would be a difficult matter, even if her husband were home.

Thomas was carrying in an armful of firewood, making sure the embers in the hearth remain lit, and saw that his mother was awake. He dropped the logs on the floor at the side of the hearth, making a loud noise – Ben stirred but continued to sleep. She realized that neither she nor Thomas had had anything to eat. The chickens and livestock hadn't been fed, and their one milk goat, Nanny, hadn't been milked. Her udder was probably dragging the ground by now.

"Thomas! Please get some water and put it in that large pot over there by the fireplace. Push it into the coals and then bring me some vegetables over in that large sac there, over on that far wall. Pull out a couple of potatoes, one or two turnips and some carrots…then bring them here with a knife. I will cut them up and you will have to put them in the pot. You can throw in some jerky for flavor…it's up on that shelf…you'll have to use a chair to reach it. Will you do that for me? You are such a good helper."

Thomas was eager to help. He knew that things weren't going well, and he was pleased to see that his mother was taking charge. He knew that she was in pain, he could see it on her face, and he winced sympathetically each time she tried to do the smallest feat or move the slightest muscle. She wanted to reach down, stretch her leg and reset it herself, but that proved to be impossible.

Isaac and Ann married when they both were twenty-years old. She was of average height, with light skin and long strawberry hair that most of the time she kept tied in a bun on the back of her head, which she covered with a bonnet. By the time she married, she had completed a classical education that included Latin, Greek and literature.

Her father was an Anglican minister who had been sent to Maryland by the Bishop of London to serve as rector of All Faith

Parish, an assignment that included all of St. Mary's and Charles Counties. He also established a school in the parish that she attended.

She and Isaac had chosen to live on the frontier, and they were both willing to face the challenges that were presented to them on a regular basis. Ann's faith always remained strong and she seemed to be strengthened by adversity. Unable to get down on her knees she lay on her back and prayed. As she spoke softly to Him whom she believed to be All-powerful, she poured out her heart, weeping, praising Him, speaking softly, asking for His forgiveness, for their daily bread, and always that His will be done. Thomas remained in the room listening intently, and he felt compelled to close his eyes also and soon he too could be heard asking that He might hear his mother's prayer. When Ann had completed her petition, she sang softly *A Mighty Fortress is our God.*

Isaac approached the concentrated settlement along the Conococheague Creek. Several residents had begun building private forts in this region: Isaac Baker, for one, had built a log fort, Evan Shelby, a noted Indian trader, built another due west of Baker's. Thomas Mills built a fort of unspecified size and configuration, and somewhere between Mill's fort and Shelby's fort, Allen Killough constructed a stockade. All four of these men were active in the militia, and their forts initially served as havens for local settlers during Indian raids.

At the outset of the settlement, there were wide-spreading plantations, fields mostly of corn or tobacco. Closer in were small farms where corn and tobacco were also being grown, and at the heart of the community were individual homes, most with large vegetable gardens bursting forth with foodstuff – beans, corn, turnips and onions. Most of the houses were of the two-story log type, with split-wood shingle roofs, three windows on the upper level and two on the lower. A few had a chimney at each end but most had only one.

As Isaac rode through the main street, there were several women and children but only a few men, mostly middle-class farmers, townsmen, mechanics and tradesmen dressed more or less the same as Isaac – wool coat, hanging waistcoat and breeches, blue, brown, gray, green or black, with pewter buttons. As he approached the far side of the settlement, he could see where several homes had been burned. This was no doubt where the seventeen were killed, and the reason for the muster. The smell of burned timbers and charred bodies still permeated the air while the tightness in his chest spoke to him of the seriousness of this call. His imagination conjured up images of savages against white men and women, bloodied tomahawks, bloodcurdling Indian yelps, exploding muskets, high-pitched cries and screams, hollers and howls, clamor and bedlam.

A medium-sized dog was rummaging through the remains – its gray coat was wet and mud-caked. Isaac pulled his horse over to the side of the road, split a part of his egg sandwich that Ann had made for him and without dismounting, tossed it down. The animal quickly tore into it, swallowing large hunks whole without chewing, then it looked up, hoping for more. Isaac too hadn't eaten and began eating the remaining portion himself. When he had finished he remembered the loaf of rye bread that Belle had given him that morning, and he tore off some of it for the dog. He then continued on toward the fort, not noticing the dog following close behind.

When Isaac Baker built his fort, he had intended it to be for the protection of his family, their lands and any of his neighbors that wished to come for their defense. It was never intended to be a military fortress. However, as the conditions began to deteriorate and the garrison at Fort Frederick remained too weak and sickly to send out so many and such large parties as the inhabitants thought necessary, Governor Sharpe in response directed a Company of Militia under the Command of Captain Joseph Chaplin to be mustered and sent to Baker's Fort for its defense until such time as the garrison at Fort Frederick could protect this western frontier. Captain Chaplin's younger brother, Lieutenant Moses Chaplin, was also commissioned and assigned to this outpost.

There were sixty names on the muster; however, on the day Isaac arrived only twenty-eight were present and accounted for. Even for such a small number there was scarcely room within the confines to garrison a company. Accordingly, the quartermaster had to obtain and erect small tents outside the front gate of the compound. This he did in traditional military fashion in a rectangular grid pattern of rows and columns.

Sergeant Meyers opened the door to the makeshift office and announced, "Isaac Leimaster is here, would you like to see him?"

Captain Chaplin was at his desk near the only window, doing what he normally did when not talking – paperwork. The backlight coming in from the window prevented Isaac from getting a clear look at the man behind the desk until he stepped forward.

Captain Chaplin wore a white ruffled linen shirt. His gray coat and matching ruffle trimmed tricorn hung on the hook behind him. Relieved by the interruption he looked up. "Yes, Sergeant, send him in."

Isaac had been instructed of the protocol for reporting in by Sergeant Meyers. "Isaac Leimaster reporting for duty, sire."

"You may stand at ease, Mr. Leimaster." Isaac made a contrived effort to look relaxed.

After placing a check mark next to his name on the roster, Chaplin looked back at Isaac and gave the same speech that he had given to the twenty-eight before him. "I would like to both welcome you and thank you for answering this call to serve His Majesty, King George II. I don't need to tell you the difficult problem we have had in defending our Ohio territories from the French, who have been actively building forts along our western frontier. With the defeat of Braddock, they have been able to convince quite a number of Indian tribes to become allies with them and to send out raiding parties against many of our settlements."

That was the second time in one day that Isaac had heard Braddock's name mentioned. He now knew its meaning but nothing of the event itself.

"This area, along Conococheague Creek, has become an area of savage uprising, the enemy being Mingo and Shawnee. They are constantly on the move, living from the land, making it difficult for us to locate them. The garrison at Fort Frederick has been unable to adequately protect this area. However, the Assembly, of which I am a member, is actively working to increase its size and scope. Until that time, we must muster local citizens such as yourself. It is my intention as your commander, together with my brother, Lieutenant Moses Chaplin, Captain Delashmutte and Captain Bealle, to organize you into small groups of rangers, to send you out to those places where we believe the enemy will pass, ambush them when they do so arrive, and kill them. Is this something that you believe you can do?"

Isaac was sure of his answer – No. "Yes, sire, (How contrary the spirit!) I would be honored to serve His Majesty and proud to be counted among those who would defend their own."

"Thank you, Leimaster, you can truly be counted as a patriot. Tell me…please…your family…I presume you have one…are they being taken care of?"

"I have a wife and two boys, five and three. They are home

alone on our seventy acres near the Flint settlement. I have made sure of provisions for at least forty-five days. There are plenty of fish in the river, and she is a crack shot with the Charleville that I left behind. My friend Red Hawk, a Cherokee, has promised to watch in on them from time to time."

"You know, you could have brought her with you. We could have put them up here at the fort."

"Sire, that would most likely have been in a tent. I understand there is scarcely any room inside the compound and no facilities either inside or out."

"Of course, you are right. Now I would like for you to have Sergeant Meyers show you to the quartermaster for your items of issue and a tent assignment. At 1500 hours this afternoon, you will report by the front gate for drill. Following that, mess will be served close by the tents. But first, place your hand on this Bible, raise your right hand and repeat after me...."

Ann remained restless, sitting up on her bed while Thomas occupied his time playing with Ben, occasionally taking an interest in stirring the stew. The warm, humid afternoon air had begun to cool, and Ann could feel a chilly breeze entering through the open cabin door. Outside, the sky began to shadow and the branches on the trees began waving about. Sudden gusts of wind would ripple through the leaves, creating a rushing sound like the soothing roar of an ocean wave sweeping onto the beach. She knew the signs well and hoped that Isaac had made it to the fort before the storm. As soon as the rain began, it swiftly changed to hail, a pounding on the roof like a snare drum, the white stones accumulating on the porch like miniature golf balls.

Both boys stuck their hands out the door, keeping the rest of their bodies inside, hoping to catch the frozen pellets and trying to examine them before they quickly melted.

Sometimes the rains come and are not appreciated, and then

other times they are the only thing able to break the momentum of things going badly. The deluge lasted only a few minutes, ending as quickly as it began, and the two boys rushed out to the porch in the clean air to gather up what they could of the pea-sized ice.

They were both so occupied that they didn't see the white and gray appaloosa slowly approaching along the same trail that their father had taken early that morning. The rider sat tall with only a blanket separating him from his steed. He wore several feathers attached to his long black hair that hung down his back in a pair of braids, leather bands on his muscular biceps, a leather vest, breeches and beaded moccasins. A four-foot bow and a quiver of arrows were attached to the side of his horse, and he wore a sheath holding a twelve-inch bone-handled knife tied around his waist.

Thomas was the first to look up, surprised to see the young Cherokee brave – he appeared to be in his early twenties. "Red Hawk!" Thomas exclaimed and ran down the steps to greet his friend.

"Hello, Thomas," the bronze-skinned native saluted while sliding off his appaloosa. "How are my two favorite white boys?"

Thomas ran up to him, wrapped his arms around his waist and then reached for his hand. Ben followed close behind and took his other hand. Thomas spoke first. "We are glad you are here. My mother, she fell…broke her leg. She's inside now…on the bed."

"Yes," Ben spoke second, "and she didn't cry. We both helped her to the house."

"Your mother is very fortunate to have two strong sons. Will you take me to her? Perhaps I can be of service."

Both boys, hand in hand with him, led Red Hawk up the steps and into the house where Ann was sitting up. Even though she was fully dressed, she modestly covered herself with the blanket that had been folded at the foot of the bed.

Ben released his grip and ran to his mother. "Mama, look! It's Red Hawk." He then started to climb onto the bed, but the movement sent a sharp pain through her leg. She gave a gasp and he backed away.

She recovered and then scolded, "Ben, you have got to be more careful! She then turned her face toward the visitor and spoke. "Hello, Red Hawk. It's good to see you."

"Hello, Mrs. Leimaster, it's good to see you. Your sons have told me that you had an accident...your leg. Can you tell me what happened?"

Ann struggled to hold back the tears. "This is so insane...he was only gone less than an hour...on his way to the muster...I slipped on those stupid planks...it's badly broken. Now it's so swollen that it will take a team of horses to stretch it long enough to be reset."

"Tell me, Mrs. Leimaster – what can I do to help?"

"I hate to ask you this, but I don't know what else. There is so much to do here, the kids and all, and I'm not able; poor Nanny is probably dragging on the ground right now. If you would ride over to Joe and Belle Flint's place, I know Belle can set a broken bone, ask her if she could come, and maybe if she could lend me one of her coloreds, one that can do barnyard chores and cook. That would be wonderful."

Red Hawk listened to her every word as if he were a trained professional. When she had told her story to exhaustion, he reassured her that he would ride to Flint's plantation as she had requested and return perhaps before dark. She thanked him and watched him leave through the front door and loose his horse's reins from the porch railing. She could see his arm muscles bulge as he mounted his appaloosa, a simultaneous leap and pull, much the same way Isaac had mounted Molly earlier that morning. She couldn't turn away and gazed intently as he pulled on his horse's thin bridle, turning it away from the porch and then digging his heels into its sides. As he rode out of her view from inside, she could feel her heart racing and she was aware that he had caused her excitement. She laid back and stared blankly at the ceiling.

When Ann saw her children playing outside, the warm feeling that had taken hold melted away faster than the hailstones on the porch. She felt ashamed; after all, she truly loved her husband. She began to question whether this savage had been sent to her in answer to her earlier prayer, or did God send him to test her? It remained unclear to her if she had sufficiently rejected satin's temptation or if she could be condemned for that short moment of euphoria that had suddenly elapsed.

Red Hawk rode fast, never stopping to rest, and arrived at the Flints' place in less than half an hour. Exactly half an hour later, he began the return trip, leading Belle, who followed behind, driving a black carriage with a canopy top, four large spoke wheels and suspended on leaf springs, which bounced along the driveway pulled by a single horse along with Abraham and Murtha, her two best slaves.

When it started to rain, Private Isaac Leimaster was standing in formation with his unit listening to the instructions being given by Sergeant Meyers. The seasoned drill instructor continued without as much as a thought about the rain, and when he shouted out his first command for the unit to do a right face and forward march, the hail began to fall. The storm was so loud that not everyone in the unit could hear his subsequent commands, and when he commanded about face, not everyone heard, and the result was mayhem with soldiers walking into each other, unaware of how to make a correction. Once the sergeant reorganized the formation, he explained that this is the way it would be out in the field, that instead of walking into each other, they would be shooting at each other, that a soldier's job does not wait for the rain or hail to stop.

Before the rain began there were several onlookers standing near the formation. Some were wives that had accompanied their husbands, some were those that had come to the fort out of fear, and there were those who came like circus or carnival vendors, selling things to eat, articles of clothing – one young girl was a prostitute. When the rain cut loose, these onlookers scrambled for shelter, which was either a nearby tent or a wagon. When the rain and hail had ceased, they returned to the site in hopes of taking advantage of what was left of the daylight sun in order to dry out.

The soldiers continued to drill, the onlookers continued to regard, and all their clothes continued to dry until a bugle could be heard sounding *Recall.* Only the seasoned soldiers understood, and as soon as they were dismissed by Sergeant Meyers, it was explained to the uninitiated about the system of bugle calls. There would next be a *Preparatory Call for Retreat,* and then the call for *Assembly*. The entire garrison would turn out for the *Retreat* ceremony and the actual lowering of the flag and playing of *Tattoo* would occur at *light out.*

Isaac stood in line holding his tin mess plate and cup, which had been given to him earlier in the afternoon by the quartermaster. When it was his turn, he held out his plate as one of the servers dished out a large dipper of stew, and another filled his cup to the top with warm wheat beer. There seemed to be nowhere to go to eat other than to find a spot and sit down on the ground, as several others were doing, or return to his tent and sit on his bedroll. He chose the latter.

The tents were all framed, two-person cabin tents, made of

canvas and supported by guy ropes connected to the ground with wooden stakes. The front flap could be rolled back for ventilation or tied shut for warmth or protection from the elements. He went inside, sat down – leaving the flap open – and began eating the stew, which had now cooled completely. Beside him, he saw someone else's gear dumped in a pile, which in a way determined which side belonged to whom, and he drew an imaginary line to mark off his side and its boundaries. The tent was perched on somewhat of a slope with the back being a little higher than the front, and Isaac noticed that a trench had not been etched around the high end to guide off any ground water, some of which had seeped in during the last downpour. When he finished his stew, he licked his plate clean and then placed it in his backpack, which had also been supplied by the quartermaster.

He fixed his bedroll and lay on his back, tired from all the day's activities, first the long journey and then his immediate immersion into duty, when he felt the dog that had followed him from the settlement he had passed through right before arriving at the fort. It was licking him on the face. He reached over, felt his damp muddy coat then opened his eyes and remembered it.

It had a forlorn look, desolate, having been deserted or abandoned. No doubt, his master had been a casualty back at the settlement, and Isaac had probably been the first to show it any compassion. Isaac returned to the soup line with his pewter plate hoping for seconds, only to receive a negative shake of the head once the server saw that it was really for the dog standing next to him. Isaac appealed to the server, who finally acquiesced and agreed that after everyone had been served, and if there were any left over, he could have it. When he returned to the tent, the person that belonged to the other bedroll had yet to appear. Isaac, tired, fell asleep with the dog at his feet.

Belle, Red Hawk and the two slaves arrived at Ann's front door. Abraham took the reins and hitched the horse to the post, while Belle and Murtha went directly to the front door. Red Hawk dismounted and took a chair on the porch. Ann had fallen asleep shortly after Red Hawk had left and she was now awakened by Belle's rapping on the opened door.

"Yoo-hoo!" Belle called softly, sticking her head partially into the room. "Ann, are you there?"

"Yes," she answered while carefully trying to sit up. "I'm over here. Please, come in."

Belle entered the cabin while the others remained outside. She had brought an apple pie with her, which she set on the table before walking to where Ann was sitting up on her bed. "My goodness, child, what have you done?"

Ann uncovered her leg and explained how she had fallen. Belle examined it closely and after returning a solemn look she spoke softly. "That bone is sticking out, it has got to be set. I can do it for you if you want. This will not be pleasant, but it has to be done. Once it has been set, I'll have to make a cast to hold it in place."

Abraham held Ann down while Red Hawk stretched her leg, and Belle massaged the two ends of the fractured tibia into position. Ann had nearly bitten the piece of wood that she held in her mouth in half during the ordeal, and when they had finished she continued to sob for several minutes. Her limb was then wrapped in wool. Pasteboard was cut into shape to provide a splint and dampened down in order that it could be molded to the limb. It was then wrapped in bandages before a starch coating was applied to the outer surface.

When Belle had finished, she leaned over and kissed Ann on the forehead. "It's all over, Ann. You can rest now. I'll watch the young ones while you get some sleep."

Ann lay quietly with her eyes closed. "Thank you, Belle.

Can I ask for one more favor?"

"Certainly, child. What is it?"

"Nanny hasn't been milked. I hate to ask."

"Don't you worry about a thing. I'll see to it that she gets milked. Now you get some rest."

Baker's Fort

The three notes of *Reveille* tooted in the key of G from the puckered embouchure of the bugler standing at the watchtower above the stockade wall. Hearing it for the first time, its trill was just as unfamiliar to Isaac as if it were the din of a Muslim cleric chanting a call to prayer. Regardless, the effect was the same, and he knew without being told that it was time to rise and shine.

The soldier next to Isaac also heard the wakeup call and sat up rubbing his eyes. Having never been introduced to each other, he turned toward Isaac and volunteered his name. "Baker, my name is Baker, Corporal Richard Baker...from Beaver Creek." His voice was that of a young boy, and it cracked as if it were in that adolescent process of changing into manhood.

Isaac lifted his head obliquely in the direction of the voice. Their tent was tall enough for an average-sized man to stand without stooping provided he stood along the centerline directly beneath the ridge; accordingly, Baker remained on his side of the tent, bent over, pulling his breeches on, balancing first on one leg and then on the other.

"My name is Isaac Leimaster. I have a small plantation farther up the river, Comare's Ramble, it's called...not really near anything unless you know where Joseph Flint's settlement lies."

Baker reflected for a moment. "No...never been in that direction. You were sound asleep when I returned to the tent last night...didn't want to disturb you."

Isaac remained partially beneath his wool blanket, "Yeah, it was a long day for me, and I was beat."

"You said your name was Leimaster – any relation to Jacob Leimaster?"

Isaac sat up. "I could be, there are a lot of us in these parts. I have a cousin named Jacob, maybe it's him. I've another cousin, Abraham, he's married to one of Captain Delashmitt's daughters. He's a recruiter, I hear. I haven't seen him for some time now."

"Jacob and I served together with the Virginia Militia, under Colonel Washington and General Braddock at the Great Meadow. I don't know if Jacob made it out alive or not – a lot didn't. It wouldn't surprise me if we see Colonel Washington here any day now. I hear that he is at Fort Cumberland and going from fort to fort throughout this frontier region. You may think this is about defending against Indian raids, but you can be sure, His Majesty King George is more concerned about the French than those savages."

Sergeant Meyers all of a sudden appeared at the front of the tent and stuck his head in. "Let's go, let's go, time to fall in! Be sure to bring your muskets...don't make me come back." He moved on to the next tent and each one down the row making sure no one missed the opening formation.

Baker scooted to the edge of the tent, opened both flaps and began pulling on his socks and pewter buckled shoes. It was a bright sunny morning and the early dampness had already burned off. In the sun's angled rays, Isaac could see that his new companion had long blond hair naturally parted at the top of his head. The air was filled with the gray smoke from several chimneys inside the stockade and from a few campfires that had been lit on the outside. Isaac could see others leaving their tents and gathering in that nearby area that would come to be known as the parade ground. Since Isaac had fallen asleep fully dressed, he only had to get up and head out with the others.

Those present stood around talking until Sergeant Meyers returned from the stockade, took his position and ordered the men to fall in. Some of the wives and their children, along with a few of the other settlers that had come to the fort, stood off to the sidelines to watch. A single vendor stood among them with hot buns to sell, waiting for the ceremony to finish. Sergeant Meyers called out the names of the men on the roster – thirty-two present. Over the next week, another eleven volunteers would straggle in one at a time.

Lieutenant Moses Chaplin arrived at the head of the formation and instructed Sergeant Meyers to fall in with the rest of the men. The regular Virginia Company, a detachment from Fort Frederick, who had already been garrisoned at Baker's Fort for the past year, led by Captain Elias Delaschmitt, numbered about twenty-eight, and they were standing in formation several feet away.

Captain Chaplin then walked out from the stockade and took his position in front of the two companies, and the sergeant called out, "Attention!" When the Captain saw that all the soldiers were in proper formation, standing at attention, he received the report, turned to the bugler, and gave the signal to sound *To the Colors*. At the sound of the bugle, the two men standing on the tower raised the *Union Jack*. When that had been completed, the commissioned officers returned inside the stockade for breakfast whilst Sergeant Meyers remained behind and led the two companies of men in early morning calisthenics and laps around the fort. That morning, the recruits trained with Sergeant Meyers. For the next thirty days, their job would be to patrol the surrounding area, and as Captain Chaplin said, "Find the savages and kill them."

Ann awoke early the next morning, before the rooster crowed, unable to sleep. She had slept a good part of the previous day and through most of the night, waking only once to nurse Benjamin. Belle was still asleep in the boy's bed, and the two boys were both sound asleep, Thomas on the bed Belle had made for them on the floor in front of the fireplace, and Benjamin in bed beside Ann; he had fallen asleep while nursing, a normal thing for him. Abraham and Murtha had made separate beds in the barn with only the livestock to spy on them. Red Hawk had returned to his home soon after having helped set Ann's leg and was not seen again for the next several days.

Ann lay awake and said her morning prayers quietly to herself. She thanked God for having sent Red Hawk and Belle, as well as for having forgiven her for having impure thoughts the previous day. She prayed that He would watch over and protect her husband as well as the others in Captain Chaplin's muster. One by one, the others awoke, and before long the goat had been milked, vegetables gathered from the garden, eggs brought in from the barn and breakfast prepared.

It seemed that everything was under control and Belle was preparing to take Abraham and return home, leaving Murtha behind for as long as she might be needed.

When she walked out the door there were three Indians rummaging through the garden, helping themselves to the watermelon. They wore paint on their faces and she was sure, by their appearance, they weren't Cherokee, they looked more like Mingos or Shawnees. She wanted to grab the Charleville from inside, but thought better of it; at best she could only stir them. She sat on the porch, in the rocker, waited and watched, hoping they would take what they wanted and then leave.

One of the braves left the garden, chased down a chicken and snapped its neck, and then the three moved across the trail by the river where they had left their horses tied. There they cleaned the chicken, built a fire and proceeded to eat their ill-gotten gains. By noon, they had finished, but still they did not leave. Belle continued to wait, going back and forth from inside and then back out to the rocking chair. When evening came they were still there, visible only from the light of their campfire, but they could be heard laughing and singing.

Inside, there were mixed feelings about what degree of danger lurked not far from their front door. Belle thought they were a remnant of some war party from the other side of the Ohio River. For some time the lands past the river had been hunted only by the Indians. Both hunting and raiding parties were common coming from across the Ohio. These three seemed peaceful enough, but then, who could tell? These war parties were known for terrorizing small, undefended settlements like theirs. Belle wasn't sure what value or benefit she served by remaining, and she had promised Joseph that she would be home by now. Nevertheless, she felt little choice but to remain and see it through.

First thing the next morning she stuck her head out the door in hopes that they might be gone, only to see one of them back in the garden again and the other two chasing down another chicken. Having made it this far with their scalps still in place, she suggested to Ann, Thomas, Benjamin, Abraham and Murtha that they try their best to go about their daily routine, whatever that was, not to show any fear and try to behave as if nothing was wrong. Certainly if these savages were going to do something to them, they would have done it by now. With that, Thomas gathered squash and watermelon from the garden.

Belle sent Murtha out to the henhouse to fetch some eggs, and when she returned, she sent her to the corral to milk Nanny. Murtha had never milked either a milk cow or a goat. Her entire life had been spent as a slave in the Flint's house. Murtha tried unsuccessfully, squeezing and pulling on Nanny's teats and finally gave up and returned to the house with an empty bucket. Belle then took Murtha back to the corral to show her how it was done.

By late morning, all but Ann gathered on the front porch, having finished the chores and preparing breakfast. They moved the table from its place in front of the fireplace out on the porch, where there was scarcely room enough for it. They would have preferred to take their breakfast in the house, where Ann could be with them, but they decided that it was important for the strangers to see them enjoying themselves, not intimidated by their presence. However, the red-skinned squatters went about their own business, paying Belle, Abraham, Murtha and the two boys no regard whatsoever.

Isaac and Richard Baker stood in the mess line together, slowly making their way to the front. It had been a long, hot, humid, late summer day, one of those days when the evening brought no cooling relief. They had each left their coats back at the tent and wore their muskets strapped to their backs.

"Have your musket clean as a whistle, hatchet scoured, sixty rounds, powder and ball, and be ready to march at a minute's warning." That was one of the rules given them by Sergeant Meyers. Actually, it wasn't his rule; he got it from having trained with Robert Rogers up around Lake Champlain. 'Roger's Rangers' they called them and Rogers had a list of 28 rules that he required each of his Rangers to know.

As they inched their way closer to the head of the queue, they could see that they would be eating stew again, this time along with an apple. The faces of the men serving the stew looked no happier than those of the men being served. The man serving Isaac remembered him and gave him an extra large serving, enough for him and his dog, but still, he was given only one apple.

The two men carried their dinner back to their tent and started to sit on the ground, however, seeing how muddy it had become, they found a log in the nearby thicket, dragged it to a spot near the front of the tent, not blocking the entrance, and sat down on it.

Ann let out a scream so loud and terrifying that the rafters in the cabin vibrated, causing loose dust to nervously float down. All heads in the cabin, except for those of the two boys, who were outside playing, turned first toward Ann and then toward the front door where the three Indians stood. Intense rays of sunlight surrounded the dark shaded side of their painted bodies, a backlight so bright that Belle raised a hand above her eyes to enable her to see more clearly. Without a second thought, she rushed to grab the Charleville hanging above the hearth but not in time to stop one of the intruders from taking it first.

Ann realized that Ben and Tom were not present and questioned frantically, "Where are my boys? Have you done something with my boys?" She attempted to rise from her bed and both Abraham and Murtha rushed to stop her. None of the intruders spoke English and pretended to ignore her.

Belle spoke to Abraham. "Go outside, look for the boys and ask them to come in the house and be with their mother." As he headed for the door, one of the intruders stopped him. Abraham tried resisting and was thrown to the floor and kicked in the stomach by the second one.

Away from the door and out of the bright backlight, Belle was able to get a better look. Two of the Indians seemed quite young to be so daring, with soft skin, perhaps twenty or twenty-one. The one that appeared to be the leader seemed older and had a shaved head except for a single black braid that hung to the small of his back beginning at his pate. His face was heavily scarred from earlier pockmarks. One side of his face was painted turquoise and the other side yellow ocher – feathers hung from leather strips attached to his braid. He was naked from the waist up and wore leather breeches, a loincloth and moccasins with a bone-handled knife in a sheath hanging from his breeches.

The other two were dressed similarly except they both wore shirts and had red stripes on their cheeks and forehead, and their heads were not shaved, rather with long shoulder length hair.

The older one spoke to the younger two, and they began rummaging through the nearby cabinet and shelves looking for anything they might take. They looked under the beds, opened boxes, and took some food, some jewelry and a clay pipe and then they quickly left. On the way out the door, the one that appeared to be in charge walked over to Ann, looked closely at her starch cast, and then mumbled a few words while looking her directly in the face. He then went to catch up with the others and as he passed the doorway he leaned the Charleville that he had been holding against the wall next to the opening, turned toward Belle and spoke the only words that she had heard from him in English, "Goodbye," and they then all left, laughing and talking amongst themselves.

As soon as they were gone, Abraham stood up and brushed the dust from his clothes; Belle asked him if he was all right. He replied that he was fine, that only his pride had been injured. As a slave, working most of his life for white men, he had never been kicked before.

As Isaac and Corporal Baker sat next to each other on the log, Isaac had a feeling that something was wrong at home. He thought that he had heard Ann's cry, and he felt helpless not knowing what was wrong or what he could do to help her. He placed his unfinished tin plate of stew on the ground for his dog. He sat on the log with his elbows on his knees, his hands holding his head up.

Each hour the temperature continued to rise, both inside the cabin and out. Abraham and Murtha both sat at the table playing whist, while Benjamin was asleep in his bunk and Thomas was busy on the floor playing with his stick people. Ann's bedclothes were wet from perspiration, and she sat up on her bed bolstered by two pillows trying her best to concentrate on the novel that she was reading – Samuel Foote - *The Englishman in Paris* – made difficult by not only the hot spell but also the tension created by those troublesome natives.

The time dragged by slowly as Belle impatiently traipsed back and forth from the kitchen chair to the porch rocker where she would sit for as long as she could force herself to remain.

She wondered if she should leave Abraham and Murtha with Ann and the boys and return to her own family. *Joe must certainly be concerned*, she thought. *He should have expected me home long ago...after all, that savage left the musket behind...kind of a sign...letting us know that they were not going to harm us.*

Eventually the day slipped into evening and then into night. The bonfire across the way grew hotter and brighter; chanting and loud whoops accompanied by the sound of a tom-tom rose above the forest din. Belle lifted herself from her chair to see what the commotion was and saw the natives dancing around the fire, naked but for their loincloths, gyrating and pounding their chests. Their banzai movements full of vivacity, potent and forceful, seemed to replicate throwing a spear, pulling a bow and slicing with a tomahawk: a war song, a call to arms. The dance seemed violent and it struck fear into her, fear of what might follow. After gazing for several minutes, she began to wish that they hadn't remained there, helpless and alone. She knew that Abraham wasn't a fighter; he had probably never held a musket. Was this the way their lives would end, she wondered, raped, scalped, their heads pushed onto pikes for the ravens to peck their eyes out? No! Never! She still had a musket and her wits, she reasoned.

After staring in their direction for the longest time, until she could stand no more, she stepped backwards to the rocker and then sat, not taking her eyes from the spectacle. She watched as more wood was tossed onto the orange-yellow flames, animated sparks zigging and zagging in all directions. Occasionally one of them would throw a handful of gunpowder into the flames, creating a dazzling white flash, a shower of burning scintillation.

Belle awoke, slumped in the rocker, unaware that she had dozed off, for how long she had no idea. Out of the darkness, the shadow of a man began to emerge, leading a horse toward her, and when she saw the outline of the feathers protruding from the top of his head she knew that he was an Indian. Before he could come any closer, she stood up, reached for the musket leaning next to the door, lowered it directly toward him and shouted for him to stop and not come any closer.

"It is I...Red Hawk," he declared. "Do not shoot."

She recognized his voice, its unique timbre, its baritone pitch, and his Cherokee accent, qualities that combined to make him easily recognizable to those who knew him whenever he spoke.

Belle lowered the musket, but just to be sure she kept her finger on the trigger and waited for him to come closer where the illumination coming from the fireplace inside the cabin could confirm his identity.

As he stepped into the dim light at the foot of the porch, she immediately recognized him and was pleased to see that it was her friend and not one of the warriors from across the way. He wore buckskin breeches and shirt, a beaded headband, and a knife in a sheath hung from his belt. His horse was a gray and white appaloosa with the image of a red hand burnt into its rear hindquarters, and it wore pieces of leather strapped to each of it hooves.

He tied his horse to the post and cut loose two brightly colored male pheasants that were hanging by their feet and tossed them onto the porch. He had trapped them both earlier in the day, broken their necks and decided to bring them to Ann and her boys rather than selling them to the French traders, which was his usual custom.

"Please come in, we are all so glad to see you. It has been several days now." Belle replaced the musket back against the wall and then stooped to get a better look at the two birds. "Those are mighty fine lookin' birds you've got. I'll see to it that Murtha takes care of them right away. Tell me, are you plannin' on stayin' for a while? We sure would like havin' you around with all that's goin' on around here."

She looked out to the spot where the war dance had taken place – it was dark. She could see no trace of the squatters.

"No, I can't. I need to continue on to Fort Frederick...I promised Colonel Washington. You need to keep your eyes open. There are several war parties circulating in this area, Mingos mostly. They come from the Ohio Territory, and they are waiting to tie up with the Shawnee and Muskingum before they move on to Fort Baker. Colonel Washington has asked me to alert him when I become aware of any movement. He is aware that these small war parties are combining in support of the French."

"They were here, there across the road, the coals are still hot. They were here for several days...helped themselves to Ann's garden and her chickens."

"That's all the more reason I can't stay, Mrs. Flint. I must be on my way." Red Hawk untied his horse from the post, placed its reins around its neck, and leaped up onto its back. While turning in the direction of the trail, he shouted to Belle, "Tell Ann that I am sorry that I couldn't stop and say hello. It looks like she's safe. I'll be back in a few days." He then dug his soft moccasin-covered heels into the sides of his horse and raced off, his horse in a gallop.

As she watched him ride away into the dark, she turned her gaze once again to the spot where the Indians had camped. *Not a sign of them,* she thought. *I hope they haven't simply moved on to my plantation. If they do, my boys will kill 'em.*

Red Hawk followed the same trail that had taken him days earlier to Flint's plantation, twisting back and forth across the river, the only difference being that it was daylight then and now it was late in the night. He continuously stopped from time to time to check for signs of the Mingos that Belle had reported to him had camped outside Comare's Ramble, reading the prints on the trail from their horses as well as their droppings. Before arriving at Flint's plantation their trace turned along a branch of the river, and he decided to follow it and catch up with them.

They had camped for the night having joined up with a small party of Shawnees. He tied his horse and moved closer on foot to where he was able to get a closer look. They had erected three teepees that surrounded a fire pit containing a few flames but mostly dying embers. A lone brave sat in front of one of the teepees, a French Charleville lying across his lap, while the others had gone to sleep for the night. It was difficult to get an accurate count, but Red Hawk estimated that there were as many as a dozen or so and was then able to confirm his estimate by checking the number of horses that had been allowed to roam and forage in the grassy meadow at the far side of the camp. Having taken a count he returned to the river and continued toward Fort Frederick.

Belle hitched her horse and carriage to return home. It had begun to sprinkle, and she wanted to get started ahead of the eventual downpour. She could hear the bullfrogs from the river, muffled by the fog, trying to out-sing the magpies fluttering from treetop to treetop. She wore a heavy overcoat and a man's roundhat with one side pinned up, as was the fashion.

Ben and Tom both sat on the porch steps, heads in hands and elbows on knees, and Murtha in the rocker, watching. Belle enjoyed staying with Ann and helping, but now that the earlier threat had passed she looked forward to returning to her family. All the morning chores had been completed, Murtha had been instructed to remain behind to help Ann maintain her household, and Abraham sat stately in the driver's seat waiting for Belle to climb aboard.

But Belle wasn't quite ready. She stepped between the two boys, onto the porch, into the house and approached Ann, who seeing her placed the book she was reading on the bed beside herself. "Well, Ann, I guess it's time for me to leave."

Ann patted the bed a few times, signifying that she wanted Belle to sit next to her. "Please have a seat beside me. I want to tell you how thankful I am for all that you have done."

Belle took a seat facing Ann, and Ann took hold of Belle's right hand, squeezing it gently. The two sat looking at each other. Belle was thirty years Ann's senior and some of the lines on her face ran deep. Some loose gray hairs hung down the side of her face. "Thank you. I owe you my life; I don't know what would have become of the boys."

"There, there child, I only did as anyone on this frontier would have done." Ann's face was soft and smooth, her hair shined. "You have your youth. I'll bet that you get your chance to do the same someday. You are a very special woman, Ann, someone I'm proud to have as a neighbor. Murtha is staying with you. She finally figured out how to milk Nanny…I hope the two of you can be acquainted. She is young, but she is strong and I think quite intelligent for a darkie. I've got to be on my way so's to beat the rains, if that's possible."

Belle leaned over and they embraced, careful not to move Ann's leg. When Belle walked to the door, she stopped, turned and winked, then walked to the carriage. "OK, Abraham, let's get started."

Fifteen minutes later the rains began to pour. The grounds were already waterlogged from the unusually wet summer and the runoff quickly filled the river.

Abraham drove the horse to its limit, causing the carriage to bounce roughly over the uneven surface that was in many places becoming like slurpy soup, roots exposed beneath puddles of collected water. The carriage top with open sides did little to protect the two from the onslaught as Belle sat stone-faced next to Abraham, who grimaced from the pelting rain. As they came to the first crossing, Abraham brought the horse to a complete stop, and he regarded the high water level, which had exceeded the river's banks.

Belle did not want to turn back and insisted that he drive on through the swell. It probably would have been better if they had driven straight through without having stopped. Slowly the horse stepped forward into the rapidly moving river, and as soon as the water level reached above the axels, halfway across, the surging current clung tightly to the carriage bottom with its muscular arms so strong, surrounding it like forest vines, impossible to break free. The cart was soon overturned and both Belle and Abraham tumbled into the swirling river, the horse dragged into the water on top of Abraham.

The horse might have been able to right itself had it not been for the carriage restraining its movement, and it whinnied and screamed as it struggled to free itself, at the same time grinding against Abraham, who was being crushed beneath it. Belle managed to grab onto a root on the far bank as she bobbed above and below the surface, taking in water and coughing. Gradually, while hanging on up to her neck in water, she managed to scan the surface, looking for signs of Abraham, but to no avail.

When she climbed up on the bank she continued to search for Abraham, her faithful servant, and not seeing him she feared the worst, seeing only the horse nearly totally submerged by this time.

No longer fearing for her own life, she was unable to stop herself from jumping back into the water and grabbing onto the horse's neck. With one hand hanging onto the bridle, her legs floating outward, she reached with her other hand and released the cinch that was holding the carriage in place. The current ripped the wooden craft away, sending it downstream where it crashed into a large rock protruding in the center of the river.

Belle let go the bridle and swam to the shore, watching as her horse was able to right itself onto four legs and onto the place where the trail crossed. She ran to the horse and took hold of its reins, attempting to calm it, checking its legs for any sign of injury. To her horror, she could see blood running down its front right ankle and the bone protruding through the skin. In normal circumstances, she would have taken it out of its misery with a bullet to the brain, but her musket was gone. She was left only with a knife attached to her belt.

Belle sat on a rock near the edge of the water, the rain continuing to downpour, debating with herself what to do about the horse. Having sufficiently agonized over the lousy options, she withdrew her blade from its sheath, walked to the injured animal and after finding the softest place in the back of its head plunged the knife in as quickly and deeply as she could. She had butchered farmyard animals this way before and death was usually instant. But the horse remained standing with the knife sticking out from the back of its head. She withdrew the instrument, found another critical spot behind its head and plunged it in a second time. It seemed as if this too had failed, and after waiting for nearly a minute she began to withdraw the blade as before when its front legs began to wobble, then buckle, collapse forward and then onto its side.

It was over, not the rain, of course. The horse could be replaced, but not Abraham. Belle walked back and forth several times looking for him, completely unaware of the continuous downpour, believing that his body had to appear somewhere, someplace. As she walked, she called out to God to help her find him. "I can't leave him here, Lord, I've got to find him, give him a proper burial. But as always, dear Lord, your will be done, not mine."

Without any success, she continued back across the river and then downstream toward Isaac's plantation. When she arrived at the rock where the carriage had crashed, a large part of it remained caught on some partially submerged rocks and a long overhanging tree branch with multiple branches and leaf clusters. She approached it slowly, thinking that she saw Abraham's head and shoulders hanging on to what was left of the broken carriage. What she was looking at was actually partially hidden by both the canvas top and the tree branch, but well enough above the water. She quickened her step and jumped into the water, hanging on to one of the limbs of the tree branch. Her heart began to pound faster and harder the closer she came to what looked like a man, a black man, a man hanging on to keep from being swept away. "Thank you, Jesus, thank you, Jesus, I think it's him! Is that you, Abraham? Oh, please, please be alive!"

Standing in water at her chest, she could tell that it was he – either unconscious or dead, it was too hard to tell. His one arm was hanging on through the spokes of a wheel and the weight of his body was perched onto the carriage platform. His head had been badly beaten against the rocks, and blood was still running from his forehead down the side of his wrinkled face. His eyes were closed, and when she started to pull his arm back out of the wagon wheel, he squirmed and she knew that there was still life in him. Once his arm was freed, she pulled him off the carriage platform into the water and dragged him by the back of his shirt to the shore while hanging on to the tree branch. While standing in the water, she managed to lift him onto the shore and then completely out of the water. On her knees Belle grasped his nostrils between her thumb and forefinger, opened his mouth with her other hand and blew her own life into him. After several breaths, he coughed up water from his lungs and began to breathe on his own. As much as Belle could tell, it was a miracle.

The rain stopped, the sun reappeared and Belle and Abraham remained on the bank of the river, thankful that his life had been spared. He was badly bruised and there was a good possibility that he had several broken bones, including an arm and some ribs. It was certain that he could not walk in either direction. Since there were no more horses at Isaac's cabin, Belle would have to walk on ahead to her plantation and send someone back with a wagon to pick him up. Overall, that didn't seem too bad at all!

"When we're on the march, we march single file, far enough apart so one shot can't go through two men." That was Sergeant Meyers' final instruction before heading out on patrol. It was also Robert Roger's rule number six.

Isaac and Richard Baker were in the middle of the queue snaking their way down the mountain to a spot where two trails crossed, a place where war parties often passed. It was late in the afternoon, and they hoped to arrive before dark in order to set up their ambush, to locate concealed upper ground positions with overlapping fields of fire, positions where they would not end up shooting at each other. Ohio Indians frequently attacked in the daylight but moved from place to place during the night. There was no certainty that anyone would pass by this location, but several ambushes had been sent out from both companies to strategic spots surrounding Baker's Fort.

Corporal John McElroy was in charge of the seven-man ambush. His low rank in no way was indicative of his talent, either as a soldier or as a leader. He had been a professional soldier for six years and had served with Washington at Great Meadows, but he had been busted several times for drunkenness and fighting, each time receiving promotion for service, only to lose his rank for off-duty shenanigans. He was tough and fearless and possessed the fighting skills that most commanders looked for. He was assigned to Fort Baker and Chaplin's Company from Fort Cumberland with hopes of quickly turning the Fort Baker recruits into Indian fighters.

After traveling on foot for about an hour, they arrived at a rocky knoll overlooking the ambush site. It provided several places among the large boulders from which to fire, each with an open firing plane. McElroy motioned for everyone to lay low and wait for him to size up the site.

He moved from rock to rock on both sides of the trail, viewing firsthand the perspective from each location, placing Isaac, Baker, himself and a fourth member of the squad on the upper side looking down onto the killing zone. The other three he positioned on the lower side of the trail, about ten yards apart to prevent any escape as well as providing firepower from that direction. Once everyone was in place, he sent Isaac and the fourth member off to observation points, one in each direction, with instructions to signal when anyone was coming and to return quickly to position.

It was usually best for the two observers to remain quietly in position; otherwise they may make too much noise and tip off the enemy. Additionally, they could stop any that were trying to escape. But this time their squad was so small that the unit needed all seven in the actual ambush. It was therefore important that the two observers be especially quiet in returning.

Isaac moved to his observation spot and found a comfortable place from which he could watch the trail. This was a good spot, he could see far off if anyone was coming, and he had a good view of Baker and McElroy when he had to signal. Later on there would be a full moon, they would still be visible to each other and they would be able to see well enough to get off accurate shots. The rule now was, "Let the enemy come till he's almost close enough to touch, and then let him have it and jump out and finish him up with your hatchet."

First, Isaac would need to signal the others, then run quietly to his firing position and wait for McElroy to start the attack. He checked his flintlocks to make sure they were ready to fire, then his hatchet to make sure he could grab it easily after firing the single ball from each of his two muskets, and then he sat back, leaning against a rock.

This was his first time on patrol, his first ambush, and the first time that he was about to kill a human being. It seemed certain to him that if the enemy entered the zone, he would be able to squeeze the trigger on each of his two firearms. That part he could do, he was sure of it, but jumping out with a hatchet...that part remained unsettled.

This section of Maryland (or perhaps it was Virginia) was much more mountainous than his plantation. He reached down to the ground, picked up a handful of soil and examined it, allowing the dirt to sift between his fingers, retaining the pebbles. He examined one of the stones closely and saw how it was somewhat a replica of the boulder that he was leaning against, only smaller – irregularly shaped, rounded edges, gray with black speckles. Funny, he thought, how he had never paid much attention to a stone up close. One of the pebbles was a dull red color, and then he noticed that there was a vein running in the boulder of a similar color. The stone seemed special, and he put it in his pocket and then remembered that he had to keep his eye on the trail. He then glanced over in the direction of McElroy to see if he was looking – he was, and he gave a nod.

He wasn't sure of McElroy's age – probably in his early twenties, a few years younger than Isaac. His features were sharp with muscular jaw and chin, pimples and brown-cropped hair. He rarely smiled, usually wearing a serious countenance. Isaac knew nothing of McElroy's personal life, only his reputation, and he wondered if he still had parents, had he ever been married, brothers and sisters, had he ever been laid? Isaac thought about how long he himself had lived so sheltered in the wilderness, just he and Ann, tending their farm, whereas this young kid could probably tell stories all night long.

Isaac looked to see if he could see Baker positioned on the other side of McElroy. No – he seemed to be hidden by some brush. He had seen him earlier from his attack position, but not now. Baker was young, too, and he had seen action, but he was no Corporal McElroy. He seemed a nice enough kid.

The time passed slowly. Evening finally crawled out from behind a boulder and sprayed mist about the killing zone and on the knoll. That place between daylight and night is a place of limbo, nothingness and uncertainty. Clear vision is put on hold for a moment.

A speckled deer walked along the trail, stopping occasionally to graze. Isaac put a bead on him and pretended to pull the trigger. At dusk, many animals in the wild come out only to disappear again, the colors of their bodies blending with their background. Something inexplicable takes hold of the hunter and keeps his bow from releasing its arrow, the boar, having eaten, is complacent. But the soldier never rests, is always either on the advance or on guard. If he isn't careful, he may stretch his imagination, see what isn't there and shoot wildly at nothing.

Isaac kept an eye on the trail, but he couldn't keep his mind from wandering. He wondered how long they would need to remain there. He realized that it would be fine with him if whomever it was that they were supposed to ambush failed to show up; McElroy, on the other hand, he was probably looking forward to making contact...Baker, now he was too hard to read, he could probably take it or leave it.

They each brought enough rations (jerky and bread) and water to last for a couple days, but that really made no difference; all around, there was plenty to eat. He had seen several rabbits in the short time they had been there.

"When we camp, half the party stays awake while the other half sleeps." (Rule #9) This wasn't camp, this was an ambuscade, and there would be no rest for anyone until daylight. Isaac was used to going to bed at dark and awaking at dawn, but not this night. At nearly midnight, the moon was shinning brightly; seventy degrees from the horizon to the zenith in the northern-eastern sky, and the knoll and trail were brightly illuminated in monochrome. His eyes had adjusted to the dark and his pupils were dilated to the size of two musket balls. He could see clearly in all directions – it was a perfect night to spring a surprise.

Red Hawk sat on the ground leaning against the eighteen-foot exterior stalls of Fort Frederick not far from the main gate. He had arrived several hours earlier and had expected to meet with Colonel Washington, but he had been turned away by the two guards in non-issued blue coat uniforms at the gate. It made no difference to them that he was on assignment for the Colonel to report on Indian movements in the area. When he presented the guards with his hand-written pass signed by Colonel Washington, one of them took it to the guardhouse for instructions. On returning, he told Red Hawk that the Colonel hadn't yet arrived from Fort Cumberland, and that he needed to wait outside.

Red Hawk was a very patient man, and he understood that the Colonel was a very important and busy person, and it didn't seem particularly strange that he would be late in arriving. However, his having to remain outside the wall didn't settle well with him. He had expected to be shown more respect than that for his position and accordingly, not to be so summarily brushed off. He had not only anticipated being invited in but to be fed and given a place to stay while there on government work.

Furthermore, he believed that he had the direct ear of the Colonel and didn't have to report through any chain of command or bureaucracy. This would soon be proven, he hoped, to be the case, but in the meantime, he was forced to remain outside until the following day when Washington finally arrived and inquired at the guardhouse if any of his scouts had reported in. Besides Red Hawk, there were two others, Queen Aliquippa of the Seneca, and Half-King, also known as Tanacharison, originally of the Catawba, and later the Seneca.

Queen Aliquippa could never be considered a scout although she provided a tremendous amount of intelligence and support. She had become good friends with a callow, twenty-one-year-old Major Washington in earlier times. She, unlike many of her contemporaries who sided alternately with whoever offered the best deal at the time, remained fiercely loyal to the British throughout her life.

While he was but a child, Half-King was taken captive by the French and later adopted into the Seneca tribe, one of the Six Nations of the Iroquois Confederacy. He claimed that the French boiled and ate his father. He had frequently accompanied Washington as a guide and as a 'spokesman' for the Ohio Indians. He traveled with Washington to meet with the French outpost at Fort Le Boeuf and accompanied him on an expedition to establish a fort at the strategic forks of the Ohio.

As Red Hawk looked around, he could see that the place bustled with people and activity, soldiers and civilians alike, much more so than the last time he was there. Outside the fort, there were two different grounds where training was taking place – target practice on the right and maneuvers on the left. The Virginia Militia hadn't adopted the Ranger's style of fighting and taught using traditional British rank and file warfare.

The fort seemed impenetrable, its exterior walls four feet thick at the base and narrowing to three feet at the top, extending

355 feet from bastion point to bastion point with at least three major buildings within the wall – two enlisted quarters and one officers' quarters or governor's house – all vastly superior to the wooden stockade at Fort Baker. The compound enclosed an unusually large area for a provincial fort. A single gateway located on the south curtain wall provided access to the interior. There were mounted eight or ten cannon, most of them 32-pounders, around a wooden platform or catwalk around the interior of the walls. In addition, there were earth embankments inside the fort. The majority of troops garrisoned there were provincial regulars from Maryland and Virginia, a force large enough to defend the fort but insufficient to patrol the surrounding settlements.

Off in the distance, on the trail leading to the front gate, Red Hawk could see a large rider arriving on a great white stallion. As the rider came nearer, he could see his white powdered wig beneath his tricorn, his crisp blue over-red overcoat, his waistcoat and black leather spurred riding boots that rose from his feet up to his knees. He was riding fast, slightly ahead of two other uniformed officers who looked equally impressive. Not far behind them followed the remaining members of their entourage. As they reached the gate, Governor Horatio Sharpe, the Royal Commander in Chief of all British Forces and commander of colonial forces for the protection of Virginia and adjoining Colonies stood there waiting to greet them. "Colonel Washington, how good it is to see you."

Isaac formed his lips and gave the signal – a bird song – similar to the black-crowned night heron, and then he looked over toward McElroy and nervously held up ten fingers. His heart was racing – they had come from his direction and he had spotted them. He could see them clearly, and they looked fearsome, savage, pagan, painted and primitive. Several carried ancient fowling pieces and tomahawks, whereas others carried only tomahawks. In the bright moonlight, he couldn't see the color of the paint on their faces, but the dark markings were there nonetheless. Those on foot moved quickly to keep up with the two mounted riders. McElroy turned toward Baker and the forth member, both of whom had heard the signal and gave a thumbs up. Isaac quickly and quietly resumed his firing position several feet from McElroy and waited for their quarry to file into the killing zone and for McElroy to fire the first volley, signaling the attack.

McElroy had done this before. He knew well not to start the attack prematurely. All seven held their positions, remaining low, hidden, each with the bead of their sights imprinted on a target, Isaac and the fourth member at each end, McElroy and Baker, ready to take out the middle.

Their enemy moved quickly yet it seemed to take forever for them to fill the zone. McElroy's gun had been primed and ready; he moved the striker from half-cock to full-cock. He could see that the zone was almost filled, and he took a breath and exhaled, checking his aim one final time. The electricity of excitement shot through his body as he squeezed the trigger, unconsciously knowing that this action would set in motion the melee that was to follow.

The trigger released the cock that held the flint that struck the frizzen, a piece of steel on the priming pan lid, opening it and exposing the priming powder. The contact between flint and frizzen produced a spark that was directed into the flashpan. The powder ignited, and the flame passed through a small hole in the barrel (called a vent, or touchhole) that led to the combustion chamber, igniting the main powder charge there; and the gun discharged. The flash and boom of exploding powder from both ends of the long barrel was seen and heard by all, team members and enemy, and three more triggers were instantly squeezed, generating a second volley, which was soon followed by the third wave originating from across the trail. By the time all fourteen rounds had been discharged, several Indians lay on the trail, one had disappeared into the opposite tree line, dashing between two of McElroy's men.

McElroy led the charge. Isaac remained and stood to reload, tearing a paper cartridge open with his teeth and pouring a small amount of powder into the flashpan. It took about fifteen seconds to finish the process, including ramming the ball all the way to the breech. He returned his ramrod and shouldered his weapon, placed it on full-cock, fired again and watched one of the savages that was about to sink a hatchet into McElroy's back fall onto the muddy path. Isaac continued to reload and fire as the others fought hand-to-hand, stepping closer each time until he was only inches away from the last remaining savage, firing directly into its bare chest. As the concussion pushed the pagan tribesman backwards onto his back, his red blood splattered onto Isaac's face, hand and overcoat; and then it was over.

While the others removed the scalps, Isaac rounded up the two Indian horses, and the detail moved out toward Baker's Fort taking a different route. (Rule: "Don't ever march home the same way. Take a different route so you won't be ambushed.") The dead bodies of the fallen Indians had been left where they fell, to be pecked, broken-up, tugged and chewed, ingested and digested by nature's cleanup crew.

Before he went after the horses, Isaac staggered week-kneed and wobbly to the side of the path where he vomited. He began to wonder, was this to be the only time that he would be called upon to perform such a horrible execution? As he and the others hurried toward the fort, he could hear only the sound of their feet rushing though the fallen pine needles, leaves and loonshit, the squish of feet in a soft, wet and muddy stream, panting as they sped up a steep incline. Occasionally, someone would trip over a root or a low-growing branch. He couldn't hear or feel his heart or pulse throbbing – he had become numb to his own feelings.

Governor Sharpe sat behind a round mahogany desk in the Governor's House at Fort Frederick. The building was new, having only been completed a few months earlier. Even though it had been built with some taste, having arched doors and windows, the décor and furnishings were still rather sparse. Anxious to get the meeting started he removed his spectacles, rose and walked to the front of his desk. "I would like to thank you all for attending this meeting, especially Queen Aliquippa and Half-King of the Seneca and Red Hawk, from the…the…"

"…the Cherokee," volunteered Captain Chaplin.

"Yes, of course, the Cherokee. In addition, I am proud to introduce Brigadier General John Forbes. The War Office has appointed General Forbes to command a combined provincial and Regular British expeditionary force. Next, we have with us the Commander of the Virginia Militia, surveyor and planter, Lieutenant Colonel George Washington. None has more experience with the land and firsthand knowledge of the conflict that exists between us and the French than this gentleman from Virginia, a bonhomme of impeccable reputation.

"And lastly, another gentleman, officer and planter, a member of the lower house of the Maryland Assembly and the present commander of the two musters at Baker's Fort, where so much of the recent troubles have been occurring, Captain Joseph Chaplin.

"I do not need to make any of you aware of the terror that looms throughout the settlements. Although we have not had any direct threat from the French forts in our region, notwithstanding the thrashing taken by General Braddock, I cannot help but believe that this escalation of Indian raids has been promoted and supported by General Francois-Marie Le Marchal de

Lignery at Fort Duquesne. Queen Aliquippa, what can you tell us about this?"

"First of all, I would like to tell you that I and my people have been continuous supporters of the British, even after General Braddock's refusal to follow my advice and wisdom. We have never flip-flopped back and forth as many of the other Mingo tribes have done accepting profit from the highest bidder, be it the French or the British. And secondly, I would like to acknowledge my friend Colonel Washington, who has always spoken to me straightforwardly and honestly, and it his friendship that is my reason for agreeing to attend this meeting."

Colonel Washington smiled and sent a nod of thanks to the Seneca chief.

Queen Aliquippa continued, "And last, my thoughts on the matter at hand. I believe that the defeat incurred by General Braddock was devastating, allowing the French to appear to be winning the great war between the French and the British. No one wants to be on the losing side. I believe that a major victory by the British, particularly the taking of Fort Duquesne, would cause many of the tribes in the area of the Alleghenies to rethink who they should be supporting."

"Thank you, Queen Aliquippa. Your thoughts and wisdom are greatly appreciated. Do you have anything else to add?"

"No, that is all I have to say."

"Then, Half-King, Chief Tanacharison; what say you?"

Half-King rose to speak. "I too would like to say good words of my friend, Colonel Washington. As you may know, the French were guilty of boiling my father and eating him, and I will never forgive them for that. I would agree with Queen Aliquippa that the French have been able to give the appearance of winning the war. I also believe that Fort Duquesne is presently understaffed and quite vulnerable to attack. The time to strike is now, not later after they have had time to rebuild."

Governor Sharpe then posed the question, "Do you think that General Forbes should use the old Nemacolin Indian trail that runs west, northerly from Fort Cumberland in Maryland as Braddock's army had done? There has been discussion that we should avoid that route and carve a new route farther to the north. I already know that Colonel Washington prefers to take the old road which passes through Virginia."

"I believe that you should move with great haste. Do not take the time to cut a new road. But you should not use traditional methods of troop movement; rather you should follow the style of Robert Rogers."

In spite of Washington's objections, Forbes decided to blaze a new trail to the west. He wanted to disassociate himself with his predecessor's disastrous campaign, and then he wanted a shorter route, one with fewer river crossings. Having learned from Braddock's mistakes, he planned to lay down a network of fortified supply depots along the route within easy reach of each other.

When it was Red Hawk's turn, he reported that a large body of troops, both Indians and French soldiers, with a number of wagons and a train of artillery were presently marching south along the Braddock Road toward Fort Cumberland. Colonel Washington had introduced Red Hawk as loyal and a valuable source of intelligence. His Cherokees would provide the expeditionary force with invaluable support in reconnaissance and guerrilla operations against the French and their own Indian allies.

More than a month had passed since Isaac had reported in for duty at Baker's Fort, fifty-eight-days to be exact. Red Hawk had arrived from Fort Frederick after having scouted out possible ways for the northern expedition to cut a road to Fort Duquesne. This new route would pass through Pennsylvania, not

Virginia, much to Washington's chagrin, after he had argued strongly against it, openly for military reasons and silently for commercial competitiveness. Actually, there was somewhat of a compromise; it would be made to look as if the main force would be following Braddock's road. Washington did not make an appearance at Baker's Fort as many had hoped and remained at Fort Frederick to prepare for the operation.

Isaac returned his musket and gear to the quartermaster. He picked up his horse at the stable. He said goodbye to his friend, Richard Baker, and to Corporal McElroy and Sergeant Meyers. As he was mounting his horse, he saw Red Hawk just outside the stockade gate. "Hey! Red Hawk, are you goin' or comin'?"

"I guess that depends; which is it with you?"

"I'm goin' home. Do you care to ride along?"

"Suits me fine, Isaac."

"Then let's get started; we can be home before sundown."

Captain Chaplin's muster was only the beginning. Several months later Isaac was called again, this time under Captain Elias Delaschmitt, and again during General Forbes' campaign against Fort Duquesne. With the capture of Fort Duquesne the threat to the Maryland frontier subsided. Baker's Fort continued to function less and less and it was ultimately abandoned. For a brief period in 1763, Governor Sharpe ordered the militia to Fort Frederick, and Baker's Fort was once again pressed into service to defend the backcountry inhabitants.

Several years later, right before the start of the War of the Revolution, Isaac got the urge to move farther west and sold his seventy acres back to Joseph Flint. It may have been that he had land coming to him from his service in the militia and, like many other frontiersmen of the time, he just couldn't sit still for long.

He settled on a four-hundred-acre parcel along Decker's Creek, a tributary of the Monongahela River, next to a larger thousand-acre parcel belonging to Zacheus Morgan. The story gets a little muddled but shortly after Isaac arrived, he went off to fight in Lord Dunmore's War. When he returned, Morgan wanted a portion of Isaac's parcel, took him to court over it, and won. Morgan began selling off lots and building the town which became known as Morgantown, Virginia.

Part III

Southampton, England, May 19, 1718

The old gentleman stood on the quay watching as his ship, *Brandywine*, pulled out from the harbor. It would be his last. He stood supporting himself with a cane, always immaculately dressed in the style of the day, and next to him was his Negro, Petrus, whom he had brought from the colonies nearly two decades earlier. He watched as the ship slipped below the horizon, and then the two climbed into his coach that was waiting to return them to his country manor. He signaled to the driver that they were ready by tapping with his cane on the window, and they were quickly on their way.

They rode through the narrow streets without speaking, quietly staring out the window, each to his own side, hearing only the sharp, metal clop-clopping sound of the horse's hoofs striking the cobblestone pavement. The old man seemed calmer than usual, appearing as if a burden had just been lifted from him. From time to time, he would turn his gaze toward Petrus and then back to the English wayside.

Petrus was sixty-five years of age, gray-haired and always neat and tidy. He usually wore a white blouse with a ruffled collar beneath a dark wool suit and today was no exception. He noticed something strange in the old man's face, a satisfied regard, something that he rarely exhibited.

About halfway home, the old man opened the door to a small liquor cabinet and withdrew a decanter of apple brandy and two small snifters, setting them on the inside of the door, which when opened became a small table. As soon as he uncorked the crystal stopper, the air at once became saturated with an indecently fruity smell – spicy, heady and extremely rich. The road had become bumpy, making it difficult to pour, causing the bottle to oscillate back and forth against the snifter and a small amount of the liquid to dribble onto the table. When both glasses were at the correct level, the old man set the decanter on the table, replacing the stopper, then handed the first glass to Petrus and took the second for himself. Petrus knew the ritual well and the two men gently began to swirl the brandy about, holding it to the light to check for its legs. Satisfied, they each buried their nose deep inside the snifter and inhaled.

As early as 1680, he had made many trips back and forth from England to Virginia, transporting his own English style brandy, and of course always a few passengers for which he would receive land credits at the Bank of London. On the return trip, he would fill his holds with Virginia tobacco and furs, often from as far away as the Ohio Territory. Over his lifetime, he had accumulated large land holdings in Prince George, York, Warwick and Isle of Wight Shires. He had apartment buildings in London from which he received rents, and he produced brandy from his fruit orchards in both England and Virginia. And from his seed came sons that would take their inheritance and cause it to multiply, become Virginia's privileged and daughters that would marry well, husbands that would become sheriffs, colonels and generals in the military, important politicians, and members of the Virginia House of Burgess.

The old man then raised his glass as if he were about to make a toast, attempted to clear his gravely throat and spoke. "This time tomorrow, Petrus, my faithful servant, you will be a free man."

Petrus thanked the man and told him that it was his pleasure to have served him. When they had finished their drinks, no more words were spoken. That evening, Thomas Haynes died.

William Haynes

W illiam Haynes was the last of ten brothers and sisters to be born. They lived together on the Isle of Wight, Virginia, on the family plantation left to them by their grandfather and enjoyed the advantages of having been born and raised into affluence, receiving an education reserved only for those children of families of high rank and a social life that included the gentility of Eastern Virginia society. By the time William was born, several of his brothers and sisters had already married and were in the early stages of building new families, some settling across the border into North Carolina. Sadly, though, his father developed tuberculosis and when William reached the age of twelve, his father died. William remained on the plantation with his mother and continued with his education until he was introduced to Catherine Baker, a daughter of another of Virginia's landed families and granddaughter to a member of the Virginia House of Burgess. A short time later, they were married.

His father's holdings had been enormous, owning thousands of acres in several locations throughout the neighboring shires, and several hundred Negroes, but when William's father died, he inherited only a lot and a small acreage of land in York along with three slaves named Samson, Jemmy and Salley. Only twelve at the time, he was the youngest of his ten brothers and sisters and was fortunate to have inherited anything at all. He acquired some of his grandfather's knack for making brandy and he was determined to turn some of his tobacco fields into peach and apple orchards. Much of the rootstock came from the northern province of Normandy, a place that was made famous for its apple brandy, or calvados as it was better known, and a place situated near the water's edge with its persistent fog.

Together, he and Samson set out the rootstocks in the moist soil that had become bankrupt of nutrients following years of overproduction of tobacco. Together they tended and husbanded each young plant using fish scraps from the nearby fisheries for fertilizer, and they watched the emerging young, green shoots turn into healthy tree trunks, then tree branches.

The first year that the peach trees began to bear fruit, he could see that it was going to be a small crop. The trees were still young, the amount of fruit was sparse, and William decided to remove all the young buds before they had a chance to mature, enabling the trees to place all their energy into tree development rather than fruit formation.

The following year the fruit production was enormous, more than he had anticipated, so great that he had to use props to keep the young branches from either dragging onto the ground from the weight or breaking off entirely. He feared that the two of them would not be able to harvest such a large crop by themselves. His fears were unwarranted. As the peaches were ready to be harvested, a large flock of black birds, crows they were, swooped in and in a matter of hours the fruit was destroyed.

At the onset, William and Samson tried running through the orchard shouting and clapping their hands, and when that did little to deter the onslaught, in rage William fired his Brown Betty into the air, still without success – the birds would fly off and then quickly return. When the birds had finally left, William saw that he could still recover a considerable amount of the fruit. Even though most all of it had been pecked and gouged it could still be mashed and pressed for making brandy.

James Baker Washington Haynes
1813

Sergant James Baker Washington Haynes' army bed was next to a window that overlooked the muddy shores of the James River. He struggled to maneuver himself around on top of the sheets to get a better view of the barracks across the river where his cavalry unit had been garrisoned three days earlier. It was one week following the summer solstice and a gray overcast ski hung above the wide river, rendering it impossible for him to make out any details on the other side. It was painful for him to make the slightest move, and he winced as a spurt of piercing torment shot through his lower leg, reminding him to remain inert. Annoyed with himself and his predicament he lay back, recumbent, his eyes looking up at the ceiling and he began to focus on a fly that had managed to find itself trapped in a spider's web, struggling to free itself. Off in the margins of the entanglement, the spider waited patiently for his victim to tire and give in to being trapped. He watched and wondered how long it would take before the spider left its position and claimed its quarry, just as he wondered how long he would have to remain trapped in his hospital bed.

There were several other men from his regiment in the ward, twelve to be exact, but Haynes was the only one from his company, at least as far as he could determine. There was one or two that he recognized from one of the other companies, but not well enough to know their names. It seemed as if everyone but he had a hand or a leg, chest, head or face wrapped with white cotton bandages. His broken leg had been set and fixed with a cast of white plaster of Paris that seemed to blend in nicely with the rest in the room, but for the lack of red bloodstains. He was thankful that he hadn't been shot or wounded. His injury wasn't quite like the others, but it was still serious enough, he thought, and he would have to remain in bed for some time. At least he still had all his body functions and he could see, smell, hear and taste.

The young soldier in the bed next to him moaned and groaned throughout the night, and the nurses continued to give him oral doses of morphine. However much he received, it never seemed to be enough to quell his discomfort. His company had walked into a British ambuscade, receiving fire from two six-pounders and a discharge of rockets. Large chunks of shrapnel had struck him in his face and chest. His column had been broken up, forced to retreat, and he was left behind. Fortunately though, he survived long enough alongside the road until a member of the cavalry made it by and found him.

This was day number three since the British had mounted their assault on the small village of Hampton, Virginia, and the town had been at the mercy of an enemy who showed no mercy and was immediately given up to plunder and outrage. Most agreed that the assault was a result of the severe tromping that the British had taken by the Americans days earlier at Craney Island.

Hampton had been a flourishing borough on the west side of Hampton Creek, two miles and a half from Old Point Comfort. It was the capital of Elizabeth City County and was defended by only four hundred and fifty soldiers under the command of Major Stapleton Crutchfield, mostly militia infantry, with a few artillerymen and cavalry. They were garrisoned on the 'Little England' estate southwest of town where they had a heavy battery composed of four six, two twelve, and one eighteen-pounder cannon to defend the waterfront of the camp and village.

The British force landed at dawn, with about twenty-five hundred troops, including several hundred *Chasseurs Britannique* – captured French who preferred service with the British to dismal months or years as prisoners of war. They landed behind a forested area near the house of Daniel Murphy, a little more than two miles from Hampton, and they moved rapidly toward the doomed town.

Admiral Cockburn of the Royal Navy remained at the other end of the peninsula, not far from the garrison, with a flotilla of armed boats and barges intended as a distraction from the real point of the attack. A patrol of Americans discovered the invading force and sent messengers to Major Crutchfield that the woods toward Murphy's were glowing with scarlet, and a grain field nearby was verdant with the green uniforms of the French. Most of the inhabitants of the village fled toward Yorktown, and there were those who couldn't leave or who were willing to trust to British honor and clemency.

Four months earlier, when he enlisted, James was eighteen years old and lived with his parents on their small plantation in Warwick, a few miles north of Hampton. He had volunteered at Hampton for six months as a private with Captain John B. Cooper's Cavalry Company. His father had served for several years in the Revolutionary War in Col. Lee's Legion as a dragoon, and James knew well the stories of how he had carried messages between Generals Washington and Lafayette. He had once been taken prisoner by the British and held for several weeks, but when he was released, they kept his horse, which he said cost him one hundred pounds.

"Colonel! How are you today?" James turned his head from watching the spider on the ceiling and saw a young girl about his age, maybe a year or two younger, standing next to his bed holding a pewter pitcher. She was quite pretty, petite and enthusiastic, wearing a nurse's uniform, starched white like everything else in the room, her hair tied up under her nurse's cap. As she stood next to the bed waiting for his response, she canted her head to one side and back and rolled her eyes. "How about a cup of cold apple juice, soldier...it's fresh, just been squeezed?"

Most of the women in the infirmary were much less

feminine, and he was unprepared to chance upon one so attractive and spirited.

With his left hand he pointed over his shoulder to the cup on the table, "Could you get it for me?"

"Why certainly, Colonel, I'd be glad to."

As she brushed by him to pick up his cup, he could detect her fragrance. However slight, it reminded him of spring lilacs and peach blossoms, and though he was scarcely able to move, he felt drawn to her redolence. Often in church on Sundays he could catch a similar bouquet on the fashionable women. She reached for the beaker and turned toward him. "So is it true you were thrown from your horse?"

"I guess you could say that." But for the surgeon, he didn't recall telling that to anyone there in the infirmary and was abashed by her mention of it. He wanted to ask her if she didn't mind telling him where she heard it, but he decided to let it go.

She could see right away that she had touched on a sensitive note and told him that she was sorry, that she should not have asked that, that she hadn't meant to embarrass him. "By the way, what's your name? Mine's Eliza Cooper."

Puzzled, James leaned forward and in her direction and asked if she were related to Captain Cooper. While she began pouring, she spilled a little of the juice on his bed and pulled a napkin from her apron pocket. Then she handed him the cup, "Yes, he's my brother, do you know him?"

"So, he's the one that told you."

"Well, if you aren't going to give me your name, I'll just go on calling you 'Colonel'. It suits you, except that you are a little young for that." She also thought that her brother probably wouldn't appreciate it.

"James, my name is James Haynes, Sergeant James Baker Washington Haynes."

Eliza was amused with his long name, and his formality, and

smiled. Shifting the pitcher to her other hand, she reached for his hand and began to shake it. "Sergeant JBW Haynes, how good it is to meet you!" The juice sloshed and a few more drops splashed onto the bed. As she firmly shook, the motion traveled to his leg, and James tightened his transverse abdominals hoping to stop the pain before it started.

"So tell me, Sergeant J, whatever the rest of it is, what really happened between you and that horse?"

Now, she was flirting and he knew it. He wondered if she were always like that or if just with him. She seemed so cool and confident that she must always be so, he thought. He began to speak to her of the British rockets, how they came from off the point, probably from the *Mohawk* and landed nearby. His horse was spooked, it reared, and he attempted to take control, but it stepped backwards onto a log and fell. He wanted to leap free, but one of his spurs caught on the stirrup, and he became trapped beneath his horse and the ground.

"That sounds horrible. How's the horse doing?"

"His leg was completely broken, and I had to shoot him."

"Oh, the poor dear."

Eliza then looked toward him warmly and lightly touched his forearm. James felt his insides jitter and wished that she would remain longer, so he suggested that she didn't need to stand. He wanted to ask her to sit next to him on the bed, but instead he asked her if she wouldn't mind pulling up a chair. He seemed very interesting to her, and she enjoyed being with him, but she had a job to do.

"Well, Colonel, I can't stay here all morning...there are lots of others waiting for apple juice, but I'll be back again to see you. Monday and Fridays are my days. So, you get lots of rest and get better and I'll see you in a few days. Goodbye, JBW."

James watched as she stepped to the next bed, the one with the patient that moaned and groaned all night. "Hey there soldier, how are you doing today? I've brought some apple juice; it's cold – just been squeezed. If you'd rather, I could get some water or tea?"

He didn't respond and she looked over at James and shrugged. She then poured some into his cup and went on to the next bed. He continued to watch her until she was gone, and then he couldn't stop thinking about her, her loveliness, her wit, and her brashness.

Now that she was gone, he had nothing to do but stare out at the river. He was certainly thankful to be near a window. A breath of fresh air occasionally made its way into the room, helping to dissolve the ubiquitous stench of infection, the strange odors emanating from the various dressings and medications, urine and loose bowels, bedpans that needed to be emptied, and the occasional farting that seemed to erupt from several of the patients. He tried to remember her fresh scent, but was he was unable to and then he put his cup near his nose hoping to detect her presence. All he could descry were the sweet remains of the apple juice.

He enjoyed looking out and watching the barges that continued to make their way up and down the river, in spite of all that had taken place. He wondered how many aboard those flat bateaux were even aware that a battle had taken place. He wondered if his father had heard anything about the battle. James was close to his father – he would probably come and visit if only he knew.

The empty barges headed upstream and returned downstream loaded with hogsheads filled with tobacco to be unloaded and reloaded onto ships bound for Europe. All the rivers connected to the Chesapeake Bay poured into it except for one, the Blackwater River, whose waters flowed south into North Carolina. His grandfather had owned land on the south side of the Blackwater River, which was at one time Indian land

and was off limits to whites.

Much of the Revolutionary War had been fought in the south, where General Nathaniel Green, arguably the war's greatest strategist, successfully waged a war of attrition against the Crown forces, keeping General Cornwallis occupied. During that period, the American economy had come to a grinding halt, yet the war had to be paid for and it was the sheriff's responsibility to collect the taxes. For several years, Lawrence Baker was Sheriff of Warwick County, during the first year following the end of the war, most Virginians were feeling quite patriotic, and the sheriff was able to collect a considerable amount that was due. However, as the years followed, the economy was slow to reestablish itself and many were either unable or less willing to pay their taxes. The government's mounting debt became the focus of attention, and it soon became apparent that taxes from Warwick County had not been paid.

This wouldn't have been important except that William Haynes had been married to Catherine Baker, Sheriff Baker's aunt. The sheriff had become the subject of investigation as to the disappearance of the taxes – Catherine and her son, William, were called to testify. The Baker family was a well-respected, landed family, as were the Haynes, which only added to the attraction of the public's attention. Sheriff Baker's defalcation of the tax dollars, his ultimate defense of insanity, and the testimony of his in-laws had created a scandal from which neither family was able to quickly recover. Much of Sheriff Baker's inheritance was gone forever, and Catherine was forced to sell off many of her slaves and much of her land in order to repay the taxes that had previously been paid. The glory days of the Haynes family were over. Out of respect and love for his mother, William added her name to his, thereafter becoming known as William Baker Haynes.

Eliza would come around regularly, just as she said, and

James eagerly waited each day for her return. When she arrived, she often brought him things that she didn't bring to any of the others – a book, paper, ink and quills – and she would take a chair next to his bed.

One afternoon he drew upon his reservoir of courage, took her hand and held it as if they were sweethearts. Her jaunty and somewhat casual demeanor quickly turned pensive. Slowly he could see her look of approval, her fondness for him, and her desire not to let go but to express her warm feelings for him by returning his gesticulation. For a brief period they remained silent, as if this was a new experience for both, a moment to savor certain feelings of ardor, and at the same time to deliberate on what to do next. Then as if she had been struck by lightning, she released her hand from his, jumped from her chair, said that she was late and had to leave and rushed out the door.

James didn't know what to make of it; but when she returned on her next regularly scheduled visit, she went directly to his bedside without stopping at any of the others in the room.

He beamed with delight at seeing her, and she pulled the chair as close as she could to his bed. She was excited and said that she had some excellent news, but that he would have to promise not to let anyone know that she had told him. She had overheard her brother, Captain Cooper, talking to Major Crutchfield in the parlor at her family plantation house, and she heard them discussing about submitting James' name for commission as lieutenant. "I know I shouldn't be telling you this," she admitted, "but I was just so excited that I had to tell someone."

James was slow to respond. It made no sense to him. Why would Captain Cooper put his name in for a commission knowing that he was about to be discharged in a little more than a month?

Eliza could see the skepticism bleeding from his hairline,

oozing down the front and sides of his face like legs on a glass of pinot noir, and she wished that she hadn't told him. "I guess that he sees you as a natural leader and thinks that you will reenlist. He got the sense that you do not want to be a farmer. He said that your fall from the horse is only a minor setback, that you could command your own regiment someday."

"I really don't think that's going to happen, Eliza. He's right about my not wanting to farm, but I suspect that I will soon arrive at the end of my military career. I do admit that I like the idea of the commission, though. But I think that I prefer being Colonel Haynes to Lieutenant Haynes."

"Well then, what do you have on your mind?" she inquired.

Growing up in Isle of Wight, York and then Warwick Shires must not have been a pleasant experience for young JBW. Furthermore, his experience of prejudice directed toward him and his family had created fertile ground for his distaste of slavery, and he was less inclined to continue the family plantation tradition.

"My mother has relatives in the Ohio Territory, a place called Licking County – it's a conclave of Welsh immigrants. I thought I might like some time to check it out, maybe move there. I enjoy reading the law and I like to argue. I think that I could be a good lawyer. Moreover, I like the idea of an adventure. Yes, I think that I could have all that there in Licking County. Have you ever thought about what you're going to do with your life?"

"I guess I never thought about it much. I should get married, have kids, you know the routine. I like doing this, though; it makes me feel good to do something for others. Good things always come out of doing good things for others; that's how I met you, you know. And no one can ever take away the good that someone has done for another. I especially like that. No one had to tell me that; I figured it out for myself. I think sometimes those are the best ideas, those that come to me without someone telling me what's so. I think that you are like that too, you figure things out for yourself, don't you?"

"How so?"

"Well, for example, when I told you about the commission, you weren't ready to jump to conclusions as fast as I was. You had to stop and figure it out. You like to think about things."

"I suppose I do. Sometimes it's a curse, though; it cuts into one's spontaneity. I often wish I were more like my brother Willy, who reacts in an instant. If you say 'let's go', he says 'yeah, let's go'. He doesn't even ask 'where to?' He really enjoys life, even though his enjoyment of it may be a bit muddled, or at least superficial."

"So where's your brother now?"

"I don't know exactly. He joined the navy the same time I signed up with the Dragoons. I think that he's busy patrolling the waters all the way from Canada down to New Orleans."

James had never been with a woman, and he was ripe with desire. Each time that Eliza left, he felt more alone than if she had not come, and he wished that he could get out of bed, even if he had to remain in a wheelchair. He wanted to be alone with her out of the sight of the others in the room, but his doctor was adamant about his not leaving the bed, not even to go to the latrine. If he could be wheeled around in a wheelchair, she could take him out to the garden. There he could speak more freely to her about his feelings and she could respond. Perhaps they might be able to touch each other – oh how much he wished he could hold her and make love to her.

Deputy Sheriff Charles Moore arrived at the beginning of the lane of the Haynes Plantation shortly before noon. He and James were both the same age and had been friends in school.

He knew William and Mary about as well as any in Warwick County, so when the news reached the sheriff's office he volunteered to ride out to let them know that their son was laid up at James Infirmary in Hampton. It wasn't an especially long ride, but it was a hot day and by the time he arrived he was drenched in perspiration and his black-spotted brown mare had ripples of white lather clinging to its sides.

William was away from the house working in one of the fields, along with Hopton, and Mary was sitting on the front porch in a rocking chair reading Susanna Rowson's popular novel, *Charlotte Temple*. William's mother, now eighty-five, was napping in a second rocker next to Mary while the Negro Hanna sat in the third rocker nursing their youngest son, Thomas, who had just turned two years old. The three sisters, Kitty, Mary and Diane were also outside, but in the back of the house playing.

Deputy Moore was quite a bit taller than James and he never seemed to stand up straight, which made it easy for Mary, peering over the top of her spectacles, to recognize him as he rode slowly up the lane, considerably slouched in the saddle. She thought it strange to be seeing him since he knew that James was away, and she had no idea what sort of official business he could be calling on.

Once he arrived halfway to the house, one of Mary's coon dogs ran out to greet him, barking continuously until Deputy Charles dismounted and began to pat him on the head and massage the sides of his jowls. Mary hadn't yelled at the dog for fear of disturbing Thomas, who had at last fallen asleep.

Hanna pressed her thumb between Thomas' mouth and her long heavy breast, which hung almost to her waist, breaking the suction around her nipple and causing a soaking up sound. She buttoned up the front of her homemade cotton dress and took him into the house to his bed as Mary rose from her chair and walked to the edge of the porch to greet her guest.

Deputy Moore had very few details and his slim report left much to her imagination, which contributed to her hasty conclusion that James had been wounded in battle. Mary quickly instructed Salley to run to the field to fetch William, a man now of some fifty-three years of age, who sauntered back with young Hopton and the Negro woman, who herself was now approaching sixty. Salley's discrepant report to William was even more off base and confusing, leaving him with the false impression that his son was dying in the infirmary at Hampton until he was corrected by the Deputy, who was sure that James was going to be all right.

The notion that they might be losing their oldest son was very distressing to both William and Mary, restoring sad memories of their having lost two daughters, Anna at age two, and Diana having almost reached her first year, and then Anthony at age seven months when a chimneypiece had fallen on him. As the two of them pressed Charles for more information that he did not have, Grandma Baker awakened from her nap and began to listen intently.

"Will, what's going on?" Her voice, weak from age, cracked as she stretched her neck forward, making an effort to refocus her watery eyes. "Is something wrong?" She leaned forward placing her hands onto the arms of her chair as if she were going to try and stand.

William turned toward her and replied with an air of confidence, "Everything's all right, Mother. James is in the infirmary at Hampton, but Charles says that he's sure that he's going to be all right." Turning back toward Charles, William invited him onto the porch for a glass of water, which he promptly accepted.

"Did you say that he was going to be all right?"

"Yes, Mother. Charles is sure of it. Salley, would you see to the glass of water for the deputy?"

"Yes, Mr. Haynes. It won't take me but a minute or two."

"Thank you, Salley."

"Did you say it was Jimmy or Willy?"

"It's Jimmy, Mother. We know that he is in the infirmary, but we really don't know exactly what has happened to him. The British attacked Hampton, and Jimmy's Dragoons were involved in holding them off. Mary and I will go to Hampton to see him, and then we will know exactly what happened. Mother, why don't you say hello to Charles? You remember him, he used to come over and play with Jimmy. He's the deputy sheriff now."

The next day, another of their Negroes, Jemmy, who was also now up in years with gray hair, drove Will, Mary, Thomas and Hanna to the James River, where they took a boat to Hampton, arriving before noon. From the river port, they walked to the infirmary, and when they entered the leeway they immediately saw James on his bed near the window, where he sat propped up busy writing on a small wooden secretary across his lap that held a small bottle of ink, a supply of quills, paper and a pounce pot. His hair was closely cropped, which was unusual as he usually wore it much longer, and his face and arms were still bronze from spending so much time in the outdoors. When he spotted his parents and his youngest brother, Thomas, walking toward him, he reached for his shirt lying on the bed next to him and put it on, leaving it unbuttoned.

His mother and father were an impressive looking couple as they entered the ward and walked past the two rows of bedridden patients. Thomas, who was only two, wore a pudding cap and held Hanna's hand as he walked clumsily but proudly alongside them. Mary was fashionably dressed with a split skirt revealing a second skirt beneath made full with several petticoats. She was obviously wearing a corset as evidenced by her thin waist and wide hips. She had doused her wig with flour before departing the plantation and used white powder on her face and rouge on her cheeks. William on the other hand was much more subdued, wearing a brown wig and a dark coat over his waistcoat and breeches; still, he walked with a cane, not because he needed it but rather a cane was a very well known and common accessory of men.

As they approached, William, Mary and James began to experience a feeling of elation, and unrestrained warm-hearted smiles appeared on each of their faces. Mary kissed her bedfast son on both cheeks then took his hand into hers as she briefly admired his handsome visage. She loved all her sons and daughters, but James was her first, and she felt a special closeness toward him. As her back began to tire from leaning over she stepped away and William quickly took her place.

James and his father shook hands enthusiastically while speaking to each other of how good it was to be together again. Hanna lifted Thomas to the bed, and James greeted his youngest brother with the same intensity and joyfulness that he had for each of his parents.

Growing up, James had never given his parents any serious problems. His teachers repeatedly praised him for his special qualities and gave his mother and father credit for having done an outstanding job as parents. They believed that they hadn't done anything differently in raising their other children, that they had been blessed by having been given one so exemplar.

Willy, on the other hand, had been a source of continuous difficulties and they couldn't understand how the two boys could be such opposites. He had nevertheless made it into the navy, and since then there had been no reports of any further grievances. William always felt especially close to Willy, even through the troublesome times, as if God had given Willy to him knowing that he needed an extra amount of love and understanding.

Both Hanna and Thomas were anxious to nurse. It had been some time now, and Thomas' stomach was growling. She took him by the hand and walked toward a door that she had noticed on the way in leading to a garden. His little legs seemed to move sluggishly along the oak-planked floor with his nightshirt nearly covering his slippers. Once they arrived, Hanna spotted a small fenced-in area where there was a bench, and she took a seat. Thomas grabbed her dress and helped pull himself into place on her lap. She began lactating before he was able to put his mouth to her, leaving a large wet spot on her dress, and she used her small blanket to wipe the spot before covering herself with it.

Shortly after Hanna had given birth to her first-born child, her husband and baby had both died of fever. She was necessarily distraught and roamed about the plantation moaning and crying out, "Who will have my baby's milk?" This was about the same time that William and Mary had their first child, Anna Katherine.

Wet nurses were common for children of all social ranks in the southern United States during the 19th century. When Mary learned that Hanna was lactating, she was brought to the house to nurse Anna, and after that she continued with Diana, their second child. When both girls died during their infant years William and Mary began to question if their deaths were caused by Hanna's milk. When James was born, Mary decided that she would nurse her own baby, only to learn that she was unable to produce a sufficient amount of milk and Hanna was once again brought into the house. From then on, Hanna would nurse all of their babies.

Once settled, Hanna began to relax, and she concentrated on enjoying being alone with the young boy as he drew from her. He lay quietly in her arms, eyes closed, his small hands massaging her breast gently, sometimes scratching her with his tiny soft fingernails, eventually rotating to the other side, looking up occasionally, large eyes opened widely, then closed again, sometimes wiggling, sometimes still. When he was finished, he pulled away on his own and did an additional swallow as if trying to catch his breath, then came the hiccups.

Mary had worked up a sweat, and she could tell that her make-up was running. She would have to excuse herself at once to repair it. When she returned to the ward, she could see her husband sitting in the chair that was, unbeknownst to her, frequently occupied by Eliza. The two men were laughing riotously, and when she drew close enough she could see that James' face was red from blushing, and there was wetness in his eyes that had come from laughing so hard. They suddenly became quiet and Will quickly rose and held the chair from behind, expecting Mary to take the seat.

Remaining standing she remarked, "I see that the two of you are getting along quite well. Well, what's so funny? Can't you let Hanna and me in on the humor?"

"I'm sorry, Mary, we were not making fun of you, we were merely relating to the first time that James had ever tried to butcher a pig, and he ended up in the mud."

Before returning to the plantation, William met with the surgeon, who explained that James would need to remain off the leg for several more months, preferably in bed. His leg had been badly crushed, and even though he had been given a cast, there was no way to brace it adequately. James' six-month commitment was about to expire, and William would need to take him home.

That evening, after his mother and father had left, Captain Cooper arrived at the infirmary to try to convince James to reenlist. He had submitted a request to Richmond that James be granted a commission as a lieutenant, hoping that he would return to the Dragoons as soon as his leg had healed. He also wanted to tell James that Major Cooper, his father, would like very much to speak with him as Eliza had expressed an interest in being courted.

James was delighted to hear this, but in the days that followed she made no more appearances at the infirmary, and he remained puzzled, unable to reconcile the irony. With so much time and little else to occupy him, he tirelessly repeated to himself possible explanations. Settling on the logical version that all was well, and that she just had other pressing matters, he began to write to her. First, he expressed his love for her. When he reread his prose and considered what he had written, he realized that he had been too carried away with his thoughts, that that sort of *billet doux* was too premature in their relationship. The next letter was about the silly goings on in the ward, and that failed to pass his merciless scrutiny as being dull, flavorless and uninspiring. He tried his hand at poetry with moderate success, and he attempted to make a sketch of her from memory, soon reminded that his better pen and quill drawings were either landscapes or architectural renderings.

At last, his father returned to the infirmary along with Hopton sitting atop a tobacco wagon into which he, Hopton and Samson had loaded James' bed from home. Even though it would have been easier to remove them, the headboard and footboard remained attached, as were the sheets, pillows and comforter. It appeared as if Salley had just finished making it in preparation for Prince Jimmy's return home.

James was placed onto a stretcher, carried out into the leeway to an exit opposite the garden door, and out to the veranda where Hopton sat waiting on the wagon seat, holding the reins.

Before leaving the ward, James had said goodbye to the friends that he had made there and thanked the medics and other medical staff for all the care that they had shown him. A total of seven weeks had passed since that day when his horse had stumbled and taken its fall.

Just as the two men began lifting the stretcher to the end of the wagon, not too far off, a woman's voice could be heard over the clop-clopping clamor of a carriage racing onto the hospital grounds, "Colonel...Colonel Haynes...Colonel JBW Haynes... wait! Don't leave, just yet."

William, Hopton and Samson all turned in the direction of the shouting and saw a young woman hanging out the side of her carriage as her Negro driver sped toward them, leaving a trail of dust behind them. "What the...?" uttered Hopton. "Who's Colonel Haynes?"

She was hanging on with her right arm and waving a handkerchief with her left hand, her blond curls trailing in the breeze. "Yoo-hoo! JBW, don't leave, please wait."

William heard what sounded like her shouting one of their names, but he couldn't be sure, and he looked down at James, who by then had crooked his neck to get a better look. "I think she's calling you, son. Any idea who she is?"

"Yes, Dad...I know her. She's a friend...sort of."

"Well, she seems rather intent on seeing you before you leave. You say she's just a friend?"

"You remember Captain Cooper, my CO? She's his kid sister...was always coming around the infirmary serving apple juice, you know? Didn't they have any *sunshine girls* around when you were in?"

"No, I don't believe they did. Then I was never in the infirmary."

All four men watched as her carriage pulled alongside their wagon. James had propped himself up with his two hands gripping the gunnels behind him. William and Hopton's arms were beginning to fatigue, holding on and balancing the stretcher with all of James' 145 pounds, and they tried to decide whether to set him on the ground or lift him on up to Samson, who was standing by ready to receive the one end.

As the carriage came to a complete stop, Eliza stood on the step, holding on to one of the metal poles that were holding up the carriage top. "Well I declare, JBW, I get the feeling that you were about to rush off without saying goodbye."

Still holding on, both William and Hopton began to feel trapped.

"I wasn't able; you stopped coming by."

"My brother told me you were leaving, I came as fast as I could."

Somewhat discomfited, William blurted in, "I hate to interrupt, but, James, do you want us to set you down or put you up into the bed? Our arms are getting tired."

"Sure, Father, I'm sorry, please put me down. And, oh, father, I would like for you to meet Miss Eliza Cooper, Captain John Cooper's sister. She helps out at the infirmary."

"Pleased to meet you, Miss Cooper."

"Eliza, this is my father, Mr. William Baker Haynes, plantation owner, father of ten and the most important man in my life."

"*Enchanté*, Mr. Haynes. James has often told me about you."

"And, Eliza, this is my kid brother, Hopton. He's the brains in the family. I think that he may become president someday."

Hopton smiled and tipped his hat. "Good morning, Miss Cooper, I'm pleased to meet you."

James asked if they could be left alone for a while, so William and Hopton moved him to a nearby, shaded bench on the lawn and then went looking for a place where they might find a bite to eat.

When they returned, James and Eliza were laughing, but inside they were both feeling dolesome. She had explained that she had been sick, but now she was feeling better. She didn't want him to leave without their saying goodbye. They agreed to write to each other, and he promised that once his leg was strong, he would contact her father for his permission to call on her. When William and Hopton lifted him to the wagon, James reached into his duffle bag, pulled out the letters that he had written but never mailed and handed them to her. They continued to exchange letters and then one day the letters stopped. She had developed tuberculosis and could no longer write. By the time he received her final note, she had passed away.

The months crawled by slowly as James waited for his leg to mend. Being with family, it offered little to offset the unhappiness that he felt for having lost Eliza. It wasn't that his parents weren't kind, loving and supportive, but they had their own load of making ends meet and taking care of his younger brothers and sisters. He became quarrelsome and argumentative; staying out late at night and sleeping-in while the rest of the family grudgingly pulled his share of the work. He struggled to discover what he wanted to do with his life, knowing only that he was sure that he did not want to remain on the plantation – he wanted nothing more to do with raising tobacco or owning slaves. Returning to the military seemed the most logical thing for him. Entering the university and studying engineering or even law seemed gainful and gratifying, but there was the question of money and the immediate Haynes family could no longer support such a venture. There were relatives farther south in Georgia and the Carolinas, the Eatons and the Joneses; they were still quite well off. Dare he go to them with some proposition?

One warm spring day he wondered off on horseback from the plantation, through the forest following on old Indian trail, a path unfamiliar to him, one that seemed rarely traveled. The path was narrow and somewhat overgrown in places with sporadic rocks and fallen logs, so he necessarily rode slowly. In places, the ground was soft and spongy with layers of fallen leaves and vegetation that had built up over the years. It was a peaceful ride and for the first time in weeks, he began to notice that he was undisturbed, almost sanguine.

When he had ridden for most of an hour, which was the customary amount of time that he would spend whenever he went ridding, he felt no compulsion to return home, rather he felt drawn forward. James was always a very rational person, even in his childhood, rarely frivolous; however, on this morning he began experiencing certain lightness, a weightlessness that he shared with his horse. Together they seemed to glide over the cushiony trail without effort, increasing in speed, without brushing against tree branches extending out onto their path. Faster and faster, they rode and there appeared ghostly images of other riders off the path on each flank, keeping pace with him passing through the thick forest without harm. At first, they seemed to be racing against him, but then he could tell that they maintained a constant pace, never falling behind or pulling ahead.

His horse splashed through a small stream onto the other side, then climbed up a steep hill when he suddenly realized that they were no longer on the trail but in the middle of a beech grove. He brought his horse to a halt, and then without dismounting he looked around. The lower boughs of each tree were still decked with the crisp, dead leaves of the previous year, reflecting the late morning sun-gleam from their surfaces of polished copper. He could hear the sounds of the ill-lighted forest – the rustling of leaves, the swaying and creaking of the trees, the babbling of the stream below, the footsteps of a rabbit, the soft flutter of a blackbird, the various sounds of a multitude of insects, all sounds that were familiar to him but this morning much crisper and vibrant. The riders were gone but his buoyancy persisted.

He felt a rush of sweet smelling air brush past his face. To his left, back towards the sunny stream, he saw a small gust of wind spinning about the ground among the trees. He thought that he saw the image of a young Indian girl in the center of the tourbillion, but then again he thought that it might have only been his imagination. A great owl gave a hoot from a high branch, swooped down near the front of his horse, landed on a lower tree in the same direction that the whirlwind had spun its way down the hill and pointed with an outstretched wing toward the stream. James dismounted and walked his horse closer to get a better view. Seeing nothing, the two continued down to the water to drink. James knelt by the stream's edge, and as he raised his cupped hands to his mouth he saw not only his reflection but also that of the Indian girl.

She stood about fifteen feet to his rear, several inches shorter than James' five-foot-five-inch stature, barefooted, fully clothed in a beaded, tan buckskin shirt, laced on both sides and short breeches revealing muscular arms and legs. Her coal black hair, unevenly parted on top of her head, hung down her back and front, uncombed, nearly to her waist.

The late morning sun glowed white like two mirrors in her large oval eyes burning brightly from her small round face equally as bright as the reflection from the buttons on his knee-length coat and the buckles on his shoes. She seemed young, like James, but her weathered skin made it difficult for him to be sure – perhaps she was a little older. She stood erect, arms by her sides, unmoved by James' sudden rise to his feet and quick about-face, and after they stared at each other for several unmeasured moments, she walked toward the water and stooped to drink.

He had no idea what to make of her and the mysterious

series of events leading up to her appearance. He wasn't sure if she were real or another illusion, as he seemed prone to creating that day. He knew of no tribes this near to home and wondered from where she had come.

Like a lioness, she drank long and slowly, scooping up the clear liquid with only one paw, paying no attention to the ends of her mane slipping from her shoulders into the water. Occasionally she would look back at him to see if he were still there. Each time she looked back, he felt a rush of warmth surging throughout his chest.

He started to remount his horse and then hesitated as she began washing her face. She lifted her shirt to her neck and shoulders without removing it and splashed water on her breasts, stomach and lower back, places he had never seen on a woman, not even of his mother or sisters. As he became aware of his excitement and embarrassment, he turned slightly, still peeking at her from the corners of his eyes until she finished and lowered her shirt.

Again he started to mount, and seeing him, she moved quickly, taking his hand and pulling him in the direction of the tree line. She motioned for him to tie his horse and follow her back up the hill, and he cooperated out of curiosity.

Continuing to hold his hand, she gently pulled him up the hillside. Beneath his blue and white top coat, his beige waistcoat, and his gray wool undershirt, he could feel his perspiration running down his chest, across his stomach, partitioned into lateral directions along his waistline, where it became absorbed into the lining of his knee length breeches.

At the top, she led him through the grove until she came to a hollowed out beech stump swarming with bees. She released his hand and motioned for him to wait as she took small steps toward the hive while chanting softly, almost reverently. Closer and closer she made her way to the honey-filled opening until she was completely enveloped by the yellow drones, buzzing about her, none of which seemed to be seriously disturbed, at least to the point of attacking her. Very slowly, she reached in with her right hand as many of the bees began to cover her arm. Slowly she sank her fingers deep into the paraffin until her palm was completely submerged, forming a cup with her fingers and pulling out a dripping mass of comb and honey.

James had never seen anyone as bold as this small one, who walked fearlessly among the bees unprotected and suffering no stings. As she turned away from the stump to return to him, the bees all flew from her arms and face back to their place at the hive. She then made a bed of watercress, which she found growing near the stream, and she placed the comb onto it, motioning for James to sit with her and eat. Never had he tasted honey so sweet; the aroma of clover and lilac filling the air, peach and apple blossoms, cinnamon and rhubarb, jam and toast. Then, as if he had been enveloped with some uncanny mist, he became drowsy and slipped into a deep sleep, finding himself aboard a flat-bottomed riverboat, much like those that he had seen at Hampton from the infirmary window. The boat was returning from Port Tobacco, Maryland filled with hogsheads of tobacco that were transferred to ships bound for Europe. He saw himself, a sailor, on the Chesapeake to the Potomac, Braddock's Road to Pittsburgh, a flatboat on the Ohio, *The Scioto*, *The Darby*, and the rich woods of the Ohio Territory…

When he awoke, she was gone. He wasn't sure that she ever existed, that he had been on a ride, had become tired, stopped to rest, fallen asleep and dreamed this transcendental dream that made no sense to him except that the remains of the honeycomb gave witness to the reality of the event, at least part of it.

He arose from the dry sandy part of the streambed where she had earlier placed the watercress, where he had sucked on her honey-laded fingers, pressed his lips to one of her breasts and had made love to her, all if only in his mind.

It was nearly sundown, and he had to look around the place to find his shoes with buckles that earlier in the day had reflected the light like her eyes, his coat, which he could only remember having placed in the fork of one of the beeches, his tricorn, which he had tossed, and his horse, who waited patiently. Even before the sun had a chance to bury itself among the trees, the forest had become quite somber.

James was fortunate that his dark brown equine was able to find the trail to lead them back to the place that he would no longer be able to call home. Early the next morning, he packed a few provisions in a cotton bag, said goodbye to his mother and father, brothers and sisters and the three Negroes and left Warwick County, taking his horse with him, never to return but to visit.

James was on his own with very little money. Unable to find work in either Williamsburg or Yorktown, he moved on to Leesburg, in Loudoun County, where he was able to earn room and board working in a creamery owned by John Hamilton.

John lived alone upstairs over the creamery and offered James a Lilliputian amount of spending money plus meals and this small room – eight-feet by ten, room enough for a small bed and a writing desk – as wages. John's barren wife, Hattie, had helped John in the business; however, she had succumbed to pneumonia during the last winter and died. Until recently, money had been scarce for practically everyone, tobacco being the predominate form of currency. Whenever possible, services or commodities were traded or bartered.

His room was located at the rear of the apartment, off the kitchen and overlooking a small barn, which gave shelter to a horse, a few chickens and a pig, all belonging to John, and where James kept his horse. The bed was quite small, even for James' small frame. It stood high off the floor, and it was covered with a heavy wool blanket and a handmade cream-colored quilt with red star patterns. There was no fireplace, and during the cold winter months he would have to rely on heat circulating from the kitchen where John would keep wood burning in the stove. The writing desk was actually a school desk that John had bought at an auction several years earlier when the public school was being remodeled. It had a slanted desktop which opened on a hinge to reveal a place for storing paper, quills and ink. The top bore the crude carving of a prior student's initials, JBH + HRT, encased in an arrowed heart, creating incessant curiosity for James.

The business of the creamery was to receive milk from the local farmers and then produce various grades of cream and milk, as well as yogurts and cheeses. It was also a retail outlet for eggs. It was one of the oldest businesses in Leesburg, actually having been first established when the town was called George Town, named after King George II, and passed on through the generations of the Hamilton family. Because of the second war with Britain, the state capital had been temporarily moved to Leesburg along with many government documents and records such as the original Constitution and the Declaration of Independence. Government workers and bureaucrats followed, all needing places to live, and most without goats or cows. The demand for dairy products increased beyond John's ability to operate the store alone. Until James could be trained, John had to do most of the backroom work, including that of separating the cream. James remained in the front taking care of customers and filling their buckets with milk. When John discovered that James was educated, he had him take care of the accounts, both the receipts as well as managing the expenses. After six months, James was able to receive extra salary – enough that he was able to sign up for night classes at the newly opened Franklin Law

School.

Opened for three months, with its small staff of only one professor, that being Phineas W. Floyd, the school proprietor, and with an initial course offering of three beginning classes on Legal Case Analysis, Contracts and Torts, the Franklin Law School was hardly to be compared to the better known one in Williamsburg. Nevertheless, with its evening class offerings, low tuition and no apparent undergraduate requirements except for a nod from Professor Floyd, it seemed to JBW that there was nothing to lose. Therefore, he and four other applicants became the first class of 1817.

The classes were held in Professor Floyd's living room where he lived in an upscale townhouse, two blocks away from the creamery on Cornwall Street, with his wife Flora, his daughter Susan and his two sons, Charles and Richard. Each evening, following his lecture, Flora would serve cider, tea, pikelets and crumpets, and in a short amount of time Phineas, Flora and the classmates became an amicable bunch. The rest of his kindred remained unseen and unheard and Phineas made no mention of them.

John Hamilton had no qualms about the night classes so long as it did not interfere with JBW's performance during the daytime; and surprisingly he eventually came to tolerate his reading case law, even while at work between customers. JBW preferred not to hang around long after class with the others since that was his only remaining time to prepare for lessons the following day. In order not to appear antisocial, he would usually have a cookie and a quick sip of cider, excuse himself and then return to his room, where he would tackle the day's homework. (Sometimes it seemed to him that the most expensive part of being a student was what he had to pay for candles each night.)

Susan Floyd's upstairs room gave over to the street below

and she made a habit of staring down at James leaving the house and turning right on Church Street. On starry nights or those late hours when the moon shone brightly, her eyes could follow him as far away as Cornwall Street, where he would turn left and disappear.

Susan arrived at the creamery one day surprised to see JBW emerge from behind the counter. She had pushed open the front door and tripped the small overhead bell, bringing him from the backend, where he was sorting eggs. As soon as she recognized him, a voice, audible only by her, berated her for all those times she had spied on him, and her face flushed pink as dawn. Believing that James did not know who she was – his vanilla countenance providing little or no contradiction – she resisted the temptation to introduce herself. Awkwardly, she made every effort to appear disinterested in him by avoiding eye contact, by looking down, then away, and pretending to read the several signs that were posted throughout the store while waiting for him to prepare her order.

When he handed her the small package of sweet cream, he smiled and thanked her. "Thank you, Miss Floyd...please come again."

He knows, she thought to herself. "You are welcomed. It is Mr. Haynes, isn't it?"

"Yes, I'm one of your father's students."

The pretense was over. Well, not exactly over, as she posed a question masqueraded as a sentence. "I'm surprised that you know who I am. We've never been introduced." which really meant, *How do you know who I am?*

"It would be difficult not to notice you. I have seen you around with your mother and at church." James then removed his apron and stepped out from behind the counter. "As you said, we have never been introduced," and he reached out his right hand. "My name is James Baker Washington Haynes, from

260

Warwick County."

Somewhat rattled and taken aback, Susan placed the sweet cream on the counter, then recomposed herself. "Enchanted, Mr. James Baker from Warwick County, and I am Miss Susan Floyd, of this here Loudoun County." She looked into his brown eyes while ignoring his outstretched hand; and, when he seemed to have nothing more to say, she turned and started toward the door. "I do hope we meet again, James."

"You can be sure of it, Miss Floyd – perhaps after class at the school."

She paused and turned her head toward him pensively. "Perhaps…" Then she smiled brightly at him. "Goodbye, James. And by the way, please call me Susan," then she headed out the door.

"Goodbye, Susan."

He saw her package on the counter and chased after her into the bright morning sun before the door had a chance to close itself. "Oh! Don't forget the sweet cream."

Having handed her the package, he remained standing on the wooden walkway with his hand shading his eyes, watching her from behind as she walked along Cornwall Street toward the church. After she made the turn, he re-entered the store and went to the counter, where he wrapped his apron around his waist before going to the rear to resume sorting the morning supply of eggs.

Unable to keep his mind from thinking about Susan, he wished that it were Monday, time for his evening class. However, when Monday arrived, she was nowhere to be seen, and he imagined that she was upstairs in her room.

When he stepped outside to return home, he walked down the front steps, turned and looked up to see if she were in her usual spot, hoping to see her peering down at him. Supposing that she might be watching covertly, he pretended to be gazing at the moon, but the only witness was Phineas gawking suspiciously from an adjacent room.

Professor Floyd kept a tight reign around his daughter and spied on her and her friends constantly. Two years earlier, he had arranged for her to marry a certain landed Virginia gentleman to the south near Richmond. The marriage would not take place until Susan completed her education at the public school on Harrison Street. She was aware of the arrangement and was quite unhappy about it. She was also aware of how her father continuously dogged her every move.

James had never known her to attend any of the after-class social hours. He thought perhaps now that James and her had met and talked, and that they seemed to have gotten along quite well together, that she might be inclined to make an appearance. When that proved not to be the case, a week later he mentioned to Mrs. Floyd that he had met her daughter at the creamery, and that he wondered why she never helped serving any of the late night snacks.

In spite of his coolness and sincerity, she discerned from his inquiry that he had more than a casual interest, and she hoped to discourage him by informing him that Susan had already been spoken for. James quickly apologized and assured her that his intentions were purely honorable, that since he had arrived at Leesburg he had been so busy with work at the creamery and studies that he hadn't had the time to develop any friendships. Nevertheless, she obediently reported her suspicions to her husband.

Due in part to his wit and charming manner, James had become quite a likable character with the local merchants in downtown Leesburg, as well as with many of the members of the Methodist Protestant Church on Harrison Street, where James and the Floyd family worshipped. James and Susan frequently exchanged quiet glances during the services, and whenever

Phineas seemed absorbed in his own after-church visiting and handshaking, the two would quietly slip off to the side where they would find their own moments of solitude.

"Good morning, Susan, how nice to see you again."

"How good to see you, James. It seems so rare a chance that we get to say hello. Father tells me that you are doing quite well with your studies and that you will soon be sitting in on your exams."

"I'm honored that he speaks well of me. And you, how are things going with you? I've heard that you are engaged."

"My studies are almost complete, and I too will be sitting in on my exams. Oh, I'm sorry, I see father is waiting for me; I must leave. Thank you for stopping to speak to me…goodbye, sweet James!"

Sunday afternoons following church were the times when James was afforded the opportunity to saddle his horse and ride to the outskirts of town. His horse needed exercise, and he needed this day of the week for regeneration – the morning for spiritual revival and the afternoon for both physical as well as psychological rekindling. Once he and his horse crossed the boundary from city to country, together they felt the urge to sprint. Down an alleyway between two tobacco fields the two would bolt, over a narrow Indian trail in the forest, invisible ghosts always at their flanks keeping pace, never falling behind or getting ahead, across a creek, a riverbed and a meadow of clover, white lather, dripping saliva and sore knees.

His cycle of living in Loudoun County continued, month following month – cream separation, crumpets and cider, torts and probates, handshakes, lather and saliva – until he received his diploma.

That was the day that he packed his few possessions and said goodbye to John Hamilton, a person to whom he would remain forever grateful, thanking him for having provided him with a room and a means of support. He mounted his horse and rode north toward Baltimore. From there, he turned west and made his way to Cumberland, then along Braddock's trail. At the Monongalia River, he boarded a flatboat to the Ohio floating down it to the Scioto where the bateau, *Scioto Princess*, had to be poled the entire distance north to Darby Creek. For the next six-months, he slowly worked his way back, on horseback, to Loudoun County, taking the trace from Chillocothe, through Newark, Zanesville, and Wheeling.

Richwood, Ohio – Winter, 1840

Susan was busy lighting the fire in her Oberlin stove while James crawled out of bed and walked to the frost-covered bedroom window. It was still dark outside; nevertheless, he could make out the fresh white snow that blanketed Clinton Street in front of their two-story frame house. He couldn't resist dragging his thumbnail through the frozen crust at the bottom of one of the panes, forming his initials – JBW. Standing back, he admired his work, uncritical of the disuniformity of the size of each letter – the J starting out small with the remaining two letters becoming progressively larger. The only heat during the night came from the single fireplace in the downstairs living room, but by early morning, the logs had become completely consumed. Once Susan got the stove going, the kitchen would be the best place in the house to keep warm.

James pulled on his shoes and walked from the bedroom in his long wool underwear and sleeping cap, along the short hall, and stuck his head in the girls' bedroom. "Eliza! You need to get up now and help your mother downstairs, so she can feed the twins. Don't make me ask again. Do you hear?"

A soft, sleepy voice emerged from under the sheets, "Yes Father, I hear...I'll be down in a minute."

"You should probably wake up your sister and help her get dressed, too. It snowed last night. The ground's covered. I'll get Jimmy to cut us a path to the barn. Put on warm clothes, it's chilly outside."

"You don't need to tell me that...I froze last night...Sue and I had to snuggle to keep warm."

"Your mother's got the Oberlin fired up now so you'll start to feel better. Are you out of bed yet?"

"Yes, Daddy, I'm almost up...I'll be right out."

"Remember to put on your Sunday dress; you know the Cantata is today."

"Oh Daddy, how could I forget?"

James passed the girls' room to where the boys were sleeping and approached their bed. "Tommy, time to get up. Rise and shine! Up and attum there, big guy. You need to get dressed and give your brother a hand clearing off the walk. It snowed last night...lots."

"Ohw, Dad, it's cold in here. Did you build a fire in the fireplace?"

"The heat will be rising soon. You know, the best way to get warm is to get busy, get that blood circulating. Let's go now, get those breeches on and get on downstairs to the kitchen."

James turned and headed down the narrow stairway to the kitchen, where bright orange flames shot out from the circular opening in the stovetop, casting shadows throughout the dark room that was otherwise illuminated by a single candle. Susan took a few pieces of firewood from the stack next to the stove and fed them through the small opening to the burning coals below. Using its coiled handle, she slid the round iron cover over the opening, sounding a loud clank as it dropped neatly into position. The flames disappeared and the room resumed its prior semi-darkness as the small flickering candle struggled to let its light shine.

James made his way through the kitchen and out the back door to the privy, wading through three inches of soft snow on top of the frozen mud ground. As he pulled open the privy door, it plowed through the upper inch of freshly fallen white stuff forming a small snow bank at its terminus. He spent very little time inside and quickly retrieved his woollies from around his ankles. He then made a dash back indoors where the kitchen was now starting to fill with the warmth radiating from the open oven door.

The previous evening, Susan had put two full cups of oats into a saucepan of water before going to bed to let them steep overnight, and she now set them on the stovetop to cook. From the hand-pump built into the counter across from the stove, she pumped water from nearly thirty feet below the house into a second large vessel and carried it to the stove for making tea as well as for heating water for the seven household members (not counting the twins) to wash-up before getting dressed. It was Sunday morning. Susan was anxious to get everyone up, dressed, fed and the cow milked in order to get an early start for church since several members of the family were to participate in the special Christmas Cantata that was being held during the morning services.

It had been six months since they had arrived in Richwood and moved into their home on Clinton Street. There was but one frame house in the village, and it had been owned and occupied by Hugh Thompson. The other dwellings were primitive log cabins. Hugh had been a farmer, and completed his in-town two-story house only a year earlier and then died. His widow returned to Newark, about eighty miles to the east, where James and his family were living at the time. James had heard about the settlement in the 'rich woods' a year or two earlier, and it sounded inviting after spending the last ten years in Newark, both teaching and as County Tax Assessor. When he heard about Hugh Thompson's home in the wilderness settlement being up for sale, he traveled several days by horseback to see if he would be able to support his family there. James returned to Newark excited about the prospects. He was able to work out the details, and he bought the farm and its newly built house from the Thompson's estate, leaving behind his mother and his brothers, Hopton and Thomas, and sisters, Mary and Diana.

"Eliza! I don't hear any noise up there. Are you up?"

"Yes, Daddy, I'm getting up now. It won't take me long."

"What about you, Tommy? I don't hear any sound coming from out of your room either."

"I'll be right down. I'm putting on my shoes now."

Not everyone in the Haynes family shared James' enthusiasm in coming to the rich woods, the least of which was Eliza. No one but Eliza protested so loudly. She may have been born in Leesburg, but her formative and teen years had been spent in Newark, and that is where she left her heart and all that was familiar to her – her school, her friends and civilization. In Newark, she boasted of having come from a plantation in Virginia; Newark now seemed an improvement. Richwood didn't even have a schoolhouse. There had been one a few years earlier, a log schoolhouse on Blagrove Street, but then it became too small and too dilapidated, and it had to be torn down. School then had to be held in the Methodist Protestant Church, where her father was her teacher.

The move from Newark to the rich woods was something near miraculous. There were no roads other than the Indian trails or the bridle paths through the heavy forest leading into town. Less than five years earlier a road had been cut from the southern to the northern line of the township. However, they only cleared away the underbrush and small trees, leaving many obstacles in the shape of large timber. There were only about twenty families living there at the time. Bears were seen occasionally, and wolves and deer were abundant.

In Newark there was a library, there were stores, and the town also boasted three newspaper offices, ten grocery stores, two gristmills, an iron foundry, a wool factory, a bookstore, two hardware stores, as well as several other business establishments. Richwood had only L.H. Hastings General Store.

More than anything, Eliza missed her friends. Her best friend, Sarah, had lived down the street from her and they would often sleep over at each other's house. She had just arrived at a point in her life where boys were starting to pay attention to her.

Eliza, Jim, Tom, Sue and Ben were all up, dressed and each had taken their turn at the privy and washing at the sink next to the hand pump. Susan had nursed Charley and Dick and placed them in the playpen where they seemed to be able to amuse themselves. Jim and Tom had returned from the outside, having finished blazing the trail to the barn, James brought a pale of fresh milk in, and Sue was placing the steaming hot oats, milk and honey on the table. At last, each family member was able to take a seat at the table. JBW took his place at the head of the table and then he asked that they all hold hands as he gave the grace.

To the average person, the Methodist Protestant Church on Franklin Street was within walking distance from the their home on Clinton, even with three inches of fresh snow on the ground. Nevertheless, Charley and Dick both would have had to be carried, and it was questionable if Ben could make it on his own. James hitched the horse to the carriage and parked it in the driveway next to the house until everyone could get aboard.

Winter came late this season and this was the first snow. As the carriage pulled onto the street, the initial rush of brisk, cold air blowing across each of their faces reminded them of what summer had enabled them to forget. Cold is something that isn't remembered and has to be re-experienced each time, repeatedly. Susan and Eliza drew their shared blanket over the twins' faces, and Sue held Ben tightly next to her. Theirs was the only house on this heavily wooded street, and the snow hung in clumps balanced on the top edges of the tall leafless elms and sycamores, and it weighed doubly heavy on the firs and pines, all silhouettes against the leaden sky. Except for the tiny footprints of a displaced robin or a red-breasted blackbird, or of a curious rabbit, the blanket of silent white lay unblemished before them, imprinted only by the steps of old Billie and the moving wheels of their carriage.

As the horse and carriage approached Blagrove Street, James pulled on the right rein and the horse began the gentle turn. He could see Jim shivering next to him. "You'll get used to it. And besides, it's excellent for your health. You will be all the better for it." Once onto Blagrove, they were only one block away from the main street, where the church stood not far from Hastings General Store, the gristmill, and Dr. Booking's residence.

Built of hewed logs the church also served as a schoolhouse and was the largest building in the north part of Union County. The seats were plain benches with no backs. The stove was new, having come from Granville in Licking County and paid for with a wagonload of wheat.

"All rise! We will begin our services this snowy Christmas morning by singing that glorious hymn, A Mighty Fortress is our Lord...." Rev. William Hamilton led off singing with his powerful voice, even before everyone had a chance to get to their feet, and by the time he reached the second stanza the entire congregation had caught up to him.

"Christmas is God incarnate! What a wonderful idea that He could reveal himself to us in human form." Rev. Hamilton had hauled the wheat to Granville and traded it for a stove, brought it back, and placed it in the church. Following his powerful sermon on temperance, the children made their way onto the platform and sang a melody of Christmas carols followed by their short dramatization of the angels appearing to the shepherds in the field announcing that the Christ was born in a manger in Bethlehem. Colonel Haynes[2] read from the scriptures, and Eliza sang *Silent Night.* At the completion of the service, the cantata and the call for tithes and offerings, and before the benediction, Rev. Hamilton introduced a guest in the back row, a new person in town, a young man from Zanesville who had just bought the Cramer Farm south of town. The reverend asked him to stand so that everyone could see him. The young man stood, raised his hand and waved as the congregation turned toward him. He wore a stylish dark gray suit with a black satin collar, a friendly smile, a thick head of hair and deep penetrating eyes.

Eliza's heart began to beat rapidly thinking that she had never seen any man so handsome.

"Ladies and gentlemen, I present to you Dr. Joshua Selmon

---

[2] There is plenty of evidence that James Washington Baker Haynes was known to all that knew him as 'Colonel Haynes', beginning with the time that he moved from Virginia to Newark, Ohio. He is frequently referred to as Colonel J. B. W. Haynes in both the 1883 and 1915 Editions of the History of Union County, Published by W. H. Beers & Co., Chicago and B. F. Bowen & Company, Inc., Indianapolis.

Even the 1869 Senate Report, prepared by Mr. Van Winkle who is identified in both the 1883 and 1915 History of Union County as a prominent attorney would have known him personally, has identified him as Colonel J. B. W. Haynes, yet chose to refer to his election as a 2nd Lt during the War of 1812.

The Newark North American on September 3, 1869, page 8 announced his passing as follows:

"The death of COL. J. B. W. HAYNES, formerly of Licking County, but for a number of years a citizen of Union County, occurred at his residence in Richwood, on the 20th of August last [1869]. Col. Haynes was born in the Isle of Wight, in Virginia, on the 9th of March 1794, and came to Ohio in 1825."

However his military records indicate that he was a Private in Captain John B. Cooper's Company Virginia Militia enlisted 4 March 1813 to 04 August 1812 (154 days) in the War of 1812. Mary R. Haynes, his second wife, in a Widow's Brief wherein she was requesting a pension based on his military service stated that he was "a private of Captain John B. Cooper's Company of Virginia."

Adding further to the confusion, his tombstone identifies him as James Haynes, Sgt 1 Regt Va Mil, War of 1812, August 20, 1869.

Gill," the reverend said.

Once Eliza returned home, she no longer gave much thought to the handsome young man. However, when she arrived at school the following day, the place triggered her awareness. By the end of the week she had forgotten him until church services the following Sunday when he appeared sitting in the back row.

Following the benediction, the congregation filed out and James approached him, introducing himself and his family. Following the introductions, Susan drifted off, carrying Charley, and joined a conversation with a nearby group of women. Eliza remained standing by quietly, holding Dick, as the two men visited.

James was interested in Joshua's purchase of the Cramer Farm and his intention of creating a subdivision that he hoped would become a southern continuation of the village. Eliza listened intently while continuing to hold young Dickey, wishing that there were some way that she could enter the conversation, and when no opportunity seemed to present itself, her mind began to drift away.

It was a warmer day than the preceding Sunday and most of the snow had melted; however, a few black-dotted, crystallized mounds remained in the shaded areas. A man nearby was laughing. Several children were running about noisily. Her mother remained off to the side with a different group of women. Eliza could see that Joshua had cut himself on the neck, no doubt while shaving that morning. His shirt looked immaculate – she wondered who took care of him. No one – he was single, unmarried, and lived all alone. As her mind drifted further away, she imagined herself standing at the dining room table at his house pouring together with him over building plans and subdivision maps. She saw herself actively participating with him in their project, the two of them dressed in elegant vestments, her hair gloriously coiffed. *Hand me that map of lot*

122, darling, she could hear him say. *What do you think about green and gold carpets?*

Dickey began squirming in her arms, wanting to be put down, bringing Eliza to her senses. When she saw Joshua and her father, now both staring at her, she wondered how long she had been daydreaming, and her pale face blushed pink with embarrassment, as if they had read her mind and knew what she had been imagining. She lowered Dickey to the ground and continued to hold his hand, wishing that she had remained with her mother. She could see her nearby, holding the other twin by his hand and talking to Mrs. Hamilton, the preacher's wife, and Eliza started to turn in that direction.

Seeing that she was about to leave and hoping to stop her, Joshua turned toward her. "Eliza, please, just a moment." Then he turned back toward JBW. "I was wondering, Colonel, if I might have your permission for Eliza here to go riding with me this afternoon? I have a new filly that is anxious to be exercised, and I would like her to join me.

Eliza beamed, and JBW turned and asked, "How about it, Eliza; is that something you would like to do?"

"Oh yes, Daddy. I would like that very much."

James felt a little stirred; after all, this was her first gentleman caller. "Well then, Eliza, you can take my horse Billie. Perhaps you should ask Dr. Gill if he would like to join us later in the afternoon for our Sunday meal. I'm sure Susan would love to have a chance to get to know him better."

Susan could overhear, and she promptly joined the conversation; Joshua agreed to come to dinner. They continued to talk together for a while longer, and then they went their separate ways, the Haynes rounding up their children and returning to their home on the north end of Clinton, and Joshua to his cabin on the corner of Clinton and Ottawa – a short walk from the church to where he lived.

All the way back to the house, Eliza couldn't stop chattering. "He just suddenly appeared out of nowhere; he seems so young to be a doctor; he likes horses, doesn't he? And he dresses so elegantly."

Susan was caught by surprise and worried that the stale bread and porridge she had prepared for their Sunday meal would not be suitable for such a distinguished guest. In the barn, she had some venison hanging, and some dried vegetables – zucchini. She could mash potatoes and make gravy. There was plenty of time, she thought, and she too was charged with excitement.

At twenty-one, Joshua had only been in Richwood a short while, arriving only a few weeks after Colonel Haynes and his family. He was born in Baltimore and moved to Zanesville with his parents, where he studied medicine. He loved working with horses, and he had set up a veterinary practice at his log cabin on Clinton Street. Dr. Brookins, who had arrived about eight years earlier, had been forced to tend to the health needs of horses as well as people, and he was relieved that he would not need to make any more calf deliveries. Dr. Gill had met several times with Dr. Brookins at his office on the corner of Blagrove and Franklin before setting up his practice, making sure that there was sufficient work for a second medical practitioner. The support that he had received in those meetings convinced him that it was appropriate for him to settle in this frontier town.

When Josh and Eliza returned from their lengthy ride, they unsaddled both horses, covering their backs with a blanket, and left them together in the barn with water and a manger of hay. It was late in the dark blue afternoon and the air had turned crisp and cold – cold enough that when they exhaled warm moist air, they could see each other's breath.

From the chimney roared the sweet smoke of white walnut and honey-baked venison, beans and molasses and through the frosted panes of the kitchen window, the warm room glowed orange.

It had been a glorious day, and Eliza was blissfully drunk. They had ridden out on Franklin Street, north along the newly carved road crossing a small stream covered with a thin veneer of ice to the boundary line, that demarcation of Indian and white lands in earlier times. There they found an old, abandoned cabin made of hewed logs and stopped to nose around and to give their horses a rest. There was no porch and the step up to the door was missing. Josh easily pushed the door open and entered, taking Eliza by the hand and pulling her up into the small interior. There were a few pieces of furniture, including a table and a bed, a stone fireplace, and one window facing the west in the rear. The plank floor hadn't been swept in years, and a large amount of dust and dirt mixed with mouse droppings had accumulated. In one corner, a few rags, the remnants of wool underwear that had outlived their usefulness, lay on top of an old newspaper dated 1832 from Newark. Eliza decided to take it home to show her father. She was certain that he would be pleased to see it, but as soon as she held it, it disintegrated and she allowed it to crumble back onto the floor.

After they had rummaged through the cabinets and shelves and found nothing further of interest, they went back out the same way they entered and walked around to the back through the dogwood and prickly ash. Hidden by bladder bush and bramble they found a hole in the ground, a well, about five feet in diameter, covered with wood planks through which an iron pipe connected to a hand pump protruded, extending down to the water table. A vine similar to clematis with several purple flowers had weaved its way up the base, wrapping itself around the handle and spout. Using both hands, Josh gently cleared it away. They took turns playfully pumping without any success – old pumps such as this one needed first to be primed – and then they sat down next to each other on the wooden cover.

Next to Josh's feet he could see a strange-looking pile of stones – black colored flint. He reached down to examine one – an arrowhead, neatly chiseled into a pointed triangular shape. There were several more strewn about in a haphazard pile, including an axe head, and the two gathered them up while joyfully speculating and conjuring up explanations about how they came to be there.

"This is so much fun!" Eliza exclaimed, and she began to dance around in a circle like she thought an Indian would do.

Josh began to beat a cadence on one of the wooden planks with the butt of his hand and chanting loudly. "Om-ba, om-ba, om-ba om-ba…" He then jumped up and joined in her dance, the two chanting and waving their arms about. "Om-ba, om-ba, om-ba, om-ba." The birds in the surrounding trees scattered, all but the owl, who gazed down at them hoping that he could somehow get back to sleep amid the commotion. Laughing, Eliza fell to the ground; the child in her was reborn. She looked up and could see the blue sky reflecting down from between the treetops. Tiny drops of perspiration had formed on her brow and a salty bead rolled down into one of her eyes.

Josh lay next to her, and after remaining quiet for a while he reached over and took her hand. She was a child again but also a young woman lying beside a handsome knight who had slain the beast that had roamed the rich woods these past several months. Unable to resist, she turned, took him into her arms and they kissed.

Unwilling to go any further, they found comfort merely being with each other. They talked quietly together. They shared their experiences coming from a world on the other side of the mountain. They had each arrived in Ohio at two different cities near each other along the same highway – Newark and Zanesville. Until this afternoon, Eliza hadn't stopped thinking about Newark; she had missed her grandmother, her uncles and her older brother Will. Throughout the past weeks she rarely laughed. This day, she was alive, full of wit and vitality; Josh was charming and full of energy and drive. Somehow, she knew that their futures would be forever woven together.

For the next decade and half, the town of Richwood grew slowly, trudging along far from any highway or waterway. Settlers rarely found their way directly there, settling first in Licking or Muskingum Counties, and then later discovering about the rich loamy farmland. It was the farmers that arrived first, settling in the surrounding countryside, and the merchants, millers, physicians, real estate agents, tavern owners, blacksmiths, and politicians that slowly followed, building their homes along Franklin, Ottawa and Blagrove Streets, replacing the early log cabins with frame houses or moving into apartments above their businesses. It wasn't until the coming of the railroad, or the rumor or promise of it, that speculators were lured to both the countryside and in town.

Shortly after his arrival and for several years thereafter, Col. Haynes held the position of Justice of the Peace. He opened the town's first hotel and soon acquired several lots along Franklin Street, including Hauk's Tavern across the street from the hotel. Dr. Gill converted his cabin on Clinton Street into a wooden bowl factory, building a new home on his acreage at the corner of Franklin and Gill Streets. He too began buying lots, investing in the small town through which the railroad would one day pass.

Eliza stood at the edge of the bed, leaned over, and spoke softly in her husband's ear. "Josh, wake up; I think it's time!" He didn't stir, and she gave him a nudge and repeated only a little louder, "Josh, wake up!"

He felt a single cold hand nudging him on his shoulder; she had just returned from being outside – from the privy. Her other hand held the bottom backside of her nightgown pulled up between her legs. The bottom half of her nightgown was wet; so was her side of the bed.

Half asleep, Josh turned and peeked out through two narrow slits. "Time for what?"

"The baby...it's time."

Several minutes earlier, Eliza's water had gushed onto her side of the bed and spread to his. He could now feel the cool wetness of his own nightgown, and he sat up, placing his feet on the floor in front of her. After rubbing his eyes, he could see the grayish haze of a November dawn out the window and hear their rooster crowing, announcing the day. "I'm sure that you have plenty of time yet. Let me have a look and see...there's no sense getting Dr. Brookins up at this early hour."

She lay on her back and raised her gown above her knees while Dr. Gill examined her, hoping to see how far the baby had dropped – if she had begun to dilate. "How long ago did you have your last contraction?"

"Right before I tried to wake you...a few minutes ago."

"It's going to be a while yet...may not be until this evening. Who knows these things? I certainly don't. All we can do is get ready for it and wait, and when it's ready, you will know it. In the meantime, let's get you out of those wet clothes and into some clean ones."

Eliza allowed her wet gown to fall to the floor, and for a moment she stood naked between Josh and the window, leaving a backlit profile of her protruding tummy. She stepped closer to the cabinet where she kept her clean underwear and gowns and paused in front of her dresser mirror long enough to notice that her bulge had in fact moved much lower down toward her pelvis.

Josh couldn't help but stare at her as he gathered up the sheets from the bed and turned the mattress over, hoping that the water hadn't gone all the way through – it hadn't. She located a clean gown and climbed into it while Josh spread clean sheets on the bed, just as the contractions returned. With her eyes closed, Eliza sat on the edge of the bed, arched her back, and exhaled slowly through parched lips until the contraction passed.

"Josh, please send for my mother. I would feel better if she were with me."

By noon, the house was full. Josh had dashed to the Haynes household and announced that Eliza's water had broken. Susan came quickly and the colonel not too long after that. Mrs. Hastings arrived and brought a loaf of fresh baked bread, chicken broth for Eliza, and bean soup for the men to eat. Dr. Brookins and Rev. Hamilton sat in the living room talking with Joshua and Colonel Haynes.

Rev. Hamilton was a very large and powerful man, full of enthusiasm and determination in all of his undertakings. Though not very cultured he was thoroughly honest and public spirited. He was perhaps more influential in creating a healthy moral atmosphere in the community by his example and teachings and of his withering denunciation of whatever was mean and contemptible. His spirit was chivalrous, and to the weak or oppressed, he was unusually kind.

He had purchased 1400 acres one and a forth miles northwest of Richwood a couple years before James or Joshua had arrived and built a log house and began the arduous labor of developing a farm. It was on his land that the Lenox Schoolhouse had been built, and Rev. Hamilton donated a lot for a cemetery.

Dr. Brookins was a very small, spare man physically, but he was very jovial. He was a social, genial spirit, and possessed an uncommon fund of good humor. He always had a good story to tell, and he usually kept a crowd in a roar of laughter. Periodically, Dr. Brookins would check in on Eliza to see how she was doing, each time returning to the living room with the news that she was progressing slowly. Finally, he told Susan that he had to leave, that he would be at his office, that she should send for him when her contractions became much stronger and closer together. When school was out, both Sue and Tom stopped by, stayed for a while, and then returned home where a neighbor was taking care of the rest of the children. By the end of the day, everyone was gone except for Susan and Joshua.

Susan was exhausted, and she lay next to Eliza trying to rest for a spell. Joshua came into the room, sat on a chair next to the bed and attempted to make conversation with Eliza, but she was edgy and irritable, flustered from all the work that she had done which seemed unproductive. When her next contraction began, Joshua tried counting as he had heard Susan do earlier, and Eliza screamed at him to shut up.

Into the night the three remained together in the room, dozing on and off between contractions, occasionally taking a drink of water or broth or a cup of chamomile tea when it became apparent that she was about ready to begin to push. Dr. Gill confirmed that the baby's head was beginning to show, and Susan began coaching Eliza when to push. The serious work had begun with an accompanying amount of pain, so much that Josh was happy to leave the house to fetch Dr. Brookins.

As Dr. Brookins entered the bedroom, Susan stood next to the bed holding a wet, wrinkled baby boy; both Joshua and the doctor had missed the delivery. Susan cleaned the baby, wrapped him in a blanket and placed him into a cradle, the same cradle in which she had once placed each of her children, as Dr. Brookins tended to Eliza. She could see out the window the grayish haze of another November dawn and hear the rooster crowing. Susan was now a grandmother.

They named the baby boy William Henry. The following year, Franklin was born, and not long thereafter, Eliza was pregnant again when William died. He was buried in a small graveyard lot behind the small wood-framed Baptist Church, several lots east of the wooden bowl factory on Ottawa Street, Rev. Hamilton officiated.

James had been appointed the official census taker for Richwood-Claibourne Township. Since the town had not yet been incorporated and there was no village government, his appointment had come from Marysville, the county seat of Union County. He had received the forms to be completed for each household and instructions on how to complete them. He was anxious to get started, but it had rained almost every day for a week, and he hated the idea of tracking mud into people's homes – there were no sidewalks and the street had yet to be paved. Since he spent most of his time managing his hotel on Franklin Street, he decided that it would be expedient if he were to put out a sign and solicit any walk-ins that might be passing by. This proved not to be such a good idea as by the end of the second week only a few heads-of-household had stopped in for the interview. By the end of the third week, the rain looked as if it was going to let up, so he headed out first to his brother, Thomas, for a trial run. There would be no better place to mess up than at the home of one of his own.

James approached the front door along the driveway that led to the small barn in the rear of the house. He knocked first and waited for a response. When no one came to the door, he rapped again, a little harder, and announced loudly, "Census taker, here!"

He could hear some rumblings inside and then a faint, "Be right there."

He looked down at his muddy shoes, realizing that he would have to remove them before being invited in, so he stooped down, untied them and placed them on a flat piece of flagstone that had been conveniently placed by the step just for that purpose. Once his shoes had been removed, he returned to his position in front of the door, and he realized that this would be all right this time, but in the future he didn't want that to be the first image that people would have of him, standing in his stocking feet, when they greeted him. The next time he would wait until he had been acknowledged before offering to remove his footwear.

It took several tugs for Harriet to get the front door opened. Since the rains had begun, the door and the surrounding framework had become swollen, causing it to stick. Besides, most everyone came in through the back, and the front door was rarely used. As the door suddenly broke loose, making a screeching sound loud enough to scare off any energetic termites, it then caught on a small throw rug spread on the inside as a place for people to wipe their feet. Harriet reached down and slid it to the side as James announced a second time, "Census taker, here."

Once inside his brother came from the kitchen to greet him. "Hello, Jimmy, come on in. We've been expecting you for some time. You must nearly be finished – saving us for last?"

"Actually you are the first – the rains, you know."

"I see you've got your shoes off already, you always were the polite one. Can I have Harriet get you a cup of tea?"

"Yes, I would like that very much." Holding up his forms for Tom to see he said, "Could we do this at the kitchen table? It shouldn't take long."

"Of course."

James carefully filled in all the information on the census form, and when he finished, he rose from his chair and slowly headed for the door. "Goodbye, Thomas, Harriet, I guess I'll see you in church on Sunday. Say goodbye to the kids."

As he stepped out the front door, he noticed that one of his shoes was missing from the rock where he had placed them.

Tom followed him out and seeing only one shoe remarked, "Oh! I didn't think to tell you, but there has been this annoying raccoon hanging around outside, and he seems to be quite the scavenger. I suspect that he's had something to do with this."

James removed his other shoe, stuffed his socks into it, rolled up the cuffs of his trousers and stepped down onto the water-soaked ground. With the weight of each step pressing downward, the brown mud felt cool oozing upward between his toes, and the small stones and twigs that served as ground cover poked the underside of his feet as he attempted to tiptoe about the neighborhood hoping that the raccoon had not carried his missing shoe off very far.

When he passed by the house of L. H. Hastings, Levin came to the door to see what was going on and had to laugh when he saw JBW holding his trousers by its knees, and he offered him a glass of port. James accepted, and they had a few more laughs before James continued farther up the street. When they finally gave up, the mud had left its mark up to his ankles, and Thomas led him to the pump in the back of the house where they both rinsed off before re-entering the house.

"Go ahead, Jimmy, and take these," Thomas said, handing him a pair of brown tie shoes that looked as if they had barely been worn. James had earlier completed the section on Thomas' line on the census form calling for 'Occupation or Trade' – Shoe Merchant.

"We both practically wear the same size. Take these and tomorrow I'll bring you a new pair from the store."

It was a new day. James rose to the lilting music of several small finches near his window, colorful small birds all in a cluster, and a bob white whistling in the distance – "ba-ba white, ba-ba white," with the sound of the -ite on the end of 'white' curving up as if one were whistling with parched lips for a kitty. It was going to be a great July day, he could tell, the birds always told the truth. All he needed was to get dressed, have some breakfast and go to the hotel, where he had errands to take care of first thing. His suit still looked fresh, and he sniffed it, just to be sure, before climbing in and buttoning it. His new shoes almost tied themselves, and his hair, towel-dried, lightly oiled and combed, was neatly parted in the middle, leaving a thin straight line of scalp exposed, starting at the apogee of his forehead back to his crown. James was a handsome man and looked good in a suit.

"Mrs. Biddle? James Haynes, here...I'm here to do the census. Is Richard home? Fine then, how about after dinner, would that be better? You folks are number 191 on my list...see you then. Goodbye."

"Mrs. Gearhart? JBW Haynes calling, I'm here to do the census. Is Harry home? OK, fine, I'll go around back. Hi...Harry...did I catch you at a bad time? I just have a few questions...the census, you know. Just look at all those horseshoes! Did you make all them yourself? One son...Jacob H. you say? ...he's 21? ...OK, you are family 192. Thank you, sir, and I'll see you in ten years. Say goodbye to the missus for me."

"Hello, Mrs. Parks...may I come in? Oh, I'm sorry to hear that; how old did you say he was? And your two sons, how old did you say they are? They don't live here any longer...you must miss them. Gee, I would love to stay, but I must be going. Gingerbread cookies...? Well, I guess one wouldn't hurt. No, I really must go...before the rain. Fifty... of course you look much younger than that, not a day over forty. Well, goodbye,

Mrs. Parks, I can see myself out. No, thank you, one cookie is enough...I don't want to spoil my supper. Thanks again...goodbye."

James truly loved going house to house, making new friends, revisiting old ones, talking politics, and of course telling his own *histoir*. Who else could have boasted of having talked with every family in the parish? Many families had similar stories, coming from Virginia, moving first to Muskingum or Licking Counties before arriving at Richwood. James was able to learn that like him, there were those who had been promised land for having served in the war and until recently had not received it.

It was an outrage! At fifty-six, he had at last received an eighty-acre parcel, but why had it taken so long he wondered? For many veterans, the bounty had come too late to be of service, as many were too old to improve it and to make use of it. Had they obtained it as promptly as it was donated to the soldiers of the Mexican War, they might have been able enjoy comfortable homes in their old age and decrepitude and not be dependent, as many of them were, upon the cold charities of the world or the kindness of friends for their lease of life.

What had started out as a hobby had turned into a profitable enterprise – more profitable than his medical practice. In Zanesville, Josh had acquired a small lathe. It was a simple machine that could be used for shaping a piece of wood, rotating it about a horizontal axis and then cutting away and reshaping the material with another tool such as a knife. It was operated by a foot pedal that the operator pumped up and down, causing a chord coiled around the horizontal axel to spin the material forward. As Josh began clearing some of the trees on his farm, he discovered several beautiful hardwoods – walnut, beech and cherry – and he began using his lathe to shape them into wooden bowls. The polished bowls were especially beautiful, and he took several samples with him back to Zanesville, where he was able to find a distributor. Unable to crank out sufficient numbers to meet the distributor's demand, he acquired a second lathe, hired his first employee, and then expanded again. With the increased production, it was necessary to move the factory nearer his source of material, so he relocated to his homestead at the end of Fulton Street where it butted up against his acreage. He experimented with wooden plates, but the distributor was only interested in the bowls.

"James Haynes, census taker here!" He knocked at the rear door of Dr. Gill's new home on the large lot at the corners of Franklin, Gill and Fulton Streets. (Franklin and Fulton Streets ran parallel to each other.) The freshly painted screen door still smelled of oil or turpentine, James couldn't tell which. He could hear the whiney of one of Josh's horses coming from the barn. It was a tall-whitewashed barn with a pulley hanging from the roof for pulling bales of hay up to the second level. On the ground level, the double doors hanging on cast iron pulleys were spread open, revealing Josh's carriage and several horse stalls.

"JBW Haynes, census taker here! Anybody home?" After a couple more minutes, the screen door at last jerked toward him, slowly swinging outward, seemingly with no one on the other side until he glanced down and saw young Frank pushing it open. Standing nearby, also barefooted and wearing a cotton nightshirt, was his younger brother Henry.

James took hold of the handle and pulled the door the rest of the way toward him as Frank felt the give and stopped pushing, nearly struggling to regain his balance. Frank beamed upon seeing his grandfather – he usually brought a piece of hardtack, a secret between the two of them, a secret known by just about everyone, including Josh and Eliza but not by Henry, who was still too young to savor its sweetness. Once inside, James hunkered down and received a hug from Frank as Henry remained off to the side.

Frank boldly hit on him, "Got any candy for me, Grandpa?"

"Not today, Frankie, I'm on the town's business."

As he squirmed toward Henry in a slow-paced duck walk, Eliza entered the kitchen having come from upstairs and hearing her father's voice. "Hello, Daddy. I hope you didn't give either of the boys any candy."

James rose from greeting Henry and approached Eliza, who was now gravid for the fourth time.

"Josh is out back. They're getting ready to send a new load of bowls to Zanesville. It's his biggest order yet."

"Hello, Eliza." James smiled on seeing his daughter, realizing that she would be delivering in another two months. "How are you doing? You look well."

"Oh Daddy, you know, I'm doing fine. If I'm not used to the routine now, I never will be. Thank goodness for the rains, though, keeps it cooler that way. I only worry that September is only two months away and that's not a good month to come to term."

"The farmers are not talking that way...the heavy rains this year. You know, 'knee high by the forth of July'. Half the corn fields are flooded and even on the higher spots of ground its only halfway to the knees."

Eliza pulled out a chair from the kitchen table and flopped down on it. "I suppose you're right, heaven help the poor farmers! So what brings you by this sun shining morning? I see you've brought an armful of forms."

"I think I told you before that I am doing the census this year. I get to talk to every household in the township, register the size of each household – important business, you know – not only the count, but also the make-up, how many adults of a certain age, men, women, all-important statistics. I need to talk to Josh to fill out the form for this household, household number 215."

"Daddy, you already know that information. Why do you need to talk to him about it."

"Eliza, you don't understand, I am representing to the government that I have visited each household and made a complete interview. To do otherwise would be a misrepresentation. Look at what I've done so far. I already know most of these families personally – Cramer, Fisher, Hastings and Rosette. How do you think they would feel if they knew that they were included in a statistic and had never been called on?"

James exited out the kitchen door and walked to the last building on the lot that fronted on Fulton Street. He expected to find Josh only to find the wagon fully loaded but no Josh. One of the workers directed him back to the barn.

"Josh! Isn't that a mule?"

"Oh, hello, Colonel. Good to see you. Yes, it is. I've always had a fascination with these animals. They are excellent beasts of burden but difficult to breed. That's why you don't see many around. I have wanted to try my luck at it. If successful, I think that I could do well with them…just have to try. So, that's not what you came to discuss now, it is?"

"Actually, not, but I still find it very interesting. We should talk more about it later."

A few days earlier, July 9, 1850 in Washington D.C. while in office, President Zachary Taylor got sick after eating cherries and milk at a July 4 celebration. The sudden accession of Millard Fillmore to the presidency brought an abrupt political shift in the administration and the sudden passage of the Fugitive Slave Act, spurring the operation of the Underground Railroad, a network of over 3,000 homes and other 'stations' that helped escaping slaves travel from the southern slave-holding states to the northern states and Canada.

Susan died in 1857, and soon after James married Mary Converse. She was a widow and they had no children together. James grandson Edwin said of Mary, "The less said of Mary the better."

Susan was buried on the western edge of Sidle Cemetery, near Bethlehem Church, two and one-half miles south of town on a slope leading down to the east bank of Fulton Creek. James purchased two cemetery lots, one for Susan and the other for himself. The graveyard on Ottawa Street behind the Baptist church where William was buried was no longer being used. James placed a marker at her head, which read:

MY WIF'S GAVEE
Sarah Floyd Haynes
Consort of Col J B W Haynes

When Col. Haynes died, the stone placed at his head read:

JAMES HAYNES
SGT 1 REGT VA MIL
WAR OF 1812
AUGUST 20, 1869

Susan's stone was quite decorative and efflorescent, while James' was stereotypical of a military stone. No one understood why the colonel's grave marker read 'Sgt'.

Many years later, his grandson Edwin wrote to Washington for a copy of JBW's military record and discovered that the colonel was only a private in the War of 1812 and that he was never a colonel of a regiment in the Mexican War as some in those later years had thought. It must have all been because of Eliza Cooper back at the infirmary in Hampton.

Rev. Hamilton passed away two years before JBW. His son, Rev. Joseph Hamilton, officiated at the colonel's funeral before a large crowd at both the Methodist Protestant Church and at the Sidle Cemetery. Rev. Hamilton spoke of James' role in the community as a lawyer, a justice of the peace, a hotel and tavern operator and real estate agent. The colonel had been one of three agents involved in the incorporation of the village and its first mayor following the completion of the incorporation. Nevertheless, James was most proud of his role in fighting for the rights of veterans, co-authoring a pension bill for the old soldiers of the War of 1812 and Indian wars.

The Bowl Factory Burns

"Josh! Josh! Wake up! The factory…it's on fire!" Eliza, her lower half still under the covers, turned and shook him by his shoulders, trying to get his attention.

Josh was a heavy sleeper and he snored loudly; however, as soon as he heard the word 'fire' he awoke without any further encouragement. He sat up and saw the bright orange flames through the upstairs bedroom window coming from the distant building. There were voices and further shouts of 'fire' coming from outside and below, and he could hear the whinnying and hee-hawing of his horses and mules.

Two of his sons, Sel and Charles Fremont, were already outside forming the beginnings of a bucket brigade from the water trough near the barn to the adjacent building that had quickly turned into what looked like a flaming haystack. As Josh looked around, he could see the dark profiles of several neighbors arriving holding empty water buckets and joining in the line – one could tell that they had done this before. By the time Josh walked out the back door, having just thrown on his trousers over his long underwear, several more neighbors had joined the brigade, including a stocky woman whom he didn't recognize and two young boys barely old enough to lift a bucket.

Sparks and burning debris swarmed though the air and into the treetops like a fireworks display, red-hot ashes fell on the ground starting mini ground fires in loose tinder.

Eliza followed Josh out the back door and began carrying

water up a ladder to the barn roof, where Thomas was busy dousing wayward sparks. It was clear that the barn was in danger. If it were to go, sparks could just as easily jump onto the house. (The house had a slate roof so the danger was more from the large amount of heat being generated so close to the wooden siding.)

As more neighbors began to arrive, those that had buckets joined in on the water line while the rest stood back, helplessly, and watched the town's only manufacturing enterprise go up in white, orange and yellow flames, all the time feeling the intense heat against their arms and faces, wondering how those battling the blaze were able to bear its intensity.

Josh insisted the children move away. At first, there were only a few standing nearby gazing at the blistering hot inferno, and then others arrived, some having known Dr. Gill and Eliza as much as twenty-three years; others not as long. Some had purchased bowls from the J. S. Gill Wooden Bowl Company; others had not. There were a few standing in the growing crowd that had had calves and foals delivered by Dr. Gill, or a molar or wisdom tooth pulled, and there were those that had discussed over their dinner table his folly of having overextended himself, investing in those useless mules that, following the war, nobody wanted.

A man stood motionless, his mouth open wide, wiping the perspiration from his forehead with the sleeve of his long underwear. His children had attended Eliza's Sunday school class, and he remembered having tasted her maple syrup pie at the annual Fourth of July picnic at Lake Baccarat. An older gentleman and his wife who had known her father, the colonel, who had passed away only a few weeks earlier, looked on weeping openly.

Henry and Josh quit the water line and began moving the horses from the barn to the northernmost corral while Charles

Fremont and Sel maintained their positions in the queue. The mules were fenced outside near the barn, but the family horses were in separate stalls on the inside; they had to be moved. Once the horses saw the flames and felt the stinting heat, they became terrified and began stammering, stomping their feet and they had to be blindfolded with towels before they could be led to safety. Surprisingly, the mules were more cooperative and moved from one corral to the other once the gate was opened.

Ed, the youngest of the five brothers, was the last to leave the house. No one had given any thought to him, and seeing him from her position high on the ladder Eliza suddenly realized that he could have been lost had the fire traversed to the house. As she began to descend, a rush of fear combined with guilt shot through her body, causing her to lose her balance. Her leading foot missed the step, and she slid downward, her chin, chest and knees grinding rhythmically against each of the rungs until she met the ground standing, her splintered hands clutched tightly onto the ladder.

Feeling doubly foolish, she reached to the ground to retrieve the fallen water bucket as Thomas rushed down having witnessed her accident from above. Shoving him aside and without further regard, she rushed to the trough for more water while experiencing the numerous body aches and pains that she had just received, especially on her chin, not realizing that both her knees were bleeding.

Thomas followed her to the trough as she struggled, carrying the heavy water-filled bucket with both hands as it banged against her knees. In the light of the nearby flames, he could see the exasperation on her face teeming with pain as well as the bleeding that was now showing through her dress. He took the bucket from her, set it on the ground and helped her over to a nearby tree where she took comfort from him.

The bowl factory was soon engulfed beyond anyone's ability

to save it or any of its contents. Occasionally, one could hear the sounds of containers filled with turpentine and resins exploding. Recently cut green logs of walnut and beech that had been inside drying sizzled loudly, making hissing noises, and when the overhead rafters gave way and the roof collapsed, the ground threw back into the air burning coals, loose dirt and material to form a fiery ball of burning debris. To Josh and Eliza it looked like the burning fires of Gahena.

It had been startling and complete. Josh, Eliza, Henry, Tommy, Sel, Charles Fremont and Ed all stood together watching as the flames were replaced by smoldering coals. The others stood behind them watching like at a burial as the darkness eventually morphed into morning dawn and the agonizing heat was replaced by the dampness of the dawning dew. The smell of burnt wood ushered the rising sun into mourning, and it refused to come out from behind the clouds for the following few days.

Those that were there that night knew that they would not soon forget the intensity of the heat, the smell of singed arms and eyebrows, wet nightshirts and long underwear, and the haunting fear that this could just as easily have been their home or barn.

Not one bowl had been saved; the lathes too were gone. The metal wheel rims and other hardware parts of their delivery wagon, a shovel, and barrel rings were melted by the intense heat and forged into hard puddles of formless castings.

Dr. Gill later explained to the *Richwood Gazette* that: 'The fire began by the spontaneous combustion of rags that had been dampened with boiled linseed oil, a fire hazard because they provided a large surface area for oxidation of the oil. The oxidation was an exothermic reaction that accelerated as the rags became hotter.' He went on to say that he would rebuild the factory and make the new plant more modern and efficient than before, taking into consideration all safety hazards.

The fire wasn't the first thing to go wrong. Josh had invested a substantial amount of time and money in raising mules, which he had been selling to the Union Army during the War of the Rebellion. However, once the war had ended, the demand for mules dropped, and Josh was left with a large herd that he had to continue to maintain with no prospects for selling.

A few months earlier, Eliza's father, Colonel Haynes, had died. Eliza loved her father dearly and hadn't yet gotten over it.

Then there was their oldest son Frank. Prior to joining the infantry, Frank helped with the farming, taught school, traded in stock (mules), and part of the time traveled – selling wooden bowls.

He had joined C Company of the 174th Regiment of the Ohio Volunteer Infantry and while on campaign during the War of the Rebellion in Decatur, Alabama, he and several of his unit had crossed the Tennessee River and were remaining in the breast works. Frank was writing a letter when they were fired upon by enemy rebels and he received a bullet wound in the wrist. The injury had bothered him ever since.

The unit moved on to Raleigh, North Carolina, and on the first night, they did not have their tents. It was cold and raining very hard, and they were compelled to sleep on the ground with nothing but their blankets to protect them from the wet and cold. Frank woke in the morning sick with diarrhea. He went on sick call, but the diarrhea continued. They then went by rail to Charlotte, North Carolina, where he went to the post hospital and stayed there for a day or two.

When he went to return to his unit, he learned that they had moved on to Wade's borough. He remained at Charlotte then later came north to Columbus, Ohio with his regiment to be discharged and then rode home to Richwood by horse. Neither the soreness in his wrist or his suffering from constant diarrhea improved.

When he returned home, his five-foot-two stature weighed only 133 pounds, and he was no longer able to work a full day as he did prior to entering the army.

Each unfortunate event, of necessity, must be offset by something good (Dr. Gill believed it to be a law of nature), and at approximately 1:25 p.m. on the day following the fire, Frank's wife Melissa gave birth to their son Willie.

When Josh and Eliza arrived at their house on Fulton Street, the living room was already filled with guests: Rev. Joe Hamilton, Irene and Levine Hastings, who stopped in for only a quick moment, and the most notable of guests, Col. W. L. Curry.

Eliza's face was badly bruised, and her sore knees rubbed uncomfortably against her dress. Josh's beard had been severely singed, and he had trimmed it close to his face, making him nearly unrecognizable. Ed and Charles Fremont came along hoping that some of the cousins would be there, which turned out to be a disappointment for them and after an hour or so Eliza permitted them to walk home. Actually, she was pleased to let them go due to all the commotion around the house.

From the beginning, Col. Curry was a close friend of both the Hayneses and Gills, and as Union County's own military laureate he took an interest in Frank, as he did all the veterans in the county. He was keenly aware of Frank's difficulties in adjusting to work, Frank having returned from the war with those nagging disabilities.

The colonel had also been a close friend of Dr. Thomas Haynes, JBW's son. At the beginning of the war, Captain Thomas was the company commander of a unit at Plain City. At about the same date, a second company was organized at New California, where W. L. Curry was elected as first lieutenant. Both their units were original Ohio units. However, Thomas died shortly thereafter of erysipelas of the throat. Therefore, it was appropriate for the colonel to stop in on that special day, if only to show his support for Frank and the Haynes/Gill families.

Eliza had become increasingly aware of the number of guests congregating in the living room. She decided that Melissa needed to rest and very politely began putting the word out, asking everyone to respect Melissa's need to be alone with her baby.

However, Joshua and the colonel continued visiting together outside in front of the house discussing the recent fire that had taken place at the factory and the need for a hook and ladder company. After all, the original plat of the town as approved by the County Commissioners provided for 'Lots 13 and 69, on Franklin Street, to the first and second fire companies that might be organized, to consist of fifty or more persons each, and own engine and hose, or buckets and ladders.'

Five years later a new engine house was built complete with all its appointments together with a hook and ladder company, a steam engine and hose cart. Col. W. L. Curry was appointed captain with J. S. Gill as engineer.

Charles Fremont Gill

The bowl factory was relocated to Indiana. The five brothers all continued to work on the farm, and one by one they each sought ways to find other means of livelihood. Frank attempted selling wooden bowls, again; however, this involved a great deal of traveling and his disabilities made it difficult for him to do most anything for any extended amount of time. Henry farmed until 1873, when he began buying grain on commission, which he continued doing until 1879 when he began buying for his own account. Sel was a natural mechanic, Thomas was a blacksmith, and together they formed the firm Gill & Brother, Blacksmith. Ed was in the first graduating class at Richwood High School in 1880, gave the commencement address and entered the military academy at West Point.

Charles began manufacturing embalming fluid in Springfield, Ohio. However, the fumes became too much for him, and he returned to Richwood and began a coal dealership with a coal yard at the intersection of Fulton, Grove and Oak Streets, near Beam's Addition. He had negotiated with the Erie RR for a spur leading into the yard. At the same time, he opened a small office and warehouse in the center of downtown Richwood on Franklin Street, where he began selling building supplies and coal furnaces. That same year, Joshua died and Eliza moved in with Charles on Clinton Street.

At the age of forty, while on a business trip, Charles met his first wife at the Union Oyster House in Boston, on Union Street. Her name was Eleanor Norris. It always puzzled his family why she followed him to Richwood. She was a dancer and the night that he first saw her, she was part of the cast performing *La Prima Donetta* at the Wang Theater in the theater district, near Chinatown. He had sat alone in the audience, three rows behind the orchestra pit, captivated, scarcely taking his eyes off her each time she crossed the stage. As she danced, she seemed to be performing for him, always looking in his direction. Her costume accentuated her figure and each time she raised it above her knees he felt an excitement rush through his body that he had never experienced before. Each time she smiled in his direction he was sure she was smiling at him.

This wasn't the first time that he had attended a professional theater production; he was a patron of the new opera house that had just been completed in Richwood.

It wasn't until his next trip to Beantown that he came across her working behind the counter in the oyster house, shucking oysters. The production of *La Prima Donetta* at the Wang Theater had closed; she had no new stage prospects and took employment at the popular historical bistro frequented by celebrities and tourists alike. He was spending the night at a small inn up the street and had wandered in unaware of the renowned reputation of the popular pub. He had an 1890's face, wore a mustache, spectacles, a top hat, a four-button suit jacket, a high-collar white shirt with a black and white polka-dot tie, and he looked perhaps a little like an underweight Teddy Roosevelt. He entered, checked his hat and was greeted by the *maitre d'hôtel,* who directed him to the only remaining stool at the counter.

There were men of various ages in various attires sitting on stools around the semicircular counter conversing together and seemingly enjoying themselves. The counter was crowded with platters of discarded oyster shells, oyster crackers, horseradish, vinegar, vessels of chowder and pewter mugs of locally brewed Boston pale ale.

The crowd was becoming energetic and noisy. There were oyster shells on the floor, probably fallen from the overloaded counter. Charles took the remaining seat and glanced around, feeling somewhat alone. Being by himself was nothing new – he was used to making business trips early on when he sold wooden bowls for his father in Indiana, and more recently when he had to make trips to Columbus to obtain coal.

Behind the counter, there were two middle-aged men and one younger attractive woman, all busy shucking large piles of fresh oysters: giant Atlantic black diamond and the smaller New England blue shell. The woman working directly in front of him wore heavy gloves and used a knife to pry open the prickly mollusks. Working quickly she pulled drafts of ale, refilled empty chowder vessels and responded to the shouts and cries of the floor waiters. He watched intently as she struggled with a tough black diamond, inserting the knifepoint between the two halves. She held the oyster with both hands and pounded the butt of the embedded knife against the counter until the sides fell apart.

He noticed that her hair seemed wiry. She wore it tied in a knot on the back of her head, and several loose ends hung down onto her face. Her long thin but muscular arms protruded from a sleeveless shirt over which she wore a brown leather apron with a kangaroo pocket where she kept her shucking implements. She didn't look up, so after a few short moments he attempted to get her attention.

"That looks dangerous."

She didn't hear him over the persistent din, so he raised his voice a little louder. "That looks dangerous! How many times a day do you slip and run that thing through your hand?"

She placed the opened shell containing the oyster on a plate that was already stacked high with shells and tossed the empty side into the barrel behind her. She then looked up and smiled, "Oh, hello…once, only once; but I've only been doing this for a week now. What can I do for you?"

"I've never eaten in a place like this. What do you recommend?"

"Do you like oysters?"

"Never had one."

"Here, try this…tell me what you think."

"It seems strange, are you sure these are good to eat?"

"Look around…that's why everyone comes here. This is the oldest oyster house in Boston, maybe even America for that matter. Winslow Homer himself sat on that same stool just minutes ago, and Oliver Wendell Holmes the night before. Just pick up the shell, put it to your mouth and let it slide in."

"Well, what do you think?" she asked when he had finish one.

"Not bad…just takes some getting used to I suppose."

"Why not let me fix you up with a half-dozen of these blue shells and a bowl of chowder…and some cornbread?"

She cleared and wiped a small place on the counter and served him his dinner along with a pint of pale ale, then she continued to shuck, draw and stack for the noisy crowd, pausing intermittently whenever possible to make small talk with him. From the start, she seemed familiar, and by the time he had finished his last oyster and spoonful of chowder he remembered.

"Are you Eleanor Norris?"

"Why, yes…how did you know?"

"I read your name in the program at the Wang Theater. That was several months ago…you were one of the dancers."

"I'm flattered that you remember."

From that day on, he became an enthusiast of oysters,

Boston clam chowder and pale ale, but of the three he enjoyed oysters the most. Never available at home and rarely so in Columbus, they were never as fresh as those New England blue shells he had enjoyed that night.

Several months after the time he tasted his first oyster, they were married and he brought her to his home on Clinton Street, where she and their first child died in childbirth.

Mr. & Mrs. John William Martin
Chestnut Drive
Upper Sandusky, Ohio

Dear Mr. and Mrs. Martin,

I was very happy to have had the opportunity to meet you last Sunday at the Methodist Church here in Richwood. I enjoyed visiting with you and your daughter Alma, and I was surprised to learn that she had recently become a widow. As you know, I too am now a widower having lost my dear Eleanor due to complication in delivering our unborn child. After returning home, I became aware of my desire to meet further with you and your daughter for determining the possibility of a marriage between the two of us.

I must confess to an age difference; however, I would hope that this would not present a barrier. My family on both the maternal and paternal sides has a history of longevity, and I have often been told that I look young for my age. I do not use tobacco or strong drink except for an infrequent glass of pale ale when enjoying oysters and clam chowder. In any event, should something unfortunate happen to me, my estate is sufficient that Alma should be able to continue her life comfortably, and the Lord willing, raise our children.

As a young boy, I was raised on a farm and instructed wisely by my father Dr. Joshua Gill, one of the early settlers of the town. *Before establishing my own coal company in 1880, I sold wooden bowls for my father and manufactured embalming fluid in Springfield, Ohio.*

I am a member of the Methodist Church and several fraternal organizations. I enjoy hunting and fishing as well as taking an occasional swim in Lake Baccarat in the summer and skating across it in the winter. I have enclosed a current picture, which you can see is a reasonable presentation of me. If you would like any personal references, I would be glad to provide you with a list of names.

I would be very happy if you would discuss this matter with Alma, and if it seems profitable to each of you, I would like very much to come visit and confer how we all might go about being better acquainted.

Sincerely,
Charles Fremont Gill

Mr. Charles Fremont Gill
W. Clinton Street
Richwood, Ohio

Dear Mr. Gill,

It was with great pleasure that we received your recent letter expressing your interest in our daughter, Alma. We have no plans to be in Richwood in the immediate future; however, it would be our delight to receive you as a guest in our home for a short stay. Anytime next month would be convenient. We are looking forward to your response.

Sincerely,
John William Martin

Mr. & Mrs. John William Martin
Chestnut Drive

Upper Sandusky, Ohio

Dear Mr. and Mrs. Martin,
It was with great anticipation this morning that I received your invitation to come to your home. Dare I be so bold to express my enthusiasm, or should I feign nonchalance? I have arranged to arrive in Sandusky on Wednesday the 30th by train. Perhaps Royal might meet me at the station at 3:28 P.M. Otherwise, I will hire my own transportation to your home. I can only hope that Alma is as excited as I, and that I will not fail to win her heart.
Sincerely,
Charles Fremont Gill

Richwood was connected to Delaware by an electric trolley, known humorously by many residents as the 'Toonerville Trolley' after a newspaper comic strip entitled 'Toonerville Folks'. It was painted bright green with red and white trim and made hourly runs.

Once in Delaware, Charles was able to board the Columbus, Sandusky & Hocking Railroad that would take him directly to Sandusky to be picked up by Alma's brother Beryl, who went by the nickname 'Royal'. She also had an older brother named Charles.

Charles was used to taking the train, usually to Columbus, and in addition to his small suitcase, he brought along current editions of the *Richwood Gazette* and the *Delaware Gazette,* an egg sandwich and a black blindfold in case he decided to take a nap. He usually preferred a seat at the rear of the car where he could see everyone without having to be stared at by any of the other passengers. It was a rainy day, and as he began to take his seat in the rear, he noticed the windows were fogged, so before sitting down, he pulled out a handkerchief and cleared a small opening where he could get a view to the outside. He could see the conductor pacing slowly back and forth along the quay checking his watch. There were also several men who looked like businessmen rushing to get aboard. He could hear the steam of the locomotive hissing loudly and the cry of the conductor, "All aboard!"

The car began to fill and three men in business suits, each carrying a briefcase, had taken one of the small tables on the other side of the aisle. They seemed to be together and were joking around and making a lot of noise. They were making so much commotion that the couple sitting in the seats in front of their table got up and moved farther to the front of the car. Charles wondered why they were behaving so distastefully – it was too early in the day for them to be drinking.

The car wasn't completely full and no one took the seat next to him, so he was happy that he had the space to himself, and that he didn't have to talk to anyone. He wanted to be alone, read his newspapers and perhaps even take a nap, wake up and find himself in Sandusky. As the train began to pull away out from beneath the shelter, he could see the rain starting to pound against the foggy window, and he reached for his handkerchief a second time to wipe it clear. The city changed into a gray and pastel countryside with telephone poles whizzing by, a most hypnotic effect.

One of the men at the nearby table turned to him and asked, "Hey mister, how's about joining us...we're getting ready to play poker?"

The three men all looked at him, waiting for him to answer. He was into his thoughts, a semi-dreamland, passively observing most of what was happening around him, yet disconnected. He wished to be left alone and slowly he responded, "Uh...thank you, but I do not care to play. You go right ahead without me. Thanks again."

He turned his head toward the window. *I work too hard for my money to risk gambling it away*, he thought to himself and stared outside, hoping to recover his former abstract state of consciousness. However, such a state can never be forced – it comes only of its own accord.

He read the Richwood paper, and when he finished he opened the Delaware paper at the inside back page, where the crossword puzzles and comic strips always appeared. The Toonerville Folks cartoon was only mildly humorous, depicting a frenzied trolley overstuffed with passengers struggling to make it up a steep hill. The skipper had just tossed out a rope connected to an anchor and said, "Git a hold o' thet rope ev'buddy, an' when I give the' word – PULL!" He smiled and went on to read the Katzenjammer Kids. When he finished the crossword puzzle, he scanned the rest of the paper, looking mainly for national news, and centered on an article that discussed the opening of Mount Rainier National Park in Washington State, the fifth national park in the United States.

"The mountain rises abruptly from the surrounding land with an elevation of over 14,000 feet. It is surrounded by valleys, waterfalls, sub alpine wildflower meadows, old growth forest and more than twenty-six glaciers. The volcano is often shrouded in clouds that dump enormous amounts of rain and snow on the peak every year and hide it from the crowds that head to the park on weekends."

I would love to go there, he thought to himself. *It would make for a great honeymoon. The winter would be over, enough...people would just have to wait for their coal, until we got back. Henry could watch the store...he's done it before.*

He consciously slumped down in his seat and tilted his head back against the soft cushion and began to see the two of them, he and Alma, in the mountains, the forest, along a swift-moving stream, a framed tent and campfire. It was daylight, early morning, and cool with the promise of being a warm day with streaks of sunlight bursting in between the trees. They were both dressed in light-colored apparel as if they were ready to walk the promenade at Atlantic City on Easter. She was holding a parasol, and he a walking stick. As the morning passed, he removed his suit jacket and hung it on the branch of a redwood tree; she took a seat on a campstool and read verse aloud to him. Feeling amorous, he began to approach her with the intention of wooing her into the tent, and when he was within reach of her, he tripped over a rock and stumbled on top of her. Startled, she dropped her book. He quickly climbed to his feet, and she reached down to recover the tome when she saw that what he had tripped over was not a rock, it was a tombstone. Surprised, she reached for his hand as together they read the inscription – Eleanor Norris Gill – died in childbirth – 1896.

Her scream was overcome by the loud whistle of the train pulling into the station at Marion. He sat up, realized that he had been dreaming, and wondered why he had conjured up such a frightening conclusion to his musing.

The train came to a stop and several of those aboard descended, replaced by a new cadre of passengers. The game at the nearby table continued uninterrupted, with an occasional slam on the tabletop and four-letter curse.

The next stop was at Bucyrus, and from there it was nonstop to Sandusky. With each rain-drenched mile that passed, the nearby poker game was becoming louder in direct relationship with the quantity of beer that was being consumed.

Charles pulled out his egg sandwich from his jacket pocket, ordered an iced tea, and began to eat. He wasn't hungry, nevertheless, it didn't take long to finish it, and he began to read the unread stories from the *Delaware Gazette*, none of which seemed interesting but served only to help make the time pass quicker. He stared out the window, gazing at the freshly plowed cornfields. In a few weeks they would be planted and then, 'knee high by the fourth of July'. He remembered his blindfold, slid it over his head and leaned against the window, stretching his legs toward the aisle.

Royal arrived at the station in the family carriage making no excuses or apologies for being late. He spotted Charles sitting on a bench, recognizing him from the description that he had received from his mother.

"Mr. Gill?"

Charles arose from the bench, "Yes, I'm Mr. Gill."

"I'm Royal Martin…here to pick you up."

Royal offered his hand; he seemed youthful, lean yet sturdy with rosy cheeks and piercing eyes. He was well dressed in a tailored suit, white shirt with rounded collar, jeweled cuff links, a silk tie and a bowler hat.

John and his wife, Augusta Martin, were standing at the door when the carriage pulled alongside the house. It was a large bright red two-story Victorian, loaded with gingerbread trimmed in white with a sweeping bay window adjacent to the steps leading up to the first floor.

Charles carried his grippe into the front door and set it down as he was greeted by John and Augusta. Standing in the entry there were sliding doors concealing a room off to the left, a long hallway leading back to the kitchen, a stairway leading up to the second level, and to the right there was a large room the length of the house containing the living area to the front and the dining area to the rear. The front room behind the sliding doors was a guest room where Charles was to stay. The family bedrooms were upstairs. After a tour of the house, Charles returned to the living room, where Royal was reading the paper.

"Will you look at this?" Royal held the paper for Charles to see. "It's a horseless carriage…they call it a 'Winton'. The article goes on to say that 'this new invention is still subject to much skepticism but to prove the automobile's durability and usefulness, Alexander Winton has had his car undergo an 800 mile endurance run from Cleveland to New York City.'"

Charles looked closely at the picture and shook his head. "It looks like an oversized plaything to me. It's probably expensive; I work too hard for my money."

"Oh I disagree; we're coming upon the twentieth century and I feel a breeze, and it's going to blow in change."

The doors to the front room opened. John and August entered the room, both holding hands with Alma between them. She appeared elegant, wearing a floor-length bolero dress, a ruffled blouse with three-quarter length sleeves that extended from beneath a petite short-sleeve jacket. Her hair was coifed high on her head, causing her to stand taller than anyone else in the room. Charles rose to his feet and stood waiting for the threesome to approach him. He appeared calm, managing to control his nervousness.

Alma smiled and spoke. "It is so good to see you again, Mr. Gill. I want to thank you for coming all this way. How was your trip?"

He was taken by her poise and beauty. "Yes, it is good to see you again, Alma; and, Mr. and Mrs. Martin, the two of you, I am glad to see you both again. Your home is beautiful, and, red, what courage; you have such good taste." Then looking at Alma and back at Augusta he continued, "Mrs. Martin, I can see now where Alma gets her good looks. Oh...yes, Alma, the trip was most enjoyable. I had a chance to see the countryside and catch up on some reading."

The following days were filled with activities, dinners, an evening at the theater and on Sunday, following church, they took the ferry across Sandusky Bay to Lakeside, a church-affiliated vacation resort, where they enjoyed a picnic and went swimming. Charles returned to Richwood certain that he wanted to marry her, and a month following his return he wrote a letter of proposal to her. She accepted and they were soon married in Richwood. She moved in with him on Clinton Street and shortly thereafter a daughter, Eleanor, was born. One year later, Alma died of consumption and Charles, once again, was a widower.

When he was fifty, he married Alice Adelle Logue, his third wife, who was also half his age. He met her in Springfield, and soon thereafter they were married; and like the others, she moved into the house on Ottawa Street. She had a very fair complexion, blue eyes and light brown hair. When she was a young girl, she fell from a wagon. It ran over her stomach and she wasn't expected to live – she recovered but always had stomach problems. They had two children – Azile Alice, whose first name was 'Eliza' spelled backwards, and Charles Franklin, named after his father, and his uncle who had served in the War of the Rebellion. After they were married, Adelle lived for another fourteen years and then died of cancer of the stomach.

When Eleanor, Azile and Charles were in their mid-teens, their father remarried for the last time. However, his new wife, who came from England, was unable to get along with Azile and left the home on Ottawa Street, never to be heard from again. No one seemed to remember her name – not even Edwin.

Martin L. Fox – Monongalia County, West Virginia – March 1900

M artin Lewis Fox passed along slowly on foot, leading the team of two gray mules, doing his best to keep them close to the shadowy mountain wall to his left, away from the edge of the lofty narrow road. One slip and the Conestoga wagon they were pulling could have easily plunged down the low-reaching mountainside, taking Mary Ellen, his wife, their three children and all their earthly possessions with it. The peaks seemed extra high this morning while the valley below appeared deeper and more penetrating; the sky seemed to be a deeper blue and the air felt especially damp, as if it had just rained.

The wagon was fully loaded with their heavy wooden furniture, an Estey pump organ, clothing, some bananas and boiled ham, and what other food provisions they had packed away before leaving Crossroads. Mary Ellen sat perched high in the air on the leaf spring mounted driver's bench holding the reins, between Ethel and Osa Ola, and she could feel the vibration on the tip of her nose and on the wooden floor against her feet as the large metal-rimmed wheels turned slowly over the rocky road. Homer, only two, remained in back playing with a stuffed rag doll, unaware of the treacherous passage. Earlier he had rolled off to the side of the wagon and was now lodged in between a sack of potatoes and two stacked bags of flour.

They had hoped to make it to Morgantown, where they had

relatives, before dark; however, at the rate they were traveling they would be lucky to arrive before midnight. Martin had taken this road many times before and knew it nearly by heart, but this was the first time that he had attempted it with a team of mules pulling a large over-sized Conestoga. Moreover, it was only this small stretch that was so narrow, the result of a large piece of the mountain having given away two winters ago, one of the coldest and wettest winters for as long as he could remember. That winter had also taken a toll on the home they were leaving behind, the strong winds having ripped a large number of shingles from its roof, allowing the rain to damage much of the upstairs rooms. Martin conjectured that as soon as they could make it through this stretch, he could rest easier.

Off to the west, there was a fuzzy view of distant bluish-green peaks, rounded and matured by time and smothered with a smoky haze, a mushroom salad covered with musty, green ferns and moss.

The morning dew hadn't yet burned off and the air was moist and cool. Mary Ellen tried not to look off, and especially she tried not to look down. In earlier times, the road at this location had been somewhat wider; the lower mountainside had been covered with trees and vegetation. The tall foliage and thick umbrage had given the allusion of being a natural barrier that would stop or at least slow down any tumble from the road. There was no longer any such feeling of security.

She held the leather reins giving just enough slack that she could quickly pull back if she had to. Martin was tall and strong, and he had a good hold of the team, but she still felt the need to keep a tight rein. Ethel sat on the outside looking down and began to complain that she was afraid, so Osa volunteered to change places with her. As the two began to make the switch, each climbing over Mary Ellen, then one over the other, the wagon tipped ever so lightly to the outside as their weight shifted. The wagon only leaned slightly and there was no real danger, but both Mary Ellen and Ethel could feel the motion. Mary Ellen said a quick prayer while Ethel let out a shriek and Martin brought the team to a stop to see what was the matter.

Ethel and Osa Ola could see the stern look on their father's face, and they both quickly settled down. He had a certain mien that brought about respect while rarely needing to raise his voice. He had the same effect with both humans and animals. "Let's take it easy up there! We'll soon be out of this narrow area, and then we can stop for a rest. Maybe Osa, you could lead the team then. How would that be for you?"

"Sure, Dad, I would like that."

Osa Ola, the oldest of the three children, was much like her father, august and self-confident except that in her face she more resembled her mother. Her thick, brown hair hung down her back to her waistline just as her homemade dress hung nearly to the ground. Martin was well aware that whether it came to shooting a rifle, riding a horse or running a footrace she could hold her own against any of the boys her age back at Crossroads, and he treated her just the same as if she had been born a son.

As the sun reached its zenith, the road widened and a soft blue-green meadow replaced the nearly vertical slope. Martin brought the mules to a halt. "Osa! Go fetch a pail of water from that stream, and, Mary Ellen, hand me those feedbags behind the bench there. We'll let Molly and Polly rest while we grab a bite to eat."

Once they had taken care of the team, Mary Ellen took some provisions from the wagon into her apron – a piece of ham, a small loaf of bread and some apples – and carried them over to the grass where Martin was spreading a wool blanket on the ground. It was an old blanket, one that had been in the family for many years, woven by Mary Ellen's mother, Nancy Haines Johnson. It was colored by the many stains that had made their way into its fibers, a few blotches of candle wax, along with a few spots singed by sparks from the fireplace in the cabin they had just left behind, all which blurred together to form a collage and give the blanket its character. Mary Ellen had made a new quilt that she kept packed away in her trunk. It was a very special quilt, one that she had made over a period of years from scraps of material sewn together in small puffs stuffed with cotton. It was large enough to cover a double bed and Martin's long legs that hung over the edge when he stretched out full length. The background was made of twelve-inch blue and white gingham squares sewn together with a fabric image of a large bush superimposed across its surface. The bush was growing from a large pot at the bottom edge with its branches each extending upward and outward, stretching to the other three sides. The bush was covered with hundreds of different flowers, carnations, roses and peonies, for example, all forming a unified plant. Each flower was made from a different piece of material and stuffed with cotton, giving the bush a certain amount of relief. It would have been a shame to place it on the moist ground, therefore, the old wool blanket showed its intrinsic value once again as each member of the Martin Fox family squatted comfortably on it, butts, feet and knees pressing the tough, fibrous weave against the grassy earth, grinding any ants, potato worms or ground moths that happpenstance would have placed at the exact spot. Martin began to say the grace.

When they had finished eating, Martin stood, preened his mustache, pushing the ends upward at a slight angle, and looked at Osa. "Well, are you ready to take the team?"

Osa nearly tripped on her long gingham dress getting up. The warm feeling that she received from her father asking her to perform this important task filled her chest and gave rise to a smile on her face. This seemed to her to be as important as the time when her father asked her to ride alone on horseback to

Peter Core's General Store at Crossroads and bring back medicine for one of their sick lambs, or how good it made her feel the first time that he had asked her to go frog gigging at night with him. It is much more common to hear about how girls are influenced by their mothers, but all it takes is a moment's reflection to start realizing the huge impact a father can have on one of his daughters.

Taking her father by the hand, she replied excitedly, "Oh, yes, I would love to." She then rushed over to Molly and Polly and began removing their empty feedbags, replacing them behind the bench on the wagon while Mary Ellen began shaking the blanket and returning Homer and the unfinished food to the wagon.

Ethel was busy watching a squirrel sitting up on its haunches. There were lots of squirrels where they came from, and even though she had never been able to get near one before, she wanted to play with this one. She began walking in its direction. The squirrel turned and ran to the nearest tree, a large, very old sycamore tree that had once been struck by lightning, and it scampered up the opposite side. The tree almost seemed human-like, its branches growing from its sides like long arms. It had a gaping hole like a yawning mouth on the trunk near the ground and several large scars above its cavity that took on the look of eyes and ears. Ethel thought that she had seen the squirrel enter the opening, and she cautiously stooped low and peered inside. From the outside, the tree appeared barely wide enough for a small girl to enter, but inside there was a large cavernous room lit by a natural luminescence emitting from its walls.

An owl perched on a large mushroom spoke to her. "The squirrel did not come this way. Nevertheless, you are welcome to stay a while and look around."

Ethel asked the owl, "Then, did you see which way he

went?"

"I didn't see him...but I can tell you that he is not here."

"This place is bigger than I thought."

"You can look around, but be careful and stay away from the frog; his tongue is very long and he can scarf you up from a distance."

Ethel was distracted by the enormity of the room, the dazzling iridescence of glowing phosphorous and the strange owl with which she had just conversed. She no longer thought of the squirrel and looked down at her feet, which had become snarled and tangled with the numerous snake-like roots that seemed to be alive, causing her to trip when she took a step. As she attempted to regain her balance her arms shot upward and both her hands pushed against the inside walls of the hollowed trunk, causing sudden darkness and evidencing that the enormity of the room was only an illusion.

Mary Ellen returned to their picnic spot for one last trip and noticed that Ethel wasn't there. Martin was back at the wagon checking the water barrel, and Osa was in the wagon changing Homer's diaper. She called out to Martin, who replied that she wasn't with him or in the wagon. Mary Ellen turned north and then south, hoping to catch sight of her, but to no avail. Unable to see her they began calling out, again without receiving any response.

Martin and Mary Ellen entered the tree line nearest the spot where they had picnicked. The undergrowth and sharp blackberry bushes made it extremely difficult to go even a few feet, but even so they pushed forward slowly and quietly hoping to hear any sounds of their little girl.

Each step produced its own crunching sound of dead vegetation, and Martin continued to take a few steps, stop and listen, only to hear the nearby crackling of Mary Ellen's footsteps and the eerie echo of two ravens crowing loudly. He called out again and then remained motionless. It was a mature forest with trees of varying sizes, some of which had grown tall. Beams of light managed to slice through the overhead canopy like alternating spikes of light and dark piercing their eyes and the lower leaves.

To Ethel, the now dark interior felt like the inside of a freshly cut pumpkin, and her hands sank inches into the soft, damp fibrous surface. She no longer wanted to remain there so she stooped down and duck-walked out of the opening. On seeing her sister, she quickly ran up to her and began explaining what had just happened while Osa interrupted and berated her for having vanished, explaining how her disappearance was creating a panic with their mother and father. They needed to find them and let them know. However, as Osa began to call out, they could hear the grunts and squeals of a boar sounding as if it were running in their direction. Neither of the girls had ever seen or heard a charging pig. As it grew nearer, the trampling and chafing of its feet and body against the brush and ground and its raspy snorts and roar mounted a fear within each of them, and they ran to the wagon screaming. Martin too heard its ugly squeals and called out to Mary Ellen for her to run quickly to the wagon. When she argued that she remain, fearing for Ethel's safety, he insisted that he would remain instead and watch for her.

The racket grew increasingly louder and Martin suddenly saw a fat, tusked, squealing pig come scurrying through the brush toward him. He pulled himself in tighter against a tree, keeping his hand on his knife, crouching lower, hoping not to be seen. Fearing that the pig, unchecked, would head in the direction of the others, Martin waited for the exact moment when it passed even with where he remained crouched, then he let out a fearsome battle cry. He leaped, screaming loudly and landed on the pig's back, plunging his knife into the back of its neck, just below its cranium.

The pig twisted, jerked and recoiled, shaking his assassin to the ground with the knife still imbedded to the hilt in its head. Having regained the moment, it began charging Martin, who now lay defenseless on the ground. The pig tore away at his leg as Martin attempted to climb to his feet. Blood began spurting from inside his thigh as the pig pushed him back to the ground and ripped at his neck. Martin tried pushing it away, but the pig was too fast, too heavy, too aggressive, and too strong. In less than a minute Martin Fox lay defeated, unconscious and soaked in his own blood while the boar continued to rip away at his flesh.

Martin awoke and sat up; he could feel his heart pounding. Mary Ellen lay facing him, asleep, the quilt with twelve-inch gingham squares and flowers covering them from the waist down. His nightgown and forehead were soaking wet with perspiration, and he was suddenly aware that he had awakened from a terrifying nightmare. He looked out the small bedroom window and could see that the sky was becoming illuminated by dawning light. This wasn't the first time that he had had this dream – it had become a reoccurring event – and the nearer the date approached that they were to leave for Ohio, the more frequently the nightmare repeated itself. He moved his feet to the floor, stepped into his slippers and walked over to the window to look out. Two red squirrels chased up and around a nearby tree, and two ravens squawked back and forth from the barn roof.

"Mary Ellen! Wake up. I have something to tell you."

Sanford Lemasters had agreed to drive the Fox family into Morgantown to the train station. He was a long-standing friend of the family, had farmed the adjacent acres, and was sad that the Foxes had decided to leave Crossroads and move to Ohio.

Martin began to work on Sanford, hoping to convince him to bring his family and make the move with him to the rich farmlands of the buckeye state. Sanford wasn't yet ready to start over and to move his family, but he did agree to help Martin make the move.

When the day finally arrived, Osa Ola and Ethel sat on the front porch steps, nervously waiting for Sanford and his wagon to arrive. Even though several years had passed since either Martin or Mary Ellen had purchased any store-bought clothes, Martin was wearing his best suit with his wide-brimmed hat, and Mary Ellen wore her usual Sunday dress and bonnet. They walked around in front, visiting and saying their goodbyes to the several friends and family members that were present to see them off – Martin's mother and father, Lewis and Charlotte Fox; Sarah Eddy, his half sister; Mary Ellen's father and mother, Amon and Nancy Johnson, and her six brothers and sisters along with their husbands and wives. Also present was the Reverend William Luke Richardson, who would one day marry Mary Ellen's youngest sister, Iva Nora Johnson. Martin, his long arms at his side, stood talking with Peter Core, Sanford's brother-in-law and owner of the Crossroads General Store.

There was an air of excitement present – many saw their move as a great adventure. Still, a certain sadness at their leaving held the buoyancy in check. Suddenly, a queasy feeling in their stomachs came over both Martin and Mary Ellen. It was as if a switch had just been set, putting in motion what early on had only been a foggy idea that had somehow matured. Up until now, it was never real, no commitments had been made, and their woolgathering could have been stopped at any time. Too many things had now gone forward for them to turn back. Martin had sold the homestead, given the down payment on the Ohio farm, and two days earlier all their furniture and possessions except for the three fully loaded suitcases they would carry on board the train had been loaded onto a Conestoga wagon to meet up with them several weeks after their arrival in Richwood. Mary Ellen clutched her worn copy of the King James' Bible tightly as she reminisced together with her mother and two of her sisters, somewhat nostalgically, about earlier times when she and her sisters were all growing up on the farm.

At last, Sanford and his six-passenger oak surrey turned onto the lane and headed in the direction of the front porch. Martin ceremoniously pulled his watch from his vest pocket. Osa Ola and Ethel both jumped unrestrained from the steps and began to run up the lane toward the fast-moving carriage. Harley sat next to his father on the driver's bench and waved at the two girls as they ran alongside. Sanford brought the horses to a halt next to the porch steps, where the suitcases and one trunk waited to be loaded.

Sanford then stood and jokingly called out, "Did anyone here order a taxi?"

"Yes!" Martin called out across the lawn. "Over here; I believe the missus needs a lift to Ohio. Are you headed in that direction?"

"Of course…well, yes…as far as Morgantown, that is." He wore a smile on his face as he and Harley dismounted.

"Come on over here, Sanford. Can I get you a glass of water?"

Sanford walked to the small table where Martin was standing filling a glass. Martin handed it to his friend and poured himself a second glass. Mary Ellen took her place next to Martin, and all their friends and family members gathered around them as if they were all about to say their final goodbye.

"Here's to my good friend Sanford, whom I will surely miss." The two raised their glasses and then took two or three long deep swallows until both their glasses were empty.

Martin removed his watch a second time and after replacing

it in his vest pocket, he turned to Mary Ellen and said, "Darlin', I think it's that time."

Rev. Richardson stepped forward and regarded the group. "Let us all move in closer and place our hands on Martin and Mary Ellen as I say a prayer. If your arm will not reach, then just place it on the shoulder of the person in front of you; the spirit will pass through just the same. Now let us pray:

"Oh Heavenly Father, we come to you this day to ask your blessing on this family that is about to depart, that their journey to their new home be a safe one. And when they arrive, we pray that they are soon able to find new friends, a new church congregation, and that they will prosper, that this land will bear the fruits that have been promised to them. We that remain will miss each one of them, Martin, Mary Ellen, Osa Ola, Ethel and Homer as they go forth to the new land…the rich woods and we thank you for our having known them, having been blessed by them."

He then raised both hands as if he were reaching to God and continued, "Now unto Him that is able to keep you from falling, and to present you faultless before the presence of His glory with exceeding joy, to the only wise God our Savior, be glory and majesty, dominion and power, both now and ever. Amen."

After a few short seconds, Martin raised his head and reached out to Rev. Richardson to shake his hand. "Thank you, Luke…that was a wonderful way to cap off our departure. I'm sure that we will see each other again, if not here, then in Heaven. We'll be back to visit…I'm sure."

As Sanford and Harley loaded the bags onto the surrey, all who came to see them off began climbing into their carriages and leaving down the long lane to the main road. Mary Ellen stuck her head inside the front room of the house for one last look before climbing aboard. Doubt suddenly caused her to wonder if she had done a good enough job cleaning the place...the new folks that would be coming, would they judge her as a poor housekeeper? She knew that a page in her life's book was being turned, and it seemed as if two pages were stuck together. She wet her thumb and index finger as though she were about to separate them, took a deep breath, turned and exited. Martin was the last to climb up and take his seat next to Mary Ellen, and when he had done that, Sanford loosed the reins and turned the two horses toward the main road.

Martin Fox and his family moved into the old house that had been built and lived in by Reverend Hamilton, northwest of Richwood on Hamilton Pike. They arrived by train with their possessions following by wagon, pulled by mules.

The land was flat and rich, full of black loam dumped ages earlier by the thawing glaciers whose migration south had reached their terminus in the counties now known as Franklin, Delaware and Union, forming Fulton Creek, the Big and Little Darby and Scioto Rivers. Shortly upon his arrival, Martin donated a small parcel of his land, on which was built the red brick, one-room Pleasanton School.

Before Martin left Crossroads, he had encouraged his friend, David Sanford Lemasters, to make the move to Ohio with him. Once he had settled in, more enthusiastically then ever, and delighted with how well matters had turned out for him, he again contacted his friend and worked out an arrangement where David could take over the Chambers' property on the Boundary Road at the end Hamilton Pike, not far from his own farm. Shortly thereafter, David arrived with this wife, Christina Core, and his two sons, Harley Clarence and Orestes Arlington.

Osa Ola – Hamilton Pike, Richwood, Ohio

T he rooster crowed at the break of dawn, and Osa lay awake in her bed, soon to be gone. It was May 10, 1902, the last day of school. She remembered there would be a photographer today to take their class picture – her mother had sewn a new dress for the occasion. Almost Edwardian, It had a dark, long sleeve bodice with a high neck, overlain with a pinafore of the same material. She would be wearing new button-down shoes. A smile came across her face as she imagined herself in her knew vestments. No doubt she would look extra special today; Mr. Shields would be so surprised to see how nice she looked. She hoped that the new shoes wouldn't hurt her feet as it was about half a mile to the red brick schoolhouse on the edge of their farm, past the cemetery, and she would have to walk along the gravel road. She might be called on today by Mr. Shields to recite her Latin conjugations: *sum fui futurus, habeo habui habitum, eo ire itum, video vidi visum.*

She could hear her parents getting up in the next bedroom. Her father snored most of the night. Sometimes she could hear her mother trying to wake him, to make him be quite. Oh how she would get so mad! But now, any moment, her mother would be knocking on her door to awaken her, so she would just close her eyes, pretend to be asleep and that would give her a few more minutes for her thoughts until her mother surely returned a second time – *sum fui futurus, habeo habui habitum….*

"Osa...Osa Ola!" The words, her name, rang from her mother's lips as if she were singing from the choir loft at the First Baptist Church. "Time to get up! You've a busy day today so let's get up and at 'em. Your dad's anxious to get started on the milking, so let's get going."

She pulled the covers over her head and then realized that it wasn't going to work, that she might as well get up and as her mother said, 'at 'em.'

Grudgingly, she climbed from her bed, slipped off her nightgown and passed in front of the dresser mirror to the hook on the wall where her blue, tattered gingham work dress hung, the one she wore when milking the cows. Its sleeves were worn thin due to her habit of sitting on a stool and resting her elbows on her knees while she milked. The last few times that she wore it, she was aware that it no longer fit; she was experiencing an increased rate of growth, particularly height, and was rapidly outgrowing all her clothes. Just as she began pulling it over her head, she stopped to look in the mirror. Other changes were taking place – the formation of breast tissue, pubic and underarm hair, body odor, and finally menarche. All in all she was pleased with most of these changes, however, she was suddenly shaken as her eyes were drawn to a single large pimple that had appeared overnight on her face. It was on the end of her nose, and she leaned closer to the mirror to get a better look, hoping that it wouldn't show in the photograph to be taken today, in her new dress and button-down shoes.

Mary Ellen returned to make sure Osa was getting ready and saw her standing undressed in front of the mirror squeezing her blemish. "Osa! What are you doing?" she exclaimed, seemingly more startled and embarrassed about her nudity and seeing for the first time how large her breast buds had become than what she was doing to her face. "Why are you standing there without your clothes?"

"Mother…I have a pimple…right in the middle of my face! How can I have my picture taken today?"

Mary Ellen picked up the milk dress that was now lying on the dresser and handed it to Osa. "First thing…please put this on…you've got to learn to be more discreet…what if your father…? As for the spot on your nose, you shouldn't squeeze it…just leave it alone. Unless you draw attention to it by squeezing it, making it red and swollen, no one will notice. If you spend your energy concentrating on it, it will sap your other beautiful qualities. Have faith, my dear, it's a matter of being bigger than it. Now let's get started."

Osa slowly walked from her bedroom down the staircase and out the kitchen door to what her father had dubbed the 'king's throne', that small square building with the moon-shaped slits.

When she returned, in through the back door to the kitchen, she could smell the oatmeal lightly simmering on the cooktop of their new Acorn cookstove. Mary Ellen had placed it off to the side so as not to boil over. It wouldn't be ready until after they finished milking and gathered the eggs. Martin and Mary Ellen had already headed out to the barn and were herding the first round of Holsteins into the milk stalls, filling the mangers with a mix of grain and hay. Osa soon joined her parents, and the three sat on their three-legged stools working quietly amid the symphony of crunching corn and the pst-pst of milk being fired rhythmically into metal pails, accented by the occasional swish of a cow's tail against a nagging horsefly. When Osa finished filling the first bucket, she poured its contents into a larger milk can to cool, then into the separator to separate the cream from the whole milk.

When they had finished, Osa gathered the eggs from the henhouse and returned to the kitchen for breakfast. Mary was busy frying bacon and scrambled eggs in a large iron skillet.

Homer was sitting at the table waiting patiently to eat, while Ethel was setting the table with plates, silverware, napkins, honey and fresh milk. Osa thought she heard a distant rumble, a little like a small object falling lightly to the floor upstairs. The second rumble was more convincing that a storm was on its way, especially as the outside sky began to darken and a cool breeze drifted in through the back porch screen door. "Oh Mama!" Osa exclaimed. "My new dress, it'll be ruined. You'll drive me to school, won't you?"

Her mother hesitated before answering. "Of course. I just hope that it doesn't blow too hard for too long or you and I'll need to put the curtains on the carriage. We still have time…it could easily blow over soon enough."

The room darkened and large heavy drops of rain pounded loudly against the rear porch roof and kitchen window, making its way, accompanied by a musty smell, in through the screen door.

Mary Ellen quickly rushed to close the door, then mopped up the floor with a towel and her feet and relit the hurricane lamp that sat in the center of the kitchen table, causing the room to take on a warm orange color. Martin remarked that he hadn't yet set out the milk cans, but then young Harley probably wouldn't be by during the downpour. The previous evening's and morning's filled cans had to be loaded onto a two-wheeled cart and taken to the milk stand at the edge of the road to be picked up by Harley Lemasters onto his horse-drawn wagon.

Harley was a couple years older than Osa and lived farther up Hamilton Pike. He picked up the milk every day for several of the farmers and drove it to the creamery in Richwood. Empty cans replaced the filled ones on the stand and the process was repeated seven days a week, 365 days a year.

By the time breakfast was over and the dishes washed, the rain had ended and the sun had resumed its position in the sky and its attendant responsibility of providing warmth and vitality to the earth, its population and vegetation. A rainbow had formed in the eastern sky, not only displaying the light's spectrum but the biblical promise that God had made to Noah. The air took on a fresh, clean quality and all the numerous earth burrowing animals and insects removed themselves from their holes in the ground and applauded the new spring day loudly. There remained potholes full of clear water in the lane leading out to the milk stand as Martin pulled the two-wheeled cart loaded with several cans, each weighing 126 pounds. His spirits were high – the cleansing rain had seen to that, and he spoke a prayer of thanks to his God as he struggled with the heavy cart.

Mary Ellen helped Osa into her new clothes and coifed her long hair onto the top of her head. Ethel also had a new dress, but she didn't share her sister's excitement and saw the day simply as just another day except for the prospect of summer vacation. When they had finished dressing, Mary Ellen kissed her two daughters and waved goodbye as they headed out down the lane to Pleasant View School.

It was a small one-room brick schoolhouse built by the newly created Pleasant View School District on a two-acre parcel donated by Martin Fox at the northern terminus of his land. Upon his arrival from Crossroads, he donated it to the district with the proviso that if and when the school ceased to function, it would revert to either him or his heirs. The Hamilton family burial ground was also situated on Martin's land and adjacent to the school. William Hamilton was the pioneer who cleared and farmed the land in the 1830's. His family had been known for having produced several generations of lawyers, physicians and ministers of the gospel. However, the great estate was now replaced with acres of corn and oats with nothing remaining except the cemetery. It was on the southern terminus of this parcel that Martin built his home along Hamilton Pike some distance away from the original residence.

As on each school day, Osa and her sister Ethel walked down the lane towards the school. The road was flat and on the same plane as the adjacent fields, not rounded and without drainage ditches running alongside, as it would appear in later years. Johnny Appleseed himself or Jonathan Alder might have passed on such a road. It was separated from the fields with an occasional tree and a thicket of low growing brush, brambles and berry bushes which served as resting spots for the many yellow canaries, redwing blackbirds and finches that filled the roadway with exquisite song and color.

The two schoolgirls walked around the few remaining pools of rainwater that had yet to be absorbed into the ground. With several gravel quarries in the surrounding area, crushed stone was plentiful and served as a first-rate road covering, keeping both dust and mud at a minimum. It was not an easy surface for walking though, so Osa ambled along slowly, holding Ethel's hand and doing her best to keep the rough-cut stones from scarring her new shoes.

In the distance she could see a two-horse wagon approaching, but it was too far to be able to make out who the driver might be. As it drew near, she was able to recognize Harley Lemasters on his milk route, and when he arrived even with the two girls he brought the team to a halt.

The wagon appeared to be quite old with large wooden spoke wheels and heavily worn sideboards all drawn by two large draft horses. Harley pressed the foot brake to keep the wagon from rolling and called down to Osa. "On your way to school?"

"Of course...isn't it obvious?"

"Actually not...you look dressed for Sunday church, but unless you are headed to Essex, you won't find any churches in this direction."

"How about turning the team around and giving us a lift…it shouldn't take long?"

"Impossible…the road's too narrow. Now I may just be able to arrange it if we might drop off Ethel at the school and you come with me on the route."

"You're teasing me, Harley! Not today…this is the last day of school, and I don't want to miss having the class picture taken. Besides, I expect Mr. Shields to call on me today to recite my Latin conjugations, *sum fui futurus, habeo habui habitum*. Ethel will be called on to give the planetary days of the week, Sunday, Moonday, Marsday, Mercuryday…you remember them, don't you?"

"Well, then, since school is out, can you come along tomorrow?"

"My parents will have plenty for me to do…I'm sure of it…see you in church on Sunday."

The Lemasters and Foxes were family friends from Crossroads. Sanford and Christina Lemasters and their two sons, Harley and Arlington, arrived only a few months after the Foxes and settled on the Chambers' farm at the opposite end of Hamilton Pike, on the corner of the Boundary Road.

Beneath his baggy trousers and worn hat Harley was a handsome boy, athletic with brownish-blond hair and muscular arms that developed from lifting the heavy milk cans on and off the wagon. Osa and Harley played together as kids back in Crossroads so the degree of familiarity shown between them had always been acceptable to each of their parents. Since arriving in Ohio the two families would ride to church together on Sundays and attend prayer services on Wednesday evenings. Only recently Mary Ellen was becoming aware that the relationship between the two needed to be guarded more closely as they began sitting together at services. Seeing her daughter's behavior

329

earlier that morning while she stood before the mirror added greater emphasis to her suspicions.

Past the cemetery, the red brick school came quickly into view. Except for the ugly wooden cold barrier that had been constructed around the front door, it was a handsome building almost looking like a small church with ceiling-height arched windows on each side. The structure sat a ways back from the road, and there was a water pump connected to a well off to the side. It was easy to tell that this was a special day since she could see several horses tied to the hitching rail and two others still hitched to carriages. Usually there would only be Mr. Shields' horse.

Once inside, one could see the small 81/2" by 11" framed picture of the late President William McKinley surrounded by red, white and blue bunting above the blackboard, on the far wall, the shock of his assassination only eight months earlier barely forgotten. President McKinley, a native son, had served as Ohio governor and later defeated his rival, William Jennings Bryan, for a two-term presidency. It would be some time before his picture would be replaced by that of his vice-president, Teddy Roosevelt. Immediately below his picture, written in cursive on the blackboard there appeared the words:

Apple blossoms whiten,
And peach blossoms fall,
Garlands are gay by the garden wall.

On an adjacent panel, there was written the date, May 10, 1902, the teacher's name, Chester Shields, names of the superintendent and directors, and the names of all ten pupils. Mr. Shields, wearing a new suit and looking especially neat and scrubbed, rushed to the door to greet the two.

"Osa and Ethel, I was getting worried. I should have known that the storm could never keep you two away. Osa…that's a new dress, isn't it…it's beautiful. And Ethel, you too. You are both two beautiful young ladies. We are going to have a wonderful time today. There are guests here, Mr. J. W. Cheney and Henry Hoxworth, both directors of the school and Mr. Clickerson, the photographer that is going to take our picture. Later we will enjoy some apple juice and some cookies that were brought here earlier by Mrs. McCrary – that will be fun. Come now, Osa, are you ready to recite your Latin conjugations?"

The Funeral

Cuba, the housekeeper, met him at the back door; she had been crying; her soft, brown cheeks wet with tears, her eyes, red and puffy, her gray-streaked hair held neatly in place with an invisible hair net. He rushed past her, with nary a 'hello', through the narrow hallway to the left that led to the living room, immediately recognizing the hanging effluvium, the same unpleasant odor that had filled the air for several weeks now: gangrene – death and decay of soft tissues from lack of blood. His father, Charles Fremont Gill, coal merchant, farmer, 32nd degree Mason, Sunday school teacher and one-time traveling salesman, had at last escaped the torment of his decomposing body.

The corpse was lying on the folding cot which had been placed downstairs weeks earlier in the small library, adjacent to the living room. He hadn't been to his upstairs bedroom since he had become unable to climb the stairs. Next to the bed was a small nightstand, which held a pitcher and an untouched glass of water, various medicines, a metal syringe, a box of Kleenex and his gold-filled wire-framed bifocal glasses. His wooden crutches, which hadn't been used for several days, lay on the floor. The library was connected to the living room with an open archway so a curtain had been constructed to shut off the light. Nevertheless, streaks of afternoon sun seeped into the room along the edges of the pulled blind that covered the remaining solitary window. The room was quite narrow, with the sagging cot pushed against the window. There was room enough for a chair at the foot of the cot, only inches from one of the two floor-to-ceiling built-in bookcases that filled the walls at opposite ends of the room. The upper shelves were lined with books read over his lifetime while old magazines and newspapers were stacked on the lower levels. One shelf held a row of Bibles of various translations together with several concordances that he had collected. His Masonic sword and scabbard, in its leather case, was stored at the very top of the bookcase, hidden behind the crowned molding.

He knew as soon as he saw his father that he was dead, lying there motionless, unshaven, body blue, his lower extremities soft, putrid, rotten and dark, his eyes wide-open and staring up to the ceiling as if there had been a last gasp captured and frozen. Despairingly, he placed his ear to his father's chest and took hold of his wrist in an attempt to see if he could discern any trace of life. His skin felt cold, however, his body had not yet begun to stiffen. He gently closed the man's eyelids and covered him with the blanket that had been earlier pushed to the foot of the bed with the final jerk. He then sat on the small space at the edge, clasped his hands together and said a prayer.

The house on Franklin Street was a new, two-story home on two acres at the northern most edge of town. Charles Franklin Gill had bought the parcel and hired his brother-in-law to design and build the Cape Cod style home for him and for his soon to be wife, Mabel Lemasters. At about the same time that the home was completed, his father had injured one of his legs while at the coal yard. At first, the wound seemed simple enough, seemingly not requiring a doctor's attention, however, it refused to heal. Infection quickly spread to other parts of his body and he became bedridden. By the time Dr. Keever was called, gangrene had set in, evidenced by crusting of his toes and fingers.

Cuba pulled the curtain back. "I called Dr. Keever, like you ask. He be here soon." Her voice was one of wanting to be helpful yet not be in the way.

"Thank you, Cuba." Outwardly, he showed no emotion, but his insides trembled with sadness. "You should probably call Charley Davis, he'll need to check with the coroner and make out a report. The number of the police department is on the inside cover of the phone book...you can call him."

"Yes, sir, Mr. Gill, I'll call him right away." As she began to leave, she paused and turned again toward him. "I'm so sorry...he was a wonderful man."

Cuba had served the family as housekeeper for several years when they lived on Ottawa Street, before the Great Depression, however, she was discharged when the three banks in town closed and the family business took a serious downturn. Charles had been a coal retailer, and one would have thought that people needed to keep warm regardless of the state of the economy; nevertheless, those were desperate times and people made do with much less, surviving on onions and potatoes, wearing heavy clothes during the winter months and cutting firewood from wherever they could find it. By the time it had bottomed, the man had aged considerably. No longer able to take care of himself, he moved in with his son on Franklin Street. That was when Cuba returned to work, but only part-time.

Dr. Keever arrived only one minute before police inspector, Charley Davis, and greeted young Charles Franklin Gill with a solemnity of both condolence and veneration. They shook hands and then he reached over and gently removed the blanket with religious assiduity. Inspector Davis quickly turned away. His short time on the force hadn't yet hardened him to the rankness of a rotting cadaver.

Dr. Keever studied the body for a while and then covered him again, his heart aching having seen what was once his friend and patient now looking forty years older than when he had seen him a week beforehand. "There'll be no need for an autopsy; the odor is sufficient proof of the cause of death."

Dr. Keever and Inspector Davis were gone when the undertaker and his assistant arrived. Cuba watched as they removed the body. She remembered how lean he had been in his early days, had grown more rotund over the years, and now his withered body seemed to weigh slightly more than a hundred pounds, easily loaded onto the gurney. *It will most likely be a grand funeral*, she thought to herself. He could be bearish at times, but his largess and the respected family name easily overcame that. He was always good to her though, never gruff as he sometimes could be with others.

Cuba was from one of the three black families in Richwood and lived with her husband in Beam's Addition, in one of the small cottages along Baccarat Lake. She wasn't completely sure when the transition actually took place, when she was no longer working for the old man; but now it was settled – death always solved a lot of problems. Not that working for the two of them was ever a problem; she always got along with both. It was that she had taken care of young Charley, as most people called him, and his two older sisters, Eleanor and Azile, when they were all young children. It seemed strange to call the one who still seemed so young 'Mister Gill'. He really wasn't that young though; to her, he just seemed like that. He had gone off to State after high school to study business, joined a fraternity and moved into the frat house when the old man asked him to come home; he had been suffering from gout and wanted Charley to help with the business.

As she stood at the front door and watched the body loaded into the ambulance, she was reminded of when Charley's mother had passed away – stomach cancer. She always seemed so young – too young for death to have its way with her. Young Charley had only been thirteen at the time, she had suffered so much before she died, endless hours of dry heaving pain that the cocaine did little to ease; now his father had taken his turn at death in a similar ugly manor.

Once the body was inside the ambulance, she continued to watch the undertaker, who remained standing there, listening to her employer, responding, and taking notes in a small notebook that he had pulled from inside his breast pocket, nodding his head. It was mid-afternoon in early October, an Indian summer and an unusually hot day, and she watched him wiping his brow with a handkerchief that he pulled from his hip pocket as he talked. Cars speeding by on Franklin Street created a flurry with the reddish-orange leaves fallen from the maple trees lining the red brick pavement. Occasionally a passing car would slow down upon seeing the ambulance parked in the drive, solemnity on their faces, wondering what had happened.

He called his sister, Azile, and conversed with her for over an hour. Since she had married and moved to Springfield, they telephoned each other regularly, usually once a week. Cuba could hear him sobbing under his breath as he and his sister lamented together, his emotion triggering her own sadness and weeping.

When they had finished, Charley went straight to the library and removed the metal box that had been hidden at the top of the bookcase, from behind the crowned molding, and he unlocked it with a key that his father had given to him when he had moved to Franklin Street. He took a seat at the desk and carefully removed the contents: cash, enough to pay for the funeral; several grant deeds covering the house on Ottawa, the office and store in downtown Richwood, the coal yard together with a railroad lease on the spur into the yard, and a commercial property on Fulton Street that was presently occupied by a service station. There were some stock certificates; totaling about 50,000 worthless shares of the bank that he had once been a director of and that had failed during the depression; and his last will and testament.

In the distance, on the other side of town, the bell at the Methodist Protestant Church was ringing. Charley removed his watch on its chain from his vest pocket, slim and elegant, a cover that opened with a touch; he was about to miss Wednesday evening prayer services.

Mabel Lemasters was on the organ rehearsing for Sunday services at the First Baptist church when Charley entered from the outside through the unlocked side door.

The muffled sound of *Nearer My God to Thee* resonated from the organ pipes, oozing its way through the sanctuary walls. He could feel its vibration on the tip of his nose and in his feet against the steps as he climbed the narrow staircase leading up to the second floor. At the top, he turned and walked past the empty dressing room and down the dark hall leading to the choir loft. The music grew louder with each step until he opened the door, entered the sanctuary and received the full power and resplendent sound of the grand organ, whose windpipes seemed to grow from the console like giant stalagmites.

Mabel sat not too far off to his right, perched on the organ bench, and he turned and regarded her for a moment as she continued playing without noticing him. Her eyes looked straight ahead at the music, never down at her hands as her fingers, drawn to each key, seemingly effortlessly moved about on their own accord, interrupted occasionally by the need to push or pull a stop or to turn a page. She wore a starched summer blouse with a pleated skirt; her bare arms appeared thin yet with well-defined muscles, like those of a swimmer, stretched out to the keyboard. Like a masseuse she performed, pushing and rubbing, pressing each key firmly, powerfully and quickly, guided by the hands of God, sometimes softly and tenderly. Her feet moved across the bass pedalboard, her tapered fingers and limbs working together, recreating Jacob's dream, a perpetual intercourse opened between heaven and earth, through the medium of Christ, God manifested in the flesh. Then as if she had just run over a cat in the road, she stopped and the house of worship fell silent but for a lingering echo while she penciled a notation in the margin of the music. Replacing the pencil to the music rack, she repeated the stanza that was giving her trouble while Charley, not wanted to interrupt, walked down the steps to the sanctuary floor and took a seat in the first pew.

Mabel Lemasters and her older sister Margaret were both pianists. The two began when their father, Harley, brought home a spinet one Christmas and they began taking lessons, once a week, fifty cents a lesson, after school, while their three brothers, Leroy, Charles and William, were at football practice. They all came to school in one car, a model-T Ford usually driven by Leroy, the older of the siblings. Mabel and Margaret usually had to remain until the boys were finished with football practice before they could go home to the farm, which was several miles north of town. On Sundays, the entire family were all members of the First Baptist church choir – Mabel at the organ, Harley, Margaret and the three boys all singing in the choir, and Osa Ola was the choir director.

Charley and Mabel had been friends for several years, and their relationship had slowly matured until they finally decided to marry. However, Charley had his hands full taking care of his dying father. Knowing that he had only a very short time to live, Charley insisted that they wait until he could give his full time and attention to the marriage. Mabel was all right with that; as a high school teacher and women's basketball coach in nearby Raymond School District and as church organist, her time too was fully occupied.

Just as he had waited these past few months, he sat patiently in the front pew, in the solemnity of the sanctuary, as his bride, not knowing of his presence, prepared herself for the following day's services. He was there to tell her that they could proceed now with the wedding. But somehow that good news did not seem to sit well with the unhappiness that he was experiencing. And the longer he remained the more uncomfortable he felt. Then, after a few minutes, without a word, he stood, turned, and dashed quietly in the direction of the vestibule.

At a certain point, as he passed up the aisle, his image became visible in the rear-view mirror mounted on the organ above Mabel's head, and she saw him disappear out the large oak double doors and down the front steps.

She continued to practice, and when she had finished and the angels returned to heaven, she exited through the side door and down the stairs where Charley had entered earlier. Still parked next to her '36 Chevy coupe, along the parking strip, she saw his blue Studebaker sedan. She wondered if he might still be around so she placed her armload of music on the passenger seat and walked to the front of the church, where she found him sitting on the lower front steps with his elbows on his knees.

He saw her as soon as she came into view and stood to greet her as she climbed the lower tier of steps that led up to his level. She was always neatly dressed, and today was no exception. Nested in her yellow hair she wore a small hat covered with jittery white sequins that glistened in the warm midmorning eastern sun, a sun that streaked yellow-orange beams of light through the upper branches of the green elm trees that lined the red brick street.

The two stood together, her high heels and lofty coif causing her to appear taller than she really was. He took hold of her hands as their lips met, aware of the slight jasmine hint of *Bal a Versailles* – an earlier birthday gift. She used a Kleenex to wipe the trace of red lipstick from him and then stuffed it back into her purse.

"Mabel...dad has passed away...yesterday afternoon. He was home alone except for Cuba. She found him and called me at the office. I tell you, I don't know how to feel except that death came for good reason. He couldn't go on living like that. Now we can be married, but I must admit that I struggled, I mean I was hesitant to tell you...unable to reconcile my happiness with my sadness."

They both gazed at each other. He reached into his jacket pocket and took hold of a small purple velvet-covered box containing a gold engagement ring, one that he had bought several months earlier and stowed away in his sock drawer. The sad event they had been secretly anticipating had arrived. Now, as they stood together, she looked more beautiful than ever. With his hand still in his pocket, using his thumb, he smoothed the velvet surface nervously while they talked. Excitement stirred through his chest as he contemplated giving it to her.

"You were both so very close...this must be difficult for you."

"It was a terrible way to die...it's finally over."

"There must be so much to do...what can I do to help?"

"Stay with me tonight."

"Are you sure?"

"Yes, quite so." He slowly removed the box from his pocket. Opening it with both hands, he took the ring from its white, padded satin slot, returning the case to his pocket, and he slid it onto her ring finger. "We can now tell your parents."

To some, it had begun to look as if Mabel Lemasters would spend the rest of her life husbandless. After all, most eligible women were married before reaching the age of twenty-six. Even so, her parents, Harley and Osa Ola, were not at all content when they became aware of her involvement with Charley Gill, whom they considered a card-playing, cigarette smoking Methodist whom had little or no chance at succeeding in the business that was handed to him by his father. His clouded standing as a feckless playboy (albeit groundless) had arrived at the farm a priori, and they believed strongly that Mabel could do much better. Additionally, they considered his casual willingness to change from the Methodist to the Baptist Church as further evidence of his instability.

The two had met several years earlier. He had returned from State when he first saw her at the creamery in town where she had a part-time job. Then shortly after that, she left for Ohio University at Athens for a teaching degree. She joined the Alpha Gamma Delta sorority, and then under the tutelage and sponsorship of a certain Dr. Peterson, she became the church organist at the Athens Presbyterian Church. Upon graduation, she returned to Richwood to share an apartment with Margaret, her older sister, above Durnel's Grocery. She began teaching at Raymond, bought her shiny new Chevy coupe, and that was when they began to see each other.

To her, he appeared successful, always wearing a freshly starched shirt, a crisp tailored suit and polished shoes. She never heard him swear, use double negatives or talk down to others. He didn't bite his nails or blow his nose at the table, and he knew to walk beside her street-side when they were together and remove his hat when he entered a building. He wore his hair combed back, and when he smiled, she thought he looked like a famous person whose picture she had once seen in a magazine. Try as hard as she might, she couldn't remember exactly who it was that he reminded her of, whether it was a major league baseball player, a captain of industry, or some other sort of celebrity or megastar. She finally gave up trying to remember and considered herself to be fortunate to have found one with so many good attributes in such a small town where (as much as she hated to admit) many of the young men wore OshKosh bib overalls and chewed tobacco.

Her so-called Aunt Sarah (she was only indirectly an aunt) lived in the farm across the road from her parents' farm, and she chewed Red Man tobacco. When they would all ride to town to go shopping or for church, Aunt Sarah would spit out the window, and it would get all over the side of the car. Harley asked her repeatedly to stop, but the brown, juicy spew had become a permanent attachment on the left rear door, trailing all the way to the taillight. It made no difference how often the car was washed, the mess resolutely reappeared days later. Mabel hated it and swore that she would never kiss a man whom had had a wad in his mouth.

Initially, there wasn't a lot for Cuba to do. She cleared the library of the curtain that separated the two rooms, the cot, the medicines and personal items no longer needed by Charles Fremont. She opened the window and drapes and raised the blind. She squeezed lemon juice about hoping to get rid of the stale, bitter stink.

Then, Azile and her husband, Paul Arthur, arrived from Springfield after first dropping their bags off at Paul's parent's home a few hundred feet up the street. Eleanor and her husband, Ernest DeLauder, arrived from Columbus and took one of the two upstairs guest rooms. Ernest was the general contractor that built the house, and he impulsively began walking around to each room admiring his work – the arched hallway, the art deco fixtures, the brick fireplace and the staircase leading upstairs.

The kitchen counter, refrigerator and dining room table were quickly overloaded with casseroles, salads, fried chicken, pies, and cookies – all customary and traditional items provided by the women of the Methodist Church and Masonic Temple, friends and neighbors.

Azile brought with her a small sheltie that yapped non-stop, and Cuba had to tie it up outside after it peed on the living room carpet. When the yapping became intolerable, she shut it up in the garage with a bowl of water and kibble.

By evening, the house was filled with visitors, well-wishers, friends and neighbors all there to pay their condolences, and Cuba carried chairs from the dining room table into the living room and placed them around the edges of the room. By eight o'clock, everyone had left except for Cuba, the Arthurs and the DeLauders. Ernest and Paul went outside for a smoke and to check on the dog. Azile and Eleanor remained in the living room and discussed arrangements for the funeral while Charley helped Cuba clean up – she washed, he dried. It was decided that they would try to hold off the funeral long enough for Uncle Edwin Gill to arrive from Seattle. There was more food than would fit in the refrigerator so Cuba agreed to take some of the extra perishables home with her. As they both stood next to the sink with only a few glasses remaining, he told her that he was getting married.

"Lawd mercy! I've been wanderin' when you would ever take a wife. Good for you, Charley Frank...tell me...who is it?"

"Mabel Lemasters...do you know her?

Uncle Ed was the youngest and only surviving brother now that Charles Fremont was resting in peace at the Mount Carmel Lodge. Colonel Gill, as he was frequently known, was the most successful of the six brothers, having graduated from West Point and served in both the regular army and the army reserves and then as the adjutant general of the State of Arizona as well as the editor of newspapers in both Seattle and Honolulu. As a lawyer, he had been appointed to serve as one of the first commissioners for the Territory of Hawaii, appearing before the Senate for hearings concerning the reformation of the Constitution of the

Territory of Hawaii. The funeral would have to wait for Uncle Ed to make the trip from Seattle to Richwood. If arrangements could be made fast enough, he could also attend the wedding as well.

Charley stood talking to the stationmaster at the train depot on Franklin Street. Outside, the 4:15 slowly passed the large open cargo doors. He had heard its whistle blowing several minutes earlier, and then as the locomotive moved forward and crept to a stop he could hear steam hissing from its brake lines and boiler. There was a loud abrasive scraping sound of metal brakes, wheels and other mechanical parts followed by a series of clangs and clanks as each of the trailing cars sequentially caught up and collided together like an accordion. Once all the clack, clatter and hisses seemed to have run their course, there was one last sigh, which signaled that the conductor could allow those who were getting off to disembark.

Charley walked to the loading platform, down the steps to the track level and stood waiting in front of a long wooden bench when he spotted a lone passenger dismounting one of the three Pullmans that had been queued behind several grain and coal cars. The man was walking slowly with a walking stick in one hand and a suitcase in the other. He took a few steps, stopped and set his grip on the ground, then he picked it back up and continued to walk toward the station.

Certain that it was Uncle Ed, whom he had not seen for several years, Charley walked quickly along the queue of cars and then began waving. He called out, "Uncle Ed?" and the colonel stopped, set his case once again on the ground and raised his hand upward in a gentle waving motion.

Charley continued toward the older gentleman, who appeared well dressed, wearing a hat, a white shirt and tie, a dark double-breasted jacket and white duck trousers. On his lapel he wore a wilted white rose that he had purchased from a street

344

vendor when the train had stopped in Indianapolis. He offered his hand to Charley. "Charles, Jr., I presume?" His stern face changed to a warm smile as the two shook hands. Up close, his face appeared pale, spotted with several sun blots, remnants of the years he had lived in Honolulu.

His face returned to a sober expression. "My heart goes out to you for your loss."

"Thank you...and thank you for coming such a long distance. Dad spoke of you often...he was always proud of you."

"And I have always been equally proud of him, after all he was the one to remain and accept the mantle of family patriarch. I suppose that has now passed to you."

"I suppose...I guess I never thought of it that way. Let me help you with your suitcase. My car is parked right over there."

Ed lifted his head and gazed around. "Looks like the same old place...probably nothing has changed...just everyone gets older, that's all. Say, that looks like a snazzy Studebaker you've got there...business must be good?"

"I've been selling a lot of those new stoker furnaces, you know, the ones with the large screw that pulls the small coal chips into the heat chamber. It's thermostatically controlled. You only have to pour two buckets of coal in it every other day and empty the ashbin once a week – the furnace does the rest...and there's no smell in house or basement with it either. Coal heat has come a long way."

Charley opened the trunk of the car, deposited Uncle Ed's suitcase inside and climbed in the driver's seat. Ed took the passenger seat and immediately began to examine the interior, paying special attention to the several knobs and instrumentation on the driver's side of the dashboard.

"The funeral is set for tomorrow morning at eleven at the Masonic Temple...Mount Carmel Lodge. Would you like to see him now or go to the house first to freshen up? I expect now you'll have a better chance of being alone with him than later this evening."

"Yes, I would like to go now; not a second to lose."

The dark blue Studebaker merged into one of the several empty diagonal parking slots in front of the gray, two-story temple and the two climbed the steps to the heavy front door that, to their surprise, they found locked. After trying the handle a second time, Charley pounded on the door, waited and then pounded again.

"Why don't you wait here while I go around to the back? It must surely be unlocked." Charley moved quickly down the steps and turned to the left and crossed the freshly mowed lawn, not noticing the particles of grass that were adhering to the tops and sides of his shoes. He pulled the brim of his Fedora forward on his head as he was straight on into the bright, late afternoon sun. After pounding on the back door several times the small peep window opened, partially exposing the face of Tiler Holloway, who announced that the temple was closed and would reopen at five p.m.

"Wait! Is that you, Tiler?" Charley raised his voice with an inflection of imputed authority. "Don't you recognize me? It's me, Charley Gill, you need to let me in...I'm here to visit my father."

The peep window closed and the door slowly creaked open. The outdoor sunlight left Charley's pupils contracted as he made his way into the darkened room. "How come the doors are locked?" The question rolled out of his mouth without waiting for an answer as he walked past Tiler, quickly heading toward the front door. The wooden floorboards squeaked, having remained dormant for several hours. He opened the front door and a late afternoon breeze snaked its way in, pushing the stale interior air to the hallway and out to the back door, which had remained open.

"Sorry about that, Uncle Ed." Charley spoke while holding open the spring-loaded door with his right arm, leaving room for the colonel to enter. "I guess they keep a tight hold on this place when there is high-ranking departed being interned…32nd degree, you know."

They moved together along the corridor into the grand hall to the left, where all the dining room tables had been removed and the chairs were lined in six rows facing the casket. Only small amounts of light made their way in through the ceiling-length stained-glass windows so Charley turned on the overhead chandeliers, illuminating the room with a dim pink light. The plainly decorated casket perched upon a purple velvet catafalque, remained closed and centered against the interior wall opposite the windows. Charley lifted the casket lid; the two couldn't help but notice the banners and temple regalia that lined the wall, forming the backdrop for the honored Master Mason, brother and father.

The two men regarded the mortal remains of that which was once alive and had possessed a soul that, presumably, had now made its way into heaven. How different a lifeless body appears compared to one whose organs are busy growing, pumping, filtering and dreaming even though those functions are carried on invisibly. Ed stared at him closely; standing erect with his arms at his side, as if he worked hard enough at it he could recreate just for one last time a certain feeling of aliveness.

It was impossible to tell that the old man had died of gangrene. The embalmer had erased the horrors of the past months, and Charles Fremont Gill had been returned to his former years. His gold-rimmed spectacles, his thick mustache and wavy hair and his uncompromising gaze, all defined his timeless visage, artfully leaving a memory picture for those who would view him in this final hour.

After a few minutes of gazing downward, Ed slowly drifted to a time when the family was together, a time before his father and Frank had died. It was the Independence Day Centennial; the entire family was there, Joshua, Eliza, Frank, Henry, Sel, Tom, Charles and Ed in the center of town, in front of Durnell's Market, all looking up at the rope stretched high above the town across Franklin Street. He was fourteen and Charles Fremont was nineteen.

The two boys stood next to each other waiting for the ropewalker about to appear. The publicity posters claimed that he wasn't only going to walk across the rope, he might even ride a bicycle or walk across it on stilts. The moment could not have been more exciting if it had been the Great Blondin, the Hero of Niagara himself, they were waiting for.

At last, the funambulist stood at the edge of the roof wearing an all white acrobats' costume. He raised his arms over his head as the announcer standing below on the back of a wagon bed introduced him with the aid of a large megaphone. The announcer began asking the crowd to give him some encouragement, and the audience began to cheer and applaud. The ropewalker then stepped back, out of the line of sight of the crowd below, and the announcer repeated for the audience to cheer more loudly. The ropewalker appeared again a second and third time and then at last stepped onto the rope, curling the arches of his feet over the twisted hemp, causing it to wobble for five or six seconds. He carried a long pole to help him keep his balance and looked straight ahead.

It was difficult for Ed to believe that he would be able to make it across the entire distance to the other side without falling – it just seemed impossible. However, after the man took his first step, he took a second, and then a third, and he glided forward smoothly with the grace and style of a ballet dancer, performing acrobatics, jumping and doing somersaults. Mesmerized, Ed took hold of Charles' hand and thought for a moment that the aerialist was looking down at him and could see the fear on his face, returning to him a reassuring smile that everything was going just fine. When Ed realized how tightly he was squeezing Charles' hand he quickly let go, feeling somewhat embarrassed. Charles then told him that it made him nervous also. Ed was closer to Charles than any of his other brothers and believed that Charles could always be counted on.

When they had finished, they thanked Tiler and left through the front door. They drove away in the Studebaker, doing a U-turn in the middle of Franklin Street, headed north and crossed the railroad tracks.

Ed spotted the tall grain elevator off to the right and lowered his window to get a better look. The elevator was a round concrete tower that rose high into the sky, looking almost like a large lighthouse except that at the top, instead of a candle, there was a square room with large bold letters painted on the front side in red and black that read 'Case Elevator'. The train had dropped off two cars on a spur next to the elevator and already there was a large chute positioned into an open door on the top of the car. A cloud of dust surrounded the opening, indicating that grain was already filling into the car. A man wearing OshKosch B'Gosh bib overalls had positioned himself on top, on a chair next to the chute, and was leaning forward, looking down into the opening.

"Now that's quite an elevator! I don't believe I've ever seen one so tall as that. Hmm…Case…is that the same as Case Implement, the tractor manufacturer?"

"No, Russell Case is a farmer with a spread north of town, on the Boundary Road. He has a heck of a lot of acres…even has a CT Farm & Country LE 1934 Stearman Bi-Wing Crop Duster and a small landing strip out there."

As the two headed north on Franklin Street, where Wood Street joined on the right, Charley pointed to the large white house on the left. "That's the home of Martin and Mary Ellen Fox, Mabel's grandfather. Mabel Lemasters…she and I are about to be married. Martin and Mary Ellen came from West Virginia to Richwood and bought the old Hamilton farm north of town, and then a few years ago he retired and they moved into town."

Ed looked surprised. "You're engaged? Tell me about it."

"You'll meet her. She's a very special woman – bright, intelligent, talented, and very attractive, if I do say so. She's the organist at the First Baptist church and teaches school over at Raymond. Of course, once we marry she'll have to find another teaching job – the District doesn't allow their women teachers to marry. She may be able teach at Byhalia – they're a lot more liberal over there."

"She sounds like a fine woman."

Since it was determined that the Mount Carmel Lodge was too small to accommodate all those that were about to attend the funeral, at the last moment it was moved to the Methodist church. The service lasted over two hours as there were many present that wished to tell personal stories and anecdotes. Edwin, Azile and Eleanor presented eulogies, and Charley served as one of the pallbearers. The coffin was then transported to the Claiborne Cemetery, where the corpse was interred next to that of Adelle, his third wife, in the ocher-colored, brick mausoleum.

On the following Sunday, Charley stood in the last row at the First Baptist church as Mabel played the doxology.

Praise God, from Whom all blessings flow;
Praise Him, all creatures here below;
Praise Him above, ye Heavenly Host;
Praise Father, Son, and Holy Ghost. Amen.

He could see Osa Ola, Harley, Leroy and Margaret all standing in the choir loft. When the doxology was over, Osa gave the signal for the choir to be seated by turning toward them and lowering both her extended arms, and they responded by taking their seats in unison. Mabel stepped down from the organ bench, took a seat next to the organ and the minister began the sermon.

Charley was unaware that Aunt Sarah Eddy and Martin and Mary Ellen Fox were sitting in the pew immediately in front of him. Leroy, who was the same age as Charley and had been in the same class in high school, spotted Charley as he entered the sanctuary. The two had made quick eye contact and Leroy had given a perfunctory nod. Mabel had earlier seen him through her rear-view mirror when he came in, and she had watched him take his seat in the last row. Now she sat facing the congregation and had a straight-on view of him. Margaret, the only member of the family to know what was going on, was teeming with excitement. She wore a continuous smile on her face and would occasionally look first toward Charley and then over her shoulder toward her sister, looking for some kind of expression. Trying as hard as she could to ignore her, Mabel seemed to find it impossible to remain stoic and had to hide her outbreaks of smiles behind her handkerchief, turning away in the direction of the minister.

Leroy sat next to Margaret and whispered to her, trying to keep his lips from moving. "What's going on between the two of you?"

Holding her hand over her mouth, Margaret was more conspicuous. "You don't know? Charley Gill is coming out to the house this afternoon, and he and Mabel are going to announce their engagement."

Unable to remain straight, Leroy's face lit up and he looked off to where Charley was sitting. "How long has this been going on?"

"Ever since she came home from university...they've been keeping it a secret."

The commotion between Mabel, Margaret and Leroy was becoming noticeable, and Harley, sitting in the second row, behind Leroy, reached over, nudged Margaret and whispered, "You two, now settle down."

His warning did little to deter the growing turmoil, and several other younger members in the congregation began to notice what was happening, perhaps not the whole extent, but they could tell that it had something to do with Charley and Mabel.

Later that afternoon, Charley turned his blue Studebaker left off Hamilton Pike, now known as Lemasters Road, onto the

Lemasters' farm. The gravel lane leading up to the farmhouse passed over a short bridge that initially traversed a narrow drainage ditch paralleling the roadway. This ditch allowed the fields to drain both from melting snow in the springtime and excessive rainfall in the summer and fall. The lane meandered slightly to the right, then ran along the adjacent pasture, continuing past the farmhouse on the left and around to the back to the barnyard, where several other cars were parked. Along the pasture fence there was a small windmill pumping water into a large watering tank, and several sheep were crowded around it taking turns. A large block of saltlick hung on the fence, inches above the ground.

The house was a white, medium-sized, two-story building to which Harley and Osa had made numerous improvements over the years, including the early addition of a basement, a furnace, a Delco generator, electrical wiring and most recently, a large porch that extended across the front.

There were several family members in the front, some sitting in chairs on the porch and others sitting on the front steps. None but Margaret and Leroy recognized the blue Studebaker, either its driver or Mabel sitting in the passenger seat as they made their way past. Mabel had told her mother that she was bringing a friend, but she had not explained whom. She suspected that it was probably Charley.

They entered the house through the back porch that served as an enclosure against the winter elements and into the kitchen. Osa, Aunt Sarah, and Leroy's wife, Esther, were in the kitchen preparing the ham, mashed potatoes, yams and string beans that would be served later in the afternoon. Minced meat and squash pies had been baked the evening before.

Osa, not surprised to see Charley, remembered seeing him in church that morning. She wiped her hands on her apron and approached the couple, not only to welcome them both but to introduce their guest to the other women in the kitchen. Charley had won the moment, however, by handing Osa a large bouquet of flowers and a pound box of Whitman's chocolates.

This was an annual event. The entire family was present to celebrate the completion of the harvest. It had been a good year as their rich farmland had produced a record crop, and the market had rewarded them with a good price, the two variables in normal years having an inverse relationship. And it was a year that the two daughters would find their husbands and the youngest son, his wife. Leroy, the oldest was now a practicing chiropractor and was married to Esther Hall. Charles, a teacher, had married Natalie Quick, and they lived in Erie, Pennsylvania. Margaret was engaged to Robert Clevenger, and Bill to Eva Davis.

They passed from the kitchen through the dining room dominated by a large oak table with a white tablecloth and ten place settings. There weren't enough chairs for everyone to be seated at the table, so it would be necessary for some to be served in the kitchen. In the middle of the walkway next to the dining room table, Leroy stood behind Margaret, who was seated in one of the dining room chairs, and he was giving her a neck adjustment. Leroy was a large man, but very gentle, and he worked her neck and backbone, massaging her muscles and eventually ending the session by giving her neck a quick snap. When he had finished with Margaret, Osa approached him and said that she too was feeling a lot of tension in her back, and asked if he could he give her a treatment, much like the one he had given to Margaret.

Bill and Eva arrived with her father and mother, Lawrence Fulton Davis and Leefa Davis from York Township. Lawrence was the maternal great grandson of Thomas Fulton, after whom Fulton Creek was named. They brought with them a large plate of deviled eggs and set it on the kitchen table before moving on in through the dining room, where Osa was getting her treatment. Lawrence said that he had known Charley's father and related that he remembered when in the winter of 1817 how he had declared one day as Farmer's Day. Because of the war effort, there had been a shortage of coal so Charles Fremont guaranteed all the farmers a half-ton of coal each that day. There had been a heavy snow and all the farmers were lined up with their sled-drawn horses from the coal yard all along Fulton Street (after Fulton Creek) to as far away as Ottawa Street.

While Bill sat on the front porch cranking a bucket of homemade French vanilla ice cream, Mabel's other brother, Charles, entered the living room from the front door. He and Natalie had been visiting with Grandpa Fox, who had come up with the idea of a horseshoe match. It would be the undefeated team of Charles Lemasters and Martin Fox vs. Harley and Charley, the newcomer. The game started with each team throwing their best 'ringers' and laying a few close shots in to score. Charles and Grandpa Fox won the first match by a narrow margin and lost the second. By the third and final round, everyone in the house but for the kitchen crew was in the back yard anxiously waiting for the outcome. Charley was last up and threw the winning ringer, dislodging Martin's shoe that was leaning against the pole. Charley had won more than the game of horseshoes, and everyone returned to the house for the afternoon lunch.

Charley and Mabel entered the parlor to be alone and to prepare for the announcement they were about to make. His attention was drawn to a small painting hanging on the wall in an out-of-the-way place. It was the portrait of a young boy, perhaps fifteen or sixteen years of age. It was a very old painting – most of the paint was cracked. The boy had wavy hair and a handsome face with rosy cheeks, and it had been painted at a time when artists gave much attention to very fine details. It was as if every hair on his head and eyebrows, each fiber of his attire, were accounted for. In the bottom left hand margin, written in the artist's hand in gold pigment, it read, *Henri IV, Le Roi de la paix, France et Navarre, Louise LeMaître, 1568.* Mabel said it had always hung there, that she would often stare at it when she would practice the piano. To her, the boy in the picture seemed to have such a serious expression for being so young. Charley agreed.

The announcement was met with jubilant expressions of congratulations. Harley and Osa, having somehow forgotten any early reservations that they might have held, gave their blessing, if not verbally, then by the smiles on their faces and by their outpouring of praise for such a gentleman, so polite and considerate, and such an excellent horseshoe thrower. They all refilled their glasses with iced tea and gathered into the parlor where Margaret played the piano and they sang songs that were popular for the time – *Jeepers Creepers, You Must Have Been a Beautiful Baby* and *My Heart Belongs to Daddy*.

The celebration and singing continued until it was drowned-out by the noisy sound of an airplane flying overhead close to the ground. It made so much racket that everyone rushed outside to see what was happening, but it had soon passed too far away for anyone to be able to make it out. Then in the distance, it made a loop and turned back toward the house. As it came straight on, it then made a turn, just enough for everyone to see that it was Russell Case, arms hanging out of his red CT Farm & Country LE 1934 Stearman Bi-Wing Crop Duster, waving his Stetson hat, dragging behind a large white banner with black and red letters that read, 'Congrats, Charley and Mabel.'

Bibliography

History of Union County Volume II, Illustrated Chicago, W. H. Beers & Co., 1883, Part V – Township Histories

History of Union County Ohio, Its People, Industries and Institutions, by Col. W. L. Curry, Published by B. F. Bowen & Company, Inc., Indianapolis, Indiana, 1915

Family Heritage Union County, Ohio, 1985, Published by the Union County History Book Committee, 1985

History of Delaware and Ohio, Illustrated, CHAPTER XXIII. – Oxford Township, Topographical and Descriptive, Early Settlements, Frontier Privations, Education and Religion, Villages. Published by O. L. Baskins Co., Historical Publishers, 55 Dearborn Street, Chicago, 1880
http://www.heritagepursuit.com/Delaware/delchapXXIII.htm

Lemasters, U.S.A., 1639-1965, Howard Marshall Lemaster and Margaret Herberger, 1965

The Delashmutte Story, Virgil D. Close, Genealogy Publishing Service, 1994

Pictorial Field-Book of the War of 1812, by Benson J. Lossing, Chapter XXX, *Predatory Warfare of the British on the Coast*, 1869,
http://freepages.history.rootsweb.ancestry.com/~wcarr1/Lossing2/Chap30.html

Montcalm and Wolfe: The French and Indian War (Paperback) by Francis Parkman, **Publisher:** Da Capo Press; New Ed edition (October 23, 2001) **ISBN-10:** 0306810778 **ISBN-13:** 978-0306810770

Archives of Maryland Online, Proceedings and Act of the General Assembly, 1757-1758, Volume 55

Defense of the Maryland Frontier 1754-1759, By Stephen R. Robertson,
http://www.friendsoffortfrederick.org/popup/defense.htm